KU-132-960

SIMON SCARROW

EAGLES·OF·THE·EMPIRE

REBELLION

HEADLINE

Copyright © 2023 Simon Scarrow

The right of Simon Scarrow to be identified as the Author of
the Work has been asserted by him in accordance with the
Copyright, Designs and Patents Act 1988.

First published in Great Britain in 2023
by HEADLINE PUBLISHING GROUP

First published in paperback in 2024
by HEADLINE PUBLISHING GROUP

1

Apart from any use permitted under UK copyright law, this publication may
only be reproduced, stored, or transmitted, in any form, or by any means,
with prior permission in writing of the publishers or, in the case of reprographic
production, in accordance with the terms of licences issued by the
Copyright Licensing Agency.

All characters in this publication are fictitious and any resemblance to real persons,
living or dead, is purely coincidental.

Cataloguing in Publication Data is available from the British Library

ISBN 978 1 4722 8711 3

Map and artwork by Tim Peters

Typeset in Bembo by Avon DataSet Ltd, Alcester, Warwickshire

Printed and bound in Great Britain by Clays Ltd, Elcograf S.p.A.

Headline's policy is to use papers that are natural, renewable and recyclable
products and made from wood grown in well-managed forests and other
controlled sources. The logging and manufacturing processes are expected
to conform to the environmental regulations of the country of origin.

HEADLINE PUBLISHING GROUP
An Hachette UK Company
Carmelite House
50 Victoria Embankment
London EC4Y 0DZ

www.headline.co.uk
www.hachette.co.uk

Simon Scarrow has been passionate about writing since an early age. After a childhood spent travelling the world, he pursued his great love of history as a teacher before becoming a full-time writer. His Roman soldier heroes Cato and Macro first appeared in 2000 in *Under The Eagle*, and have subsequently fought their way through over twenty novels, including *Rebellion*, *Death to the Emperor*, *The Honour of Rome*, *The Emperor's Exile* and *Centurion*.

Simon Scarrow is also the author of the Criminal Inspector Schenke thrillers, *Dead of Night* and *Blackout*, set in Berlin during the Second World War, as well as: the *Wellington and Napoleon* quartet, chronicling the lives of the Duke of Wellington and Napoleon Bonaparte; *Sword & Scimitar*, the epic tale of the 1565 Siege of Malta; and *Hearts Of Stone*, set in Greece during the Second World War. He is the co-author with T. J. Andrews of Roman era bestsellers *Pirata*, *Invader* and *Arena*, and the co-author with Lee Francis of the contemporary thriller *Playing With Death*.

Find out more at: www.simonscarrow.co.uk and on
Facebook: /OfficialSimonScarrow
and
X: @SimonScarrow

Praise for Simon Scarrow's novels

'A good, uncomplicated, rip-roaring read'
Mail on Sunday

'An engrossing storyline, full of teeth-clenching battles, political machinations, treachery, honour, love and death . . . More please!'
Elizabeth Chadwick

'A new book in Simon Scarrow's long-running series about the Roman army is always a joy'
The Times

'Scarrow's rank with the best'
Independent

'Utterly authentic characters; a gripping plot. The perfect way to bring history alive'
Damien Lewis

By Simon Scarrow

The *Eagles of the Empire* Series
The Britannia Campaign
Under the Eagle (AD 42–43, Britannia)
The Eagle's Conquest (AD 43, Britannia)
When the Eagle Hunts (AD 44, Britannia)
The Eagle and the Wolves (AD 44, Britannia)
The Eagle's Prey (AD 44, Britannia)

Rome and the Eastern Provinces
The Eagle's Prophecy (AD 45, Rome)
The Eagle in the Sand (AD 46, Judaea)
Centurion (AD 46, Syria)

The Mediterranean
The Gladiator (AD 48–49, Crete)
The Legion (AD 49, Egypt)
Praetorian (AD 51, Rome)

The Return to Britannia
The Blood Crows (AD 51, Britannia)
Brothers in Blood (AD 51, Britannia)
Britannia (AD 52, Britannia)

Hispania
Invictus (AD 54, Hispania)

The Return to Rome
Day of the Caesars (AD 54, Rome)

The Eastern Campaign
The Blood of Rome (AD 55, Armenia)
Traitors of Rome (AD 56, Syria)
The Emperor's Exile (AD 57, Sardinia)

Britannia: Troubled Province
The Honour of Rome (AD 59, Britannia)
Death to the Emperor (AD 60, Britannia)
Rebellion (AD 60, Britannia)

The *Criminal Inspector Schenke* Thrillers
Blackout
Dead of Night

The *Wellington and Napoleon* Quartet
Young Bloods
The Generals
Fire and Sword
The Fields of Death

Sword and Scimitar
(Great Siege of Malta)

Hearts of Stone (Second World War)

The *Gladiator* Series
Gladiator: Fight for Freedom
Gladiator: Street Fighter
Gladiator: Son of Spartacus
Gladiator: Vengeance

Writing with T. J. Andrews
Arena (AD 41, Rome)
Invader (AD 44, Britannia)
Pirata (AD 25, Rome)
Warrior (AD 18, Britannia)

Writing with Lee Francis
Playing With Death

To Michele and Silvano, thank you for all your kindness, friendship and Italian cuisine.

THE ROMAN PROVINCE OF
BRITANNIA AD 61

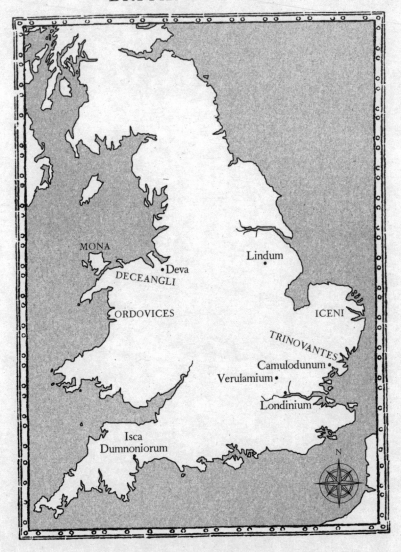

MONA

DECEANGLI

• Deva

ORDOVICES

Lindum
•

ICENI

TRINOVANTES

Camulodunum •

Verulamium •

Londinium

Isca
Dumnoniorum

N

CHAIN OF COMMAND

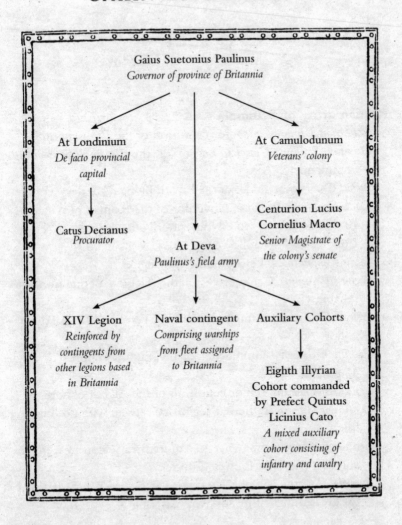

Gaius Suetonius Paulinus
Governor of province of Britannia

At Londinium
De facto provincial capital

At Camulodunum
Veterans' colony

Catus Decianus
Procurator

Centurion Lucius Cornelius Macro
Senior Magistrate of the colony's senate

At Deva
Paulinus's field army

XIV Legion
Reinforced by contingents from other legions based in Britannia

Naval contingent
Comprising warships from fleet assigned to Britannia

Auxiliary Cohorts

Eighth Illyrian Cohort commanded by Prefect Quintus Licinius Cato
A mixed auxiliary cohort consisting of infantry and cavalry

CAST LIST

Roman army of Britannia

Centurion Bernardicus, senior centurion of the IXth legion

Quintus Petillius Cerealis, Legate of the IX legion, a rash commander

Prefect Cato, commander of the Eighth Illyrian Auxiliary cohort

Gaius Suetonius Paulinus, Governor of the Roman province of Britannia, wrongfooted but utterly determined to crush Boudica and her followers

Cestius Calpurnius, Legate of the XX legion

Poenius Postumus, Camp Prefect of the II legion, of questionable reliability

Prefect Thrasyllus, commander of the Tenth Gallic Auxiliary cohort

Centurion Tubero, commander of the Eighth cohort's cavalry contingent

Centurion Galerius, senior centurion of the Eighth cohort

Centurion Hitetius (retired), a legionary veteran with nothing to lose

Centurion Macro (somewhat less retired), a legionary veteran and best friend of Prefect Cato

Agricola, Tribune on the governor's staff, green but destined for great things, if he survives that long

Centurion Vespillus, acting commander of the Londinium garrison, barely able to cope

Phrygenus, surgeon of the Eighth cohort

Roman civilians

Claudia Acte, lover of Prefect Cato and former exiled mistress of Nero, now incognito

Petronella, wife of Macro, fearless and formidable, the love of Macro's life

Portia, mother of Macro, equally fearless and formidable, though frail

Lucius, son of Cato, a chip off the old block and shaping up nicely

Denubius, Portia's handyman, a loyal retainer

Decianus Catus, Procurator of the province, a scheming opportunist with devastating consequences

Maecius Grahmius, a civilian rather too much in love with the sound of his own voice

Rebels

Boudica, Queen of the Iceni, the proud leader of those cruelly oppressed by Rome

Syphodubnus, a noble of the Iceni who thinks he should be in charge

Bardea and Merida, daughters of Boudica

Bellomagus, champion of the Iceni tribe

Tongdubnus, an Iceni warrior, but a poor swimmer.

CHAPTER ONE

Roman province of Britannia, summer 61 AD

The column was in trouble. Centurion Bernardicus, commander of the First Cohort of the Ninth Legion, sensed it the moment he caught sight of the enemy, shading his eyes in the bright sunlight. A distant line of riders regarded the approaching Romans from a low ridge half a mile ahead. At first the centurion mistook them for some of the legion's scouts screening the advance of Legate Cerialis and his soldiers. But there was something irregular about the disposition of the riders, and then he noticed the absence of any standard or the red crest of an officer's helmet.

How in Hades had a party of rebel horsemen managed to slip through the line of scouts? he wondered. The officer in command of the mounted picket was going to feel the sharp edge of the legate's tongue when the column made camp that night. Assuming the enemy made no mischief before then. Bernardicus squinted up at the sun and calculated that there was another three hours to march before the legate gave the order to halt and erect the defences of a marching camp. Maybe longer, given the late halt the day before. Then there had only been time to set up the stockade of sharpened stakes to guard the camp. No ditch, nor rampart.

Bernardicus had fretted at the legate's failure to follow the army's doctrine for preparing defences when marching into hostile territory. There was little doubt in his mind about such dangers, given Cerialis's briefing on the eve of their advance from the legion's base at Lindum two days before. A message had arrived from the senior magistrate of the veterans' colony at Camulodunum reporting an uprising by the Iceni tribe and their Trinovantian allies. The magistrate had learned that the rebels were making for Camulodunum and had begged the Ninth Legion to march to the veterans' rescue.

As the senior centurion of the legion, Bernardicus had put his concerns to the legate and been rebuffed with haughty disdain.

'We're dealing with a ragtag mob of armed peasants,' Cerialis had scoffed. 'Led by the scrapings of whatever warrior caste has survived the conquest. We have nothing to fear from such a rabble. They'll take one look at the vanguard of the Ninth and turn tail and bolt for the safety of the woods and bogs of their territory.'

'I hope you're right, sir.' Bernardicus nodded diplomatically. 'But if they stand and fight?'

A cold smile formed on Cerialis's lips. 'Then we'll crush them, scatter any survivors and crucify the ringleaders. After that, I doubt that any tribe on this island living under our rule will have the balls to ever rebel again.'

Bernardicus could not help a small degree of bitter mirth at his superior's words, given the gender of the enemy's leader. He had seen Queen Boudica several months earlier when she was amongst the tribal leaders declaring their annual homage to the emperor before the provincial governor in Londinium. Tall, haughty and flame-haired, she had stood out amongst the others. A woman to be reckoned with, Bernardicus had thought, and he had been proven right. Where Boudica led, her people, men and women, old and young alike, would be sure to follow in their desire to humble Rome and its ruler, Emperor Nero.

Rome had a history of fearing powerful women and, fortunately for the Empire, triumphing over them. Yet the centurion could not help a tremor of anxiety. Under other circumstances he might have shared the legate's easy confidence. As things stood, the bulk of the Roman army occupying Britannia was campaigning against the mountain tribes far to the west of the island. Governor Paulinus had stripped the province of the best soldiers to fill out the ranks of the army, including four of the cohorts from the Ninth. The only forces available to confront Boudica and her rebels comprised the raw recruits being trained at the Second Legion's base down at Isca Dumnoniorum, a handful of poor-quality auxiliaries and the six remaining cohorts of the Ninth at Lindum.

Proud as Bernardicus was of his legion, he was aware that the cohorts marching behind him were under strength and their men had not made the cut to join their comrades now serving under Paulinus. He was also aware of the limitations of his superior. Legate Cerialis had only recently been appointed commander of the Ninth and had arrived in Britannia wreathed in the customary arrogance and ambition of his class. His only combat experience had been a brief punitive expedition across the Rhine during his time as a tribune. He had yet to earn the hard-won experience required to make a decent legate of him.

All this flowed through the veteran centurion's mind in a matter of heartbeats before he drew a deep breath to give the order. 'First Cohort! Halt!'

The men, bent slightly forward under the burden of the kit on their marching yokes, took a pace and a half further along the track and drew up. Some regarded him with surprise. They had stopped for a rest break less than a mile back, and it was too early in the day to make camp. Bernardicus ignored them and strode on another twenty paces ahead of the column before he paused to scrutinise the distant horsemen.

The dull thrumming of hoofbeats heralded the approach of Legate Cerialis and his small band of staff officers, fresh-faced tribunes who had yet to see any combat. Maybe that was about to change, Bernardicus mused.

'What's the bloody meaning of this?' Cerialis snapped. 'Who gave the order for the column to halt?'

The centurion turned and nodded a salute. 'I did, sir.'

Cerialis frowned. 'Why?'

Bernardicus gestured towards the ridge. The legate straightened and squinted briefly. 'So?'

'The enemy, sir.'

'Nonsense. Those are our scouts.'

'Look again. They're no more Roman than I am a Druid, sir.'

Cerialis and his tribunes stared ahead of the column before one of the latter cleared his throat. 'The centurion's right, sir.'

'Then where are the scouts? They're supposed to clear the way ahead of us.'

Bernardicus took a deep breath before he responded. 'I'd say our lads are either dead, taken prisoner or have been forced to flee. Some of 'em might make their way back to us, but the scouts are gone, sir.'

'Gone?' Cerialis stared back as if the centurion were quite mad. 'Impossible.'

Bernardicus shrugged and there followed a strained silence as the officers waited for the legate to give fresh orders. Nearby, the legionaries stood ready, still shouldering their yokes. At length, the senior tribune edged his horse alongside his superior.

'Give the word, sir, and I'll lead the rest of our mounted contingent forward to drive those rebels off the track.'

Cerialis chewed his bottom lip for a moment before he shook his head. 'If they have dealt with our scouts, then I'll not throw any more men away or send them on a wild goose chase. No . . .

4

We'll continue the advance. The rebels wouldn't dare attack the column. Besides, we must reach Camulodunum as swiftly as possible and save our comrades there.'

And no doubt claim a civic crown for saving their lives in the process, Bernardicus thought cynically. Like most of his kind, Cerialis was eager to win military decorations to add lustre to his family's name.

'Pass the word for the column to close up,' the legate continued. 'The mounted contingent is to form up at the rear.'

'Yes, sir.'

As the tribune trotted back along the ranks of the waiting legionaries, Bernardicus made his own way down the track, cupping a hand to his mouth as he bellowed, 'First Cohort centurions! On me!'

When he was safely out of earshot of the legate, he stopped, and the other centurions of his cohort gathered round.

'Looks like we've seen the last of our scouts, lads. Cerialis is determined to reach Camulodunum nonetheless. Reckons we can see off any rebels that try their luck. So we keep closed up and keep a good look out for trouble. We're the spearhead of the Ninth, so it's up to us to set the example. No slacking or grousing from our boys, understand? If the other side try and block our path, we go through them quicker than shit through a sheep.' He glanced at his subordinates and was met with steady gazes. 'Our comrades at Camulodunum are counting on us. They're good men. I knew their chief magistrate back when we both served in the Second Legion. Macro's one of the best. If our positions were reversed, he'd give his all to save us.'

'Do you think there'll be any trouble?' asked a well-built centurion.

'There's always trouble in this shitty island, Timandrus.'

There was a chorus of chuckles and some smiles from the other centurions.

'Without the scouts, we're blind,' Timandrus continued. 'Who knows what we're marching into? Could be a trap.'

'Could be,' Bernardicus conceded. 'But we've never let those hairy-arsed barbarians get one over us yet, and they ain't going to do it today. Right?'

The other man nodded.

'That said, if I give the order to down packs, I want the boys formed up in a heartbeat, with their shields out and javelins ready. Now get back to your men and be ready to move as soon as Cerialis gives the command.'

Bernardicus returned to the head of the column and strode out boldly the instant the legate called the order to resume the advance. The legionaries of his century tramped steadily behind him. Ahead, on the ridge, the horsemen held their position as they observed the approaching Romans. The track inclined slightly, and as Bernardicus came within two hundred paces of the rebels, he felt the first icy trickle of concern slide down his spine. At the same time, he stiffened his shoulders and continued to advance without the slightest sign of hesitation. He had always striven to appear fearless and bold to provide a reassuring example to his men. Even now, he resisted the urge to call for his manservant to bring up the mule carrying his heavy rectangular shield, while he handed over his cloak so that the folds did not encumber him if it came to a fight.

Closer still, no more than a hundred paces from the crest of the low ridge, he could make out the grisly trophies the horsemen now raised for the Romans to see. Severed heads, gripped by the hair. Brandished at the legionaries as the rebels jeered and shouted insults.

'Bastards!' a voice cried out close behind Bernardicus. 'They'll pay for that.'

'Silence in the ranks!' The centurion glanced over his shoulder. 'Next man to open his mouth gets latrine duty for a month!'

The horsemen lowered their heads, then turned their mounts away and trotted down the far slope and out of sight. Bernardicus had marched along this route many times before and knew the lie of the land beyond. There was a sharp dip into a wooded vale where the ground had been cleared by the army's engineers for sufficient distance on either side of the track to deny any attacker the chance to spring a sudden surprise. It also provided the Romans with space to change into a more defensive formation if necessary. The vale was also as good a place as any to ambush the column, but three thousand heavily armed soldiers of the finest army in the world should be more than a match for any force the tribes could scrape together, Bernardicus reassured himself.

Glancing back, he saw that the gaps between the six cohorts had narrowed, and their small baggage trains of carts and mules were now flanked by the legionaries of the rearmost century of each cohort. The column was now little more than half the length it had been before the halt, when it had been strung out along the track.

The centurion reached the crest and looked down into the vale. He could see that the horsemen had increased their distance to half a mile ahead of the column, but there was no sign of any other rebels. He scanned the treeline on either side of the track, but there was no sign of movement. Then his eyes fell upon a cluster of bodies lying halfway between himself and the horsemen. The headless corpses of the scout squadron. They had been stripped and their weapons and horses taken, and their pallid flesh was spattered and streaked with blood under the bright sun. As the column drew closer, he heard the muttered curses of his men rippling through the cohort and angrily demanded silence once again before turning to his second in command.

'Optio Severus, my compliments to the legate. Tell him that we've found what's left of the scouts.'

'Yes, sir.'

Bernardicus paused while the optio trotted back along the column, then gave the follow-up order. 'First Section, First Century . . . Fall out and get the dead off the track and loaded onto our wagons.' The funerals could be arranged once the legion had made camp at the end of the day. Identifying the bodies, though, would be a problem, especially if the enemy had taken the scouts' identity tags as trophies.

The men of the leading section dropped their packs at the side of the track and jogged forward to take care of the bodies as the centurion continued leading the column into the vale. He spared the corpses laid out beside the track a brief glance as he marched past, then resumed scanning the way ahead for signs of danger. The wooded slopes on either side blocked all but the lightest puffs of breeze, and the air in the vale was still and hot. Sweat trickled from under the felt skullcap beneath his crested helmet. The bracken and undergrowth on either side was parched and dry after many days without rain. Overhead, the sky was cloudless and the afternoon sun grilled the marching men without pity as two kites swooped languidly against a cerulean backdrop searching for prey. Every so often the horsemen would rein in and taunt the Romans with their gory prizes before trotting off again. Each time Bernardicus felt his blood run hot in his veins, frustrated that he was powerless to avenge his comrades.

The column had advanced nearly two miles into the vale when he saw the first swirl of white ahead. An instant later, there was another, and another, until several trails of smoke were visible across the width of the open ground either side of the track. He could make out figures with torches moving to set alight yet more of the dry bracken and undergrowth. Soon the flames beneath the smoke could be discerned, brilliant flares of red and orange that swiftly spread from side to side until there was a curtain of fire and smoke blocking the way ahead. Now and then

Bernardicus could see the figures of the rebels beyond, shimmering in the heat haze.

He halted the column once again a hundred paces from the blaze and ordered the cohort to down packs and stand to along the track.

'Sir! Look!'

He turned to see Timandrus gesturing towards the rear of the column. Above the cloud of dust stirred by thousands of boots and the hooves and wheels of the carts, smoke billowed from yet more fires stretching across the vale behind the legion. As the Roman soldiers looked anxiously in both directions, there was a deep roar from the trees on either side. Bernardicus felt his guts twist as he saw figures emerge from the gloom beneath the boughs of the trees and pour out onto the open ground.

Hundreds, then thousands of the rebels were massing on each side of the Ninth Legion, roaring their battle cries, jeers and insults as they brandished spears, swords and axes. In amongst them, their chiefs and Druids urged their followers on.

'First Cohort! Form square!' Bernardicus had to strain his lungs for the order to be heard above the din that filled the stifling air. He waved his servant forward and took up his shield, handing his vine cane over before ordering the man to fall back to the baggage train. Around him the men of his cohort changed formation, his century facing the fire, two more on either flank and the last closing the rear of the formation. Their large, heavy shields formed a wall, and between each shield, the point of a short sword protruded. The javelins were handed back to the men of the rear rank, ready to hurl over the heads of their comrades.

The other five cohorts of the column were still completing the manoeuvre when the rebels' war horns sounded. The rearmost unit surrounded the baggage train and the mounted contingent, as well as the legate and his staff. Bernardicus could just make out the glint of the gilded eagle standard and the bright red falls of the other standards of the legion.

The horns sounded again and the Romans braced themselves for the enemy charge. Instead, hundreds of men advanced to within a hundred feet of the legionaries. Each carried a torch, and they bent to thrust them into the dry undergrowth, surrounding the Ninth with fire. Only now did Bernardicus realise that the ground in front of the trees had been cleared of most of the combustible material, which had been cunningly concealed amongst the parched bracken close to the track.

'Shit,' he mouthed softly before turning to steady his men with a forced grin. 'Hold fast, boys! We've some hot work ahead of us!'

The cordon of fire was still some distance away, and he caught glimpses of the enemy through the wavering flames and searing air. The blaze prevented any attack for the present, he mused. Then the truth of their predicament struck home. The enemy did not intend to attack the legion directly; they meant to let the fire do the work for them before picking off the survivors. Already the flames were working their way towards the Roman column in an uneven ripple of smouldering, then roaring bursts that crackled and hissed like some demonically possessed monster. There was only one path to salvation that occurred to Bernardicus, and he sheathed his sword and turned to his men.

'We have to create a fire break. Cut away as much of the undergrowth as we can and dump it close to the fire. Severus, set the men to it!'

Leaving the optio to obey his orders, the centurion moved along the column to pass on the instructions. As he reached the Fifth Cohort, he saw Cerialis riding towards him.

'What in Jupiter's name is going on, Centurion? Why are the men breaking ranks? They need to be ready to receive an attack.'

Bernardicus explained briefly, and concluded with a warning. 'We have to do it, sir, or perish in the blaze.'

The legate looked towards the head of the column and observed the frantic efforts of the legionaries before he winced and nodded. 'Very well, carry on. Once we have tamed the fire and it burns out, we'll teach those barbarians the price of defying Rome.'

As the centurion turned away, a blast of scalding heat from a nearby flare-up made him flinch. Along the column, the legionaries had downed their shields and were hacking at the undergrowth, using their swords to loosen roots and strip the combustible material away from the bare earth before hurling it into the flames. Still the fire crept closer, the heat forcing the men back into an ever smaller space each side of the track. Nor was the blaze the only danger. The enemy were hurling rocks and spears and loosing arrows through the flames and smoke, shooting blind but striking Romans who had been forced to set down their shields to work on the fire break. The casualties were hauled onto the track, where the legion's medics attended to their wounds as best they could while smoke and cinders swirled around them. The mules of the baggage train were braying with terror as they pressed together, the drovers trying to prevent them becoming entangled. The disciplined cohesion of the legion was beginning to break down as the men were steadily driven back by the heat.

Bernardicus turned to the legate. 'We're going to have to break through the blaze, sir. We can't stay on the track. The fire's getting the better of us.'

Cerialis glanced at the cordon of glittering flames and smoke. 'We can't get through that.'

'We have to, sir. And quickly. Before it closes in.'

'How?'

'The men will have to use their cloaks to beat paths through the flames.'

11

'Even if that works, the enemy will be waiting for us on the far side.'

'Yes, sir. That's the choice before us. We either stay put and roast, or we take our chances with the rebels. I'd sooner die with a sword in my hand than be burned to death.'

The legate shuddered. 'Then there is no choice. Re-form the cohorts and tell the men we're going to fight our way out of the trap. We'll head to the right,' he continued. 'That way we'll only have to face half their number before the rest see what's up and work their way round the blaze to join the fight.'

'Yes, sir. Good idea,' the centurion conceded. 'We'd better move all at once to make the most of it, sir.'

'I'll have the bucinas sound the advance when the men are ready.' Cerialis gestured to the men carrying the brass instruments who were formed up behind the legion's standards. 'Go and give the order, Centurion.'

Bernardicus hurried back up the column, pausing to relay instructions to the commander of each cohort, and the men fell back from the flames, faces gleaming with sweat as they took up their shields and waited for the signal. When he reached his century at the head of the column and explained the plan, his optio glanced at the fire, no more than twenty feet from them, and shook his head. 'We'll never make it.'

'Maybe. Maybe not,' Bernardicus replied laconically. 'We can discuss that afterwards. Get the men ready.'

'Yes, sir.' The optio forced a grin. 'Later, then.'

The men of the First Century formed up, four deep, to the right. One section had their cloaks ready while their comrades carried their shields. The cloaks were hurriedly soaked with water from the canteens. Three more sections stood with javelins, ready to unleash them against the enemy on the far side of the blaze as the way was opened for the century to pass through and engage the rebels. Looking down the column, Bernardicus could see the other centuries making their preparations, and the legate and his men in the distance.

'Give the order,' he muttered to himself. The flames were close enough that he had to squint to protect his eyes from the searing heat. 'For Jupiter's sake, man, give the fucking order . . .'

He saw that his men were pressing closer together and raising their shields to protect themselves from the scalding air that stung their exposed skin. He raised his own shield and ducked his head behind it.

'Sir!' a voice called out. 'Your crest's alight.'

He smelt the sudden acrid odour of burning horsehair and snatched at his canteen, removing the stopper and dousing the top of his helmet with what was left. The strident notes of the legion's bucinas sounded above the roar of the fire, and he let the canteen drop to his side as he shouted to his men, 'Beaters! Get forward!'

The men with the dampened cloaks bent double to keep the heat off their faces as they scurried forward and started striking out at the burning grass and bracken, then cast the cloaks onto the ground to smother the flames. Within moments, only a thin line of fire separated them from the enemy.

'Javelins!' Bernardicus called out. 'Loose!'

The legionaries hurled the weapons in a shallow arc and the shafts disappeared into the smoke. An instant later, there were cries of alarm as the points penetrated the enemy's ranks. Long experience had taught the centurion the importance of striking home while the enemy was still recoiling from the impact of a javelin volley, and he snatched out his sword and shouted for his men to follow as he ran towards the smouldering cloaks on the ground. He heard a man close behind him call out the legion's battle cry, 'Forward Hispania!'

Bursting through a thin screen of flames, heedless of their sharp sting, he charged across the ground on the far side, where wisps of smoke curled from the blackened earth. The first of his men ran close behind and fanned out on either side as they made for the nearest rebels. The enemy were loosely massed and had been cheering at the prospect of their foes being burned alive. Now they were taken by surprise as the Romans surged through the flames and slammed their shields into the tribesmen, stabbing at them with their short swords.

Bernardicus saw a tall figure with helmet and armour to his right and took the man for one of the enemy leaders. He swerved towards his opponent, who had time to raise his kite shield so that they clashed with a jarring thud. The momentum was with the Roman and the rebel stumbled back. Bernardicus seized the advantage and thrust his sword into the other man's throat, driving the point through the back of his neck. Recovering the blade, he did not spare his enemy a second glance as the rebel fell to his knees, sword and shield dropping from his hands as he gurgled blood. On either side, more of his men were throwing themselves at the enemy after braving the thin curtain of fire. To his right, the other Roman units were following suit, charging home with desperate fury to shatter the rebels' morale.

The centurion turned to face a younger rebel warrior, tall and skinny, barely old enough for stubble to grow on his jawline. The youth's eyes were wide with fear and the point of his spear trembled as he confronted the Roman officer. Bernardicus smacked the flat of his sword sharply against the trim of his shield and noticed his opponent flinch. He feinted with the sword and gave a vicious snarl, and the youth backed away hurriedly and disappeared amongst his comrades.

The enemy's battle horns sounded in answer to the bucinas, their flat notes overwhelming the sound of the Roman instruments. The air filled with the battle cries of the Iceni and their Trinovantian rebels, who pressed towards the scattered groups of legionaries desperately fighting for a foothold beyond the flames. Glancing over his shoulder, Bernardicus could see that almost all his century had passed through the fire and were holding their own, for the moment. Other units of the legion were not faring so well. Some had not even breached the flame wall. Others had, but were being forced back on the blaze. He felt a leaden sickness in the pit of his stomach as he realised that the fight was already lost. The odds were against the Romans and worsening with every heartbeat. The only hope for himself and his men was to try and cut their way through the enemy and escape into the trees.

'Form a wedge on me!' he cried out above the din of battle. 'First Century, on me!'

His men edged toward him in tight formation, with the century's standard two ranks behind Bernardicus. He waited an instant to ensure that the last of them had escaped the flames, then called the pace as the wedge of overlapping shields, punctuated by the tips of the legionaries' swords, tramped into the dense mass of tribesmen. Bracing their shield arms, the Romans punched and pressed their way forward, stabbing at any enemy warrior who came within reach. Sword and axe blows thudded off the curved shields and rang sharply where they struck the large hemispherical hand guards.

Steadily the wedge cut its way through, leaving a trail of bodies in its wake. A handful of legionaries were wounded, and those who could still walk fell in behind the standard and did their best to keep up. Those who could not were borne away by their comrades in the middle of the formation, but as the latter were called on to fill the gaps, the injured men were left behind to be slaughtered by the enemy.

Bernardicus steered the formation towards the nearest trees, noting that there appeared to be a narrow track that ran up the slope towards the ridge. That would be the century's best chance of escaping the fate of the rest of the legion, he decided. All around the enemy continued their assault, increasingly frustrated

15

by their failure to break up and crush the wedge as it carved its way through. Only a handful of rebels now stood in the centurion's way, and he battered one to the side and cut through the arm of another before those left backed away and left the path unguarded.

'Stay with me, lads!' he called out. 'Keep on the path!'

He moved swiftly between the trees and trotted up the incline, his lungs burning with the effort of his exertions. His men followed him, the rearmost turning to cover the retreat as the enemy pursued them closely. The undergrowth began to thicken as the path penetrated the trees, hampering any attempt by the rebels to harry the flanks or cut round the Romans and block their escape. The sounds of the fighting in the vale began to fade as the trees muffled the noise.

After half a mile, the trees began to thin out, and a short distance ahead Bernardicus could see the bare crest of a hillock that formed part of the ridge. If they could occupy the high ground, his men could catch their breath while he considered the next move.

'Set the standard up there,' he panted to the century's standard bearer, then stepped to the side to urge his men on as they stumbled past him, gasping for breath. As the stragglers came up, labouring under the burden of their armour and shields, he pointed to the standard.

'Up there, lads. Then you can rest a while.'

He could hear the sounds of fighting drawing closer: the clash of blades and the thud of weapons on shields. He headed back down the path, rounded a corner and came up against Optio Severus, who was commanding a section that made up the rearguard. Beyond them, he could see the enemy, desperate to hunt down and slaughter their prey. The six legionaries were falling back in relays, using their broad shields to block the path while they stabbed at any rebels reckless enough to come within range.

'Good job, Severus,' he greeted the optio.

'Hot work, sir.'

'I've got the rest of the century on top of the ridge. Delay that lot as long as you can before you fall back to the standard. I'll have two sections ready to cover you once the path leaves the trees. Understood?'

'Yes, sir.'

'Good.' Bernardicus patted him on the shoulder and left him to his task. Trotting back up the path, he came across a straggler who had slumped to the ground just before it reached open ground. One of the younger men who had only recently joined the Ninth. He was on his knees, leaning forward as he fought for breath, his sword sheathed and his shield lying on the ground beside him.

'On your feet, boy!' Bernardicus smiled at him. 'Don't let those barbarian bastards think we can't go the distance.'

'So tired . . . sir. So fucking tired . . .'

'There'll be plenty of time to be tired later.' He bent to haul the legionary to his feet and picked up his shield for him. 'You'll need this. Trust me.'

He gave the youth a gentle shove, and together they climbed the short distance to the crest of the ridge, where the other men were gathered around the standard.

Bernardicus took a deep breath to ensure his order would be clearly heard. 'First two sections! Fall in on me! The rest of you be ready to stand to the moment the enemy come out of the trees.'

The men rose wearily to their feet across the crest of the hill. Bernardicus could see the flames and smoke that were engulfing the rest of the column and the baggage train. A panicking team of mules emerged from the blaze, their manes on fire. As they careered across the open ground, driven mad by their agony, the enemy scattered to avoid falling under their hooves and the heavy wheels of the burning cart. Amid the flames he could see legionaries pressing together in small groups, trying to shelter behind their shields until they too caught fire. Others, singly and in small groups, dashed through the fire and were cut down by the enemy waiting beyond.

At the rear of the column, several more carts drawn by mules bolted through the enemy, clearing a wide path. Immediately after them galloped a body of mounted men. Bernardicus smiled bitterly as he realised that must be Cerialis, his staff and the rest of the mounted contingent, saving their own necks while the infantry were burned alive or slaughtered by the enemy. A handful of the riders were pulled from their horses as the party cut their way through the scattered rebels, but the rest escaped and raced back down the track in the direction of the fortress at Lindum. The legate would live to tell the tale. Bernardicus could only hope that his reputation would die along with the thousands of good men he had led into the trap.

He turned to the two sections he had summoned to cover the optio's retreat. 'Let's go, lads.'

They were no more than ten paces down the slope when Severus and two of his men came running out of the trees ahead of the enemy, sprinting hard towards the crest. The rearmost man stumbled and fell to his knees. An instant later, he was knocked onto his face by a brawny warrior wielding an axe. The second blow smashed into his helmet, pulverising his skull. A handful of the warrior's companions paused in their pursuit to hack at the body and stab it with spears before resuming the chase. Their bloodlust was the salvation of Severus and the last survivor of the rearguard section as they ran through the narrow gap in the line of shields, which closed behind them. Bernardicus and his men had recovered their breath and easily held off the rebels who reached them, cutting down several before he gave the order to break contact and withdraw to the crest.

18

A steady stream of rebels spilled out from the path, and more joined them from amongst the trees, flowing swiftly across the slope and beginning to encircle the crest. Bernardicus considered rousing his men to follow him in an attempt to cut their way out again, but there was no chance to escape now. Better to make their last stand here than be slaughtered like dogs in a futile attempt to outrun the enemy.

He spat, then called out, 'Close up around the standard!'

He estimated that little more than forty of his men remained. At least a thousand rebels surrounded them, and more were appearing all the time. A mounted chieftain rode up from the trees and reined in safely beyond javelin range as he surveyed the Roman position. He shouted an order to his followers, and those closest to the legionaries drew back and began to jeer and throw insults at the small knot of soldiers defending the hilltop.

Bernardicus regarded them silently. Even as he looked over the mass of warriors and those in the distance still gathered around the conflagration in the vale, his mind was calm. This was the moment that all soldiers contemplated many times during their service. There was always the question about how they would face the end, in whatever form it took. A sudden merciful death, the lingering agony of a mortal wound or, as was now the case, the certainty of annihilation. He knew that he had enjoyed better fortune than the majority of those who served in the legions. He had survived battles and skirmishes when many others he had known did not. Promotion, decorations and loot had come his way and paid for the modest farming estate in Gaul where his wife was raising his sons. He thought of them fondly, and the only thing he found himself regretting was that he had not been able to join them for one last Saturnalia.

'Ah well,' he muttered to himself. 'The gods will play their games.'

19

The enemy chieftain slowly approached the crest, accompanied by one of his men. They halted some thirty paces away, and the chieftain thrust his finger at the centurion and spoke loudly and clearly in the native tongue. He paused, and the man beside him cleared his throat and translated in slightly accented Latin.

'My lord, Syphodubnus calls on you to surrender and save your lives! Throw down your weapons and submit to his mercy and you will be spared.'

'Oh, I believe that!' said one of the legionaries cynically.

Bernardicus was about to silence him, then thought better of it and addressed Severus instead. 'Optio, take that man's name. Latrine duties for a month.'

The men laughed, as he had hoped they would.

'Romans! What is your answer?'

Bernardicus leaned on the top of his shield. 'What shall I say, lads? He's inviting us to become slaves. I say fuck that. But what do *you* say, eh?'

The air filled with loud raspberries and contemptuous laughter, and the noise from the enemy massed about them died away for a moment as the rebels took in the Roman soldiers' response to their chieftain's offer. Looking surprised, Syphodubnus spoke again, and waited for his warrior to translate.

'My lord offers you one last chance. Surrender or die. What say you?'

Bernardicus paused a moment to find the right words to sum up his feelings about bowing to the enemy, his anger at the foolishness of his legate, his despair at never seeing his family again, and the comradeship he felt for the tough men who were about to die along with him.

He smiled, and bellowed his answer. 'Bollocks!'

The chieftain frowned and turned to his translator, and there was a brief exchange. Then he shrugged and gave a sad salute to Bernardicus before turning his horse and trotting down the slope to his followers. The centurion's smile faded as he called out to his men.

'Take as many of those barbarian bastards down as you can. Let those that survive never forget the men of the First Century, First Cohort of the Ninth Legion!'

The legionaries let out a loud cheer and brandished their short swords as the standard bearer raised the standard high.

A war horn sounded and a savage roar erupted all around them as the rebels charged up the slope.

'Shields up!' Bernardicus shouted. 'Close ranks!'

The legionaries hoisted their broad shields and braced their boots, ready to absorb the impact of the charge. They raised their swords to the horizontal and drew their elbows back, muscles bunching. The centurion offered a swift prayer to Mars that he be permitted to die with honour and without undue suffering, then gritted his teeth and faced the enemy.

The rebels came in the wild rush favoured by the Celts, lips stretched wide as they shrieked their war cries, eyes blazing and their limed hair rising in spikes from their scalps. Many bore the swirling tattoos of warriors on their limbs and chests and carried the shields and spears that had been concealed from their Roman overlords for many years. They closed the last few paces in a heartbeat and slammed into the legionaries' shield wall with a rippling series of thuds and sharp, splintering cracks as their blades bit at the leather-covered laminate.

Bernardicus let his body sway under the impact and then thrust back, slamming his shield boss into the sword-wielding rebel before him. He heard the man grunt, and stabbed his short sword round the side of the shield, angling the point towards where he estimated his opponent's torso to be. He was rewarded with the judder up his arm that indicated a solid strike. Twisting the blade, he tore it free and drew his arm back to strike again. Around him the clatter of weapons and the shrill ring and scrape of blade on

21

blade filled his ears. He could hear the grunts and gasps of his nearest men and those of his foes.

The first of the Romans fell as his shield was ripped from his grip before a spear thrust tore through his thigh and opened an artery. He staggered a moment as blood gushed from the wound, then his knees folded beneath him and he pitched forward amid the rebels.

'Close the gap!' Bernardicus shouted, and the small formation shrank a little tighter as the fighting continued.

As the men were cut down one by one, the wounded were dragged to the centre and sat or lay at the feet of the standard bearer, who cried out constant encouragement to his comrades: 'For Rome! For the emperor!'

Bernardicus knew that this skirmish would be forgotten almost as soon as it was over, and that though he and his men would be mourned, no history would ever relate their last stand. He was no longer fighting for Rome and emperor. He was fighting for his men, and because that was what he was trained to do until he drew his last breath.

A sudden surge of enemy warriors forced a break in the shield wall a short distance to his right, and then the rebels were in amongst them, striking at the sides and backs of the legionaries still trying to hold the perimeter. In an instant the formation dissolved into a series of unequal duels as the enemy overwhelmed the position. Bernardicus saw the standard bearer stagger under an axe blow from behind; his fingers spasmed and the standard slipped from his grip. As it began to fall, the centurion threw his shield aside and leaped forward to catch the wooden shaft and keep it aloft, slashing wildly with his sword at any rebels who came close.

As his men died around him, butchered where they lay on the bloodied grass, Bernardicus was surrounded by several attackers. He managed two parries and blocked a feint before a blade cut deep into the wrist of his sword arm, almost severing it. His weapon dropped at his side and the enemy rushed forward, hacking and stabbing. He felt the blows, and the warm rush of blood as he was driven to his knees. Still he clutched the standard tightly in his left hand, resisting the first attempt to wrestle it from his grip. Then his strength gave out and he fell onto his side and rolled onto his back. As his vision darkened, he could only gaze up in despair as an enemy warrior brandished his trophy against the clear blue sky while his comrades roared in triumph.

CHAPTER TWO

The straits of the island of Mona

Dusk was closing round the mountains to the east, while in the other direction the sun was setting over the gentle hills of Mona, bathing the scattered clouds in a warm red glow. The final squadron of the cavalry contingent of Prefect Cato's cohort was being ferried across the strait aboard the shallow barges that had been used to invade the island. The Eighth Illyrian cohort was one of the auxiliary units made up of both cavalry and infantry that were the workhorses of the Roman army across the Empire.

Cato was watching the sunset from a small hillock overlooking the straits and the fortified camp where the rest of the cohort was feeding and grooming the horses before they attended to their own needs. Men drawn from a number of mounted units made up the flying column escorting Governor Suetonius in his bid to reach Londinium before Boudica and her rebel horde. Cato had been obliged to leave his infantry with the main body of the army while he and the mounted contingent of the cohort raced ahead with the governor's column. He could easily make out the headquarters tents where Suetonius had planned the attack on the enemy's defences across the strait less than a month before. He could imagine the fevered atmosphere at headquarters at this moment, and what might be said at the briefing for senior officers that was due to take place later.

He had taken advantage of this moment of inactivity to find a place where he might be alone. There had been so little time to think over the months since the campaign to defeat the hill tribes and their Druid allies. The enemy had resisted with desperate courage and had come close to frustrating Rome's ambitions. They had fought to the last to protect the sacred groves of the Druids that had stood for longer than history could record. Now those groves had been destroyed, the sacred oaks cut down and burned and the Druids and their followers massacred. Most of the warriors of the mountain tribes had been killed, though a handful had managed to flee the island and escape to the mainland. Only a few hundred had been taken prisoner, to be sold into slavery. The proceeds would be meagre, and along with such booty as had been gleaned from the battlefields and the settlements, it was doubtful that Emperor Nero would have much to rejoice over when news of the victory reached Rome.

Cato sighed. It was the emperor's reaction to the other news from Britannia that would set the cat amongst the pigeons in the capital. In fact, reports of the outbreak of the rebellion led by Boudica was more likely to reach Nero first, and there would be shock and outrage over the destruction of the veterans' colony at Camulodunum. The announcement of Governor Suetonius's victory over the hill tribes and the conquest of the Druid stronghold of Mona would be overshadowed. There would be no celebration, no vote of acclaim for the governor in the Senate. Indeed, the emperor and his advisers would be looking for someone to blame, and Suetonius would be the first in line for that.

Moreover, Cato was aware of the political cross-currents in Rome. There were many senators, some of whom had the ear of the emperor, who advocated the abandonment of Britannia. He appreciated the arguments made in favour of withdrawing the legions – mostly to do with the imbalance between the costs of operating the province and the revenues it generated. At the same time, the damage to Roman prestige would be formidable. The perceived influence of the Druids over the Celtic tribes of the mainland had prompted the invasion of Britannia. To withdraw before the Romanisation of the island was complete would be seen as weakness and embolden the enemies that surrounded the Empire's thinly held frontier. Besides, there was a more human argument in favour of retaining Britannia. Much blood had been shed by the men of the legions and auxiliary cohorts to tame the new province and put an end to the Druids. If Rome pulled out now, it would mock the sacrifice of her soldiers, including the veterans who had died at Camulodunum.

As his thoughts turned to the colony, as they had many times since the news had reached Mona only the day before, a shadow passed over Cato. The small circle of family and friends he had loved most in the world had been living in Camulodunum when he had been called away to fight in the campaign. A great burden had been lifted when he had learned that the women and children had been sent to the relative safety of Londinium. However, his best friend, Centurion Macro, Camulodunum's senior official, had remained to defend the colony, and had undoubtedly perished with the rest of the defenders when the rebels took the place.

Macro, his grudging mentor when Cato had first joined the Second Legion nearly eighteen years ago. Macro, who had been there to share the chilling dangers of each campaign they had fought. Macro, who had been so proud when Cato had been promoted above him, and who had handled the new arrangement with a sensitivity that belied his gruff, hard exterior. Macro, who had toasted the birth of Cato's son, Lucius, and who had invited Cato to be his guest of honour when he married his woman, Petronella. Macro had been friend, father figure and brother in arms for most of Cato's life, and he found it hard to accept that he was now gone. It pained him so much that he was tempted by the conviction that it could not be. That somehow Macro had survived. But cold reason mocked such a slender hope. Macro would not have abandoned his post. He would have gone down fighting, since nothing else would have occurred to him. He would have scorned flight or surrender.

'Macro is dead,' Cato muttered to himself. Then, more bitterly, as the urge to deny it rose in his heart, 'He is dead . . .'

He must accept that and use it to harden his resolve to avenge his friend and defeat the rebels before they marched on Londinium. As for his love, Claudia, and his son, he earnestly hoped that they had the good sense to leave Londinium and take ship to Gaul until the rebellion was crushed. He smiled ruefully and corrected his line of thought. There was no certainty that the rebels would be defeated. Given the disposition of the forces in play, Boudica and her followers would have a free hand across the richest and most vulnerable areas of the province. They could devastate Britannia to such an extent that it would be beyond salvation. Worse still, if they moved swiftly and boldly, they could pick off the Roman forces before the governor had a chance to concentrate them into an army powerful enough to confront the rebels. The situation looked bleak indeed.

His thoughts were interrupted by the notes of a bucina announcing the change of watch at sunset. The last of the barges had grounded on the shore and the auxiliaries were unloading their mounts and kit and leading the horses towards the camp. Cato stirred and rose stiffly to his feet before striding down the slope to the nearest gate. He exchanged a salute with the sentry before crossing the timbered causeway that stretched across the defence ditch. The fortified camp had been built to accommodate two legions, and so there was plenty of space for the mounted column and their horses, and the air was thick with the sour odour of horse sweat and manure.

He made his way to his tent and took off his helmet, cloak and scale vest. It had been a hot day and it would be some hours before the temperature became more comfortable. His dark curls were plastered to his scalp, and he cupped his hands in the water bowl his orderly had prepared for him and doused his face, scalp and neck, enjoying the cool trickles that found their way under his tunic. Mopping his brow with a rag held out to him by the orderly, he instructed the man to prepare a meal for when he returned from the briefing.

'Roast pork or mutton,' he decided. 'Take whatever coin is needed from my purse. But get a good price.'

The parsimony of the long years before he had acquired wealth had stayed with him, much to the initial amusement of his orderly. The latter was used to the string of aristocratic officers he had served before being appointed to Cato's cohort as a replacement after the costly fight to secure a foothold on the island.

'Yes, sir. I will see what can be done. But I dare say the other officers' servants will have a head start on purchasing what meat there is to be had.'

'You haven't failed me yet, Trebonius,' Cato responded, half in praise and half in warning. He handed the rag back and made his way across the camp to the cluster of large tents where Governor Suetonius and his staff were quartered.

As he passed the tent lines, where the men of the column were lighting cooking fires, there was a palpable tension in the air, different from the customary quiet good cheer of men relaxing after a day's march. There was no singing and little of the usual humorous banter. The disaster at Camulodunum and the danger posed to the lightly defended territory of the south and east of the province preyed on every man's mind. Many had family in the settlements that had grown up around the garrison forts dotted across the land, now under threat from the rebels. Some, like Cato, had friends who had lived at the veterans' colony. He

28

shared their sense of helplessness, being so far away from where they were needed to protect those they knew and loved. The same concerns were being played out in the camp of the main army that was following in the footsteps of the mounted column, only they would be more acute for the infantry, who would be marching at a slower pace and would take longer to cross the straits, then head through the mountains and across the province to Londinium, in the unlikely event that the town had not been sacked by the enemy by the time they arrived.

The flaps of the governor's tent had been rolled up to take advantage of the light breeze blowing across the camp, bringing with it the sweet scent from the heather growing on the nearby hills. Most of the summoned officers were already present, and Cato sat on the end of one of the benches as he waited for the briefing to begin. He could see Suetonius talking earnestly to two tribunes outside, clasping the forearm of each before they climbed onto their mounts and rode off towards the gate giving out onto the coastal path that ran along the sea to the north of the mountains.

As the governor entered the tent, the officers within stood to attention. It would be light for some hours yet, and there was no need for any lamps as Suetonius glanced over his officers.

'Be seated.' He paused while Cato and the others eased themselves back onto the benches. 'The last elements of the column will reach the mainland soon. The mounted column will be leaving the camp at first light and riding hard. I've sent men ahead to make sure that remounts are made ready for us at Deva and the larger forts along the way. With luck we should be in Londinium in six days. The rest of the army under Legate Calpurnius will reach the straits tomorrow evening and follow our route at the best pace they can manage. I've emphasised that I want the units intact when they catch us up – it's not a race. I can't afford stragglers. Every man will be needed when we face the enemy. Assuming they can keep to a pace of twenty to twenty-five miles a day, the infantry will reach Londinium in twelve to fourteen days' time. That's if there are no contacts with the rebels or mountain tribes who still have any fight in 'em.'

He rubbed his left eye and blinked wearily. 'It's possible, even likely, that Boudica will reach Londinium before us. I've just sent a tribune with orders to the procurator, Decianus Catus, to evacuate the town as soon as the enemy scouts are sighted. I've sent a second tribune to the Second Legion at Isca Dumnoniorum to order them to march on Londinium. Hopefully, the commander there will have already acted on his own initiative and set off. If the town has been taken, they are to turn north instead and meet the main column marching down from Mona. A message has already been sent to Lindum to order Cerialis to march the Ninth Legion to Londinium and fall back on us if he finds the rebels there. With the best part of three legions and the auxiliary cohorts, I will have enough men to risk battle.'

'Surely that is ample to deal with a tribal uprising, sir,' one of the cavalry prefects commented. 'After all, it's only the Iceni and some of the Trinovantes we're dealing with. What can they muster, a few thousand men armed with farm tools and hunting weapons?'

'If that was the case, then I dare say the veterans at Camulodunum would have been able to hold them at bay for much longer. The truth is that we . . . I have underestimated the Iceni. Both in terms of number and the amount of weapons they have concealed from us. I received a dispatch from Decianus this afternoon. A merchant has seen the enemy camp outside the ruins of Camulodunum. He's a former officer of scouts, so he knows his business, and he reckoned their number at no less than eighty thousand.'

His audience stirred anxiously before the governor continued. 'How many of those are first-rate fighters, I don't know. But with the defeat of the veterans at the colony, it's likely that many more will flock to Boudica's standard. There are plenty of warriors in other tribes who will be keen to join her cause. I dare say they will also have hidden their weapons in the hope that the day would come when they could use them against us.'

Cato could see that the scale of the peril posed by the rebels had shocked some of the other officers. Rome had not faced a tribal army of that size since the time of Caratacus. The fate of the province was balanced on the edge of a knife and every man there knew it. For a moment he felt a degree of sympathy for Suetonius, who should have been enjoying the victory that had eluded his predecessors. Instead he would be seen as the man who failed to spot the danger and whose campaign to take Mona would now look like reckless adventurism. If he defeated Boudica, he would still be accountable for the destruction and loss of life she had caused. If he was defeated, his name would enter the annals of infamy. Not that he would be alive to mourn the fact. Nor would Cato and all the other officers contemplating the desperate situation they were facing. Nor the thousands of legionaries and auxiliaries who served under Suetonius and the tens of thousands of Roman citizens who had settled in Britannia. Not to mention the people of the tribes that had allied with Rome, and as a result would surely be treated with greater cruelty than the rebels unleashed against Romans. All were at risk, and the killing had only just begun.

Suetonius continued. 'The danger is that the longer the rebellion lasts, the more those tribes whose loyalty to Rome is uncertain will be tempted to join Boudica. It'll be like an avalanche, gathering pace and growing as it sweeps all before it. So the best chance we have of stopping the rebels is to move to confront them as swiftly as possible, before they can turn almost every tribe against us. To that end, my intention is to see if we can meet them at Londinium and repel them there. A sharp setback will hit their morale and discourage others from joining their cause.'

Cato raised a hand. The governor turned to him. 'Yes, Prefect Cato?'

'Sir, the defences in Londinium are in shit order. Every one of us who has been there knows this. There's hardly anything left of the rampart and ditch that protected the original settlement. Only the governor's palace compound has any walls that could be defended. Even then, a determined assault made by the enemy will overwhelm them. Besides, there wouldn't be enough room to shelter the people of the town.'

'Thank you for your contribution,' Suetonius replied flatly. 'There's truth in what you say about the defences. Once we reach Londinium, I will assess what can be done to make good. If there is time, we may effect repairs sufficient to keep the rebels out. Besides, the Second Legion will be on hand a matter of days after our arrival. A few thousand legionaries manning the rampart against the rebels could well be enough to stem the tide until the rest of the army catches up. Then we'll be on the offensive and will crush those treacherous bastards who have stabbed us in the back.'

'And if you judge that the defences can't be made good, sir, what then?'

'I'll order the civilians to evacuate, abandon Londinium and fall back on the main body of the army.'

'Where will the civilians go, sir? Where would they be safe?'

'Verulamium . . . Calleva. Any place they can stay ahead of Boudica and her horde. They'll have to shift for themselves, Prefect. My concern is safeguarding my forces until I can concentrate them on the enemy. I cannot and will not waste men on futile attempts to delay the rebels. If Londinium cannot be held, it must be sacrificed. You all know how it is – we must trade space for time if there is to be any hope of winning the day.

32

If that means we lose Londinium, Verulamium or any other town or settlement in the path of Boudica and her army, that is a price that has to be paid. There may be some in Rome who will question my decision, but they are not here and I'll be damned if I will let the prospect of grumbling from some dining-couch generals decide my strategy. They'll be grumbling even more if we go down to defeat and lose the entire province.'

'Yes, sir,' Cato said with feeling. He was relieved that the governor's grasp of the overall situation was sound and that he was not prepared to take unnecessary risks out of concern for how his actions might look back in Rome. For an instant he felt a spark of anger over Macro's refusal to give Camulodunum up and evacuate the colony. The veterans might still be alive if he had. Then he felt ashamed for second-guessing his friend. Perhaps Macro had managed to repair the colony's defences to the extent that they were sound enough in his professional judgement. He had been there and Cato had not, and in the absence of accurate knowledge it was unfair to question his judgement. At the same time, he understood Macro well enough to know that he would have found it hard to give up a position. It was one of the qualities shared by all men promoted to the centurionate. The first into a fight and the last to leave it. That was why they were the backbone of the Roman army. It was likely that Macro knew he was a dead man when he made his decision to remain and defend the colony, and whatever Cato might think, that decision was the inevitable consequence of his character and every value he held dear.

'Very well,' Suetonius concluded. 'Make sure your men are ready to ride at first light. They are to leave all non-essential kit here. Just two days' rations from the stores, weapons, armour and cloaks. Nothing else. Any horse that goes lame will be left behind along with its rider. They can make their way to the nearest garrisoned outpost and wait for the main body to catch up. Better let them know as soon as you are dismissed. I don't want them dealing with a nasty surprise come the dawn. Very well, there's nothing more to be said. Goodnight, gentlemen.'

The officers stood to salute and made their way outside. There was a rosy hue across the horizon to the west, and the evening air was still and humid. To the north, the sky was gloomy and there were no stars. As Cato turned to make his way back to his men, there was a faint rumble of thunder, culminating in a sound like a discordant and uneven drum roll that ended with a resonating boom. He stared towards the gathering storm, wondering if this was an omen, and then pushed the thought out of his mind. There were preparations to be made for the tough march to come. The demands of the next few days would test every man and horse to the limit of their endurance and beyond. But they must reach Londinium before Boudica and her rebels if the town and its inhabitants were to be spared the fate that had befallen Camulodunum.

CHAPTER THREE

The storm broke early in the morning, not long after the mounted column had ridden out of the camp. The air was oppressively still and heavy as the first rolls of thunder echoed off the hills to the right of the cavalry units. Low clouds covered the sky from horizon to horizon and obscured the heights above the track. Despite the constant clop of hooves, the champing of snaffles and the snorts of the horses, the men were aware of the imminence of the deluge and rode in silence for the most part, muttering quietly when they spoke. The rain came on a sudden chilly breeze that bit through the sultry summer air, heavy drops that pattered onto the cloaks of the men and the coats of their horses and impacted with a light ping on their helmets.

Cato and the two hundred men of his mounted contingent formed the vanguard of the column, riding a short distance ahead. He pulled his cloak more tightly across his shoulders and tilted his head to the side so that the water ran off the brow guard of his helmet and did not obscure his view ahead. Even though the local tribe, the Deceanglians, had been defeated in the recent campaign, there were still war bands at large, and they were capable of launching hit-and-run attacks before melting away into the hills. He hoped the enemy would be deterred by the fact that the column was comprised solely of cavalry, unaccompanied by any slow-moving baggage train. There would be little to tempt any raiders and much for them to be wary of. The greater danger was the possibility of an ambush or a more concerted attack that would hinder the column's progress and cause casualties that the governor could ill afford in his bid to save Londinium.

Cato heard the drumming of hooves above the hiss of the rain and glanced over his shoulder as one of the staff tribunes reined in and eased his mount alongside him.

'Governor Suetonius's compliments, sir. He says the horses should be warmed up by now and to increase pace to a canter.'

'Does he now?' Cato looked up just as lightning lit the interior of the clouds a short distance ahead. The thunder came with a tearing metallic crash and ended with a deep blast whose reverberations he could feel. The track ahead of the column was already covered with puddles and would quickly be churned up by his men to leave a sucking, slippery quagmire in their wake. Dangerous ground for any horse to attempt at a canter.

'Inform the governor that in my judgement it would be ill advised to advance any faster until the rain has passed and the ground is firm enough to risk an increase in pace.'

'Sir?'

Cato could see that the tribune was not used to the governor's orders being questioned. He fixed him with a steady gaze and the young man nodded.

'Yes, sir.'

He wheeled his horse round, rather too sharply, and the beast caught a hoof in a rut and stumbled a few paces, forcing the tribune to bend forward awkwardly to remain in the saddle. The men behind Cato snorted with derision at his poor horsemanship, and once the tribune had recovered his seat, he walked his horse off at a sedate pace with as much dignity as he could muster.

As he rode on, Cato wondered how well the governor would take his response. Over the course of the campaign, he had observed his commander closely and learned that Suetonius was

36

a man in a hurry, driven to secure a successful military reputation before age obliged him to return to Rome and retire from his army career. Like all members of the Senate who could trace their family across many generations, he aspired to outdo the achievements of his ancestors and add to the reputation of his clan. In Cato's long experience, such men were inclined to disregard the safety and lives of those who served under them if such considerations clashed with the opportunity to win fame on the battlefield. Or, in the present predicament, reverse a setback and avoid disaster.

Thankfully there were other senators, particularly those more recently elevated to the aristocracy, who were not so profligate with the lives of their men. Vespasianus was a case in point. He had been the legate of the Second Legion when Cato had first enlisted, and his concern for the well-being of his troops had impressed his men, who repaid him with loyalty and courage. If Vespasianus had been appointed governor, Cato reflected, he would surely have proceeded with more caution and ensured that the rest of the province could be adequately garrisoned before even considering an attempt to take Mona.

It was pointless to wish for such things. The dire situation was as it was and had to be faced, whatever the outcome. That was the nature of soldiering. Forever dealing with the contingencies of fate, while at the same time hoping that the high command did not discover any new means of buggering things up.

'Sir, the governor's coming forward.'

Cato turned to Centurion Tubero, the officer in command of the cohort's mounted contingent, a younger man who had begun the campaign headstrong and foolhardy but was now seasoned and more reliable as a result of the harsh lessons he had learned. Tubero nodded his head to indicate the small party of horsemen cantering along beside the column. The red crests of the helmets of the governor and his staff officers and their finely woven cloaks were now drenched and dark, presenting a pitiful portrait of discomfort.

'Prefect!'

Cato sucked in a breath and turned his mount off the track to let the cohort continue on its way. He raised a hand in salute, but Suetonius ignored the gesture, his expression hard and his eyes glinting beneath the rim of his gilded helmet.

'Why have you countermanded my order?'

'It would be dangerous to risk any increase in pace with the track in this condition, sir.'

'I don't give a damn about the condition of the track! In any case, it looks fine to me. We must increase the pace.'

'It looks fine at the front of the column, sir. But conditions will get worse as the leading horses churn the surface up. If we try to increase the pace, you will lose more men and horses to injury than we can afford.'

Cato watched the other man's jaw clench as he weighed up the situation. It was a marginal call, but given that there was still a remote chance that the column might reach Londinium before the enemy, it made sense to look to the safety of the men and their horses.

Suetonius's nostrils flared in frustration as he stared up at the sky, blinking away raindrops. 'Very well, we'll wait for the bloody rain to stop and then decide. In the meantime, I'll thank you not to question my orders next time.'

Cato gave a non-committal grunt.

'And I'll have the vanguard advance another mile ahead of the column. You are supposed to be scouting the way ahead, Prefect, not clinging to the front of the column.'

It was a harsh rebuke, especially in front of the men from his own cohort, and Cato stiffened in his saddle and managed to bite off the urge to object to this affront to his courage. No good would come of protesting the slight.

'Yes, sir. I'll see to it.'

Suetonius turned his horse, with some difficulty, and led his officers away.

Tubero met Cato's gaze and rolled his eyes. 'That was uncalled for, sir.'

'Perhaps. The governor has a lot on his shoulders at the moment.'

'Still . . .'

Before the centurion could comment further, Cato drew a deep breath and called out to his men, 'The Eighth will advance at a slow trot!'

He tapped his heels into his horse's flanks and urged it to increase the pace. Tubero and the others rippled forward in turn, and the cohort edged ahead of the main column, leaving a glutinous layer of churned mud in its wake. Cato led the way until he estimated they were far enough ahead to satisfy the governor, then raised his arm and called out the order to reduce speed. The condition of the track improved as it climbed to higher ground, and they were afforded a view over the sea, grey and white-capped as the wind blew in from the north.

Shortly before noon, as far as Cato could estimate in the gloom, they reached a fork in the track. To the left, the route continued along the coast to a bay where a wide river with a strong current emptied into a bay. The right fork led into the mountains before reaching the ford at Canovium, guarded by a small fort, one of many that covered the army's coastal supply lines leading back to the fortress at Deva. He posted ten men at the fork to make sure that it was not missed in the rain. Tired men, hunkered down in their cloaks, could easily ride by without noticing the junction of tracks.

As the route climbed between the hills, the thickly forested slopes provided some shelter from the breeze, but the rain continued to fall in steely rods that hissed on the leafy boughs of the trees and occasioned competing ripples of water in the puddles along the track. Higher up, the trees gave way to open slopes covered with bracken. They passed a few farms surrounded by empty pens, and a village, abandoned and looted by Suetonius's army as it marched on Mona. Only once did Cato catch sight of one of the tribesmen, a solitary figure with a staff watching them from the top of a crag as the cohort wound its way towards the pass that looked down on Canovium. The hard country where the hill tribes eked a living must have been desolate enough at the best of times, Cato mused. Stripped of its sparse population and grimly illuminated by the weak daylight that struggled to pierce the low clouds and rain, it did not feel like a prize worth having for the Empire. There was little of value to tax here, and the appalling climate had him longing for the comforts of his villa in Italia.

The rain gave way to a light drizzle late in the afternoon and bright patches appeared amid the clouds as the sun tried to break through. The highest point of the pass ran a short distance from the foot of a long stretch of crags, and Cato kept a wary eye on the heights as the cohort approached the top of the incline. He saw several figures appear above them, and a moment later a volley of small rocks was hurled at the passing auxiliary cavalrymen.

'Shields up!' Cato shouted the warning and stabbed a finger towards the top of the crags. The stones landed short and thudded amid the spiky tussocks of grass to their left. A number of the horsemen whistled and jeered at the enemy as more stones failed to reach them. Ahead, Cato could see that the crags loomed almost directly above the track where it reached the top of the pass. That would be the danger point if the enemy were planning an ambush.

'Keep your shields up!' he ordered.

Tubero came alongside him. 'Want me to take some men up to deal with that lot, sir?'

Cato dismissed the idea. 'No point. They'll be gone to higher ground long before you could climb up there. Besides, it'll only cause a delay, and you can imagine what Suetonius will have to say about that. Let 'em go. A few more dead Deceanglians is not going to change anything.'

Tubero looked disappointed.

'I thought this campaign had cured your bloodlust, Centurion.'

'Just concerned to do my duty and take the fight to the enemy, sir.'

'We defeated the enemy on Mona. That lot are just the scraps left over. Besides, the way things are, you are going to be in the fight of your life when we go up against Boudica. You should concentrate on saving your courage and strength for that and not squandering it on some pointless skirmish with a bunch of hill farmers.'

'Yes, sir.' Tubero's tone was more chastened, and he let his mount fall back to rejoin the head of the cohort.

Cato felt the familiar tension as they approached the narrow point between the crags. There was no sign of movement above them, but still he had to resist the temptation to reach for the strap of the oval shield hanging from his left saddle horn. Despite the rain, the clop of the horses' hooves echoed off the rocks rising on either side, and the noise was alarming as Cato strained to detect any sound of voices. He thought he caught snatches of native tongue on the wind blowing through the gap, but they were too few and too faint to be certain that this was anything more than imagination testing his overtired and anxious mind.

He passed through the crags without incident and looked back to see that the handful of enemy warriors who had lobbed the rocks at his men earlier had disappeared, perhaps in anticipation of the pursuit that Tubero had been so keen to launch. Before him, the track zigzagged down towards a stretch of flat ground before dropping out of sight beyond the far edge. The rain was

41

falling harder, borne on a biting wind stronger than anything they had endured that day. He hunched down in his sodden cloak and pulled the folds about his body with his left hand.

As he rode on, he tried to distract his mind from the acute discomfort of the day's march by turning his thoughts to the tribal rebellion threatening the rich lands of the south of the province. Few towns and larger settlements had any garrisons of Roman troops to protect them and would be easy prey for Boudica and her followers. Those that were garrisoned had had the best men stripped from their ranks to serve with Suetonius's army. The men that remained were the oldest, or least experienced and least fit, and Cato doubted they would put up much of a fight. The best hope for those living in the path of Boudica's horde was that the Second and Ninth legions moved swiftly to block the rebels' way, or at least give their scouts cause to report back to Boudica and cause her to advance more cautiously and so delay her descent on Londinium.

Once again his mind was filled with thoughts of those he loved, and he prayed to the gods once more that they had the good sense to abandon Londinium and retreat to safety, or take a ship for Gaul, where he might find them when – if – the rebellion was defeated.

They approached Canovium at dusk, just as the rain finally eased off and became a soft mizzle that beaded the cloaks of the men and the manes of their horses. Ahead lay the river, tumbling over rocks to their right before spilling out into a wide, smooth flow that looped through the hills to the left. They had journeyed little more than twenty miles, Cato estimated with frustration. If the weather and the poor condition of the tracks endured, it might take as many as twelve to fifteen days before the column reached Londinium.

A bucina sounded the stand to as the column approached the ford opposite the supply fort, and a moment later the men of the garrison were lining the palisade and clambering up into the timber towers. Cato nodded to himself in approval. The commander of the fort was clearly a man who played safe. As well he should here in the heart of Deceanglian territory. The challenge sounded faintly across the water washing the shingle of the ford, and Cato cupped a hand to his mouth to announce their identity, even though they were surely close enough to be recognised as Romans. He edged his horse into the water, which splashed around the beast's hooves as it picked its way to the far bank followed by the rest of the column.

A centurion of auxiliaries emerged from the gloom beneath the gate tower and saluted as he crossed the ditch to greet Cato.

'Centurion Raminus, sir. You've picked a fine evening to visit us.' He leaned aside and glanced past Cato. 'Is that the general back there?'

Cato nodded. 'And he's not in the best of moods.'

'I can imagine. That Boudica business has got everyone rattled.'

'You've heard the news, then?'

'The imperial courier gave me the outline when he changed horses here two days back. Sounds serious, sir.'

He was prompting for further details, but there was not much Cato could add, and in any case he was tired and needed to see to his men. He edged his horse to the side and waved Tubero and the others towards the open gate.

'The column will need feed for the mounts and three days' marching rations.'

'Yes, sir.'

'And a meal for tonight. Be good if the garrison took care of that. I want my men rested as much as possible before we leave at dawn.' Cato jerked his thumb back towards Suetonius. 'I'd do whatever it takes to make the general comfortable.'

The centurion nodded, taking the point. 'I'll give orders for my quarters to be cleared out straight away.'

'Do that, and make sure you see to our other needs directly.'

They exchanged a salute, and the garrison commander was about to turn and trot away when Cato stopped him.

'Wait. Your men are keeping a sharp lookout and were at their positions quickly enough. Has there been any sign of trouble here?'

'Nothing we can't handle, sir. A few parties of enemy horsemen have had the fort under observation the last few days. No attempt to attack, but I've been keeping the men handy just in case.'

'Very wise.'

'Will there be anything else, sir?'

'No. Best get to it at once,' Cato replied.

The centurion trotted between the horses as he made his way back into the fort. He was already shouting for his optio to issue the orders. Cato looked at the column of riders stretching back across the ford and snaking up the slope beyond, already dissolving into the gloom as night approached.

Canovium was one of the larger depot forts along the supply lines leading back to the fortress at Deva. As the campaign was drawing to an end, there was plenty of space within its ramparts to accommodate the extra horses and men, and the latter could even shelter in the empty prefabricated granaries that had been erected in the heart of the fort. Later, as food was brought to the men in steaming iron pots carried by the auxiliaries of the garrison, Tubero marched up to Cato at the end of the granary that had been assigned to the Eighth Cohort. One of the rankers was following a few paces behind.

'What is it?' asked Cato.

'Beg your pardon, sir, but you've still to decide on the punishment for Trooper Faustinus. The deserter.'

Cato glanced at the thin young man with sallow features who stepped forward and stamped to attention. Taking in the anxious expression on the man's face, he recalled the details. Before they had left Mona, Tubero had reported that one of the men had been caught trying to leave the camp under cover of darkness. Cato found it hard to believe – where would a soldier desert to in these barren, hostile hills? – and had told the centurion to wait until a quieter moment before bringing the matter to his attention again.

'What's the story, Faustinus? You were intercepted on the picket line with a horse and several days' supply of feed and rations.'

'Yes, sir.'

'Where did you imagine you were going to desert to?'

'Wasn't deserting, sir. I was headed for Londinium.'

'Londinium?' Cato arched an eyebrow. 'Leaving aside for the moment the fact that that's where we were headed in the first place, how in Hades did you think a single Roman rider would make it through hostile country on his own?'

'I knew it would be risky, sir.'

'You are a master of understatement, Faustinus. Pray continue.'

'It's like this, sir. My woman's in Londinium, with our first kid. She's got another on the way. She lives with her folks. Her father's got a bakery in the town, but there's no other family in Britannia for her to go to and be safe from the rebels.' The words tumbled out in an anxious torrent, and the man drew a quick breath before he continued. 'I can't leave them there to face them barbarians, sir. I have to get them somewhere they ain't going to be at risk.'

'I see,' Cato said. 'If you think there's anywhere in Britannia that is safe from Boudica and her friends, then I'm afraid you are mistaken. The only hope for the province is if we can gather men quickly enough to defeat them before the rebellion spreads much further. To do that, we need every man we can find to face them in battle. That includes you, Faustinus. Do you understand?'

The young soldier hesitated before he replied. 'But it'll take too long for the column to reach Londinium, sir. If I ride alone, I can get there faster and get my family out of the town before the general and the rest arrive. Then I can rejoin the ranks to fight the enemy.'

'That's your plan?'

'Yes, sir. I swear on my kid's life I was going to rejoin the Eighth as soon as they were safe.'

Tubero gave a snort of derision.

'I mean it, sir. The lads of the Eighth are like a second family to me. Brothers in arms and that.'

Cato regarded him with a neutral expression as he considered the man's explanation. 'How long have you served with the cohort?' he asked.

'Three years, sir.'

'Then you've no excuse not to understand your duty and your obligations, have you?'

There was another brief hesitation. 'No, sir.'

He softened his tone. 'Listen, Faustinus, you are not the only man in the cohort with family in Londinium. There must be many others in the same situation, and you don't see them deserting the ranks, do you?'

'No, sir. But—'

'But nothing. The others understand that the best chance their families have of staying alive is if we defeat the rebels. They know that they have to put their fears to one side and place their trust in Suetonius, their training and their swords. If they all acted as you did, there would be no chance of victory and every single member of their families would be hunted down and slaughtered by the rebels as a result.' Cato let the man dwell on his words briefly. 'Do you understand now, Faustinus?'

The trooper nodded.

'Answer the prefect directly, damn you!' Tubero snapped.

Faustinus flinched. 'Yes, sir. I understand.'

'Then you'll give me your word that you'll make no further attempt to leave the ranks?'

'Yes, sir. I swear it, by Jupiter, Best and Greatest.'

'Good.' Cato scratched his scalp. 'That brings us to the punishment. Desertion in the face of the enemy is a capital offence . . .'

He saw the man's eyes widen and waited a moment for the gravity of his position to sink in.

'However, we are not yet in the face of the enemy, and you have sworn on your child's life that you intended to rejoin the ranks to fight. That stands in your favour, but I cannot overlook the seriousness of the offence. In other circumstances I might condemn you to be beaten to death by your comrades. But as I said, we need every man we can find to face the rebels. So my decision is that you will return to the ranks, pending reconsideration of your punishment when the rebellion is over. Provided you prove yourself in battle, I am prepared to set aside a death sentence in favour of whatever lesser punishment is deemed suitable in the event of our victory. In the event of our defeat, well, your offence will cease to be of any concern to me or the rest of the army.' He allowed himself a thin smile.

'Yes, sir. Thank you, sir.'

'Dismissed.'

Tubero frowned and seemed to be on the verge of protesting, but then clamped his lips together as Faustinus quickly saluted, about-turned and marched off before his commanding officer could change his mind. Cato turned his gaze to the centurion.

'You disapprove.'

'It's not my place to pass judgement on a superior, sir.'

'Quite right. Nevertheless, your reticence is eloquence itself.'

Tubero hesitated before he spoke again, in a quieter, urgent tone. 'Discipline is the backbone of the army, sir. Without it our men are no more than an armed rabble.'

'A highly trained armed rabble.'

He conceded the point with a nod and continued. 'Show a man how to wield a weapon and he becomes a warrior, but show him how to do it and obey regulations and orders and he becomes a soldier, part of a unit that is part of an army that is the basis of our empire. There's a world of difference between being a warrior and being a soldier, sir. As the poor sods we defeated over on Mona discovered to their cost. Discipline matters,' he concluded.

Cato was impressed by the succinct argument the centurion had presented. But there was another aspect to the situation that he needed the man to understand. 'All of what you say is true, and the purpose of training, rules and discipline is to make men fight well, yes?'

Tubero nodded.

'Do you not think, given what is at stake for Faustinus, that he will fight like a lion when the time comes? Whether to protect his family or to avenge them. Right now, Suetonius needs men who will fight, and fight fiercely. Faustinus is such a man. If I was to condemn him, we'd lose a fighter. And we'd undermine the morale of the men. It does them no good to witness, to be responsible for, the death of a comrade.'

'He deserted, sir. There has to be a consequence to that, otherwise it sets a bad example. The men know what he did. Do you want to risk more of them following his lead now that you have failed to condemn him?'

'I haven't failed to condemn him; I have merely deferred my decision. And as I pointed out to Faustinus, where does a man desert to in an island full of enemies? That's what he'll be repeating to his comrades, along with what I said about the need for us all to stay together if we are to have any hope of defeating Boudica. It's better for the men to hear that from one of their own than for me to make the case from a podium . . . Understand me?'

'Yes, sir.' Tubero stirred slightly as a thought occurred to him. 'Do you have family in Londinium yourself, sir?'

'Yes, but that makes no difference to how I deal with Faustinus.'

Tubero considered his superior's words silently, and then said, 'I understand. But I still don't like it.'

'You don't have to like it. Just as long as Faustinus fights.'

'If ever you grow tired of the army, you'd make a fine politician or lawyer. You're a canny cunt, sir.'

Cato's expression hardened. 'How dare you use such language to address a superior officer?'

Tubero stiffened and stuttered. 'Sir, I—'

'Silence!' Cato stepped towards him until their faces were inches apart before continuing in a menacing whisper. 'If I ever catch you comparing me to a lawyer again, I'll have your bollocks for breakfast. Dismissed.'

The rain eased off as night fell over the fort at Canovium and the weary men propped themselves up on their saddles, wrapped in their cloaks, and slept, their bellies filled with warm stew. Outside, their mounts stood or lay in dark clusters within the roped-off enclosures that had been prepared for them. Cato took a last turn around the fort, noting the vigilance of the men keeping watch from the rampart and towers. Lamplight glimmered round the shutters of the garrison commander's timber hut, and he felt a moment's sympathy for the burden weighing heavily on Suetonius's shoulders. He was the man who could save, or lose, the province in a single day when his army came up against Boudica and her followers. History would remember him as the heroic victor, or the failure who betrayed the reputation of Rome. Only the Fates knew which man he would be.

49

Returning to the granary, Cato settled down to sleep, heedless of the stirring and occasional coughing and muttering of the men in the gloom around him. Rest did not come easily. He was haunted by the expression of terror on Faustinus's face as he talked of the family he had left behind in Londinium when he marched off to war, little knowing that they faced an even greater peril than he did. It was the same for Cato himself, who had hoped that Claudia and Lucius would be under Macro's protection in the quiet backwater of the colony at Camulodunum. The rebels could have taken Londinium already and they might all be dead for all he knew. At once he thrust the thought aside and struggled to suppress it, as the night hours dragged until finally he slept.

CHAPTER FOUR

'Sir!'

A hand shook his shoulder vigorously, and Cato's eyes snapped open. He sat up instantly, looking at Tubero by the faint flicker of the flames in the nearest brazier. Glancing round, he saw no sign of light around the frames of the shutters and the small gaps in the timbers of the granary. It was still dark. Around him, the men were stirring as their officers began to shout orders to arm themselves and form up outside.

'What's happening?' Cato demanded as he reached for his scale armour and sword belt. He was still wearing his boots from the previous day. His back and limbs ached from yesterday's ride, and he stood stiffly and rolled his neck.

'There's movement outside the fort, sir.'

'Movement?'

'Hundreds of 'em, as far as I can make out. Just beyond the ford.'

Cato's ears strained to pick up any sounds of fighting, but there was nothing. 'Has Suetonius been told?'

Tubero nodded. 'Sent a man to him before I came to find you.'

'Right . . .' Cato briefly closed his eyes as he fought off the weariness clouding his thoughts. 'Get our men on the rampart facing the river and tell them to be ready to receive an attack.'

51

Tubero hurried off. With his sword belt over his shoulder and carrying his scale armour under his left arm, Cato joined the dark mass of men tumbling out of the granary into the cold night air. Men from other units in the column and those of the auxiliary garrison were also squelching across the muddy ground as they made for the ramparts. He strode in the direction of the river and climbed the ladder of the gate tower facing the ford. The three sentries moved aside for their superior, and he scanned the dark landscape to the west. He could easily make out the black sweep of the river and some of the details on the rising ground beyond the ford. He stared for a moment at a dark mass that seemed to be shifting across the slope, and realised he was looking at a large body of men; hundreds, he estimated, just as Tubero had reported.

He glanced over his shoulder to the dark line of mountains to the east, dimly visible against the stars and skeins of cloud. It was still an hour or so before dawn. If the enemy meant to attack the fort under cover of darkness, they would have to strike soon, and without the element of surprise. He caught a flicker of light from the corner of his eye and turned to see a soldier carrying a blazing torch aloft as he led Suetonius and his staff officers towards the gatehouse. He turned to the nearest sentry.

'Call out the instant that lot make any move towards the ford.'

'Yes, sir.'

Descending the ladder, he hurried towards the governor and saluted.

'Prefect Cato, what's the situation?' Suetonius demanded. 'Are we under attack?'

'Not yet, sir. There's a large body of enemy warriors gathering on the far side of the ford. If they attack, my men will be ready for them. But even if they try, I doubt they'd have the strength to break into the fort.'

'Then what are they doing out there?'

'I don't know, sir. We'll have a better idea when there's enough light to see by.' He pointed to the east, where he was sure he detected a clearer distinction between the dark mass of the mountains and the sky above. 'Not long now.'

The brief exchange was interrupted as a young auxiliary from the garrison came running up, breathing heavily. 'Centurion Raminus's compliments, sir. He says to inform you that there's another enemy force forming up to the east of the camp.'

'How many of them?' asked Cato.

The auxiliary shook his head. 'The centurion didn't say, sir. I didn't see.'

There was a brief, tense silence before Suetonius said, 'Seems they have us caught between the two forces. We could hold out until the main body of the army arrives. They should reach Canovium no later than midday tomorrow . . . Damn, this delay is the last thing we need.' He glanced to the eastern skyline. 'We'll make our move when dawn comes. In the meantime, I want the men to have their mounts prepared to march. We'll do it two units at a time. The rest are to man the rampart. We'll start with your lads, Prefect Cato, and yours, Fortinus. Go to it, gentlemen.'

Cato strode towards the cohort's standard, where Tubero was positioned, and passed on the orders. Once his men had fallen back from the rampart, the remaining auxiliaries of the garrison looked woefully spread out, but there was still no sign of movement from the enemy. He rested his hands on the palisade as he reflected on the governor's predicament.

Suetonius was right about the main body of the army reaching the fort the next day, and Cato felt confident the mounted column could hold out until then. The Celts often relied on a wild charge into battle, and it rarely paid off against well-trained and resolute defenders. The critical issue was the loss of a day and a half while the governor waited for the infantry to come up and clear the way to Deva. Of course, he might choose to try and break through the enemy line on the other side of the camp and continue the march, but that would entail losses he could ill afford. There was also the danger of the garrison at Canovium being overwhelmed and the depot sacked, with the prospect of a significant haul of supplies and weapons falling into enemy hands. Though Mona had been taken and heavy losses inflicted on the mountain tribes of the region, it was possible that even a modest victory over the invader might give sufficient encouragement for the surviving warriors of the tribes to renew their struggle.

There was a finely balanced choice to be made between sacrificing time or men. Cato felt a moment's sympathy for his superior. If Suetonius delayed, the emperor and the Senate might put it down to lack of courage. If he attempted to break out and suffered heavy losses, he might be judged too rash for not waiting until his infantry arrived. It was always easy for those far away and after the fact to pass judgement – an inevitable burden for commanders in the field. It would be interesting to see what he decided. The fate of Londinium, the largest Roman settlement in the new province, must be the critical element informing his choice.

A break-out, then, Cato concluded. As long as the enemy force blocking their way was not so numerous as to make the attempt suicidal.

There was a sudden cry from across the ford, and a moment later a roar of laughter followed by shouts of challenge and insults directed at the defenders in the fort. Cato smiled grimly. He had heard it many times before: the bravado of the Celts as they began to work up their courage for the coming fight. It would build gradually, rising to a crescendo as the war horns joined in before the enemy chiefs chose to unleash their warriors.

'Fuck . . .' muttered the auxiliary standing closest to Cato. Cato saw that his javelin was trembling in his grip. He eased himself towards the man and could make out enough of his features to see that he was another youth.

'It's all bluster and bollocks,' he said. 'They need to fire up their fighting spirit. Roman soldiers don't need any of that bullshit because we have the right training, discipline and kit. Stand firm and put your faith in that, soldier. All right?'

The young man nodded and took a deep breath.

'Of course,' Cato continued, 'you might also offer a few prayers to the gods while we're waiting. For insurance.'

He was rewarded with a nervous chuckle, and he patted the youth on the shoulder before turning away in search of Centurion Raminus.

The commander of the garrison was in the gatehouse on the far side of the fort, and he turned and nodded a greeting as Cato climbed onto the platform. The sky was beginning to lighten to the east, and details were emerging of the landscape and the enemy force positioned aside the route to Deva. Cato could now readily estimate the number and composition of the enemy forming up on the rising ground outside the fort. At least two thousand men, many bearing helmets and shields, and some even wearing armour. Like their comrades on the far side of the fort, they were making a lot of noise, brandishing fists and weapons at the defenders rather than preparing any fieldworks. Cato gave a thin smile of satisfaction at that small advantage already conceded. Even so, the enemy line stretched across the vale through which the route passed, and the slopes on either side were sufficiently steep and rock-strewn to make them impracticable for Suetonius and his men to attempt to get round the Deceanglians. If the Romans attempted to ride around the base of either hill, they would expose themselves to a flank attack, with disastrous consequences.

'Looks like they have us bottled up,' he said. 'The only way out is through that lot.'

'Yes, sir.' Raminus nodded. 'You think the governor will attempt it?'

'Almost certainly. It'll be a bloody business, even if we manage to break their line. Tell me, have you any stocks of javelins in the depot?'

Raminus thought a moment, then nodded. 'I'll have them brought up to the ramparts in case those bastards come within range.'

'Good . . .' Cato allowed himself a small smile. 'And if they won't come within range, then maybe we'll just have to take the javelins to them.'

'Sir?'

'Never mind. Let's wait until dawn and see what happens.'

As the light strengthened, the noise from the enemy continued unabated. Cato could see their leaders moving along the front rank, shouting encouragement to the men. There was something different about the battle line, he realised, and then it came to him. Not a single Druid was in sight. Presumably they had all perished with their followers on Mona in their final stand against the Roman invaders. The absence of their fanatical invocations and curses was bound to be felt by the enemy, who had previously counted on them to inflame the passions of their warriors and invoke the support of the Celtic gods. In equal measure, the more superstitious amongst the Roman ranks would have less reason to fear their opponents.

Inside the fort, the horses of the mounted column had been saddled and loaded with kit and supplies, and now stood in clusters of four, their reins held by riders while their comrades remained on the ramparts.

Not long after Raminus had left to see to the procurement of the javelins, Suetonius climbed the tower and joined Cato. He scrutinised the enemy line before he sucked in a deep breath.

'We'll have to fight our way through them. I cannot let them keep us in here.'

'Yes, sir.'

'You don't seem very surprised, Prefect.'

'I don't see you have much choice in the matter, sir. Given the wider picture.'

'Indeed. The mob in Rome have little grasp of strategic realities but a decided appetite for snap judgement of those of us who know our trade. You'll do well to understand that if ever you achieve a senior command.' Suetonius grimaced. 'Perhaps that's something to be avoided.'

'Perhaps, sir. With my background, I doubt I will ever have the chance. Small mercies and all that.'

'Don't bet on it. You have a fine reputation, and times are changing. The emperors have been playing fast and loose with such traditions ever since the Republic fell. You may surprise yourself one day, Prefect Cato. If that day comes, you'll find out what it's like to have every man in the army look to you for salvation and victory.'

Suetonius turned and cupped his hands around his mouth as he shouted down into the fort. 'The column will prepare to march! Recall all the men to their units and stand ready to mount!'

As the officers repeated the order and bellowed at any man moving too slowly, Cato looked round the perimeter of the depot and saw how thinly the garrison was spread. 'If we break out, Raminus and his men have no chance of keeping the enemy at bay.'

'I know,' Suetonius responded. 'I've given him orders to burn what he can before he retreats into the garrison fort. He and his men will be able to hold that until the main column comes up.'

'I hope so, sir.' Cato gestured to the enemy waiting some two hundred paces beyond the outer ditch. 'May I ask how you intend to break through?'

'We'll send in Fortinus first, since his cohort is strongest. A wedge formation should do the job and the rest of the column can charge through the gap.'

Even as Suetonius spoke, there came the braying of a war horn, and both officers turned to see the enemy pulling back up the slope to higher ground, where the vale was narrower. For a moment, Cato's spirits lifted at the sight of the enemy moving out of the way rather than risking a fight. Then their true purpose became apparent as they halted and adjusted their line so that it was deeper and better able to resist the coming attack by the Roman cavalry. Along the front rank, almost every man carried a shield and a spear. The odds against Suetonius and his men had just taken a turn for the worse.

'Seems like we've lost the element of surprise.' The governor clenched his jaw in frustration, then turned abruptly to climb down from the gatehouse. Cato followed him.

The men of the four cohorts that made up the column, together with Suetonius's escort and staff officers, mounted and settled into their saddles. The horses snorted and champed as their riders clasped the reins to the forward grip inside their shields, adjusted their sword belts and readied their spears. As Cato waited next to Tubero, ahead of the standard bearer and the bucina man, he pulled his helmet down securely and tightened the chin strap before taking up his own shield. Once each of the cohort commanders had called out that their men were ready, Suetonius nodded to the auxiliaries at the gatehouse.

'Open up!'

The gates creaked on their wooden pintles as the grunting auxiliaries dragged them inwards and stepped aside for the cavalry to trot through. Fortinus's cohort, nearly four hundred strong, led the way and advanced a short distance before he bellowed the order to form a wedge. Behind them rode Suetonius and his party, then Cato's unit and the remaining understrength cohorts, forming a line behind Fortinus's spearhead. Once the last of the men in the wedge formation was in position, their commander shouted the order to advance. There was a scant hundred paces between the point of the wedge and the enemy's shield wall, where lowered spears bristled, ready to receive the attack. Fortinus allowed a moment for the formation to ripple forward, then increased the pace to a canter. As the gap between the two sides closed, he bellowed the order to charge.

Above the thrumming of hooves on muddy soil, Cato heard the thud of weapons striking shields, the panicked whinnying of the horses and the battle cries of the Deceanglian warriors. He turned in his saddle to face his men.

'Prepare to advance!'

When he turned back to follow the fighting further up the slope, he saw that Fortinus and the head of his wedge had cut their way into the enemy line, but the charge seemed to have stalled and the Deceanglians were pressing in against the flanks, darting forward to stab at the riders or their mounts, some trying to haul the Romans from their saddles to be cut down on the ground. For their part, the cavalrymen were thrusting their spears as they wheeled their horses to one side or the other in an attempt to drive the enemy back.

'They're not going to make it through,' Tubero said quietly.

Cato had already reached the same conclusion, and looked towards Suetonius, willing his superior to have the recall sounded. But there was no need to issue the signal. The first of Fortinus's men fell back, then more followed as the Deceanglians sensed victory and thrust at the head of the wedge, forcing it down the slope until the formation, as of one will, hurriedly disengaged and trotted back towards the fort, leaving behind the bodies of men and writhing horses. The air filled with a triumphant roar as the enemy celebrated the repulse of the charge. Cato was relieved to see Fortinus still alive as the prefect followed his men and called out to his officers to re-form their squadrons.

'So much for that,' said Tubero before spitting to one side. 'What now?'

Cato was instinctively minded to tell the man to shut his mouth, but he was too busy thinking about the predicament facing the mounted column. The slope, already muddy, was now churned up by the hooves of Fortinus's cohort, and any fresh charge could not hope to strike the enemy line with sufficient impetus to break through it. A different tactic was needed. He turned to Tubero.

'Take twenty men and go back into the fort. Fetch as many light javelins as you can carry and issue them to our men.'

Tubero hesitated, and then saluted. 'Yes, sir.'

As the centurion turned his horse and called on the nearest troop to follow him back towards the gatehouse, Cato urged his own mount forward and made for Suetonius. He reined in beside the governor as the latter was giving orders to one of his tribunes to tell Fortinus to re-form his wedge for a second charge.

'Sir!' Cato interrupted. 'That won't work. The ground is against us and the enemy line is too strong.'

Suetonius glared at him. 'How dare you—'

'There is another way to break the Deceanglians down, sir. With your permission . . . ?'

The governor nodded for him to continue.

Once Cato had outlined his intention, Suetonius considered the change in tactics and then gave his assent.

'It might work. We'll still have to make a charge, though.'

'At least we should have a better chance next time, sir.'

'Very well. Prepare your men, Prefect Cato. And may the gods grant you good fortune. If you fail to achieve what we need, we'll have to abandon the attempt and wait for the infantry to arrive and clear the way for us.'

There was no need to spell out the delay that would entail, and Cato touched the brim of his helmet in salute and turned his horse away to rejoin his cohort, where Tubero and his party had returned with the javelins.

'Officers on me!' he shouted.

As the centurions and decurions gathered around him, Cato explained his plan. 'The vital part of this is to keep the formation moving and feeding the javelins to the men going forward. If all goes well and we disrupt their line, the column should be able to cut their way through.' He paused and glanced round. 'You're all clear on what must be done?'

His officers nodded.

'Let's get ready to move. I'll lead the First Squadron off.'

Tubero opened his mouth to protest, but Cato had anticipated his subordinate and spoke first. 'You'll be handling the re-arming. Make sure you send for more javelins in good time if they're needed.'

'Yes, sir.'

Cato rode to the First Squadron. 'All right, lads, set down your shields and spears. You won't be needing them.' He indicated the bundles of javelins that had been fetched from the fort. 'Each man is to take two of those and be ready to follow me in single column. We'll let those bastards up there have it as we ride along their front. There is to be no attempt to engage them. Throw your javelins, then circle back to pick up more. If any of the enemy try to rush us, target them and ride on. All clear? Good, then prepare your weapons and wait for my order.'

He handed his shield to Trebonius and took two light javelins, shorter and more slender than the cavalry spears and the heavy legionary variant he had been trained to use when he first joined the Second Legion many years before, though they still had the four-sided beaten-iron tip and the slender shaft leading back to the weighted grip. Transferring one to the leather sheath hanging from his saddle, he took the other in his right hand and hefted it to get a feel for its balance before holding it firmly.

When he saw that the rest of the cohort was similarly armed and standing ready, he called out, 'First Squadron will advance at my pace!'

He urged his horse forward, trotting then cantering towards the enemy. Ahead, he could see that the advance of the single line of Roman riders had provoked renewed brandishing of weapons, and fresh jeers and war cries swelled to a deafening crescendo that echoed off the steep slopes on either side of the vale. He focused on a point in the enemy ranks twenty paces to the right of the centre, and chose his target, a large bare-chested warrior with spiked limed hair and swirling tattoos on his cheeks. Steering his horse round to canter along the front of the shield wall, he hurled the first javelin at the warrior. He did not wait to see if the shaft struck home, but snatched the second weapon from his left hand and threw it so that it arced over the line of shields and plunged into the dense ranks beyond.

As he turned his mount in a broad curve towards the rear of his cohort, he looked back to see the men following him unleashing their javelins at the enemy before steering away. He reined in by Tubero and watched as his men continued their easy ride in single file, inscribing a rough oval across the ground, unleashing their javelins before returning to pick up fresh weapons.

The steady infliction of casualties soon had its effect on enemy morale. The boastful cries and jeers of earlier faded, and when frustration caused individuals and small groups to break ranks and charge, their leaders had to force them back into line with harsh shouts and brutal shoves. Meanwhile, the Romans sheered away whenever the enemy tried to rush them, causing further frustration to the Deceanglians, who began to shout angry insults after the retreating riders. Every so often, one of the javelins that had missed a target and was still intact was thrown back. One struck a horse, whose rider was thrown and instantly charged upon and cut down before he could rise to his feet. Another man was unlucky to be hit in the neck, the javelin bursting through flesh and spine so that he slumped motionless in his saddle for a short distance before tumbling to the ground.

The light had been steadily gaining in strength, and now the sun appeared above the crest of the hills behind the enemy and burnished the scene in a tawny red glow. Cato had to raise a hand to shield his gaze as he regarded the enemy line. His men had concentrated their efforts against the centre, and he could see that the ranks there had thinned out and a number of warriors were limping to the rear, some assisted by their comrades, who were doubtless keen to withdraw out of range of the javelins. The moment to strike was close, he judged, and he trotted over to Suetonius.

'Your men are doing fine work,' the governor observed with a satisfied nod. 'Scores of casualties for the loss of two of our own.'

'Yes, sir. Their centre should be weak enough to risk a fresh charge now.'

Suetonius scrutinised the disruption in the centre of the Deceanglian line and nodded. 'Very well, keep at it. Fortinus's cohort can lead the charge through your men. Do them good to get revenge for the first repulse. Your lads can follow when we break through.'

Cato rejoined Tubero and the cohort's small command party. He explained the governor's intentions.

'Charge through our lads?' Tubero questioned. 'Could be risky, sir.'

'Agreed, but if we call them back before the charge, it'll give the enemy a chance to firm up their centre. The risk is acceptable.

63

Pass the word to the men: once more round and then they are to retrieve their shields and spears and form in column.'

'Yes, sir.'

Cato gestured to his orderly to return his shield and held it ready. Three of the tribunes had ridden to the commanders of the other cohorts to issue the governor's orders as Cato's men continued their harassment of the enemy line. A series of notes blasted from the bucinas behind Suetonius, echoed an instant later by the bucinas of Fortinus's cohort. The First Squadron rippled forward in a wedge formation, followed by the rest in a broad column, ten abreast. They cantered up the slope, partially screened by Cato's men riding across their front. At the last moment, the latter wheeled aside and the wedge passed through without incident, to Cato's relief. The bucina sounded the charge, and the riders of the leading squadron advanced their spears, leaning forward in their saddles and urging their horses on. The enemy's war cries faded as they braced themselves to receive the charge amid the muffled thrumming of hundreds of hooves across the churned soil of the slope.

There was an instant where time seemed to slow perceptibly, then came the thudding crash of spears and horseflesh against shields, followed by the sharp clatter of blades and the whinnying of horses. This time the Roman formation ploughed through the weakened enemy ranks, carving the line in two.

'They're through!' Tubero punched his fist into the air. 'Give it to 'em, Fortinus!'

Cato kept his gaze on the fighting up the slope. The follow-up squadrons had arrived in the breach and were fighting to widen it and roll up the enemy line before they recovered enough to offer any spirited resistance. The governor and his escorts led the second cohort forward, passing through the gap without trouble and moving up the slope, cutting down enemy wounded and others attempting to flee. The last of the men to throw javelins at the enemy had returned to the Eighth Cohort and were retrieving their shields and spears. Only a handful of javelins remained, and Cato hoped that Raminus would have the sense to retrieve them before they could be seized by the enemy.

'Prepare to advance!' he called out. The riders eased their mounts into position, and he swept his arm forwards. 'Advance!'

He led them up the slope at the trot, then at the canter. He did not increase the pace any further, wanting to keep the men in good order as they reached the battle raging in the centre of the enemy line. The cohort ahead of them had also passed through, but Cato could see that the impetus of Fortinus's men had faded, and already they were being forced back. He swerved round the horse that had been struck earlier, and reached the cordon of dead and injured where the enemy centre had once been. The flattened grass was splashed with blood. Javelins lay strewn across the slope, some shafts embedded in the soil and presenting a hazard to the riders passing through the gap. He had nearly reached the open ground beyond when several warriors burst between Fortinus's men to his right and charged towards him.

'First ten men on me!' he shouted, and turned to meet the enemy, drawing his cavalry sword and jerking his reins towards the danger. He urged his mount at the knot of warriors, forcing them to scatter, and then lashed out with his sword as he wheeled his horse from side to side, using its bulk to keep the enemy at a distance. His first blows were easily avoided or blocked with shields, but his opponents were unable to strike back for the few heartbeats it took for Tubero and the others to come to his aid. The brief skirmish was one-sided, and three of the warriors were cut down before the others backed off and turned to rejoin the fight against Fortinus's auxiliaries.

Tubero made to follow them, but Cato halted him. 'No! Get through the gap and re-form the cohort up by the governor!'

The centurion growled in frustration, but called on the men to rejoin the column of riders passing through at the trot, picking their way through bodies and the detritus of battle.

Cato held his position, scanning the fighting before him. Fortinus's men were steadily losing ground. He picked out the prefect's red crest, and as the last of the riders from the Eighth passed him, he urged his horse towards Fortinus, who sat in his saddle momentarily aside from the flow of the fighting. His face and shoulders were spattered and streaked with blood and his chest heaved from his exertions.

'It's time to recall your men,' said Cato. 'The rest of the column has got through. We have to go.'

'Go?' Fortinus responded through gritted teeth. 'For fuck's sake! We could wipe these bastards out if Suetonius orders the whole column in.'

'We can't afford to lose any more men,' Cato countered. 'Now get your cohort out of here. Follow your orders,' he added with emphasis.

Fortinus turned to look for his standard bearer, and urged his horse over to the man as he bellowed, 'Rally on the standard!'

Cato steered his own mount clear of the battlefield and increased his pace to a canter as he urged it up the slope to rejoin his command. The first two cohorts were already advancing along the vale, with Suetonius and his party riding between them. Cato deployed his men across the slope either side of the track to cover Fortinus's cohort as they disengaged from the enemy and withdrew to rejoin the column. As many of the wounded that could be saved were assisted by their comrades, while others drove off any warriors nearby. Then, with a last defiant cry of 'Long live Rome!' the prefect turned his horse and trotted away from the Deceanglians. Cato was relieved that the latter showed no willingness to continue the fight, but instead saw to their own wounded and plundered the bodies of the Romans. As was the way of the Celts, there was a scramble to claim trophies from their fallen enemies, and he felt his guts tighten with anger as he saw warriors holding up severed heads to show off to their comrades.

Fortinus exchanged a nod with Cato as he rode past to join his cohort forming up on the track before they followed the rest of the column. Cato waited a little longer to give them time to put some distance between themselves and the enemy. Satisfied that there was no attempt at rallying the warriors to begin the pursuit, he gave the order for the Eighth to file back onto the track and leave Canovium behind. Already columns of smoke were rising into the morning air as the garrison set fire to the remaining supplies before withdrawing into the fortified compound in the corner of the depot. With luck, the Deceanglians would realise there was little to gain from taking the depot and would retreat into the mountains before the main column of Suetonius's army arrived. Cato muttered brief prayers to Fortuna and Mars for the preservation of Raminus and his men, and then cantered up the side of his cohort to take his place at its head.

Over two hours had been lost, he estimated, as well as at least fifty men. And they had only covered a fraction of the distance to Londinium. His heart was heavy with concern for all those who stood in the path of Boudica and her rebels. Amongst them his son and the woman he loved.

CHAPTER FIVE

A small party of mounted warriors on shaggy ponies followed the column as it emerged onto the coastal track that skirted the mountains. Every so often they would charge at any stragglers, and Cato would have to take command of a squadron and wheel round to chase them off. On occasion, they were too late and the Deceanglians would catch up with an isolated auxiliary and cut him down before he could escape. When such incidents occurred, it was difficult for the Romans to resist the urge to charge after the enemy and avenge their comrade. Which was why Cato took personal command and ordered his men to rein in and let the enemy go, rather than risk running into an ambush and suffering needless losses. All the same, he was aware of the damage to the morale of his men, and looked forward to leaving the mountains behind.

On the first night, the column camped outside one of the forts that had been built along the supply route that stretched back to the army's base at Deva. The weather remained fair, and they made good progress, covering over thirty miles the first day and forty the next as they followed the route that snaked along the coast. The injured were left at the first fort in order not to slow the column's pace.

At dusk on the third day after reaching the mainland, they came in sight of Deva. Cato felt a weary relief as he looked down on the vast rectangle of ditch and turf rampart topped with a sturdy palisade. The glow of braziers illuminated small patches within the fortress, and smoke curled from openings in the buildings and dissipated into the gathering gloom closing over the landscape. Tiny figures patrolled the walkways and made their way across the interior of the fortress. Beyond, an arrow-shot from the outer ditch, lay the sprawl of crudely constructed buildings and tents that marked the inevitable makeshift civilian settlement where the camp followers lived. Women and children of men serving in the army, traders, fortune-tellers, innkeepers, prostitutes and entertainers. A peaceful enough setting, he reflected. He wondered if they knew about the fate of Camulodunum and the threat posed by the rebels. All that stood between them and annihilation were the widely spread men of the Roman army, desperately trying to concentrate in sufficient numbers to confront Boudica and her followers.

The weary column entered the fortress and was directed to the horse lines and empty barracks. As his men dismounted, removed saddles and blankets and rubbed their mounts down, Cato made his way to the quartermaster's office to draw the necessary supplies needed for the rest of the march to Londinium. According to his memory of the itinerary, the distance to cover amounted to nearly two hundred miles. An imperial messenger with regular remounts might do it in two days, three at the outside. For a mounted column it would take twice as long, at least. Four days' supply then, he decided, weighing up the trade-off between the weight of the men's food and the horses' feed and the need to move as swiftly as possible. If supplies ran out, they would have to go without for a day before they reached Londinium.

As he entered the courtyard of the headquarters block, he was immediately aware of the atmosphere of urgency. Lamplight glowed from behind the shutters of the main building and offices and storerooms on either side of the courtyard, and there were many orderlies and officers from the garrison and the mounted column talking in small groups or hurrying to prepare for the long march to come. There were already a number of officers in the cramped room where the quartermaster was trying to deal with their requests. As Cato had anticipated, he was the senior officer present and was able to shoulder his way through to the desk unchallenged by the centurions and decurions sent by the prefects of the other cohorts. Rank did indeed have its privileges, he reflected with some small satisfaction.

The quartermaster, a gaunt veteran centurion, stood up. 'Can I help you, sir?'

'Prefect Cato, commanding the Eighth Cohort. I need rations for two hundred men for four days. And feed for the horses.' He paused to let the man record the details on a waxed tablet. 'There'll be some who need replacement tack and possibly saddles. They'll report to you later.'

'Yes, sir.'

'What about remounts? How many do you have in the fortress?'

The quartermaster sat on his stool and reached for a larger tablet from a chest behind his desk. He flipped it open and scanned the records. 'After the governor's escort has been provided for, there's another three hundred available, sir. Provided you have the governor's authority for me to release them.'

There was a muted groan from some of the officers from the other cohorts, and Cato could guess why. No doubt they anticipated that he would make the first claim on the remounts, leaving a mere hundred for the other three cohorts to share. Another prefect might have put his own men before the others, and Cato was tempted by the prospect, but maintaining the morale of the entire column was of paramount importance. They knew they were riding against impossible odds, and there was no point in adding resentment to that burden.

'I'll return with the governor's authority within the hour. In the meantime, you are to allocate a hundred remounts to the Eighth, another hundred to Fortinus, and fifty each to the two remaining cohorts. My senior centurion, Tubero, will report any further requisitions that are required.'

'Yes, sir. Is there anything else you need?'

'Any further news from the south of the province?'

'Last thing we heard, the rebels were still celebrating their capture of Camulodunum. No doubt drinking themselves insensible while they argue over who gets to keep the heads of our lads they've taken for prizes.'

Some of those heads would belong to Cato's closest friends, and he hurriedly thrust the thought aside before any grisly images presented themselves to his imagination.

'No word of Boudica moving on Londinium, then?'

'Not as far as I know, sir.'

That was something to be grateful for, thought Cato. It was also something of a surprise. If he had been in Boudica's place, he would have acted as quickly as possible to destroy the main Roman settlements and then hunt down and defeat the Empire's scattered forces before they could concentrate to offer battle on more equal terms. The warriors of the tribes in Britannia had proved that they could move swiftly and strike hard, especially under the leadership of Caratacus. The situation seemed to be different now. Perhaps there was division between Boudica and those who followed her. Or maybe the uprising was dominated more by expressions of anger and desire for revenge for their treatment by Rome than by any coherent and clear-sighted plan for the conflict they had unleashed.

Cato believed he knew Boudica well enough to know that she understood the cardinal importance of striking fast and hard and keeping up the momentum if the rebels were to succeed in driving the Romans from Britannia. There was a victory to be had, but every moment wasted edged the balance back in favour of the Empire. If the rebels had delayed their advance from Camulodunum, it was most likely because there was dissent and confusion in their ranks and Boudica was struggling to exert her authority over those who had flocked to join her rebellion, driven by various motives: revenge, the prospect of loot, the desire to humiliate Rome and restore the honour of the Celtic peoples. Such a variety of reasons to fight could be a source of strength or of weakness. As long as Boudica could feed her followers with the fruits of victory, the rebels were a force to be reckoned with. Perhaps that had made her too cautious to advance. It was impossible to know with the scant information available. Maybe when Suetonius's column reached Londinium, the situation would be clearer.

He nodded to the quartermaster. 'Very well. You have a note of what I need. You can deal with the others now.' He turned on his heel and strode from the room. The moment he passed into the corridor outside, the clamour of demands resumed as the officers from the column vied to get preferential treatment for their units.

Keen to learn if anyone else at headquarters had further news of the rebellion, Cato passed through the main hall towards the modest suite of offices allocated to the commander of the fortress. That was where he expected to find Suetonius and his staff this night, and sure enough, the governor had taken over the rooms and was busy reading reports that had come in from across the province, dismissing some and issuing urgent responses to others. He looked up as Cato entered and gestured to the sheets of papyrus and waxed tablets piled on the desk.

'As you can see, all Hades has broken loose thanks to the uprising. Every town senate has sent demands for reinforcements to protect them, while the officers commanding the smaller garrisons in the south of the province are asking for permission to retire to the safety of the main legionary bases. Can't wait to see what fresh confusion will be sown when Rome gets to hear what's going on and issues their instructions.' He tossed his stylus down and leaned back, yawning briefly. 'To make matters worse, I've had a message from Postumus, the acting commander of the Second Legion at Isca. He is still in camp, waiting for orders to move. The fool should have set off for Londinium as soon as he received news of the uprising. I just hope that Cerialis and the Ninth Legion make it on time. Then we might be able to hold on until the Second and the Fourteenth and the Twentieth and the rest of the main column arrive on the scene.' He shook his head. 'What a fucking mess.'

Cato's tired mind was considering the perilous position of Rome's newest province. The mess in question might have been avoided if Suetonius had left stronger garrisons behind, if he had not pressed Boudica for more tribute than the Iceni could afford, if he had punished Decianus for letting his men flog Boudica and rape her daughters. But that was all 'blood under the bridge', to quote the playwright Albeus. Regardless of who was at fault, the Roman army in Britannia would have to resolve the mess or be crushed and killed in the attempt. There would be time for picking over the details later.

Suetonius leaned forward again and rested his arms on the edge of the desk. 'We'll be marching at dawn. Make sure your men have sufficient supplies for a few days. We can pick up more in the forts and settlements along the way. Won't amount to much, but it'll have to do. We'll not be slowing down for any stragglers. They should be able to fend for themselves, as we'll be passing through pacified territory.'

'Let's hope that is still the case, sir. There will be elements within those tribes allied to Rome who will have sympathy with the rebels. In some cases enough to take their side.'

'That can't be helped. And they will be dealt with after we have defeated Boudica. If they harm any of the stragglers, there will be consequences. All the same, it would be advisable if the men were made aware of the danger.'

'Yes, sir.'

Suetonius fixed Cato with a direct stare as he continued. 'We will not be stopping for anyone. If any tribesmen get it into their heads to try and harass the column, we take the casualties and keep to the road. In the unlikelihood that we encounter a strong force, there will be no attempt to engage them. We ride round and continue to Londinium. Gods willing, we reach the town in time to defend it and protect the lives of our people there.'

'Yes, sir.'

'Is there anything you need from me?'

Cato relayed the quartermaster's demand for authorisation for the release of the remounts, and Suetonius rolled his eyes.

'I sometimes wonder if one day Rome will burn to the ground for want of a quartermaster's document agreeing to provide fire buckets.'

'Yes, sir. Quite.' Cato smiled grimly. 'But quartermasters serve their purpose, or so I'm told.'

The governor gave a brief dry chuckle before he gestured towards the door. 'I dare say there are arrangements you need to make for the next stage of our advance, Prefect.'

It was a polite but curt dismissal, and Cato saluted and turned to leave the office, making his way back to his quarters at the end of the barracks assigned to his cohort. The men were already settling in for the night, and the smell of cooking wafted towards him, making him aware of how hungry he was. He found Trebonius waiting for him, having prepared his bed. He undid the clasp of his cloak and handed it over.

'Get the mud off that as best you can. Same goes for the boots and cuirass.'

'Yes, sir.'

'And I want something to eat. Stew with some fresh bread.'

'Yes, sir.'

He noticed that Trebonius was hesitating. 'What is it?'

'It's the death rights, sir.'

'Death rights?'

'Yes, sir. The two men we lost at Canovium. Troopers Heromanus and Faustinus. Their comrades have asked me to put the matter to you.'

It was a routine enough request. Soldiers had the right to make a will, and it was the duty of their commanding officer to execute it if they fell in battle or died through accident or illness. Such meagre possessions as a man might have with him he would leave to his comrades, while most of his savings would pay for his funeral, or memorial if the body could not be recovered. The balance was handed to any family that might be living where the soldier was garrisoned. Sometimes the comrades of a fallen man would auction his weapons, armour and kit in order to raise money for his family. This was what they were now asking permission to do.

It was the second name that caused Cato to pause in his thoughts. 'Faustinus?'

'Yes, sir. Young lad. The one who was presented to you for punishment.'

The young soldier who had been spared punishment for deserting to save his family in Londinium would never have the chance to redeem himself now. It was always harder to accept a man's death when you knew something about him that singled him out from the ranks. Cato recalled Faustinus's features and the earnestness of his desire to fight. He was no coward and had proved it on the battlefield.

There was no question of dealing with his will, as it would be with the others in the cohort's administration chests on the baggage train of the main column, along with his funeral club savings. His body had been retrieved at Canovium and buried that evening at the next fort the mounted column had reached. Cato recalled giving the order, but had not asked the men's names at the time. He felt a twinge of guilt over such a lack of consideration, but there had been little time to spare them much thought. The least he could do now was give Faustinus's comrades the chance to do right by his family.

'Tell them they have my permission.'

'Yes, sir.'

'Then bring me my food straight away.'

Trebonius saluted and crossed to the door.

'Just a moment,' Cato called after him. 'Take ten sestertii from my strongbox to add to the auction proceeds.'

'Very kind of you, sir.'

'Don't say the money is from me. Just use it to buy a few small items and pay well over the odds. The others will be doing the same in any case.' Cato had worked to present himself to the men under his command as a stern disciplinarian. That image had been compromised by his earlier treatment of Faustinus. To openly make a donation for the man's family would make matters worse.

Trebonius frowned. 'Why not just let me tell them it's yours, sir? They'll be grateful.'

'I don't want their bloody gratitude.' Cato affected a growl. 'I want their obedience and I want them to do what they are trained to do.'

'But sir—'

'Just do as I say, then damn well bring me my food! Go!'

As Trebonius hurried away, Cato felt leaden fatigue settle on him. He untied his laces and eased his boots off, then stretched his toes for a moment before lying down on the cot with a sigh. He folded his arms behind his head and closed his eyes while he waited for his orderly to return with the food.

It felt good to rest for a moment, he decided. He turned his thoughts to the coming march and the challenges he and his men might face before they even reached Londinium. One thought blurred into another, and then into random incoherence, before he fell into a deep sleep.

He did not stir even when Trebonius returned with his meal, bumping the door open before setting the tray down on the small desk opposite the bed. The orderly waited a moment, then cleared his throat.

'Sir?'

Cato muttered a few incomprehensible words before starting to snore.

'All right then, sir,' said Trebonius quietly. 'You've earned your sleep, may the gods bless you.'

The column left Deva at first light. The horses were laden with nets of feed, while the men's haversacks bulged with extra rations and two full canteens hung from their saddle horns. The Eighth Cohort were once again honoured with leading the column, and Cato, feeling refreshed by a long sleep and a cold meal, was relieved to be resuming the advance.

The pallid dawn light soon gave way to a clear azure sky with fine skeins of white cloud to the north. Birdsong sounded cheerfully from the trees along the route, and for a while, Cato was content to watch the birds darting from tree to tree. The mountains were left behind and the rolling landscape on either side consisted of ancient forests interspersed with broad sweeps of cultivation, with small clusters of huts and the occasional villa nestling amid the farmland. Every so often they passed travellers, who hurriedly drew aside to give way to the military traffic. Cato stopped to question those coming from the south in case they had any news of the rebellion. Some repeated alarmist rumours that the rebels controlled the entire south of the province and were even now marching north, destroying everything in their path. Others merely shrugged and said they had heard nothing, or treated events with the same fatalism they had the conflicts that had swept the island for as long as its people could recall.

Midday came and went, and Suetonius allowed a brief rest as the column arrived at a river. The men watered their mounts and stretched their limbs gratefully as they drank freely from their canteens and replenished them upstream of the horses. It had turned into a baking summer's day, and Cato felt the sweat pricking on his brow, while the linen tunic under his armour was drenched down the spine. He could feel the tingling sensation on his forearms from exposure to the sun, and he shifted himself into the shade of a willow growing by the river, which glided around the thin curtain of leaves. It was not easy to enjoy the peaceful setting, however, as his mind was once again preoccupied by the grave peril hanging over the province.

At the sound of a bucina from the direction of the governor's command party, the men capped their canteens and returned to those assigned to hold the horses before leading their mounts back to the dry, dusty road. As Cato was about to climb into his saddle, he noticed a distant figure a mile or so ahead of the column, riding hard towards them, his horse's hooves kicking up a thin veil of dust in his wake.

Tubero, already mounted, pointed up the road. 'Who's that, I wonder?'

'We'll know soon enough,' Cato replied, handing his reins to Trebonius before walking forward a short distance and waiting.

As the rider approached, he slowed and then stopped a short distance away. He wore a military tunic, but no armour, and was armed only with a short sword. Small sidebags hung across the rear of his saddle. His face was streaked with grime and he looked tired and anxious.

'Who are you?' Cato demanded.

'Optio Rutilius, sir,' the man panted. 'On the procurator's staff. Carrying an urgent dispatch for the governor. May I pass?'

'Suetonius? You're in luck.' Cato pointed down the road. 'You'll find him at the head of the next cohort.'

The optio glanced along the line of men mounting their horses. 'He's here? I was told to make for Mona. Where's the rest of the army, sir?'

'On the march from Mona, some days behind. You'd better deliver your dispatch,' Cato concluded.

Rutilius urged his horse into a gallop, and Cato returned to his mount and swung himself up into the saddle.

'Tubero! Get the cohort formed up ready to march.' He flicked his reins and made off along the column.

As he approached the governor's party, he saw Suetonius taking a leather tube from the rider. He opened the end and extracted a scroll. Breaking the seal, he unrolled the dispatch and read it in silence as Cato and the others looked on in anticipation. At length, he shook his head and then read the contents aloud.

'"To Governor Suetonius Paulinus from Procurator Catus Decianus, most urgent.

'"Sir, I have the duty to inform you of news of a great misfortune that has arisen subsequent to the capture of Camulodunum by the forces of the traitor who calls herself the Queen of the Iceni. In the days preceding the capture, I took the precaution of sending a contingent from the Londinium garrison to the colony the moment I was made aware of the rebellion. At the same time, I sent orders to the commander of the Ninth Legion to march to the aid of Centurion Macro and his comrades at Camulodunum. In the event, the enemy reached the colony first. Regrettably, Macro proved inadequate to the task of defending Camulodunum, even with the additional soldiers I sent to help with the defence. As yet, there is no news of any survivors, and I can only assume they were massacred once the colony was overwhelmed.

"'I am afraid, sir, that I must now impart tidings of an even greater calamity. In accordance with their orders, elements of the Ninth Legion marched to the relief of the veterans at Camulodunum. While still two days' journey from the colony, the legion was ambushed and virtually destroyed. The legate was fortunate to escape with the men of the legion's mounted contingent and has retired to a fort on the road to Lindum, from where he sent me news of the defeat. I am sure it will be apparent to you, as it is to me, that the emboldened rebels will march on Londinium next.

"'I have given orders to the garrison that remains to strengthen the town's defences, and I am confident that my men can hold off the enemy's scouts should they arrive before the walls, such as they are. Nonetheless, I have decided to sail for Gaul to appeal for assistance from the governor there. I do not take the matter of my temporary absence lightly and am firmly resolved to return the instant it is prudent to do so, and to take charge of the defences until you are able to reach Londinium and assume command. However, if I should fail to return from Gaul as soon as I would like, I have every confidence in the valour of the garrison and the sound leadership of yourself. The rebels will be driven off and victory will be ours! All hail the emperor . . .'"

Suetonius paused and crumpled up the scroll. 'Et cetera, et cetera . . . Damn the coward.' He looked up. 'So there it is, gentlemen. The Ninth Legion is lost and we are the only force capable of reaching Londinium before either the rebels or the Second Legion can arrive on the scene.'

There was a stunned silence as the other officers digested the governor's words, and then one of the youngest of the junior tribunes spoke up.

'This changes everything, sir. We should wait until the main body of the army catches up before we march to the aid of Londinium.'

'If we wait,' Cato intervened, 'Boudica will surely arrive first. We must press on, sir. After all, we are the only soldiers capable of giving Londinium a chance. If we fail the people of the town, they are surely doomed.'

Suetonius smiled grimly. 'My thoughts precisely, Prefect Cato.' He looked round at the other officers. 'We ride to Londinium, come what may. The column will continue the advance at once!'

CHAPTER SIX

Camulodunum, three days later

Little remained of the colony the Romans had intended to be the capital of the new province of Britannia. Where neat rows of tiled and shingled roofs had spread out between the two rivers, there were now only charred timbers and stretches of grime-streaked plaster walls. Smoke still drifted from several fires amid the smouldering ruins. In the heart of the desolation, the columns and pediment of the half-built temple dedicated to Emperor Claudius rose above the ruins. This was where the garrison had made its last stand.

Opposite the scene of devastation, beyond the river, sprawled the camp of the rebel army, led by Boudica. Most were from the Iceni and Trinovante tribes, but increasingly fresh bands from tribes further afield were swelling the ranks of the rebellion. There was an atmosphere of gaiety amid the wagons and shelters. Victory had emboldened them and erased the desperation that had motivated them to take up arms against Rome. Now, their ambition to drive the Romans from their lands seemed within their grasp, and they eagerly awaited Boudica's order to march on Londinium.

In the heart of the camp was a small farm. Its owners had fled before the rebels reached Camulodunum, and now the main hut served as the quarters of one of the tribal chiefs. A short distance away stood a few pens and a cattle byre covered with a thatched roof. There were no animals within, the only occupants being the handful of prisoners taken when the temple complex had fallen. They were guarded by four Iceni warriors, who were currently sharing a jar of wine looted from the colony. The drink had encouraged their cheerful mood, and they were happy to allow passers-by to stop at the entrance of the byre and briefly gawk at the forlorn figures within. Some hurled insults at the prisoners, while others threw clods of mud or manure at them. Most of those inside raised their bound hands to shield themselves from the missiles, but one was made of sterner stuff and returned the insults in kind as he spat his defiance at his tormentors.

'Try that again, and I'll make you bastards eat that shit when I get out of here!'

The prisoners had been kept bound around the ankles and wrists for two days. Centurion Macro was propped up in the corner of the cattle byre, trying to loosen his bonds to ease the discomfort. Around him huddled the other twelve men who had been taken when the temple complex had been overrun by the rebels. Their armour, weapons and boots had been stripped off, and only their loincloths and tunics remained, streaked with filth and torn by the rebel mob as they were led into captivity. The prisoners were bloodied and bruised, and one man had been stabbed in the eye by a frenzied woman brandishing a small dagger. He sat opposite Macro, groaning with pain every so often.

They had been given no water nor any food since they had been bundled through the gate and left under guard. Besides the gnawing hunger, Macro was desperate to slake his thirst, and once again he ran his tongue over his dry lips as he thought about water. His torment was made worse by the aromas from the cooking fires that drifted across the byre. The captives could hear frequent bursts of cheering and laughter as the rebels celebrated their victory, and the acrid stench from the burned ruins filled the air even after two days. Indeed, parts of the town were still burning, or new fires had started, and the columns of smoke were visible through the entrance to the byre.

'What are they going to do to us?' a voice rasped softly.

Macro flexed his hands and lowered them into his lap as he glanced towards a sallow young man, one of the civilians who had stayed to fight alongside the veterans.

'Best not think about it, lad.'

It occurred to Macro that he did not know the man's name. Even though they had been held prisoner in the confined space for two days, most of the men had sat staring in silent despair, and there had been little conversation. In the early hours of their captivity he had considered trying to raise their spirits by talking of escape, but there was no realistic chance of that, and false hope when exposed was even more damaging to morale. Even if they managed to untie themselves, they would still have to fight their way through the enemy camp. No, there was no hope of that, he conceded.

'What will they do to us?' the youth asked again. 'I have to know.'

'Really?' Germinellus, one of the veterans, rounded on the civilian. 'Very well then. It's likely they'll sacrifice us to one of their gods. Andraste, most likely. If it's the Druids who do the deed, they'll either cut our hearts out or have us burned alive, maybe in one of those wicker men they use occasionally. And we are quite the occasion. The tribespeople don't get to sacrifice Romans every day. They'll want to make a memorable event out of it. That's why they haven't killed us yet. Saving us for something special. Whatever the reason, we ain't getting out of this alive. Happy now?'

The young man said nothing, but lowered his trembling chin and turned his face to the lime-plastered wall to hide his tears.

'Best make your peace with the gods, boy,' the veteran continued in a gentler tone. 'While you can.'

The silence resumed, and Macro began to move his legs to stave off the numbness in his feet. He stared through the gap above the byre gate, trying to concentrate on the wider context. The fall of Camulodunum had demonstrated that the rebels were a force to be reckoned with. Many more tribesmen would now be flocking to join Boudica, while others wavered, waiting to see if there was a realistic prospect of crushing the invaders and driving the Romans out of Britannia. In order to gather a host strong enough to achieve that ambition, she needed to feed her followers with fresh victories and spoils of war. So why was she not yet advancing on the next most obvious target, Londinium? There was no sign that the rebels were getting ready to continue their advance; just the sounds of revelry. Macro could not help thinking that some other factor was in play. Perhaps Boudica was apprehensive. It was possible that the Ninth Legion had received orders to put down the rebellion and was already marching on Camulodunum. They might be too late to save the colony, but they would be sure to exact a terrible revenge. There was grim satisfaction to be had in that, he reflected, even if he was not around to witness the outcome.

That brought his thoughts to the fate of those in the byre. That they were doomed was certain. All that remained was to choose the manner in which they met their deaths.

'Boys,' he said, 'there's something we need to discuss.'

He shuffled round so that he could see his companions. Some of them looked at him with a hopeful gleam in their eyes, as if they expected him to have formulated some plan to escape this foul, stinking place and the fate that awaited them.

'We're going to die. Most of you have accepted that. For the rest, it's important that you resign yourselves to it. What matters now is that we show those bastards out there how Romans die.

There's a lot riding on it. They'll want us whining like whipped curs and begging for mercy. They'll want us to die like cowards so that it gives them less to fear when they next go into battle against Roman soldiers. We can't let that happen, d'you hear? For the sake of our comrades, for the sake of revenge, we have to die hard, hard as nails. Every man of us. They'll probably want to finish us off one at a time. No matter what you see or hear, you must grit your teeth and show no fear.' He paused to let his words settle in their minds. 'I'm not saying we'll all manage it, although that would be for the best. But enough of us set an example that shows those barbarians that Roman soldiers face death without fear, it'll shake 'em to the core. Are you with me on this?'

There was a pause before Germinellus nodded, then one after another the other veterans grumbled their assent. Macro turned his gaze on the sallow young man again.

'What's your name?'

'Batillus . . . Publius Batillus.'

'All right then, Publius Batillus, are you with me like the other men?'

There was a pause as Batillus worked his jaw, then he said, 'Why should I be with you? It was you that led us into this mess. You made us stay here. We could have escaped with the women and children. You trapped us in Camulodunum when there was no hope of defending it. All those other men died because of you. Why should I listen to you now?'

His voice had taken on a shrill edge as he spoke, and Macro could hardly blame him. How was he to know that Macro had been promised support from the garrison at Londinium and the prospect of the Ninth Legion marching to their relief, only to be let down on both counts. He could use that now as an excuse, but Macro had never been the kind of man who instinctively looked for others to blame for the situations he found himself in.

After all, what difference did it make and what good would it do?

'Listen to me, lad,' he responded in a gentle tone. 'We're here now. That ain't going to change. What's happened has happened. You might be right about everything you just said, but you having a go at me, and me saying sorry changes what exactly?'

Batillus opened his mouth to reply, then shook his head.

'Well?' Macro prompted.

'Nothing,' the young man muttered. 'It changes nothing.'

'Right, so where does that leave you? Are you with the rest of us on this?'

'I . . . I'll do my best, Centurion.'

'Good man. You know what, Batillus? I think you'd have made a fine soldier if you had joined the legions. With the right training and attitude, I'd have been proud to fight alongside you.'

His words of encouragement prompted a faint smile from the young man. Hopefully his resolution would last until the time appointed for his death, and throughout the torment that was sure to entail if Macro was any judge of Celtic tastes for dispatching captured enemies.

Silence fell once more, and the prisoners tried to find comfortable positions in which to rest and relieve the pressure of their bindings. Macro closed his eyes and attempted to ignore his raging thirst and the irritable rumblings from his starved stomach.

The light faded and night closed in, and the byre was illuminated by the glow of the rebels' campfires. Once again the prisoners endured the loud din of celebration, laughter, singing and boastful exchanges mingled with the crackle of flames. Shuffling across to the entrance, Macro peered out through a gap in the timbers and saw four fresh guards posted immediately outside. They stood to with spears and shields grounded. They were not drinking, he noticed, and were obviously under strict orders to attend to their duty of keeping a close watch over the prisoners.

He moved away from the entrance and sat against the wall,

trying to shift his thoughts from the death that awaited him. He pictured his wife, Petronella, safe for the moment in Londinium at the inn owned by his mother, Portia. If the Ninth and Second legions arrived before Boudica did, then Londinium might be successfully defended and the rebels driven off. If not . . . He hoped that Petronella and Portia would have the good sense to take passage on the first available ship sailing for Gaul. If they waited too long and panic seized the inhabitants of Londinium, there would be a fraction of the berths needed to evacuate the population. The rest would have to flee the town, and if the rebellion grew, there would be no safe haven for them anywhere on the island.

He cursed under his breath. His attempts to distract his thoughts had only resulted in him feeling worse. He closed his eyes and tried to think of nothing at all, visualising a century of legionaries on a parade ground and counting each man off in turn until he fell asleep.

Despite the discomfort of the manacles and his hunger and thirst, Macro slept through the night, and was woken by the crash of the door striking the wall. His eyes blinked open and he squinted at the dark outlines of two burly warriors as they stood against the backdrop of the morning sun. They had dispensed with their shields and spears and bent down to seize him by the arms, yanking him to his feet before dragging him towards the entrance. He was wide awake now and just had time to call over his shoulder.

'Goodbye, lads! See you in the shades. Don't forget what I said!'

Then he was outside, being hauled away from the byre, the short length of chain at his ankles clinking. As his eyes adjusted to the glare, Macro glanced at his surroundings. He was on a slight slope that gave a clear view over the vast sprawl of the camp, nearly twice the size of the one he had seen when the rebels first pitched up before the walls of Camulodunum. The sight caused his pulse to quicken with concern. At this rate, the Roman army of Britannia would be hopelessly outnumbered by the time it concentrated enough men to face the enemy. He felt an aching sense of loss as he recalled the comrades he had lost in the final struggle. The spy Apollonius, whose qualities he had only begun to appreciate at the end of the time they had known each other. The veterans he had lived amongst since he and Petronella had settled in the colony a year before. And Parvus, the mute boy they had taken in and who had preferred to return to Macro's side rather than flee with the women and other children. All had perished in battle, and perhaps he should be grateful for that. It was almost certainly a better end than the horrors the rebels had in mind for the handful of survivors they had captured.

His thoughts were interrupted by a shrill cry, and he detected a blur of motion out of the corner of his eye. Too late to attempt to defend himself. A blow landed on the side of his head. He twisted and saw a woman, perhaps in her forties, dark hair tied back with a scrap of cloth and wearing a checked tunic cinched at the waist. Her features were screwed up in fury as she shrieked abuse and struck out at his head. Macro raised his hands to protect himself and was rewarded with a howl of pain as her fists made contact with the iron manacles about his wrists. But already others were rushing in, men, women and even children, some lashing out at him in anger while others jeered in contempt and spat.

'Fucking brave of you all to go for a man in chains!' he shouted back. 'Bloody cowards! Take these bloody chains off and we'll see what you're made of!'

One of the guards cuffed him on the temple and snarled something in the Iceni dialect that Macro's ringing ears could not catch, even though he had a good grasp of their tongue. But the warning was clear. He hunched forward and did his best to ward off further blows as the guards dragged him onwards, shoving away those trying to hit him as the trio passed by.

At length, Macro could see a tent ahead at the top of the slope. He recognised it as one of Roman design, much like those used by senior officers of the legions. Probably looted from the stores at Camulodunum, he surmised. Or perhaps spoils from one of the villas owned by the wealthier Romans in the region. There were carts lined up around it, creating a modest enclosure with an opening overlooking the slope guarded by several warriors. As he was dragged through the opening, the warriors closed up behind him to keep out the small mob that had followed them across the enemy camp. He lowered his manacled hands, grateful that he was no longer being targeted by the rebels, and looked up. Two more warriors stood either side of the parted tent flaps.

He was given a shove by one of his handlers and stumbled forward, just managing to stay on his feet. The man thrust his finger towards the tent and snapped an order. Shuffling forward, Macro approached the opening, and one of the guards leaned inside and called out. A woman's voice replied. He felt a chill of expectation as he recognised Boudica's voice. The guard turned to him and waved him inside.

There were three women within. Boudica was sitting on a cushioned seat of Roman design, while her daughters, Bardea and Merida, perched on stools either side of her. They were eating off a low table bearing silver platters of meat, bread and fruit. Macro licked his lips at the sight of the food and the jar of wine standing to one side. The women stared coldly at him for a moment before Boudica spoke quietly to her daughters and they left the tent by a side flap.

Macro stood before the Iceni queen and tried not to grimace as he stiffened his spine and felt the pain of the blows he had received on his way from the byre. Boudica was still as she scrutinised him with an expression of distaste. Her nose wrinkled, and he was aware of a faint sickly-sweet odour from somewhere, and a muffled droning sound.

'There was a time I would never have dreamed we would meet as enemies.' She spoke in faintly accented Latin. 'When you and I first met, and later fought side by side against the Dark Moon cult all those years ago.'

'I haven't forgotten,' Macro replied evenly. 'Happier days.'

'Quite.'

There was a long silence as they stared at each other. Macro tried to moisten his dry lips. 'Why have you brought me here?'

'I wanted to see you one last time before you die. And die you must, like all Romans on this island. That is the only way for our tribes to be rid of you. Die, down to the last woman and child, so that your emperor learns the price of trying to impose his will here.'

'If you do that . . .' Macro cleared his throat before he continued, 'you will have made an enemy that will not rest until every one of your victims is avenged ten times over. The blood of your people will drown that shed by ours.'

'Brave words. You truly think the ultimate victory will not be ours?' Boudica's lips lifted in amusement. 'I have thousands more joining the rebellion every day. Every victory will swell that number.'

'Mostly farmers, their women and children. How many warriors are joining you, I wonder?' Macro countered as his gaze shifted to the food and drink.

Boudica nodded at the table. 'You may come closer and eat. It will be your last chance.'

He was too hungry to care if this might be his final meal. He dropped to his knees in front of the table and reached for the nearest goblet, draining it in one go before grabbing a chunk of

91

roasted pork and tearing at it, chewing furiously. She watched him with a sad expression for a while, and then her features hardened.

'I wonder how you live with the guilt.'

Macro glanced up and frowned. He swallowed quickly. 'Guilt?'

'Every one of the deaths of your comrades and the other Romans we have slaughtered since the rebellion began lies at your door.'

'How so?' Macro could already guess where her remarks were headed.

'When Decianus led your column into the Iceni capital and took me and my daughters prisoner before his men raped them and flogged me, it was you who arranged our escape. If you had not done that, we would have been taken to Londinium in chains and left there to rot. I would not have been able to persuade my people to revolt. Therefore, the blood of your people is on your hands. I wonder what your Roman friends would say if they knew.'

'I don't accept that,' he responded. 'I have thought it through. The Iceni are fond of rebellion. If it had not been you that provoked the uprising, it would have been someone else.'

'You think so?' She gave a dry laugh. 'You'd *like* to think so, at any rate. In truth, I have a firm hold over my followers. Most of them. I think you underestimate what it meant to them when they discovered the outrages perpetrated against their queen and her daughters. Decianus and his men could not have picked a more provocative target. And you can be sure that I milked that sense of outrage for every drop. Their souls are on fire and they will not rest until Rome has been swept from our shores and we are free once again. For that, you and the other prisoners must die. You will be handed to the Druids to sacrifice. I dare say they will not be inclined to show much mercy, given Suetonius's campaign to wipe out their sacred groves on Mona and eliminate their cults. I imagine your deaths will be agonising and lingering.' She picked up a goblet and took a sip before she continued. 'If it's any consolation, I will grieve at your death.'

'I bet.'

She glared at him. 'You fool . . . You still don't understand, do you?'

'Understand what? That we were once lovers? That was a long time ago.'

'Yet you still felt enough to help me and my daughters escape.'

'I did that because it was the right thing to do. I hoped it would teach you that not all Romans are the same. Some still know right from wrong. I hoped it would undo some of the damage caused by Decianus. Seems I was mistaken. Any affection I once had for you perished along with my comrades who died here. If you spared me because of our past friendship, you are wasting your effort. We share nothing now.'

'Nothing?' Boudica shook her head. 'Macro, you are so wrong. Tell me, have you never been curious about the contrast in appearance between my two daughters? You can clearly see that the younger one takes after Prasutagus, but the older one is markedly different.'

'So?' Macro felt an anxious twinge in his gut. 'What of it? Have you been playing the field? I've heard that you Celts like that sort of thing.'

She winced and sat back, lips pressed tightly together as she struggled to control her anger and hurt. 'I never gave myself to a warrior who did not deserve me, whether he was an Iceni or a Roman.'

'Thanks for . . .' Macro's eyes widened as the import of her comments struck home. He continued quietly, 'What are you saying to me?'

'Don't play the fool, Macro. You know. Bardea is your daughter. Your child. You're her father.'

'No . . .' He did a quick calculation of the girl's age and then allowed for the time he had been Boudica's lover. He shook his head even as the disbelief began to evaporate. 'I can't be.'

'You are. You'll know it the moment you set eyes on her again now that I have told you. I'm surprised it hadn't crossed your mind already. For my part, I swear by all the gods of my tribe that it is true, and may I be torn apart by horses should I lie.'

Macro felt dazed. 'Why tell me this now?'

'You deserve the truth before you die.'

'Does she know?'

'She suspects that Prasutagus was not her father. How could she not? She saw how you and I were around each other when we travelled to Londinium to renew the oath of allegiance to Rome, and again when you helped us escape. She can also add up. She's not a fool.'

'What have you told her?'

'Nothing. But she will ask one day.'

'And what will you tell her then? The truth?'

'Yes. Why wouldn't I?'

He raised his bound hands and gestured around him. 'Given the circumstances, I doubt she will be pleased to discover her father is Roman.'

'Her father is a man to be proud of. Even if he is the enemy.'

'What if others find out the truth? They will turn on her and tear her to pieces.'

'Not if they don't know. Even if they did, I am sure I could sway their feelings by presenting it as yet another example of Roman abuse of our people.'

Macro felt his throat tighten. 'You'd claim that I raped you?'

'If I had to. I would not wish to dishonour my memory of what we shared, but I would do it for the sake of Bardea and the interests of my people.'

94

He slumped back on his heels. 'Sweet Jupiter . . . I don't recognise you any more. What happened to you, Boudica?'

'Rome. Rome happened to me. To my people and every tribe in Britannia. You treat us as your property to do with as you wish. You offend every value we hold sacred. Your arrogance and ignorance of our ways hang over us like a foul, clinging stench . . . We will wash the stain of dishonour away with your blood and be clean again.'

'No you won't,' Macro countered. 'All that will happen is that you will wallow in blood for a while before Rome sends more legions to Britannia to hunt you down and annihilate every last one of you who dares to rebel against the emperor. That is as sure as the rising of the sun. You cannot win. I have no doubt about the bravery of you and your people, and your willingness to fight, but your victory here at Camulodunum was because you had overwhelming numbers and faced a handful of aged veterans and volunteers. What do you think will happen when you go up against the men of the legions? They are the best-trained soldiers in the known world. A killing machine that crushes all before them. You know this to be true. You have seen how they fight at first hand. Your rabble won't stand a chance against them.

'For the sake of your people, for the lives of your children, for our daughter, I ask you to end this rebellion and spare the lives that will be lost if you continue to fight. If you agree, I will do what I can to plead for mercy for you. There will be repercussions, that is inevitable, but far fewer will die. You and your daughters can escape. Go to the tribes in the far north, you will be safe there—'

'Enough!' Boudica cut in as she rose from her chair with a frown. 'I have heard enough of the boasts of Romans. Whatever you may say about your legions, Macro, they are still made up of men of flesh and blood who can die as easily as anyone else, even my rabble,' she added with a sneer. 'On your feet!'

He struggled to rise and stood before her as she regarded him coolly. 'Follow me.'

She crossed to the flaps at the rear of the tent with Macro shuffling behind her. The sickly odour he had noticed on entering grew stronger, as did the buzzing, which he now recognised as that of insects. Boudica paused as she turned to address him.

'You say my people won't stand a chance against your legionaries . . .'

She drew back the flap and bright sunshine flooded the tent, causing Macro to squint. Gradually the scene before him came into focus. It was a pile of severed heads, perhaps two or three hundred of them. As far as he could make out, most had the cropped hair of Roman soldiers. The skin was pale and covered with blotches and dried blood, indicating that the men had perished a few days before. The dark blots of flies swirled over the pile, while more crawled across the flesh and sightless eyes of the dead. The odour that Macro had detected earlier now washed over him in a putrid aroma and caused his stomach to clench in revulsion, and for an instant he feared he might throw up. He swallowed hard, his gaze moving to the shaft rising from the middle of the heap. There were the familiar iron handles protruding at right angles, then higher up the gold and silver medallions awarded to the legion. At the top was the gilded eagle, and below it the plaque that identified the Ninth.

As he stared at the eagle, the full import of what he saw before him struck home.

Boudica gestured towards the heads and the standard. 'As you can see, my rabble − as you put it − has come up against your precious legionaries. They marched straight into the trap we set for them and my warriors crushed them. Only their legate and a handful of his men managed to flee. The rest were killed. I would say that our second victory in as many days is proof that Rome can be beaten. Even now, word of the destruction of your Ninth

96

Legion is spreading across Britannia like wildfire, kindling the spirit of rebellion in the hearts of every man and woman who is proud to be a Celt.'

Boudica's eyes gleamed as she stared into the middle distance, beyond the terrible trophies piled about the eagle standard. 'A host is gathering the likes of which this island has never seen. We shall destroy your legions, one after another, and decorate our halls with the trophies of war. We shall drive the Romans into the sea, which will run red with their blood. We shall be avenged for every insult, every theft, every rape and other humiliation that Rome has heaped on us since her shadow fell across our lands. The day has come, Macro . . .'

She turned to him and released the tent flap, cutting off the grisly sight beyond. Her expression softened with pity. 'It is a shame that you will not live to see our great victory. But be comforted by the thought that our daughter will bear witness.'

She sighed heavily, and Macro saw that she looked very tired. Then she called out, and a moment later, the two guards who had brought Macro from the byre entered the tent. She gave a quick order, and they grasped him by the arms, pinning him between them.

'Farewell, Macro. When you are returned to your comrades, let them know that they die on the morrow.'

CHAPTER SEVEN

A s dawn broke over the rebel camp, the prisoners in the cattle byre waited in anxious expectation to be taken to meet their death. Macro had been assailed by questions when he had been brought back the previous evening. He described what had occurred, sparing them any mention of the food and wine, and concluded with Boudica's pronouncement of their execution. The other captives had been stunned by the news of the Ninth Legion's defeat. There had been the faintest of hopes that they might be saved by the legion's intervention. Now there was none.

The night had passed largely in silence. Most of the men were consumed by their thoughts. One of the veterans tried to raise their spirits by breaking into an old marching song, but only two others joined in, half-heartedly, and when the last verse concluded, there was no attempt to continue with another. In the darkness, Macro could hear occasional muttering, and later muted sobs, which seemed to come from Batillus. He hoped that everyone would hold true to their word when their time came to die. Despite the revelation about the fate of the Ninth, it was important to make some show of courage and defiance. That, at least, they could do before they died.

As the sun rose, its warmth seeped into the byre, making the fetid stench within ever more unbearable. Outside they could hear the camp coming to life, and there was an unmistakable festive edge to the rebels' voices; an excitement that added to the dreadful anticipation of the captives as they waited. The morning hours passed with agonising slowness, a kind of torture, Macro reflected. It was strange how when faced with death he found himself wanting the moment to be over, rather than eke out what should be the last precious moments.

'When are the bastards coming for us?' Germinellus growled as he rocked gently. 'When?'

'They'll come,' Macro replied. 'Just be ready when they do. I'll lead the way and go first. Is that understood?' He looked round at the others, daring anyone to defy him. It was vital that he set the example for the others to follow.

'Why you?' Batillus demanded. 'Shouldn't we draw lots or something?'

'Why me?' Macro responded. 'Because I'm the one giving the fucking orders. This ain't a democracy, lad. There isn't going to be any debate over it. Just play your part, along with the rest of us. In any case, it'll make it easier for you to see what you must do when it's your turn.'

'Easier?' Batillus laughed drily. 'Sure, Centurion. That's a relief to know. A big bloody relief. You've really put my mind at rest.'

'Shut your mouth!' Macro bared his teeth. 'I've heard enough of your prattling, boy. One more word of that nonsense and I swear I'll come over there and knock your teeth out, y'hear me?'

Batillus opened his mouth.

'Just nod,' Macro growled in a menacing tone.

The young man dipped his head.

'That's better.'

'We shouldn't take this lying down,' said Germinellus. 'We should show those bastards there's still plenty of fight in us. When they come for us, we should go for them, try and take some of them with us.'

'How?' Macro demanded, raising his bound hands.

The veteran clenched his fists. 'We can still use these! And we have teeth!'

'We're not Spartans,' Macro scolded him. 'What do you think we can achieve? Most of us are old men. You've seen the guards outside. Biggest, meanest-looking fuckers they could find for the job. We won't stand a chance against them. They'll laugh at any attempt we make to fight them. All you'll get is a few more bruises for your efforts, and bruised pride into the bargain. No. Our best weapons are dignity and courage. In any case, they're our only weapons, and we must use what we have to hand.'

A series of shouts from outside ended the exchange, and a moment later the door to the byre swung open. Two warriors entered and pulled the nearest captive to his feet before thrusting him outside into the hands of other warriors waiting to take the Romans away. One by one, the captives were dragged into the bright midday sunshine. Macro was one of the last to be removed from the byre, and he looked up at the clear blue sky and smiled as he saw some swifts swooping high overhead.

'A fine day, lads,' he said loudly. 'It is as good a day as any to die.' He tried to shuffle towards the head of the group, but was held back. As the last of the captives emerged, he grinned at the warriors grasping his arms. 'Well, let's get on with it, shall we? Don't want to keep the queen waiting.' The warrior to his left snarled something and raised his free hand, making a fist.

With the captives and their guards formed in a loose column, a tall, broad-shouldered Icenian with the tribe's distinctive blue tattoos on his cheeks waved his arm in the direction of Boudica's tent, and the small procession set off through the rebel camp.

At first there were few people about, and they looked up and either scowled and shouted insults or stared with mute hostility at the Romans. Ahead, however, a vast crowd had gathered.

Macro saw that Boudica's tent had been struck, and in its place a large scaffold had been constructed, with the platform a good eight feet above the ground so that a clear view of the coming executions would be afforded to all. He could make out the glint of the eagle to one side of the scaffold, and hoped that he had prepared his comrades for the moment when they saw the trophies piled around the base of the standard.

As they approached the crowd gathered across the slope, the first of the rebels to see the captives and their escort cried out in excitement. The cries were taken up by others, and in no more than a few heartbeats, the din had swelled to a roar of triumph as fists and weapons punched into the air above the crowd. A group of warriors trotted round the edge of the densely packed rebels and forced an opening. Forming a cordon and pushing the crowd back with their spears thrust out horizontally, they created a rough oval about the prisoners, sparing them from any blows that might fatally injure them or render them unconscious before they reached the scaffold. The shouts and screams from all sides were deafening, and Macro forced himself to look directly ahead, refusing to meet the savage glares of any of the men, women and children lining the route. Something struck the shoulder of the guard to his left, and he instinctively looked aside and saw the brown streak on the man's cloak. The warrior paused to shout angrily at the crowd, and Macro laughed loudly.

'Seems I'm not the only one in the shit today, eh?'

The warrior muttered something under his breath and thrust Macro forward to catch up with the others.

The prisoners and their escort reached the open area around the scaffold. A ring of warriors, again using their spears horizontally, formed a barrier to keep the people back. The space was some thirty paces across and dominated by the structure, which was ten feet wide and fifteen in length. A crude set of stairs led up from the rear. Atop the platform were two posts with iron rings at the top and bottom. A brazier stood at one end and the air above it shimmered.

As the prisoners were led around the rear of the scaffold, they came in sight of the standard and the heads piled beneath. The putrid stench of decaying flesh was more pronounced in the close heat of the day, and a dense halo of flies swirled in a dark blizzard about the heap.

'Oh fuck . . .' Germinellus said from two places ahead of Macro.

'Steady there!' Macro called out. 'You knew this was coming. Don't give these barbarians the satisfaction of provoking a reaction.'

The captives were lined up a short distance from the scaffold and made to wait as the noise from the crowd rose and fell. Even though he had eaten a few mouthfuls of meat and drunk some wine the day before, Macro began to feel faint and had to force himself to stand erect, chin up and shoulders back. He saw that some of his comrades were struggling to do the same, and the oldest of the veterans simply hung in the grip of the warriors on either side, his head lolling as his lips muttered in meaningless delirium. Batillus was still with them, Macro was pleased to see. The young man stared straight ahead, unflinching.

As close to noon as he could estimate, he caught sight of a blue banner with a white horse on it rippling gently as it was moved from side to side. The roar of the crowd swelled to a fresh crescendo as the banner approached the scaffold. The crowd parted, and Boudica, her daughters and a small retinue of nobles and Druids appeared. Macro turned towards the queen, but she refused to meet his gaze as she climbed onto the scaffold to acknowledge the rolling cries of acclaim from her followers. One of her retinue scrambled up the steps with the chair that she had sat on in the tent the previous day and set it up at one end of the platform. Once she was seated, with the banner shimmering in the light breeze above her, she gestured towards her retinue and three Druids stepped forward.

Macro regarded them with hostility. The Druid cults had been an ominous presence ever since the Romans had first encountered them in Britannia. They had remained the most fanatical of enemies and the most cruel and ruthless. Many Romans who had fallen into their hands had been brutally sacrificed to satisfy their gods. The Romans had repaid their brutality in kind and ensured that any Druids who were taken alive were swiftly put to death. Macro had not encountered the cult associated with the Iceni, and noted the five-pointed star within a circle that had been branded onto the Druids' foreheads as they passed by him and climbed the steps.

As they appeared in full view of the crowd, Boudica's followers fell reverently silent and still. The tallest of the Druids stepped to the front of the scaffold, raised his arms to the sky and began to chant in a high-pitched sing-song voice, imploring his gods to accept the sacrifice of the Roman prisoners and to bless the tribes with good fortune in their struggle against Rome and her legions. He concluded by lowering his arms and extending them to the sides as if to embrace the crowd as he spoke to them directly. Once more they cheered and began to press forward so that the warriors in the cordon struggled to hold their ground, and had to brace their feet and lean back to keep their people at bay.

The tall Druid turned and crossed the scaffold, looking down at the line of prisoners. He stared intently at each in turn before suddenly thrusting a finger towards the limp figure of the oldest of the veterans. Before Macro could intervene, the guards dragged the man forward and up the steps onto the platform. There the rope binding his wrists together was untied and the other Druids helped the guards to tie his wrists individually with fresh cord. This was then passed through each of the rings at the top of the posts, and the veteran's arms were forced up and out in a crucifixion posture. He let out a cry of pain as his shoulders took the strain. The process was repeated for his ankles, and he hung between the posts in agony as his limbs were stretched to the limit. Macro was relieved that, true to their pledge, he clamped his mouth shut and refused to cry out again.

The tall Druid parted his dark robes and drew a long, curved dagger from the sheath at his belt. Approaching the veteran, he grabbed the neckline of his tunic and cut downwards, tearing the woollen fabric until he reached the hem at the bottom. Then he parted the folds and cut away the man's loincloth, screwing it up and hurling it towards the crowd, where hands shot out to snatch the trophy from the air. At the rear of the scaffold, the prisoners were mercifully shielded from sight of what happened next, only able to see the back of the veteran from the midriff upwards as the Druid bent down and began to work on his victim's groin with the curved knife.

The man managed to hold out for a moment before he screamed in torment as his genitals were cut from his body, held aloft to the cruel, rapturous cheers of the crowd and then tossed into the brazier. There was a sudden hissing sizzle, and a puff of smoke curled into the air. The veteran had slumped in his bonds and fallen silent. Macro hoped he had passed out. The Druid went to work again, cutting and tearing, and then held up his victim's heart, blood running through his fingers and down his arm. The crowd cheered again as the heart was added to the brazier.

Macro had witnessed this with as much self-control as he could muster, but inside his guts clenched and an icy chill gripped his spine. He risked a glance to both sides and saw that some of the others were staring rigidly ahead, while others looked down, but none had cracked yet.

On the scaffold, the Druids had released the ties holding the veteran to the posts, and the body slumped out of sight, blood dripping through the timbers onto the grass below. A moment later, the corpse was swung off the platform to land on the pile of heads. The Druid leader returned to the top of the steps and pointed his now bloodied finger at Batillus.

'No!' Macro shouted, trying to tear himself free of the guards on either side, but they held him firmly and his effort was futile. 'Me! Take me!'

The Druid's lips parted in a sneer as he stared at Macro, and he raised his finger and waved it from side to side in a mocking gesture before returning his attention to the young man.

'You Druid bastard!' Macro shouted. 'Take me, I said!'

Without warning, the warrior to his right swung his fist into Macro's gut. The impact made him double over as the air was driven from his lungs, and he was left gasping for breath and only able to make his protest in a whisper that no one could hear.

Batillus was escorted to the steps and climbed them stoically. Macro watched him with wary admiration, fearing that the youth's resolve would buckle the moment he first felt the blade. He was bound and his limbs stretched in the same manner as his predecessor. Macro could not bear to look upon the scene, and instead fixed his gaze on one of the support posts, forcing his mind to empty itself of thought.

One by one the captives were mutilated and dispatched, to the delirious delight of the crowd. The grass beneath the scaffold was slick with blood, and flies feasted on the fresh corpses sprawled over the ghastly heads at the foot of the standard. An hour passed, and then there was only Macro and Germinellus left behind the scaffold, while the Druid was doing his utmost to slow proceedings to keep the crowd entertained for as long as possible. The veteran he was dealing with held out for as long as he could, and then began to howl in agony as the Druid cut him again and again.

'Kill him!' Germinellus suddenly called out. 'For the love of Jupiter, kill him and be done with it, you barbarian bastards!'

Macro was no longer capable of admonishing his fellow prisoner, so numbed by the horror had he become, and would have yelled something similar if Germinellus hadn't beaten him to it. The protest was silenced by a blow to the veteran's head and the threat of more if he continued.

On the scaffold, the latest victim had finally fallen silent. His heart was cut out and tossed on the smoking brazier, and the smell of roasting flesh vied with the stink of the pile of heads. Macro felt his stomach lurch and fought back the urge to vomit. The Druid appeared above them, dark against the bright afternoon sky, and paused a long time before making his selection and gesturing towards Germinellus.

'No!' the veteran shrieked, recoiling and trying to thrust himself back from the steps as his minders struggled to drag him forwards. Their captive writhed one way, then the other, the weathered sinews of his arms and neck straining within the gleam of his sweaty skin. He suddenly turned his head and thrust it at the hand of the guard holding his left bicep, biting down on the warrior's knuckles. The man cried out in surprise and instinctively released his grip. Germinellus swung his manacled fists up and struck the guard a glancing blow on his chin, then lurched to one side and tried to run, but his ankle chains snagged and he fell headlong. The guards were on him before he could rise to his knees, and pummelled his limbs and head, dazing him, before dragging him up the steps and fastening him to the posts.

Germinellus stirred and then strained his muscles against his bonds as he saw the Druid turn towards him. 'Don't! For pity's sake, spare me! I can't do you any harm. Let me go! I'll leave Britannia and never return. I swear it! By all that's fucking holy, I swear it! Let me live!'

The Druid grinned and raised his knife. There came the sound of tearing material above the terrified screams of the veteran, accompanied by the laughter and jeers of the crowd, though they

106

were quieter now, their initial bloodlust having withered in the oppressive heat of the afternoon. As the Druid set about torturing his victim, Germinellus alternated between begging for mercy and screaming when the knife cut into him.

Macro could not bear it any longer. He closed his eyes and tried to shut the noises out of his mind. He feared that his courage was failing him, and an imagination that had always shied away from visualising the harm and pain that might come to him in battle now began to give way to the most awful speculation. It took every bit of his self-control not to call out for mercy, to beg Boudica to save him. He turned his thoughts to prayer and began to mutter under his breath.

'Almighty Jupiter, Best and Greatest, please grant me the strength to do honour to those comrades who have gone before me. Give me the courage to face death without flinching. Give me the mercy of a quick death and the strength to deny my enemies the satisfaction of seeing a Roman beg for his life. All this I ask in return for the service I have given Rome. For the blood I have shed to honour the gods . . .'

He was so focused on his request for divine intervention that he was unaware of the death of Germinellus and the casting of his body on top of the others. A sudden jerk of his arms snapped him out of his prayers, and he found himself stumbling up the steps. There was blood all over the platform and splashed and smeared on the arms and face of the Druid holding his gory blade. Charred lumps of flesh sizzled in the brazier. At the other end of the scaffold, Boudica sat regarding him impassively.

Two warriors removed Macro's bindings and tied his wrists and ankles with sturdy ropes before feeding the ends through the iron rings on the post. At a signal from their leader, the other Druids pulled on the ties, stretching his arms out painfully and causing him to gasp. He clamped his jaws together and stared fixedly towards the blackened columns of Camulodunum's half-built temple in the distance. He felt his legs being forced apart, and the insides of his thighs burned under the unaccustomed stretching. Tightly held in position, he was utterly powerless and unable to breathe easily.

The Druid leader slowly circled him, chanting softly, then turned to speak to the crowd. His words were in the Iceni dialect, which Macro had developed some understanding of in the year he had lived at Camulodunum. Here was the last of the captives, he announced. The Roman chief of the veterans at the hated colony. His death would be the most precious of sacrifices to be offered to Andraste.

The Druid turned and stepped slowly towards the centurion. When their faces were no more than a foot apart, he narrowed his grey eyes and shifted so that Macro could no longer see the temple's columns and had to return his piercing gaze. Summoning up his last reserve of defiance, Macro tried to hawk up some phlegm and was rewarded with enough to spit into the Druid's face.

'Fuck you and all the sheep-shagging rabble that follow you!'

The Druid blinked as the spittle struck his cheek, and then raised his knife so the point was an inch from the notch in Macro's collarbone. He did not strike, did not make to cut Macro's tunic open. Instead his eyes flickered towards Boudica, as if waiting for a word of command.

'Do it!' Macro challenged him.

Boudica rose from her chair. Hand raised to stay the Druid's blade, she spoke distinctly for the benefit of those who had stayed to witness the death of the last of the captives.

'Enough!'

The Druid lowered his knife and stepped aside as Boudica approached the front of the platform. She waited until there was silence before she continued.

'Andraste has had her fill of sacrifices for the day! This one, this last of the Romans, the leader of those we defeated at Camulodunum, is too rich a sacrifice to be shared with the curs who died before. Andraste's appetite has been sated by today's offerings, but soon she will be hungry for more. The centurion will be saved for a special ceremony, when the true mettle of the Roman warrior will be put to the test and all shall witness the cowardice and hollow courage of Rome laid bare. This scum is supposed to be the best of his kind. Yet he will beg for our mercy like a child when his end comes!'

Macro followed the sense of her words with numbed disbelief. He had committed himself to accepting death, and now he was to be spared for today, only to face the prospect of an even more grim end. He felt sick and his limbs trembled as he fought to keep his expression coldly defiant.

'Cut him down and take this animal back to his pen!' Boudica ordered.

As the Druids began to untie the bindings, she approached and spoke quietly to Macro in his own tongue.

'I will not let you die bravely. Not you. I need you to be broken and despairing, crying to be released from life, for all my people to see. You will beg for death. Be in no doubt, you *will* die, Macro. But you will die on my terms, not yours.'

CHAPTER EIGHT

Macro was left alone in the byre for the next two days, but this time he was brought food and drink in the morning and at dusk. He was no longer manacled, although there were four men on guard around the byre at all times, and their nervous watchfulness made it clear what penalty lay in store should he escape or attempt to harm himself.

After he was returned to the byre, he had slumped down, arms folded across his knees, head bowed, unable to control his trembling any longer. He felt an exhaustion that went beyond the consequence of physical effort. His mind was as numb as his body, and he found it hard to concentrate on anything for more than a few heartbeats before his thoughts were overshadowed and smothered by pure dread. He would be reminded of some detail of the events that had taken place on the scaffold, and it pierced his mind like a dagger, causing him to flinch instinctively and gasp. His heart raced, and sweat pricked on his brow and the nape of his neck.

By the time night had fallen, he was more in control of himself, and stood up and stretched before attempting some light exercise to loosen his muscles so that he might be better prepared for whatever fate Boudica had in mind for him. As his mind cleared, it became obvious to him that she had never intended for him to die with his comrades. That was why he had been left to the last.

She and the Druids had played him, convincing him that he was about to die, perhaps hoping that he, like Germinellus, would break down and beg for mercy. If that had happened, she might not have spared him. The fact that he had held out, as far as they could tell, might have been the reason he had been saved for a later day. If they had only known how close he had been to crumbling, how brittle his courage had been at the last moment as the Druid raised his blade . . .

He had achieved a minor victory of sorts by the narrowest of margins.

Any relief turned to bitter anger at Boudica for reducing him to the pitiful state he found himself in immediately afterwards. She had humiliated him more than she knew. Of all the wounds that Macro had endured through his career, and there had been plenty of them, this was the worst, even though he had not shed a drop of blood or endured any physical pain. He now knew that he had been at breaking point and that Boudica intended to push him beyond it to make him an object of ridicule in front of her followers. He cursed her at the prospect. At the same time, he could not help recalling that they had been lovers once, and friends and allies thereafter. If she was telling the truth about her daughter, then Bardea shared Macro's blood. How could Boudica dishonour that so comprehensively? he wondered.

Anger churned in his stomach and became rage. She had almost brought him down, and would ensure that when the time came for him to be sacrificed, he would give way to his dread entirely and die a bawling coward in full view of his enemies.

'That is not going to happen,' he muttered fiercely to himself. 'I forbid it.'

His heart filled with fresh resolve and he stepped up his exercises, driving himself harder than he had for years. Now and then one of the guards would look in and comment in their own tongue, or laugh at his activity. Perhaps they already knew of his fate and were amused by the futility of his efforts. He did not care. All that mattered was to be ready for whatever came next, and to face it in a manner that did honour to himself and to Rome.

Two days after the execution of the prisoners, the rebels broke camp and prepared to advance in the direction of Londinium. The hot, dry weather continued and there was a palpable mood of excitement amongst Boudica's followers, as if they were embarking on a public holiday such as Macro had experienced in Rome as a child, when much of the population had left the city to enjoy a spectacle featuring gladiators fighting in rival fleets on one of the nearby lakes. The warriors and their families packed their belongings onto wagons and handcarts. Many were further burdened by items they had looted from Camulodunum before fire consumed the colony: pieces of furniture, fine goblets, cups and crockery, bales of cloth, jewellery, clothes, jars of wine and preserved food – including garum, which was as highly prized amongst the tribespeople as it was amongst Romans. Then there were the weapons and armour taken from the Roman dead, now borne proudly by their new owners.

It wasn't until the host began to move off that Macro was taken from the byre and made to stand by an Iceni chariot while his hands were manacled again. A long tether was attached to the short iron bar between his wrists and the other end tied to one of the posts at the rear of the chariot. As the wagons around him were loaded, he recognised the campaign tent that Boudica had claimed for herself, as it was folded and placed over the table, chair and stools that he had seen the night before the executions. He saw a group of warriors setting up the standard of the Ninth Legion on the bed of another wagon. The shaft was held in place by a simple wooden frame, and the Roman heads, including those of his fellow captives, were piled around it.

After a while, he made to sit down, but a guard shouted angrily and kicked him in the side, gesturing for him to get back on his feet.

'All right, sunshine,' Macro retorted. 'The exercise will do me good.'

Boudica and her daughters appeared ahead of the rest of her retinue and the warriors clad in blue cloaks who served as her personal bodyguard. Macro deliberately fixed his stare on Bardea as she passed by, but the girl did not spare him even a glance. While her daughters mounted another of the chariots, Boudica approached Macro and regarded him coolly.

'Leashed like the mangy dog you are . . .'

'Be careful, I bite.'

'I'll have you tamed in short order, Centurion Macro. Eating out of my hand and rolling over on your back at my command.'

'I roll over for no man. Let alone some barbarian hag and her peasant rabble.'

'You mean to provoke me.' Boudica gave a laugh and gestured towards the ruins of Camulodunum and the cart bearing the eagle standard. 'Not bad work for a peasant rabble. And we've only just begun the humiliation of Rome and your emperor. Even now, word of your defeats will be speeding its way to the heart of your empire. I wish I could be there to witness the moment when Nero hears how the colony his father founded has been razed and its veterans wiped out along with the men of the Ninth Legion.' Her face lit up with a triumphant gleam. 'What will happen, I wonder, when further news arrives of the sacking of Londinium and the destruction of the remaining legions occupying Britannia?'

'Don't count your chickens, as the saying goes.'

'I don't have anything to worry about on that score. Andraste has had her blood sacrifice and the Druids have read the signs. Great victories lie ahead of my people. Andraste has spoken.'

'I'm sure Jupiter, Best and Greatest, will have something to say about that.'

Her expression darkened. 'We'll see. Or at least I will. You won't live to witness the outcome.'

Macro felt his pulse quicken. 'What fate have you decided for me? To be sacrificed like my comrades?'

'Sacrificed, yes. But differently.'

She turned and climbed onto the chariot Macro was tied to as a warrior, stripped to the waist, jumped up ahead of her and sat astride the yoke. He picked up the reins and turned to his queen, and she gave him a nod.

'Yah!' he called out, flicking the traces, and the gleaming black horses walked forward.

Boudica gripped one of the wicker side panels to steady herself as she stood tall on the bed of the chariot, where her people would be able to see her clearly as she and her retinue joined the broad column picking its way westwards across the sun-drenched landscape. Macro hurried a few steps to keep up and allow himself some slack with the tether. Behind them came the chariot carrying Boudica's daughters, then her nobles on horseback, before a modest baggage train, with the wagon carrying her grisly trophies at the rear. Her bodyguard mounted and formed up on each side of the procession to keep the other rebels and their vehicles from impeding the queen's progress as she made her way towards the vanguard. Bands of warriors, some mounted, others riding chariots, most on foot, led the way. Many of them were equipped with Roman armour and weapons, and their polished helmets gleamed in the sunshine.

For the rest of the day, the horde moved across the rolling landscape, joined by individuals and small groups arriving from the north and west to swell the ranks of the rebellion. There were so many women and children present that it was hard for Macro to estimate the fighting strength of Boudica's force. They passed a handful of villas whose occupants lay dead, stripped of their clothes. Columns of smoke besmirched the clear blue sky. And always more loot – supplies of grain, as well as cattle, sheep and pigs – was added to the column, which looked to Macro less and less like an army marching to victory and more like the migration of an entire people.

By the time Boudica gave the order to make camp at the end of the day, he estimated that they had covered no more than eight miles. A poor effort, and he took comfort from the slow progress. At this rate it would take them several days to reach Londinium, whose inhabitants would have enough advance warning to ensure that most escaped long before the first rebels arrived in the town. He knew his mother would be loath to abandon the inn and the other businesses she had built up since settling there, but trusted that Petronella would persuade her to flee. There would be time for Portia to collect her savings and valuables and for both women to quit Londinium for a safe haven. Preferably in Gaul. Even if he never saw them again, he was reassured to think they might survive the approaching storm. With luck, his mother would have enough silver to start a new business when the rebellion was over.

He had few doubts about the eventual outcome. If Boudica triumphed over the legions in Britannia and drove every Roman from the island, the emperor was sure to send a fresh army to retake the province. An army powerful enough to crush even as great a host as the Iceni queen could ever hope to gather. It might be the case that Nero and his advisers were still considering abandoning the province, as had been rumoured these last few years. It was ironic that had Boudica waited long enough, Britannia might have been rid of Rome without a blow having to be struck. If she achieved the victory she sought, it would only be a prelude to her bloody defeat, the destruction of her followers and the devastation of her lands. Rome would never tolerate the humiliation of being forced out of the province and would exact the harshest revenge. An example would be made of the Britons so that Rome's allies, her subjugated peoples and her enemies alike understood the price to be paid by those who had the temerity to defy her will.

Macro was left tied to the rear of the chariot as the horses were released from their yoke and taken to a nearby stream to be watered and fed. Boudica and her daughters went to sit in the shade of some oak trees while her bodyguard unloaded the wagons and erected her tent. Others were sent to forage for wood for the campfires, while a pig was slaughtered for the queen's retinue to feast on. Macro had spent the day walking in the sun and subjected to the choking dust thrown up by the horses and wheels ahead of him. His throat was parched and he gratefully took the canteen that was brought to him at dusk. There was some food too: stale bread and a hard chunk of cheese. He ate hungrily and relieved himself beside one of the chariot wheels before lying down to rest.

All around him, as far as he could see, sprawled the rebel camp. The air was filled with the sounds of men talking and laughing, the shrill cries of children, the banter of women, the lowing of cattle, bleating of sheep and grunts and occasional squeals of pigs. There were familiar smells of woodsmoke and ordure, and then the aromas of stews and the heavenly richness of roasting meat that set Macro's stomach grumbling. He rolled onto his back, resting his manacled hands on his chest as he stared up at the twilight sky, where the first star had appeared. Closing his eyes, he settled into as comfortable a position as he could manage.

Something struck him lightly in the side, and he opened his eyes as he heard a giggle. A small group of young children were standing a few paces away, looking at him with wide eyes. They wore ragged tunics and were barefoot, and most had an unkempt appearance. The oldest, who could have been no more than eight years old, held a stick in her hand that she jabbed at Macro as she bared her teeth.

'Ah, you've come to goad the ferocious Roman beast,' Macro chuckled. 'As fine a bunch of warriors as I have ever seen.'

They regarded him with blank expressions, so he repeated his comment in Iceni as best he could. The girl with the stick, who appeared to be their leader, puffed her chest out proudly.

'Looks like a fine sword you have there,' Macro said. 'May I see it?'

She hesitated, then took a step towards him and held out the stick. He took it gently and turned it over as he pretended to examine it closely.

'Very good . . . Fine craftsmanship.' He offered it back to her, and when she went to take it, he gave a sharp tug and she stumbled onto her knees beside him. He laughed and smiled at her. 'The first thing a warrior learns is never to give up her sword to anyone.' He released his grip and patted her head. 'There, take it back and guard it well. Make Boudica proud.'

The girl retreated with a scowl that gave way to a look of pride as she made a show of tucking the stick into the strip of cloth about her middle that served as a belt. Macro ran his eyes over the others. They were the same kind of kids that could be found amongst any band of camp followers tagging along with an army. One of them, a boy of five or so, was eating an apple, and he could not help staring at it. The boy reached into a pouch on the front of his tunic and brought out another one. Extending his arm, he warily approached Macro and tossed it into his lap.

'Why, thank you, lad!' Macro beamed. 'What's your name?'

The boy mumbled something. Macro cupped a manacled hand to his ear.

'Taconala.'

'Taconala, eh?' He picked up the apple and took a bite, savouring the sweet tang. He chewed and swallowed, and then bowed his head in gratitude. 'Centurion Macro salutes you, Taconala, warrior of the Iceni.'

The boy smiled as he took another bite of his own apple, and his round cheek bulged as he chewed.

'Why don't you all sit down so we can get to know each other better?' said Macro.

There was some hesitation, and the children looked to the oldest girl, ready to follow her lead. She regarded him suspiciously.

'You are the enemy. This might be a trick.'

It was true that Macro had an ulterior motive for befriending the children. There was a small chance he might learn something useful from them. He made himself smile as he held up his manacles. 'I am your prisoner. I give you my word, as a Roman officer, that I mean you no harm. Sit down and rest your legs.'

The girl paused long enough to let Macro know that she was not obeying an order from an adult but making up her own mind, and then sat down, beyond arm's length. The rest of the children followed, squatting or sitting cross-legged.

'That's better. Now we can talk, warrior to warrior. Are you all Icenians?'

The girl shook her head. 'Just me and my brothers.' She indicated two small boys sitting beside her and then pointed to the others. 'Trinovantes, Atrebates and Catuvellauni. They only joined us this morning. There are kids from other tribes in the camp too. Regni and Dumnonii.'

Macro kept his expression neutral as he nodded. The rebellion was spreading faster than he'd thought and drawing support from tribes across Britannia.

'What's Rome like?' asked the girl. 'What's it *really* like? Some grown-ups say it's a very big place, far away.'

'Very far away,' Macro replied. 'It would take many months to reach it.'

'Is it bigger than Camulodunum?' asked the boy with the apple.

'At least two hundred times the size.'

He saw the confused expressions on their faces and realised that the number was meaningless to them. He laughed. 'Much bigger, at any rate! With temples and markets and theatres and the greatest horse-racing track in the whole world. People come from across the Empire to see the marvels of Rome. You should travel there and see it for yourselves when you are older.'

The girl nodded. 'I would like that.'

'Me too!' one of the boys echoed. 'I want to see it.'

'Maybe you will one day. When there is peace again in Britannia.'

'You mean after Boudica has beaten the Romans,' said the girl.

'What's your name?' Macro asked.

'Cardella. Daughter of Erbagnus, charioteer of the Iceni,' she added proudly.

'Do you think Boudica can beat the Romans, Cardella?'

'Of course! My father says so. After all, we beat you at Camulodunum. And we beat that legion. That shows our warriors are better than yours.'

'Fair point,' Macro conceded, albeit a painful truth to accept. 'But there are many more Romans who will come to fight you. Far more than you can imagine. They will not give in and you will not be able to beat them all.'

'We beat you once and we'll do it again! And again!' she responded fiercely. 'Our warriors are better than any Roman soldiers. You'll see when you fight Boudica's champion tomorrow.'

Macro gave her his full attention. 'Tomorrow?'

'That's right. My father says that Bellomagus will defeat you easily. He has never lost a fight. He is the best warrior in Britannia. He will take your head as a trophy to hang outside his hut.'

One of the boys, a year or so younger, snorted. 'The champion of the Atrebates is better.'

She turned to him fiercely. 'No he's not! If you say so, I'll fight you for it!'

Much as the prospect of discord amongst his enemies, young as they were, was pleasing to Macro, he needed to find out more.

'I am sure that all the champions of every tribe are fine warriors. There's no need for friends to argue about it, eh?'

The two children glared at each other for a moment before the boy gave way and muttered, 'I suppose not.'

'That's better,' Macro said. 'Tell me about this Bellomagus. What is he like?'

'He's a giant. He's ten feet tall.'

'Ten feet? I see.' Macro glanced round and saw one of Boudica's bodyguards outside her tent. He pointed the man out. 'Taller than him?'

Cardella looked at the bodyguard. 'Maybe a little. And maybe older. He has a fine moustache and tattoos. He has been the champion for as long as I can remember.'

That was some small comfort to Macro. He had bested many such giants during his time in the army. That said, his best years were behind him and he was far from complacent as he considered his combat against Boudica's champion. No doubt her intention was to mount a public display of her man's superiority over a Roman soldier. Not just any Roman soldier, but a centurion, one of the elite who formed the backbone of the legions that her people must face in battle. It would be a big boost to their morale to see Macro comprehensively beaten by their man. And he would not be given a quick death. Bellomagus would be sure to kill him by inches and make him beg for a merciful end. Just the kind of spectacle her followers needed to maintain their resolve to see the rebellion through to victory.

While it was obvious that Boudica had chosen a man she believed would easily defeat Macro, he felt a surge of hope. The odds were against him, but there was a slim chance that he might defeat Bellomagus, as opposed to no chance if he faced the same fate as those executed by the Druids.

'This Bellomagus, have you ever seen him fight?'

'Yes, once.' Cardella nodded excitedly. 'He fought a duel with a Trinovantian champion at our capital. The place you call Venta Icenorum. But it was not to the death. Not like your fight will be . . . Oh.' She glanced away guiltily as she was struck by the insensitivity of the remark. Then she looked back at Macro. 'I wish you didn't have to die tomorrow.'

'I will do my best not to.'

'You are a nice Roman. I would be sad if you died. Are there other nice Romans?'

'Yes. Many. Just as there are many fine Britons, like you and your friends.'

'It's a shame we have to fight each other.'

'Yes. Let's hope that your queen and my emperor find a way to end their quarrel. Tell me, what weapons did Bellomagus like to fight with when you saw that duel?'

'He had a large axe, and a small one. He won the fight with the small axe. He threw it and hurt the other champion in the arm.' She mimed the blow by striking the edge of her hand below her right shoulder.

'Ouch,' said Macro.

They were interrupted by a harsh shout, and he turned to see one of Boudica's bodyguards striding towards them, waving his arms at the children. They scrambled to their feet and scurried away. Cardella, though, held back a moment.

'I will cheer for you tomorrow, Centurion.'

'No. I wouldn't do that, if I were you,' Macro cautioned. 'Besides, he is your champion. It is only right that you cheer for him. I won't mind. Now go! Before that man catches you and you get in trouble.'

She waved a farewell and sprinted after her friends. The bodyguard came trotting past Macro, and he thrust his feet out, tripping the man so that he fell headlong with a heavy grunt, the air driven from his lungs. Some of the children stopped to laugh, and then ran off between the wagons as the bodyguard regained his feet and shouted angrily after them. His wounded pride made him turn on Macro, and he delivered several kicks before backing off, breathing heavily. Snarling, he raised his thumb and drew it violently across his throat.

'We'll see about that,' Macro answered in the Iceni tongue.

The bodyguard snorted, then turned and shouted for one of his comrades to guard the Roman prisoner and make sure that the children did not return.

As night fell over the camp, and campfires flickered across the landscape in every direction, Macro could not sleep as he pondered the information he had gleaned from Cardella and her friends. Tomorrow he would face Boudica's champion, and he resolved to make sure it would be a contest that did not go the way the queen intended. Whether he won or, more likely, lost the fight, he was going to die like a soldier of Rome. On his feet. Defiant to his last breath.

CHAPTER NINE

The site picked for the duel between Macro and Bellomagus had been chosen to afford the greatest number of rebels a chance of following the contest. The crest of a small hillock had been cleared of undergrowth, and chairs and stools had been set up to one side for Boudica, her daughters, her nobles and the Druids. Her bodyguards, reinforced by over a hundred other warriors, formed a cordon below the crest, where they would be able to keep the crowd back but not obstruct the view of the fight that was to take place above.

It was mid morning before Macro's hands were untied and he was led away from the chariot and through the camp to the hill, some half-mile distant. As he walked between the four men sent to escort him, he stretched his muscles and rolled his neck in preparation for the duel. He had few illusions about the outcome. The principal reason for the success of the Roman army was how it trained its men to operate as units. Man for man the Roman soldier was as good as most, but Macro was going up against a Celtic warrior, from a caste dedicated to the ideal of individual combat and raised to fight in that style from an early age. If that was not challenge enough, he was going to face a champion of their people. At least he would have a fighting chance, he told himself firmly. The odds were stacked against him, but he would face his foe the same way he had faced enemies throughout his career, however hopeless the odds seemed: with a sword in his hand and iron determination in his heart. He would die in a way that honoured the courage of his profession and his people.

As they neared the hillock, he saw that it was surrounded by a tight ring of wagons and carts, peopled by those who had clambered up for a better view of the coming contest. A small gap had been left between the wagons nearest Macro and his escort, and they made for the opening. At their approach, a cry went up and faces turned towards them. Macro's gaze swept over their expressions of excitement, anger, contempt and hatred. Some jabbed their thumbs or pointed at him. Others brandished their fists, and some even waved what looked like a friendly greeting but was in reality a mocking farewell, he realised.

The group pushed through the gap between the wagons and thrust their way up the gentle slope – no easy task due to the densely packed crowd waiting for the entertainment to begin. Macro could not help wondering what might happen if there was a sudden panic or surge. There was nowhere for people to escape, and many would be crushed against the wagons. If only he had a century of men to charge that crowd, it would be a massacre. He smiled grimly at the thought. He might as well wish for the moon.

The small group pushed on, and Macro's senses were assaulted by the din surrounding him, the raw stench of sweat in the sweltering heat beneath the glare of the sun, and the seething press of humanity on all sides. Some attempted to strike at him through the gaps between his minders, and a few glancing blows landed, but it was nothing he could not shrug off. It occurred to him that being forced to fight his way up to the makeshift arena might be a deliberate ploy by Boudica and her advisers to unsettle him before the duel. If so, it was a futile tactic, given that he was well used to fighting for his life in close combat, and he made his way calmly through the excited mob until the small group reached the cordon formed by Boudica's warriors and emerged onto open ground.

Macro shrugged and pulled the hem and sleeves of his tunic down in an automatic gesture of parade ground neatness. He looked for his opponent, but there was no one to be seen apart from Boudica and her retinue to his left. Some of her nobles were scrutinising him, while the others, closer to their queen, were drinking wine from goblets and laughing as they vied for her attention. Boudica smiled thinly, affecting an aloof expression. A Druid leaned towards her ear and muttered, and her gaze swept across the open ground and fixed on Macro and his escort. There followed a brief exchange with the Druid, while the noblemen she had cut dead drained their cups and sat in awkward silence at her demonstration of their dispensability.

Boudica rose from her seat, adjusted the folds of her long blue and green checked robes and strolled up the rise to the crest of the hillock. She waited for the attention of the multitude who had gathered within the ring of wagons, and there was a roar as she was acclaimed by her followers. She indulged them before waving her hands to call for silence. The cheers died away and there was only the sound of children before they were sharply hushed by the adults around them.

'Today is the feast of Andraste!' Boudica began. 'The time when we Celts gather to honour the victories of our tribes and the deeds and valour of our greatest warriors. We celebrate the humbling of our enemies and proudly show off the trophies we have won in battle.'

She paused, and Macro saw a Druid emerge from behind her seated retinue holding the standard of the Ninth Legion, the gold of the eagle glittering in the sunshine. He slowly proceeded around the crest of the hill to ensure that everyone in the crowd had the chance to see the proof of the humiliation of Rome, and once again the air reverberated with the triumphant roar of the rebel horde. Once he had completed his circuit, he planted the spiked end of the standard in the ground behind Boudica's chair. Again she raised her hands to signal silence, and the crowd waited for her next words in eager anticipation.

'This glorious day we make a very special offering to Andraste to celebrate and honour her feast day. Today we offer her the life of one of the most formidable enemies we Celts have ever faced in battle. A Roman soldier. A man of their legions. One of their famed elite – a centurion of Rome!' She swept an arm towards Macro.

One of his escorts nudged him in the back, and Macro, who had followed the sense of most of her words, stepped forward, punching his fists into the air as he paced towards the crest as if he was a famous boxer being introduced to the crowd.

'For Rome!' he grinned as he bellowed. 'For the emperor!'

He saw a frown on Boudica's face as he approached. Before he could reach her, he was restrained by his escort and held ten paces back from the Iceni queen. The crowd booed and jeered. Macro looked round, wondering if Cardella and her young friends were somewhere amid the ocean of faces that surrounded him on all sides. They had been a nice bunch of kids and he hoped they might be spared the spectacle of his death. Then he put thoughts of them aside as Boudica quietened the crowd and spoke again.

'Against this hero of the legions, this champion of the pampered child who calls himself Emperor of Rome . . .' the sneer in her tone was impossible to miss, 'against this centurion we have chosen to pit a warrior of the Iceni. Our champion, victor of many duels, taker of scores of enemy heads in battle, famed from coast to coast, revered and feared by his enemies and beloved of his tribe. I present to you . . . Bellomagus!'

She turned to the side of the makeshift arena from where the eagle standard had emerged. Macro looked in that direction and heard the rising cheer of the crowd as their man made his way through them towards the crest of the hillock. As the cheers swelled, Bellomagus strode into view: a giant with broad shoulders and muscled chest. He was stripped to the waist, and his torso was covered in swirling tattoos of blue ink. Unusually for a Celtic warrior, his face was untouched, but there was no need to tattoo his features to make him look fierce. Nature and a hardy life had done that for him. A wild mane of curly red hair framed a thickly ridged brow, beneath which his deep-set eyes glared fiercely. Macro judged him to be of middle age, perhaps early forties, and still in the prime of his life. His nose was broad and uneven due to being broken many times, and above his bearded jaw his thick lips parted as he let out a roar of greeting to the crowd.

As the Iceni champion crossed the open ground, Macro was able to appraise his physique more closely, and felt his hopes sink.

'A monster and no mistake,' he muttered to himself. 'Jupiter, Best and Greatest, if you could just see your way to unleashing a bolt of lightning to fry this one to a crisp, I'd be passing grateful to you . . .' He glanced up, but the sky remained a serene azure, with only a handful of puffy white clouds floating peacefully across the heavens. Of Jupiter and the requested lightning bolt there was no sign. Macro shrugged. 'You can only ask.'

Bellomagus strode across the crest of the hillock, raising his fists and flexing his muscled shoulders for the delectation of the huge crowd.

Turning to one of his minders Macro spoke in stilted Icenian. 'Your lad's a bit of a show-off. Bet his dick is as small as his opinion of himself is huge, eh?'

'At least he'll have a dick when the fight's over.' The warrior smiled. 'He's going to cut you into little pieces before this is done. What's left of *your* dick will be stuffed in your mouth.'

Macro made a show of cradling his groin. 'No chance. Not nearly enough room.'

He saw Boudica make a gesture to her champion, who took up his position opposite Macro. The queen stood between them and addressed the heavens.

'O Andraste, revered goddess of victory. We offer you this battle of champions for your pleasure! May you savour the blood shed here this day and favour our cause as we seek to sweep the Roman scum from our shores!'

'Andraste!' the crowd echoed in response, shouting the name in chorus.

Boudica retreated to her chair and sat down. The Druid who had whispered in her ear nodded to the bodyguards standing behind the retinue, and two of them stooped and picked up some weapons and shields from the ground, holding them aloft as they paced towards the crest of the hill where Bellomagus and Macro stood. The men on either side of Macro grasped his arms, while a third drew his dagger and cut away at his tunic, tearing the soiled folds aside so that Macro was left only with his loincloth. He saw his opponent sizing him up with a scrutinising stare, and realised that the Iceni champion was no mere braggart, but a seasoned fighter who knew his craft well and fought with a wary regard for his opponent. He played his part as the breezily confident champion of his people, but a shrewd mind lurked behind his brutally intimidating features.

One of the warriors carrying the weapons approached Macro and held out a Roman short sword in one hand and a legionary shield and javelin in the other. He tossed the sword and shield at Macro's feet with a snort of derision, then paced past him to the edge of the open ground and thrust the base of the javelin into the ground, testing it with his fingers to ensure that it would remain standing before returning to his place behind Boudica. The other warrior was carrying a long Celtic sword with a wide blade inlaid with swirling designs, and a heavy spear with a broad leaf-shaped head, as well as a kite shield, smaller than that of his opponent. Unlike Macro's weapons, the champion's sword was laid reverently before him, while his spear was planted point first on the far side of the arena.

As the warrior went back to join his companions, an expectant hush settled over the vast audience. Macro's minders scooped up the shredded folds of his tunic and fell back to the cordon, leaving him alone and exposed before his enemies.

The Druid began to chant in a sing-song tone, extending his arms towards Macro and Bellomagus. Macro saw his opponent plant his feet apart and brace his legs in readiness to explode into action. Muscles tensed and heart beating hard, he cleared his mind of all thought other than killing his foe.

The Druid suddenly let out a sharp word of command and swept his arms down. The Celt snatched up his sword and shield and faced Macro in a crouch, shouting his battle cry. Macro had moved just as quickly and confronted him in silence. They stared at each other for a few heartbeats before Bellomagus stood tall and moved in a slow circle, urging the crowd to cheer for him.

'Bellomagus! Bellomagus! BELLOMAGUS!' The champion's name thundered across the open ground and Macro could feel the reverberation of the chant on his exposed skin. As he weighed up his opponent, he noted the arrogant look on the man's face. Clearly Bellomagus placed a high value on his reputation. But not everyone in the crowd was from his tribe, and Macro knew enough about the Britons to understand the depth of tribal rivalry, even if they were presently united in their hatred of Rome.

As Bellomagus completed his circle, Macro took two paces forward to be more easily seen by the spectators, raised his arms in imitation of the Icenian and bellowed as loudly as he could, 'Macro! Macro! MACRO!'

There was a roar of laughter from sections of the crowd, and then, as he'd hoped, some of them called out his name, keen to see the haughty Icenian humbled a little before he killed the Roman.

The anger was clear to see on Bellomagus's face, and before Macro could complete half a circle, the champion charged him, sword raised, shield held to the side and muscles defined as they stretched beneath his skin. Macro spun to confront him, holding up his own shield, raising his sword arm, the flat of the blade against the trim of the shield, while his feet were apart and at right angles to brace himself against the impact. At the last instant Bellomagus swerved and swung his blade down in a ferocious arc. Up went Macro's shield to block the blow and deflect it away to his left, briefly striking the kite shield, and he swung his short sword round in an effort to stab the Icenian as he rushed by. But Bellomagus was too fast, and Macro's blade cut through the air. Both men turned immediately to face each other as the crowd cried out with excitement.

Macro hefted his sword, keeping the point up and his body covered by the curved rectangular shield as his mind raced. *Fuck, he's quick for a man of his build and his age . . .* Then he noticed the crack, fringed with small splinters, on the inside of his shield, and was aware how the blow had jarred his arm. Neither the shield nor his arms would endure many more attacks like the first. He must try not to give the Icenian space to charge. He slapped the flat of his blade against the metal trim again and advanced on his opponent, who stood no more than ten feet in front of the edge of the ring of warriors forming the cordon.

There was a brief flicker of surprise on Bellomagus's face as he registered the temerity of his Roman enemy, and then he swung his kite shield to face him and raised his sword, ready to strike. Macro pressed forward before the Icenian could rush him again and unleashed a series of blows with his heavier shield, interspersed with several thrusts and cuts from his sword, driving his foe back a few paces. Bellomagus leaped aside and opened some space between them before facing his opponent again. Once more Macro marvelled that so large a man could move so nimbly.

The effort put into his attack had left Macro breathing deeply, the blood pounding in his ears. His opponent seemed hardly affected and his breath came easily, although any hint of arrogant mirth had disappeared from his expression. He regarded the Roman intently and gave a brief nod to acknowledge his respect. For his part, Macro realised that he had to conserve his energy. The legionary shield was far heavier than his opponent's, and while it offered greater protection, it was more unwieldy, designed more for formation fighting than individual combat. Unless he could get close enough to batter Bellomagus with it, he would be better off adopting a more defensive stance. Let the Icenian attack and expend his energy in the hope that he might tire himself enough to make a mistake.

Bellomagus must have been thinking along similar lines. He eased his arms apart to reveal his expansive tattooed chest and shouted a challenge to Macro, inviting him to strike. The Roman held his ground and made no response. Boudica's champion snorted with contempt and called out over his shoulder.

'The Roman dog fights like a puppy! Playful snaps that tire him out!'

There was laughter, and then his supporters in the crowd began to shout his name again. Macro paid them no attention, fixing his gaze on Bellomagus. The Icenian lowered his shield and sword and stood tall in a relaxed posture, then raised his arms and began another circle to encourage his people. As he came side-on to Macro, the Roman was tempted to rush in and strike, but realised that this was what his foe wanted. To test that assumption, he feinted with his shield, and at once Bellomagus jumped round ready to face him. His reactions were flawless, Macro conceded, more aware than ever how one-sided this contest was.

Warily backing off a few paces, he lowered his shield and repeated his earlier imitation of the Icenian, causing more laughter and a few ragged cries of his name. Bellomagus's expression darkened, and he tensed, lowering himself so that he was ready to charge once again, or deal with Macro should he attempt the same. But he had revealed his weakness; a pride that brooked no mockery.

Macro called out in broken Iceni, 'This cur fights like a coward! Runs from the fight! All mouth and no heart!'

With an outraged roar, Bellomagus surged forward, whipping his sword arm back to strike a mighty blow. Macro raised his shield just in time to block the slash aimed at his head, and the edge of the long sword shattered the trim at the top and split the laminated wood beneath, showering him with splinters. At once he twisted the shield one way, then the other, trying to tear the sword from his opponent's grip. At the same time the Icenian was desperately trying to keep hold of his weapon as he strove to wrench it free. Working it viciously up and down, he eventually succeeded in tearing the blade out, leaving a jagged gap six inches deep in the top of the shield.

The two men drew apart as the fevered cheering about them rose in pitch and the crowd surged forward, putting the warriors of the cordon under pressure. There was a shrill scream to Macro's left, and he glanced round and saw a thickset woman rushing towards him with a small knife clenched in her hand, her features contorted by rage and hatred. He leaped back and just managed to avoid the weapon, but in doing so stumbled and fell, landing heavily on his back and driving the air from his lungs. The woman turned to make another attempt to stab him, but before her blade could strike home, a powerful fist closed around her forearm and hauled her aside. Bellomagus shouted at her angrily before shaking the knife free from her fingers; it dropped close to Macro as Bellomagus thrust the woman back towards the crowd. One of the warriors grabbed her and shoved her into the packed ranks of spectators.

Macro was still on his back, looking up at the sky as he gasped for breath, expecting the Icenian's sword to fall at any moment and end his life. Instead, Bellomagus loomed over him, reaching down to grasp his hand and hauling him back to his feet. He said something in an apologetic tone that Macro could not hear above the din, and nodded in the direction of the woman. Then he picked up Macro's damaged shield and handed it back to him before retreating to recover his own shield and sword from where he had dropped them as he dealt with the interloper. Macro nodded his gratitude and leaned on the edge of his shield, catching his breath. The Icenian watched him, poised to continue the contest. After a moment, Macro ducked quickly to pick up his sword.

As soon as he was re-armed, Bellomagus came on again, the point of his sword inscribing an oval in the space between them as he prepared his next attack. It came in a flurry of blows. Macro parried some of them, and the others glanced off the iron bulge of the hand guard or crashed onto the curved shield with splintering thuds. Step by step he was forced back under the onslaught, his shield weakening as the top edge was progressively shattered and split apart. The Icenians roared encouragement to their champion as they anticipated the imminent defeat of the Roman officer. A fresh blow sent a large chunk of Macro's shield flying to the side, while another section threatened to fall off. It was not much use to him now, and he threw it at his opponent. Bellomagus deflected it with his own intact shield and paced forward brandishing his blade.

Turning to his side to minimise the target area of his body, Macro raised his sword and desperately parried the next few blows, the impetus of the heavier weapon jarring his arm with every strike. Then Bellomagus made a neat undercut inside his opponent's weapon and struck it hard on the flat. The move caught Macro by surprise, and before he was even aware of it, his sword handle was snatched from his grasp and the weapon fell to one side and he was disarmed.

'Sa!' the Icenian hissed triumphantly, and stepped over to stamp his foot on the blade before Macro could retrieve it.

Shaken by the savagery of his opponent's attack, Macro backed off hurriedly, then turned and sprinted towards the javelin to his left. Bellomagus surged at an angle towards the shaft rising from the ground, but Macro reached it first and snatched it from the soil, turning to thrust the point towards his pursuer. For an instant he was tempted to hurl the weapon, as it was designed to be used. But there would only be one chance, and if he missed, he was as good as dead, so instead he brandished it as if it was a spear.

Bellomagus drew up sharply, out of reach, and raised his kite shield. Holding the shaft firmly in both hands, Macro jabbed the javelin at his opponent, feinting towards his face and any exposed part of his body. His foe blocked him effortlessly each time, to the cheers of the crowd. Then he tossed the shield aside and slapped his chest, daring Macro to strike at him.

'All right, you bastard, if that's what you want . . .' Macro advanced, thrusting the head of the javelin at his opponent's torso. Keeping pace, Bellomagus stepped back, alternating parries with lithe movements to dodge the thrusts. The pair edged up to the centre of the cleared ground, at the very crest of the hillock, where they were in full view of the multitude watching the action in anticipation that the end was nearing. There, Bellomagus stopped abruptly and counter-attacked, swinging his sword at Macro's head. There was only one way to block the blow, and Macro shifted his grip and thrust the shaft of the javelin up as he rushed forward. The haft caught the Icenian above the wrist before he could develop much momentum, and as the blade fell to the side, Macro released his right hand, balled it into a fist and smashed it into the other man's jaw.

It was a solid punch that caused Bellomagus to stagger back and shake his head. Macro stepped away and stood, boots braced and javelin point lowered, ready to continue the fight. There was blood oozing from the corner of the Icenian's mouth. He wiped it away with the back of his left hand and glanced at the crimson smear. As he spat a gobbet of blood onto the grass at Macro's feet, there was no mistaking the cold glint in his eye.

'First blood to you, Centurion . . . Now it's time to put an end to the show.'

'Sure. Do your best. All you Celts are full of bluster and bullshit.' Macro hoped to provoke a mistake. Or at least provoke Bellomagus to kill him swiftly and save him the agony of a lingering death, one cut at a time.

'Enjoy your last words, Roman.'

Bellomagus came on again, swinging his sword in a powerful arc. Once more Macro raised his javelin to block the blow, but before he could try to rush his opponent again, Bellomagus stepped back nimbly and the blade landed on the slender iron shaft that ran from the grip to the point. The blow cut into the metal, bending it, and the end of the sword came perilously close to Macro's ear before he scrambled backwards. The next blow would surely destroy the shaft, and he was forced to shift his grip and use the javelin as if it was an unwieldy cross-staff. The next blow struck the wood halfway between the grip and the small iron point at the base, sending splinters flying into the air.

Macro sensed imminent defeat and death but even now shouted a war cry for Rome before another blow could land. This time it shattered the javelin, and he had to release the upper end to save his arm from being cut wide open by his opponent's blade. Throwing himself aside, he rolled over, still grasping the short fragment at the base of the weapon, barely eighteen inches in length. He was lying on his stomach adjusting his grip when Bellomagus reared over him, standing just to his right.

'Turn and face your death, Roman! Or take my sword in the back like a coward!'

Macro tensed his muscles and spun his body, thrusting himself up on his left hand and stabbing the small iron point at the bottom of the javelin up at the Icenian. The tip tore through his leggings and loincloth and then the soft flesh of his scrotum, and pierced his groin. Macro rammed home the splintered length of wood as hard as he could and twisted it violently for good measure before tearing it free.

Bellomagus let out a roar of surprise and agony and staggered back, his sword half raised as he looked down at himself in horror. Blood gushed from the wound and spattered the trampled grass at his feet. Macro, back on his feet, powered forward and hurled himself on the Icenian, grasping his right wrist as he stabbed the end of the ruined javelin in a frenzy. Over and over the iron tip plunged into Bellomagus's chest, shoulder and neck, and blood sprayed across the faces of both men. Around them the crowd had fallen deathly silent as they beheld the sudden reversal of fortune.

The Icenian was bellowing like a stricken bull Macro had once seen killed in an animal hunt put on for public entertainment back in the Rome of his youth. He had dropped his sword and was flailing with his fists as he tried to beat Macro off, to no avail. Then he stumbled and fell to his knees, his arms swinging drunkenly. Macro backed away, his makeshift weapon dripping blood as he held it ready to strike again. But he could see that Bellomagus was finished. He was bleeding out. All that remained was to give him a merciful end. He owed him that much, he decided, after the chance the Icenian had given him when the woman from the crowd had attacked.

Working his way around and behind his swaying opponent,

he reached over Bellomagus's broad shoulder and placed the iron point in the soft flesh behind the collarbone to the left of his jaw. The Icenian rolled his head back and looked up at him, then gave a nod and muttered, 'Sa . . .'

Bunching his arm muscles, Macro rammed the spike and the splintered end of the javelin down into Bellomagus's heart. The Icenian's arms lurched and he let out a deep groan as Macro released his grip and stepped away.

All around there was silence as the crowd stood still and looked on, stunned. Bellomagus's chin slumped onto his chest and his arms dropped to his sides, then he toppled forward face-down onto the ground and gave a final shudder before his body lay inert. It was a swifter death than that intended for Macro if the fight had gone the other way, but the Icenian had fought honourably, and that was something Macro respected.

He saluted the fallen champion coolly, not quite accepting that he had survived the ordeal. He could feel the trembling in his limbs and he drew a deep, calming breath before he raised his right fist into the air and shouted as loudly as he could, 'Victory! Victory for Rome!'

His words broke the spell, and the first angry shouts sounded from the crowd. Boudica had risen to her feet and was hurriedly conferring with the Druid before she snapped an order to her bodyguards. Two men came trotting towards Macro as he continued to shout his cry over the rising hostile din that surrounded him. They grabbed him by the arms, forcing them behind his back and half lifting him so that the strain caused instant agony as they made their way to Boudica.

Her eyes were wide and glaring and she was shaking with rage as he was set down on his feet before her. He made to speak, but she slapped him hard and shrieked, 'Silence, you Roman dog!'

Macro's cheek was burning as he turned his head to face her and lifted his chin arrogantly. 'So much for your champion . . .'

She struck him again, and then backhanded him, and he tasted blood on his tongue.

'Why couldn't you just die, Macro?' She spoke in a harsh undertone. 'You fool. You cursed fool. I was trying to spare you the worst. You had your chance to die well, like a soldier.'

He frowned. 'I thought the point was to humiliate me.'

'I knew you'd never let that happen. I was certain you'd want to die quickly and spare yourself that.' She paused. 'Now nothing can save you from the Druids. After this, they'll visit every torment on your body that can be imagined. And when they're done, what's left of you will be burned alive in a wicker man.'

She stared at him a moment longer, then turned to the men holding him. 'Take him away. Take him back to my chariot and tie him securely. No one is to be allowed near him. No one is to touch him, or I'll have your heads. Go!'

As he was marched away, the fury of the crowd was growing to a dangerous pitch, and a score of Boudica's warriors had to clear a path down the hill and form a screen between the rebels and the object of their rage. Macro stared ahead, shoulders back, spine stiffened, as he offered a silent prayer of thanks to Jupiter, Best and Greatest, for his divine mercy.

CHAPTER TEN

For the rest of the morning and most of the afternoon, Macro lay in the shade under the chariot. There was a marked change in the atmosphere of the rebel camp. A sullen quietness had settled over Boudica's followers. Ten of her bodyguards stood around the chariot keeping the rebels at bay and moving on those who loitered to hurl threats and insults. Some attempted to throw stones at the prone tethered figure but were quickly chased off by the guards. In any case, the distance to the chariot and the cover it afforded Macro meant that he was not struck once as he rested and reflected on his situation.

The defeat of Bellomagus had bought him no more than a day, and if he failed to escape, the rebels would ensure his death on the morrow. Already he had heard the distant sounds of sawing and hammering as the Druids oversaw the construction of the wicker man that was to be used for the sacrifice to Andraste.

Late in the afternoon, he emerged from beneath the chariot to take the bowl of thin stew that was brought to him. He sat on the rear of the chariot as he ate. He had a good view of the wicker man atop the hillock where the duel had taken place. Already the framework had been completed and stood like a skeleton against the sky. Several figures were at work threading branches around the frame, while others were piling faggots at the base of the structure. Once complete, it would stand some thirty feet high, and when it was lit, the blaze would be seen for many miles. His death would serve as revenge for the defeat of the Icenian champion, and at the same time, by virtue of his victory, he would make a fine sacrifice to their god, who was said to have a particular taste for the burned flesh of warrior heroes.

He gazed speculatively at the wicker man. It was clear that he was to be burned alive only after being subjected to the grossest tortures the Druids could conceive. Death would be a mercy, but the prospect of death by immolation sent a shiver down his spine. As a child, he had seen criminals burned at the stake in Rome, and recalled hearing that sometimes they were overwhelmed by smoke and perished quickly. Otherwise they died a lingering death amid the flames, screaming in agony until their lungs burned out. He had no intention of submitting to such a fate while he could still fight. But in order to do that, he needed to set himself free. His hands and ankles had been manacled this time, and he was bound to the chariot by a short length of rope, securely tied.

All was not lost, however, he thought as he finished the stew, then eased himself off the chariot and resumed his position beneath it. Besides sheltering from the sun and the occasional missile flung at him by passing rebels, there was a good reason for Macro to find somewhere he could lie still and undisturbed. He felt the hard lines of the knife across his buttocks where it lay concealed between his flesh and the folds of his loincloth. It had been the work of a moment to roll close to the blade and retrieve it from the grass where the woman had dropped it before slipping it down the small of his back, where it had been hidden since. Though he had kept as still as possible, the point had still nicked his buttock a few times, but the discomfort was easy enough for him to bear.

As the afternoon dragged on, he became aware of a heavy stillness in the air as a faint haze obscured the sky. It seemed that the run of fine weather was coming to an end. The sun drifted down towards the western horizon, and slanted light burnished the landscape and the vast rebel camp sprawled across it. He could make out a dark band of clouds to the north, and as he watched, there was a flicker of sheet lightning, a pause, then a muted roll of thunder. He smiled briefly. If he was lucky, the storm would pass directly over the rebel camp and distract attention from him. He smiled at the thought that it would also drench the wicker man and the faggots piled at its feet. Moreover, if it rained hard enough, the sodden ground would turn into a quagmire beneath the feet, hooves and wheels of the rebel host. They would make little progress, if any, until the ground dried out, which bought a little more time for those in Londinium. He hoped that Petronella and his mother had already left the town, but there would be many others who remained out of a sense of duty, reluctance to abandon their property, or illness or infirmity, as well as some who hoped to hang on long enough to loot the houses of those who had already fled before the rebels arrived. It would also buy time for Governor Suetonius to gather his forces to confront the rebels.

A moment later, the first drops of rain fell.

'May it piss down,' Macro muttered vehemently.

The light faded quickly, even though dusk was hours away, and the rain hissed down in a dull glimmer, occasionally illuminated by flashes of lightning. Thunder followed, crackling and crashing before breaking into booms that resonated against the flesh of those out in the open and sent them running for cover. The breeze steadily strengthened, and there were cries and shouts across the camp as the rebels struggled to find shelter. Those who had looted tents or made makeshift covers fought to keep them from being torn from their fastenings to trees or pegs and carried off into the darkness. There was confusion amongst the horses, draught animals and stock, and whinnying, braying and the barking of dogs competed with the shouts of people and the terrified crying of children.

There was scant comfort for Macro under the bed of the chariot as water dripped through the gaps between the planks above him. His tunic had not been returned, and his bare flesh was exposed to the cool wind and the angled rain borne upon it. As the sun set, he lay shivering. However, his spirits had risen. Such a storm as this worked to his advantage and that of Rome, and to the detriment of their enemy. As the storm continued to rage, several of the warriors tasked with guarding him retreated to the tents clustered about that of Boudica, and of the three men that remained, two were huddled against the trunk of an oak tree twenty paces away while the last stood guard over the chariot, no doubt having drawn the short straw.

Macro stretched his manacled hands towards the small of his back, grunting with the strain. The fingers of his right hand felt their way beneath the folds of his loincloth and under the tight line of the cord that held them up. Then the tip of his forefinger found the metal of the short blade, and he worked his hand around the knife until he had a good grasp before easing it out of the loincloth and bringing it round in front of him.

He rested before checking to make sure that his movements had not attracted any attention. The legs of the warrior standing beside the chariot had not moved. Reversing the knife, he set the haft against the end of the pin that fastened the iron hoop around his left wrist, then drew it back and struck hard. The sound was alarmingly loud to his ears, and he froze as he stared towards the guard. A moment later, there was another dazzling burst of lightning, and almost at once the concussive rumble of thunder as the storm raged directly overhead. Macro struck again and again, and then stopped as the thunder died away. Groping with his fingers, he could feel that the head of the pin was now flush with the locking bar.

Now came the trickier part. Positioning the point of the knife against the pin, he began to press it home as steadily as he could, mindful of the injury he might do himself if the blade slipped and the point stabbed into his left arm. At first the pin held firm, then he felt it give fractionally and applied more pressure until it gave a tiny lurch and the point of the blade jarred up against the slot. Moving the knife round to where the other end of the pin protruded, he worked it free, and a moment later the manacles came apart with a faint clank.

He glanced anxiously in the direction of the warrior, but once again there was no reaction. With his free hand he made quick work of removing the other manacle, then cut his feet free. The knife was too small and its edge too dull to be any use in dealing with the guard, so he set it aside and picked up the length of rope he had cut from his leg bindings.

Looking out from beneath the chariot, he could make out the forms of the men huddled beneath the oak tree, cloaks pulled up over their slumped heads as they tried to sleep. He eased himself to the front and crouched beside the yoke, rising high enough to look down the length of the bed of the vehicle. The guard was leaning against the right-hand post fixed to the back of the chariot. He had pulled the hood of his cloak up over his helmet, and his spear rested against his shoulder as he served out his watch and waited to be relieved. Macro had thought to use the space between the side screens to cover his approach, but now realised that the instant he grappled with the guard and pulled him back onto the chariot, the rear would tip down and the yoke would rise sharply into the air, betraying what was happening to anyone looking vaguely in that direction. Instead, he moved round to the side furthest from the oak tree and worked his way towards the rear, where he paused and made ready.

With the ends of the cord wrapped around his fists, he took one last glance at his surroundings to make sure no one was watching. Then he rose swiftly and looped the rope over the guard's head, ramming a knee into the small of his back and pulling him down with him beside the chariot.

He landed heavily on the sodden ground and grunted as the full weight of the guard crashed on top of him. The man had released his spear, and his hands were groping for the tight band biting into his throat and crushing his windpipe. Macro's biceps bulged as he used all his strength to tighten his grip. The guard's legs flailed desperately, and a strained keening escaped his gritted teeth as he tried to cry out for help. As his thrashing increased in intensity, he reached out and found Macro's hair. His fingers clenched tightly as he tried to yank his assailant's head to the side, and Macro abruptly turned and opened his mouth, finding the guard's thumb and biting down on it.

The man's struggles began to fade and become more feeble, then he slumped heavily against Macro and fell still. Macro continued to pull the cord for a while longer until he was sure that the guard was dead. He eased the body over onto its side and took a deep breath before letting go of the rope and sitting up. The storm was already moving off to the south, but the rain and wind remained, and would keep the rebels' heads down for a while yet.

He unfastened the man's cloak, tunic and sword belt, then removed his leggings before dressing himself. When he was done, he hoisted the body onto the back of the chariot, hurriedly tying the guard's right arm to the post with the length of rope used to throttle him. Angling the helmeted head so that it looked as if the man was dozing, he picked up the spear and rested it against the guard's shoulder, then crouched down to examine his handiwork. In the darkness of the night, the body would pass for a man on guard unless someone came right up to the chariot.

Keeping low, Macro moved in the opposite direction to the oak tree, towards a horse line stretching in front of a mass of

144

rippling shelters and wagons. On his side of the line were tethered cattle and mules, and beyond them more wagons and tents. He made his way along the horses, whose dark forms remained stoically still in the downpour. When he had put a hundred paces between himself and the chariot, he paused and breathed deeply to calm his swiftly beating heart and ease the tension in his aching muscles. Retirement from the army had not done him any favours in terms of his fitness, he chided himself, and he resolved to exercise more frequently if he escaped, before dotage put an end to that.

Raising the hood of the cloak over his head and pulling the folds about his shoulders, he rested one hand on the handle of the sword and continued along the horse line until he found several mounts clustered together. Untethering the bridle of the largest of them, he stroked its cheek and whispered soothingly as he led it away from the others, keeping the horses between him and the camp until he passed over a low rise and saw more tents and wagons blocking his way.

'Shit . . .'

There was no way of avoiding passing through the heart of the rebel camp now, and he stiffened his back and stood as tall as he could manage before setting off, heading in a roughly westerly direction. The wind had moderated to a stiff breeze as the rain continued to fall, and he felt the ground squelch beneath his boots as he led the horse past wagons and makeshift tents consisting of leather hides stretched over crude poles and any convenient limbs of the trees that darkly dotted the night landscape. Many of the rebels were out in the open, sheltering as best they could under their cloaks and animal skins, and few bothered to pay any attention to him. A man standing by the trunk of a tree called out to him in a dialect he could not understand, and then laughed. Macro snorted loudly in disgust and made a show of shrugging as he continued on his way.

All the while, he was waiting for the alarm to be raised. It would not take long for word to spread through the camp and for the rebels to be roused up to look for the Roman in their midst. His identity would be obvious the moment he was challenged or his hood drawn back, and he would have no chance of fighting his way free. For the moment, though, his luck held, and he continued on, making for a forest that covered a hill half a mile ahead, as far as he could judge the distance in the darkness. He noticed that the breeze had almost died away and the rain was starting to ease and subside to a light drizzle. Surely the guards sheltering under the oak tree would soon emerge, and one of them would go and relieve himself, or speak to the man who had been left to guard the chariot alone during the worst of the storm.

He picked up the pace, and soon he was approaching the edge of the woodland. There were a number of dark shapes huddled at the foot of the nearest trees, but none bothered to address him as he led the horse into the depths of the forest. After a short distance, he came across a track heading in the direction of Londinium, and he followed it, guided by the faint loom of the night sky between the treetops on either side. After a quarter of a mile or so, he emerged into the open and saw that the track continued up a slope. At the top, a horse and rider worked their way along a low ridge.

He stopped dead at the edge of the forest, trusting that the picket would not be able to see him against the dark mass of the trees. The rider continued to make his way along with frustrating slowness, but Macro dared not make his move until he was sure that there was no chance of him being spotted and chased down on the cusp of making his escape.

Then he heard the distant braying of a war horn from far behind him. The signal was picked up by other horns, closer, and the urgency in the notes splitting the night was unmistakable. The body of the guard must have been discovered. On the ridge, the picket reined in, and Macro swore under his breath. He hesitated for an instant, waiting to see if the man rode back to the camp or remained at his post. Infuriatingly, he stayed where he was, even as the muted sounds of shouting carried over the forest. Now there was the chance of being discovered by men coming from the camp, Macro realised. It would be dangerous to wait any longer.

He took the reins and clambered onto the horse, settling as best he could bareback, then urged the animal into a trot up the path towards the ridge. A moment later, the picket spotted him and turned his mount to intercept him. There was a sudden flash of sheet lightning as a fresh storm edged down from the north, and the rain began to seethe a little more as Macro rode steadily towards the crest. He shifted the reins to his left hand and drew the guard's sword from its sheath, holding it point down beneath the cloak so that only the tip protruded behind his leg.

As the two riders drew close to each other, just below the ridge, the picket called out to Macro and pointed in the direction of the camp. An instant later, thunder crackled, drowning out any reply Macro might have made. He shook his hooded head and continued forward. As the thunder died away, the warrior called out again and trotted closer. There was another burst of lightning, and for a heartbeat both men were illuminated in its harsh glare. Then the rebel reached for his sword and Macro swung his out, free of the cloak, as he tugged the reins to steer his horse alongside the other man. He slashed horizontally, aiming at the rebel's throat, and the latter threw his arm up to protect himself and took the blow on his elbow. The impact sounded with the sharp crunch of shattering bone, and the man let out a cry as Macro rode past.

He swerved the horse to turn and strike again, but the rebel had gathered his wits and had already urged his horse into a gallop down the slope, his right arm hanging uselessly at his side.

147

Macro was tempted to chase him down and finish the job, but the foolishness of riding back towards danger stayed his hand.

As he looked towards the rebel camp, there was another burst of light directly over the hillock where the nearly completed figure of the wicker man loomed like a sinister giant striding across the storm-battered landscape, tiny figures dashing around the bottom of his legs. Macro took grim satisfaction at having escaped the fate intended for him, and then spared a thought for those who had been tasked with guarding him. If Boudica held to her threat, one or more of them would be sacrificed in his place. That was too bad for them, he mused without much sympathy. If they had been Roman soldiers caught sleeping on guard duty, they'd have faced death, and rightly so.

He trotted his horse onto the track and turned it in the direction of Londinium before increasing the pace to a canter. Then he sheathed his sword and settled himself as comfortably as he could as he made his escape into the night.

CHAPTER ELEVEN

As the mounted column neared Londinium, the road was choked with wagons and carts and people on foot, women carrying infants and dragging children behind them. The wagons were overloaded and the draught animals strained in their harnesses to keep the wheels rolling. Cato, riding at the head of the column, considered ordering the civilians aside to make way for the Romans, then realised it would be quicker to ride alongside the road even if that slowed their pace. A glance over his shoulder revealed that Governor Suetonius and his retinue had followed the Eighth Cohort without attempting to clear the road. That was a small relief for Cato. In fairness, he reflected, Suetonius had displayed less arrogance with every day that had passed since the column had left Deva.

There had been some hard riding and long days, and the men and horses of the column were exhausted and covered with mud and grime. The storm that had raged on and off for a night and most of the next day had added to their discomfort by drenching their kit and clothing and turning the unmetalled stretches of the road into a quagmire that sucked at the boots of the men obliged to dismount and the horses they led, slowing the advance to a crawling pace. The rations they had been issued at Deva and supplemented along the way had been exhausted a day earlier, and the riders and their mounts were hungry as well as worn out.

For the first two days, only a handful of men had had to drop out of the column when their horses had gone lame, but the numbers had grown as the march went on, and of the thousand or so men who had set off ahead of the main body of the army trudging back from Mona, less than half remained. Although the Eighth cohort had suffered the fewest stragglers, that included Trebonius and Cato missed his servant's foraging skills as he made do with the standard rations for the rest of the march.

Suetonius and his staff had been obliged to sleep in the open with the rest of the men, since the governor's tents and the comforts afforded by his personal baggage had been left behind, and now they ate the same rations and used the same hard ground for a bed as the common soldiers around them. Lacking the slaves they were used to meant they had no one to shave them or clean their kit either, and now they were as bearded and filthy as those they commanded. The only thing that distinguished their rank was the limp crests of their helmets. Yet the governor had not complained once, in Cato's hearing. Indeed, he had even paused to offer a few words of encouragement to a straggler who had fallen out of the column.

In the last few days, Cato had developed a little more respect for his superior, as well as a little more sympathy. Dealing with the rebellion was going to be the supreme test of the governor's career. Few men in his position were responsible for the fate of an entire province. His decision to invade Mona in the hope of achieving lasting fame had played into the hands of the rebels. Only a complete victory offered him the chance of saving his reputation. If, gods forbid, he was defeated, then honour would demand that he at least die like a hero in battle. Failing that, he would have to take his own life to atone for his failure and salvage what little honour he could from the catastrophe, as Varus had done when he had led three legions to their doom in the depths of the German forests.

A milestone a short distance ahead caught Cato's eye, and when he saw that Londinium was only five miles distant, he felt a surge of relief that the hardships of the past days were over, together with an aching anxiety over what he would discover there. He had been trying not to think about what fate might have befallen Claudia, Lucius and Petronella, or to dwell on the fall of Camulodunum and the annihilation of the Ninth Legion, though he had allowed himself the flickering hope that somehow his friend Macro had escaped the fiery end of the veterans' colony.

Some half an hour later, the day drew to a close and the long shadows of dusk stretched across the gentle landscape, bathing it in a lurid blood-red glow. The road climbed the final low ridge, and the largest town in Britannia was sprawled out ahead along the bank of the great Tamesis river, which glimmered as it flowed placidly in wide loops towards the distant sea. Cato was surprised to see that the wharfs and piers were still crowded with ships. He had anticipated that most would already have sailed off to safety, decks packed with those fleeing the town along with their portable wealth. There were many people and vehicles on the road ahead of him, and also spread out along the road leading to the west. The narrow bridge that crossed the river and marked the furthest navigable point for seagoing vessels was packed with people crossing to the south bank and taking the road from there to the coast.

With so many leaving the town, Cato wondered how much of the population remained and how safe the streets would be as order began to collapse. It was possible that the arrival of the governor and the mounted column would boost the morale of the inhabitants and provide the authority and muscle needed to maintain control. At least until the rebel horde reached Londinium.

From his vantage point he had a good overview of the

town, and it was clear that it could not be defended. Only the administrative quarter was protected by a wall, but sections of that had crumbled away, and the spoil and other rubbish had filled up stretches of the ditch so that an enemy could easily walk across. The defences had belonged to the fort built to protect the original military bridge that had crossed the Tamesis. That had been dismantled when the outpost became a thriving port. At the same time, a new wall and ditch had been constructed to encompass the wharf, warehouses, shops, bathhouses and homes of the rapidly growing town. Within a few years, Londinium had overflowed these additional defences and they had fallen into neglect. Now the town was open to attack from any direction north of the Tamesis. The failure to maintain the defences was due to the arrogant assumption by successive governors that the lowlands of the new province had been pacified and there would be no need to protect the largest settlement in Britannia. Now their folly was laid bare.

Cato waved Tubero on and drew aside to wait for Suetonius to catch up. The governor scrutinised the town and squinted to the east, where there was no sign of the enemy or even any parties of scouts.

'It's hard to believe we beat them to it.' He scratched the bristles on his chin. 'The rebels had to cover only a fraction of the distance we had to. I feared they would be here long before we arrived.'

'Yes, sir. That was my fear too.'

'So what has delayed them? It makes little sense. Where in Hades are they? Surely they can't have remained around Camulodunum. The initiative is with them. Why are they squandering the opportunity before them?' Suetonius's eyes narrowed. 'What is that Iceni witch up to?'

There was no obvious answer to his superior's question, and Cato shrugged. 'We're not facing a conventional army, sir.

Boudica may be more of a figurehead than the leader of the rebels. Who can say how much authority she commands over those who follow her? And if her followers are more concerned with looting what's in front of them rather than thinking about the strategic situation, then it's likely they'll only move on once they have run out of food. That said, Londinium offers rich pickings, and I dare say the prospect will draw them here sooner rather than later.'

'There's another possibility,' one of the tribunes volunteered. A tall young man with high, delicate cheekbones and sensitive eyes, he looked as if he was about to continue, but then lost confidence.

Suetonius turned wearily towards him. 'Do please share your thoughts with us, Tribune Agricola.'

'Yes, sir.' The tribune hesitated. 'It's possible that the enemy lack the nerve to continue their advance, sir. They might doubt that they have the strength to attack a major settlement. Also, they must know that you'll be concentrating your forces to crush the rebellion.'

'I doubt it is a question of a lack of nerve, young man. They dealt with the veteran colony at Camulodunum and the Ninth Legion well enough. If anything, they'll be enjoying an excess of nerve.'

'With respect, sir, the colony was defended by old men, and the Ninth Legion was mostly comprised of those deemed unfit for the Mona campaign. I dare say the rebels will be aware of that, and they'll be far more anxious about facing a much tougher proposition once they come up against the cream of our forces here in Britannia.'

Cato was irked by the casual dismissal of the veterans commanded by Macro, and felt compelled to defend his friend's honour as he addressed the governor. 'With due respect to Tribune Agricola's point of view, sir, I doubt the rebels had an

153

easy victory over Centurion Macro and his veterans. There's a reason why veterans get to be veterans. That's something the tribune may learn one day, if he lives that long.'

Suetonius stifled a look of amusement as he turned away from the tribune. 'Let's all hope he lives that long, eh?' His expression became serious again. 'Whatever the reason for the enemy holding back, we should be grateful. For now, we need to steady the nerves of our people in Londinium and see what can be done to prepare for the attack. Let's go.'

The column had to wait at the northern gate leading into the town while a harassed section of men from the garrison cleared the refugees from their path. Once they were able to enter, they passed down one of the main thoroughfares of the town. Many of the civilians in the process of leaving, and those who were undecided or had chosen to remain, regarded them with surprise and relief.

A cry went up. 'The governor's returned! The army's here! Now we'll show those bloody rebels!'

Others were less convinced, and called out as Suetonius rode by, 'Is it true about the Ninth Legion? Is it true? We deserve to be told!'

Suetonius made no reply as he sat tall in his saddle and tried to look as dignified as possible despite his weary and filthy condition.

As they reached the crossroads and prepared to ride left towards the governor's headquarters, Cato hesitated and looked in the opposite direction, towards the Deer and Dog inn. That was where he hoped to find his son and his friends, and he felt his heart lift at the prospect before he turned away. He would have to see to the quartering and provisioning of his men, and attend the governor while the latter assessed the situation, before he was permitted to deal with private matters. He considered sending a man to the inn with the message that he had arrived, but decided he would prefer to do that in person.

The mood of the town was overlaid with a fearful tension that he observed in almost every face as he rode past. Halfway along the street leading to the headquarters compound they came across a shop that had been looted. The doors were splintered and smashed and broken pots and glassware were strewn across the threshold and the interior. An elderly man in an embroidered tunic was sweeping up, and he paused as he saw the governor and his officers riding by.

'Where's the army when we bloody need it?' He stepped into the street to call after Suetonius. 'I'm a Roman citizen! I pay my taxes! Why isn't Rome protecting us?'

'Want me to silence the old fool, sir?' asked Agricola.

'What good would that do?'

'The town needs order, sir. Discipline and respect for authority. Once we let the plebs abuse us in the street, that starts to go.'

'Once we start beating up the plebs who have a right to demand our protection, that's when respect for authority goes, Tribune.'

'I suppose so . . .'

Suetonius shot his subordinate a glare, and Agricola nodded.

'I mean yes, sir!'

The governor exchanged a quick look with Cato and rolled his eyes.

Cato chuckled. 'It seems the boy can be taught after all, sir. He may go a long way yet.'

'The longer the better,' Suetonius growled.

They encountered two more shops along the street. Both had been broken into and stripped of what was left of their stock. No one was in either establishment, and Cato reasoned that their owners had abandoned them.

The fortified gateway at the entrance to the compound was

guarded by a full section from the garrison, eight men under an optio. As the officer recognised the rider at the head of the column, he quickly called his men to attention and saluted. Suetonius nodded wearily as he rode past into the huge courtyard beyond, followed by the rest of the column. He paused to order his small group of staff officers to find themselves quarters in the barracks, and then dismissed them. There were several carts to one side of the main block, and men from the garrison were busy loading them with chests and items of furniture. The governor reined in at the steps leading up to the entrance of the main building and dismounted, rubbing his backside in relief. There was a clamour inside, and he sighed to himself before he turned to Cato.

'Prefect, have your centurion see to the men and join me inside.'

'Yes, sir.'

Cato dismounted, handing his reins to one of the orderlies who had hurried over from the barracks to the side of the courtyard as soon as they saw the governor. He stretched his back as he made his way to Tubero and passed on the order.

'And make sure the lads stay in the courtyard. I don't want them swanning off into the town looking for tarts and drink once they're off duty. They need to be ready to get back in the saddle first thing tomorrow. I don't want to be sending parties out to hunt them down and bring them back in.'

Tubero arched an eyebrow. 'Tomorrow?'

'Who knows? Whatever happens, I want the Eighth ready for it.'

'Yes, sir.'

They exchanged a salute before Cato turned towards the headquarters entrance and walked stiffly up the steps. Inside, the noise swelled to a deafening volume as a crowd of civilians remonstrated with a line of clerks and several men from the garrison who were holding them back from the offices of the procurator at the far end of the building. Already a number had spotted Suetonius and turned to approach him. Cato paused on the threshold and called back to Tubero.

'Centurion! I want ten men up here on the double!'

He hurried over to the governor, who was already being harangued by a round-faced man with porcine features who was jabbing his finger as he declaimed, 'We demand that you protect us! Protect our businesses! Or we'll take our complaints to the emperor himself.'

Other men nodded in agreement as the round-faced man drew himself up, cheeks quivering with indignation.

'And who exactly are you?' Suetonius asked with icy calm.

'Me? I am Maecius Grahmius, sir. Owner of the fastest-growing concrete importing business in Londinium. I am the leader of the Merchants' Guild. When I talk, people listen! And I say we demand protection!'

More of the crowd had gathered around and now called out their support. Cato could see the anger and anxiety on their faces, and glanced over his shoulder as he heard Tubero and his men enter the hall and march towards the confrontation. Suetonius swept his gaze over the merchants before pinning his eyes on their spokesman.

'You certainly talk a lot, Grahmius. I wonder if you fight as well? You and your friends here. Because that's what it may come down to in the days to come. Are you attached enough to your businesses to defend them? Or will you leave it to others to do the job for you?'

'That's what we pay our taxes for, sir. Taxes that are a damn sight higher in Britannia than they are in other provinces where I have traded in the past. We have fulfilled our side of the arrangement. It is now up to Rome's governor and his soldiers to fulfil their obligations to us.'

There was an enthusiastic burst of support for Grahmius, and Cato could see that as many as a hundred men were pressing forward around the governor. He took his place at Suetonius's shoulder and indicated to Tubero to form his men up on either side. The arrival of the soldiers was met warily by the crowd, and their shouting began to die down. When it was quiet enough for him to be heard, Suetonius continued.

'Enough of your blather! I am the governor of Britannia and my power derives from the emperor and the Senate of Rome. I will not be spoken to as if I was a petty bureaucrat. How dare you think you can make demands of me?'

Grahmius's indignation was momentarily checked by the hard edge to the governor's words, and he responded in a more moderate tone.

'Sir, I respect your authority. In your absence, the procurator acts in your place, but he has refused to act on our demands. Why, he has refused to even meet us these last few days. No one has seen him. He has disappeared when he is needed most, and we want answers. We need to know what steps he has taken to protect us, our businesses and our families.'

'Disappeared?' Suetonius frowned.

'Oh, he's here all right.' Grahmius pointed down the hall beyond the clerks and the men from the garrison. 'He's been seen at the windows of his offices, but he refuses to come out to deal with our demands . . . I mean requests. Something must be done, sir. Action is needed. Authority is breaking down in the streets. There is widespread theft, looting and violence. Only yesterday, one of the wine importers' warehouses was broken into, and within hours there was a drunken mob moving down the main street while the men of the garrison did nothing. The house of my friend Kephosullinus here,' he indicated one of the better-dressed men at his side, 'was broken into, and his wife and family were terrorised. The mob stole everything and then burned the place to the ground. It was a miracle that Kephosullinus and his family escaped alive. What do you have to say to that?'

'I say I will not tolerate lawlessness. I will bring order back to the streets. Order and respect for authority.'

'What authority?' Kephosullinus interrupted.

Suetonius indicated Cato and the soldiers either side of him. 'That authority. And I will not tolerate being told what my duties are by some gang of money-grubbing merchants moaning about their businesses when the future of the entire province is at stake. Now get out of my sight and go and tell the people of Londinium that the governor is back in charge and that I will deal with those who threaten disorder with utmost severity. Do you understand?'

Grahmius nodded.

'Then go, before I order my soldiers to start here and now and make an example of you all.'

There was no need for Grahmius to take the lead as the crowd melted away and scurried for the entrance. The merchant offered an obsequious bow and made off after them. Suetonius gave an irritated hiss. 'That's them dealt with. Now to find out what in Hades that damned fool Decianus is playing at. Centurion Tubero.'

'Sir.'

'You and your men are to clear the compound of civilians. See to it.'

As the auxiliaries made off, the governor gestured to Cato to follow him and strode towards the orderlies and armed men still forming a loose cordon across the hall.

'Who is in charge here?'

A young man stepped forward and saluted. 'Optio Labinus, sir.'

'Where is your commanding officer?'

'Centurion Vespillus is in with the procurator, sir.' He indicated the corridor leading to the suite of offices assigned to Decianus and his staff.

The other men hurried aside to let Suetonius and Cato by, and they entered the corridor. There were clerks in some of the offices busy packing scrolls and other records into boxes and baskets, while other offices already lay empty and silent. At the end of the corridor was a door with benches on either side: the office and quarters of the procurator. Suetonius lifted the latch and entered brusquely.

Inside was a generously proportioned room with a large desk, behind which sat a thin, bald man reading a waxed tablet. The desk was piled with more tablets and scrolls. He looked up at the intrusion with a surprised expression, then stood up smartly and saluted as he recognised the governor.

'Sir, I was not informed—' he began in an apologetic tone.

'Where's Decianus?'

'The procurator?'

'Who else do you think I'm asking about, you fool? Where is he? He sent a dispatch to say he was taking ship to Gaul, yet I hear he is still in Londinium.'

'Yes, sir, the procurator is in his private quarters.' Vespillus indicated the door in the corner behind him. 'Been there for the last ten days, sir.'

There was a beat before the governor continued. 'What, in the middle of a fucking crisis? Is he ill?'

'No, sir. I was obliged to, er, confine him,' Vespillus said nervously, and it was obvious that he was consumed with anxiety. Cato, however, was delighted that Decianus had been prevented from fleeing. After all, the procurator had been mainly responsible for the outbreak of the rebellion. Now he would have to face the consequences of his actions along with the rest of them.

'What on earth for?' asked Suetonius.

'Begging your pardon, sir, but the procurator attempted to leave the province. He had requested that his personal possessions be loaded onto a ship he had chartered to take him to Gaul, and had written orders for me to take command in his absence, until you returned or a more senior officer arrived on the scene.'

'He left you in charge?' Suetonius asked with incredulity.

'Yes, sir. I told him that he shouldn't go, sir. I told him that he was needed here and that it was his duty to keep order until you came back. When he said he still intended to leave, I pointed out that a procurator was not allowed to leave his posting without permission from the emperor.'

'Quite so. And then?'

'Then he dismissed me, sir. So I gathered some men and confined him to his quarters.'

'Very good.' Suetonius eased up on his stern tone. 'You did the right thing, Centurion Vespillus.'

Cato saw Vespillus's shoulders slump in relief, and wondered if the man's true motivation had been to avoid being held accountable. As long as Decianus remained in Londinium, willingly or unwillingly, the blame for what happened to the town would fall on him.

'We saw evidence of looting on the streets,' continued the governor, 'and I understand from the cabal of merchants I've just had removed from headquarters that it's been widespread.'

'That's right, sir.'

'Then what steps have you taken to restore order, Centurion?'

Vespillus was taken aback. 'We've only just been able to keep control of the compound, sir. The garrison has barely fifty men left.'

'Fifty? Where are the rest? There was almost a full cohort here when I left. Over four hundred men. What's happened to the others?'

'The procurator sent two hundred men to reinforce the veterans' colony at Camulodunum, sir. That was the last we heard of them. I imagine they died with the other defenders or were ambushed on the way. As for the rest of the missing men, well, they all had family here, sir. They left Londinium over the last few days.'

'Deserters.' Suetonius frowned. 'I want a list of their names so they can be charged when the rebellion has been dealt with. Hand it over to Tribune Agricola as soon as you have drawn it up.'

'Yes, sir.'

Cato glanced at the governor, impressed by the confidence he expressed about defeating Boudica and her followers. Perhaps it was real, or perhaps the governor was playing up the importance of discipline and procedure to instil a greater sense of order and raise morale.

'Now go and bring Decianus to me.'

'Yes, sir.' Vespillus saluted and disappeared through the door in the corner.

Suetonius sighed impatiently. 'It's bad enough having to deal with a bloodthirsty bunch of barbarians intent on taking our heads for trophies without having to sort this mess out too. We'll need to restore order on the streets. Stop the looting.'

'Yes, sir.' Cato nodded. 'That's true. But if we can't hold the town, then it's not going to make much difference in the end. We'll need to think about evacuating.'

Suetonius rounded on him sharply. 'I don't want to hear that kind of talk, Prefect. Not yet, at least. There's enough panic out there as it is.'

Cato felt his temper rise, and in his weariness he could not restrain his protest. 'I'm not panicking, sir.'

The governor stared at him. 'No. Of course not. You are a man of nerve, Cato. I know that. And you are right about having a plan to evacuate the town, if we have to, but we need to handle the situation with caution. At the moment, there are many people in Londinium who are counting on us to protect them. They still believe I can do that. If that belief crumbles, there'll be wholesale panic as all those left try to get out at once. One step at a time, eh? We reclaim control of the streets, assess what can be done about the defences and wait for the arrival of the Second Legion. An extra five thousand legionaries might make all the difference.'

'I hope so, sir.'

They were interrupted by the sound of footsteps and the angry voice of Decianus. 'I'll have you flogged for this outrage! I swear it, on the honour of my family . . .'

The procurator came into the office, addressing the hapless Vespillus over his shoulder. He smiled as he saw Suetonius. 'Governor! I'm so relieved you are here. I have to report that this man, Centurion Vespillus, has committed an outrage. Nothing less than mutiny. I demand that he be put in chains and tried under your authority. Thank Jupiter that you have returned to right this dreadful wrong.'

'Be quiet. I've already had enough of people making demands today.' Suetonius turned to Vespillus. 'You may go. Make sure we're not disturbed.'

'Yes, sir,' the centurion said eagerly, stepping out of the entrance to the office that gave onto the corridor and closing the door. Decianus's sharp eyes followed him before shifting to the governor.

'That scoundrel needs dealing with. He had me kept in my living quarters under armed guard for ten days.'

'You're lucky he didn't have you locked up in the cells.' Cato jerked his thumb towards the floor to indicate the dank chambers below the headquarters building. He felt his guts tighten in disgust as he looked at the scrawny figure of the procurator, his cheeks covered in stubble. It was not the man's appearance that affected him, but the knowledge that he had tried to save his own skin and abandon his position without any regard for the people he was supposed to serve and protect in the governor's absence. Furthermore, this was the man who had treated the Icenians harshly in the past and might well have played a pivotal role in provoking the rebellion, thereby sealing the fate of Macro and his comrades at Camulodunum.

'I beg your pardon?' Decianus affected a look of indignation.

Before Cato could reply, the governor intervened. 'I'll deal with this, Prefect Cato . . . Firstly, Centurion Vespillus is in the right. You had no permission to leave the province.'

'Not under normal circumstances,' Decianus cut in. 'But this is a time of great peril and normal rules do not apply.'

'We'll have to let the emperor be the judge of that. You'd better hope he doesn't decide that your motive for fleeing Londinium was based on cowardice.'

'Not cowardice, but prudence, sir. It was my intention to raise the alarm in Gaul and ask for reinforcements to be sent to Britannia. Reinforcements you desperately need.'

'A message would have sufficed.'

'I felt I needed to plead the case in person, sir.'

'The message will be sent, even if word has already reached Gaul. But you will stay here until the rebellion is crushed, or die with us if we go down to defeat.' Suetonius smiled grimly. 'You've enjoyed the privileges of your office, Decianus. Now it's time for you to earn them. I'll need every available man when I face the rebels, although in your case, I use the term lightly. You have proven yourself a force for chaos and corruption in this province. A low, slippery, self-serving scoundrel you may be, but you'll have a chance to redeem yourself once a sword is placed in your hand and you take your place in our ranks.'

Decianus shook his head. 'I'm an imperial procurator. I serve at the emperor's pleasure. You have no right to force me to fight like a common soldier.'

'I'll let you take that up with Nero, if we both live to see that day. For now, I want you out of my sight. Prefect Cato, escort the procurator back to his quarters and make sure that his room remains guarded.'

'With pleasure, sir.' Cato took a step forward and saw the man flinch. 'Let's go.'

With a last hostile glare at the governor, Decianus walked towards the doorway in the corner of the room. Cato gave him a gentle shove. 'Pick up the pace.' Outside in the corridor, he fell into step beside the procurator and spoke in a low, menacing tone. 'I don't yet know precisely what part you have played in this disaster, but I'll tell you now, if I discover that you were in any way responsible for the deaths of Centurion Macro and the other veterans at Camulodunum, I will kill you.'

Decianus shot him a fearful look, but made no reply, and a moment later they reached the two rooms at the end of the corridor that served as his living quarters. One of the men from the garrison was standing outside the door, and made an effort to snap to attention as Cato approached and gestured to Decianus to go inside. He closed the door and turned to the sentry.

'He stays in there until the governor says otherwise. He is not to be allowed out or to have any visitors. Clear?'

'Yes, sir.'

Cato returned to the office, where Suetonius had made himself comfortable on the padded stool behind the desk. The governor folded his arms and thought a moment before he spoke.

'I'd say that friend Decianus has bequeathed us a fucking great mess.'

There was no debating the proposition, Cato conceded. 'Yes, sir.'

'Mind you, Vespillus has not helped. He may have been right to prevent Decianus from leaving, but having locked the procurator up in his quarters, he's let control of the town slip out of his grip.'

'He can't be held accountable for sending the contingent to Camulodunum, sir. Nor the desertions.'

'I don't know about the latter . . . In any case, he should have done something to remedy the situation.' Suetonius looked at Cato searchingly. 'I'm sure you'd have done a better job.'

It was as much a question as a statement, and Cato knew that he was being tested by his commander. He racked his weary brain for a credible response.

'In his position, I'd have recruited some good men from the town to replace the deserters. Made them swear the military oath and then kitted them out from the stores. They might not have been proper soldiers, but they'd have looked the part and been out on the streets in sufficient numbers to keep things in order.'

'Quite. That's what any decent commander would have done. Vespillus falls well short of that description, but that's why he's serving with the garrison and not in a front-line unit. If only I had sufficient men of quality that I could afford to leave some behind to keep the province safe while the army was on campaign. Instead of having to rely on the incompetent, like Vespillus, or the corrupt, like that reptile Decianus.'

'Yes, sir.' Cato had often wondered about the wisdom of the campaign, and its timing, but there was everything to be lost if he dared to raise the matter now. Besides, what difference would it make? All that remained was to make the best job of it with the resources at hand. And pray.

'Well then,' Suetonius continued. 'Our first duty is to take back control of Londinium. I want you to get a hundred of your men out on the streets tonight. I'm imposing martial law and a curfew. They are to use whatever means necessary to impose my authority.'

'Sir?'

'You understand me perfectly well, Prefect Cato. I don't care how many we have to kill, but we must restore order. See to it. Dismissed.'

CHAPTER TWELVE

It was dark before Cato had assigned the zones of Londinium that his men were to patrol until they were relieved at dawn. Those selected for the patrols made no secret of their anger, and there was an ugly chorus of protest before their officers shouted at them and waded in with their staffs until order was re-established. Cato could fully sympathise with their mood. After the exhausting march from Mona and the arrival late in the day, they had expected a rest, however brief, before preparing themselves for what was asked of them next. The Eighth Cohort had performed with distinction throughout the recent campaign and had suffered the lowest number of stragglers of any unit in the column that had set out from Deva. And now the governor had tasked them with trying to keep order on the town's streets.

Cato regarded his men from the podium on one side of the compound as they settled down and stood at ease under the wary eye of their officers. By the light of the torches and braziers arranged around the open space, he could make out their weary faces in the ruddy glow of the flames. They needed something to stir their spirits for this fresh call on their endurance. He had served long enough to be able to read the mood of his men and how best to call on their reserves of strength and courage. He knew what he must say, and at the same time felt a degree of contempt for the cynicism at playing on their sense of self-esteem. Nonetheless, it had to be done.

'I understand how you feel, men. It seems as if the Eighth gets chosen for the toughest jobs in the army. No task is so dangerous, uncomfortable or tough that we don't get called on to do it. The decorations on our standard are eloquent proof of that. And that has come at a high price when we remember the comrades we have lost and the wounds we have borne in our service to Rome . . .' He paused, and saw men nodding, while a few muttered and grumbled. 'However, there is a reason why the Eighth is asked to deal with these challenges before any other unit. That reason being that we are the best in the army. We march harder than anyone else and then fight harder when battle comes. When Suetonius needs the best, he calls on us. He knows we will not let him down. The whole army looks to the Eighth Cohort to set the example, and there are many men in other units who regard us with envy and who wish they had the honour of serving in our ranks.

'We've earned our reputation the hardest possible way. Now we are called on to face the greatest peril of our time.' He raised his right hand and thrust it towards the east. 'Our enemy is marching on Londinium. They vastly outnumber us and they are sufficiently arrogant to think that that alone will weaken our resolve and cause our courage to fail enough to guarantee our defeat in battle. When that time comes, our fate will hang in the balance. As will the fate of Rome. If we are defeated here in Britannia, our enemies around the Empire will be emboldened to attack us on every front. That is why we must make our stand here. That is why we must win our victory here.' He indicated the ground at his feet to emphasise the point. 'And victory will come to those who fight hardest, those who inspire their comrades, those who give the very last measure of their strength and courage to the service of Rome. Those who are honoured to serve in the ranks of the Eighth Cohort! To victory!'

He punched his fist into the air and repeated the cry, and it was taken up by his men and echoed back from the walls of the buildings around the compound.

He let the cries die away before he continued. 'Men, the battle that will be the most glorious hour of the Eighth Cohort is still to come. Until then, our duty is to deal with the enemies of Rome here on the streets of Londinium. Those who would use the shadow of the rebel host as cover to commit their crimes. Those who loot and rob and abuse the civilians it is our duty to protect. Those who undermine the laws of Rome and who would weaken the morale of our people. Those whose actions serve the purpose of Boudica and her barbarian horde. We must hunt them down and drive them from the streets. We must deal with them without mercy.

'The governor has declared martial law and has ordered a curfew to be imposed on Londinium from dusk until dawn. Copies of the order will be given to each patrol to set up on the main crossroads of the town. If you see any civilians, you are to tell them to return to their homes. If you encounter resistance, or catch any looters in the act, your orders are to use lethal force. Kill them and leave the bodies beneath the nearest curfew notice to make sure that people understand the price to be paid for challenging the authority of the governor and Rome. We control the streets. Not the criminal rabble who are out there stealing, burning and abusing the townsfolk. Let them know that the Eighth Cohort is here and is in charge . . . Good luck, men.'

He nodded to Tubero, who called the men to attention. Cato returned their salute as they filed off behind their officers to begin their patrols. There was a noticeable spring to their step now, he saw with relief. It was a tactic as old as the hills for a commander to paint a picture of his men's virility and exceptionalism, and yet it worked its magic on the rankers almost every time. He could not help wondering what it was about such an appeal that made it so readily attractive to those in the military when a civilian audience would usually be much harder to persuade. Whatever it was, he was glad that it made his life easier.

Once the men had left the compound, he made a tour of those resting in the barracks and ordered them to extinguish lamps and get some sleep. Then, his obligations to duty met, he set off to the Dog and Deer, full of hope that he would find Claudia, Lucius and Petronella there along with Portia, and hopefully find out something more about Macro's fate. He kept his helmet on so that any patrols he encountered would spot his crest and recognise him as an officer before they were tempted to cut him down in an overexuberant application of the governor's orders.

Londinium was a study of contrasts under normal conditions, but that night contrast seemed to have slipped into chaos. Stretches of the streets were silent and dark, whereas elsewhere fires burned and chains of civilians passed buckets of water drawn from troughs and wells to fight the flames. Some of his men from the patrols were helping out while their comrades guarded against any gangs of criminals who might cause trouble. When he set off, Cato had been content to walk alone, but every so often he detected movement and heard muttering, and was careful to keep away from the openings of the narrow alleys that led off the main thoroughfares. Halfway to the inn, he stopped to take a torch from one of the patrols he encountered and made the remainder of the short journey holding it aloft, using the wavering loom of its flames to light his way and let any looters know that a soldier was coming.

The doors and windows of the inn that opened onto the streets on each angle of the crossroads had been boarded up, and there was a faint glow in the gaps between the sturdy timbers. Making his way round the corner and down the street to the entrance of the yard at the rear, Cato tested the latch, but the gate was bolted on the far side. He extinguished the torch in the drain that ran down the middle of the street and tossed the iron bracket over the wall before clambering up. Heaving himself over the top, he dropped down into the yard and adjusted his helmet, which had slipped forward.

'Stand still or I'll gut you!' a voice called out close by.

Cato stepped back against the wall in case there were more men concealed in the darkness. He drew his sword and held it ready.

'Get out of here!' the voice growled. 'Now! We won't give you another chance . . . Go, before I order my men to deal with you!'

There was a false note in the words, and Cato realised that the speaker was bluffing and that he was alone. There was also something vaguely familiar about the voice, and then he recalled the nervous and not very bright individual who worked for Macro's mother and on occasion warmed her bed.

'Denubius, it's me, Prefect Cato.' He smiled. 'You can call your men off.'

'Prefect Cato?' the other man responded with instinctive suspicion. 'Is there anyone with you?'

'I'm alone. Like you.'

A figure emerged from the gloom, a sturdy club raised in his right hand. 'Thank the gods it's you, sir. We've had so much trouble ever since news arrived about Camulodunum.' The relief in Denubius's voice turned to sadness. 'We've been grieving for the centurion and the others ever since, sir.'

'The others? You mean Apollonius?'

'Yes, sir. Him and the boy, Parvus.'

Cato recalled the young mute Macro and Petronella had taken into their household and raised like a son. Parvus had played with Lucius, who had hero-worshipped the older boy. His mind raced on to a pressing question. 'What of Claudia Acte, Lucius, Petronella?'

'All safe, sir, and inside. You know the way.' Denubius waved the club in the direction of the door across the yard that Cato recalled from previous visits to the inn.

'You're not coming in?'

'Not yet, sir. I'll be keeping watch here until after midnight. That's when things quieten down. Mostly.'

Cato sheathed his sword and patted the older man on the shoulder, then picked his way over the cobbled yard to the far corner and groped for the iron latch. The hinges squealed as the door swung inwards, revealing a short, narrow corridor dimly lit by an oil lamp hanging from a bracket. The door at the end was closed, but an instant later, Cato heard a woman's voice call out from the far side.

'Denubius? Is there something wrong?'

He closed the door to the yard and made his way down the corridor. 'All's well.'

'Who are you?' the woman demanded. 'Where is Denubius?'

'On duty in the yard. It's me, Cato. Let me in, Portia.'

'Cato? Cato!'

There was a rattle of bolts being slid back, and then the door swung open and Macro's mother stood there, looking thinner and more frail than he had ever seen her. But there was a gleam in her eye and a grateful smile on her lips. 'It *is* you, by the Fates. Come in! Come inside, my boy.'

She stepped aside, and Cato ducked under the door frame into the main room of the inn as Portia closed the door and slid the bolts back into position. In front of him was the heavily scored bar, and beyond lay the open space that had previously been filled with tables and benches. That crude furniture had now been stacked against the door and windows facing onto the crossroads. Only one table remained in the middle of the room, where two

173

women were seated facing each other, over bowls of stew and cups of watered wine.

The younger woman, with shoulder-length dark hair, pushed back her bench and leaped up, rushing across the room and into his arms. She buried her face in the scale armour of his cuirass as her hands pressed against his back, drawing him tightly to her.

'Cato, my love . . . You're safe.'

He bent to kiss the top of her head as he hugged her and breathed in the scent of her, and felt a familiar lightness in his heart and a surge of overwhelming affection that welled up from the depths of his soul as he murmured, 'Claudia, my darling . . .'

They held each other for a long moment before drawing apart to look into each other's eyes.

'I heard the news about Camulodunum,' said Cato. 'I hoped you'd all got away before it was too late.'

'Not all of us . . .' Claudia gave the slightest movement of her eyes to indicate the woman still sitting at the table. Petronella had pushed her bench back and looked as if she could not decide whether to remain seated or come over and risk interrupting their reunion. 'Macro sent all the non-combatants away from the colony before the rebels arrived. Except that Parvus left us, and it's almost certain that he returned to Camulodunum, along with the dog.'

'Cassius?' Cato recalled the huge beast he had encountered as a stray on the eastern frontier and that had attached itself to him, saving his life once. Now that he thought about Cassius, he was struck by grief over the fate of the dog along with that of Parvus. But most of all his grief was for Macro, and he struggled to contain his feelings as he made his way over to Petronella.

She stood up, her expression torn between relief at seeing him and the emotional devastation over the loss of her husband and Parvus. Her bottom lip quivered, and then, as Cato went to embrace her, she shook her head and began to weep, covering her face with her hands. Cato hesitated, feeling awkward, not knowing what to do. Fortunately, Claudia hurried over and put an arm round the older woman, drawing her close. For a moment, the only sound in the interior of the inn was the deep, sobbing and animal groans, until Petronella eased herself back, rubbing her eyes, and looked at Cato apologetically.

'It's just that seeing you reminds me . . . of the two of you together. Through thick and thin. He always said you were half friend, half son and all comrade to him. Maybe that's the way a soldier's life is. He might have been my husband, but in a way, it felt like he was also married to the army.'

'I understand.' Cato nodded. 'Yes, it is like that. But don't ever think you are second in his emotions. I know Macro well enough to know that you are the love of his life.'

Petronella smiled faintly. 'You speak of him as if he was still alive. Is that what you feel? As I do?'

There was a gut-wrenching hope burning in her eyes, and Cato was torn between the cold, rational likelihood that his friend was dead and the yearning in his heart that by some extraordinary miracle Macro still lived. His heart won out, partly from compassion for Petronella and partly out of the need to believe that Macro had survived.

'I know he would never have deserted his post at Camulodunum. As long as the men there held out, Macro would have stood with them, until the end. At the same time, I've served with him long enough to have escaped greater perils and overcome greater odds. If there is any way a man could have come through it alive, that man is Macro.'

Petronella nodded. 'I agree.' She touched her breast over her heart. 'I feel it here, that he is still with us.'

Cato turned to Claudia. 'Where's Lucius?'

'Asleep. I've put him in a room upstairs. It's the safest place for him.' She indicated the barricaded doors and windows, and on closer inspection, Cato could see that knives and cleavers had been placed close by.

'If anyone tries to break in, they'll regret it,' said Portia. She picked up one of the cleavers and brought it down heavily on the end of a bench propped against the entrance. 'I'll not let any of those bastards loot the Dog and Deer. Or do harm to any of us.'

'With your reputation, they'd be fools to try,' Cato grinned. He noted the lack of any other sound of life in the building. There were no noises coming from the corridor that led through a curtain partition into the brothel attached to the inn. 'What about your women?'

'If there's ever any trouble, it's the women who suffer most,' said Portia. 'I put them on a ship to Rutupiae as soon as things became difficult here. One of the older women is in charge. I've given her enough money to look after them for a few months. Let's hope the governor has sorted out the rebellion by then and things return to normal. Even if Macro . . .' A pained expression crossed her face then she turned towards the passage leading to the kitchen. 'You must be hungry. I'll get you a bowl.'

Cato sat down opposite Claudia and Petronella. 'How is Lucius coping?'

'He's a kid,' said Petronella. 'You know what it's like at that age. Everything is an adventure and you don't really understand much of what is going on outside of playing, eating and sleeping.'

'He thinks it's exciting,' Claudia added. 'Poor soul.'

'Perhaps that's for the best.'

Portia returned and set a samianware bowl in front of Cato before ladling some stew from the pot at the end of the table. 'There. Now tell us how you come to be here. I thought the army was still fighting against the Druids up in the mountains.'

As he ate, Cato related the broad details of the campaign and the landing on the island of Mona that had marked the final conquest of the heartland of the Druid cult. He told them how, at the very moment that Suetonius and his battle-weary men were celebrating victory, the news of the outbreak of the rebellion and the fall of Camulodunum had reached them, and of the race to reach Londinium before Boudica and her horde.

'The governor is here?' Portia asked excitedly. 'And the army too?'

'No. Only the mounted men of my cohort and a few other units. The main body is several days behind us.'

'Will they arrive in time to stop the rebels?' asked Claudia.

'I don't know. The rebels are much closer to Londinium; they could be here within days if they wanted to be. Long before the main column arrives. Our best hope is that the Second Legion gets here first. The governor sent for them before we left Deva. They could arrive at any moment, and then there's a chance of holding the town long enough for the rest of the army to arrive and give us a fighting chance of defeating Boudica.'

'And if the Second Legion doesn't arrive in time, what then?' Claudia paused. 'Can Londinium be held?'

'No. Suetonius has enough men to restore some semblance of order to the streets but far too few to have any hope of holding the headquarters compound, let alone the rest of the town. If help doesn't arrive soon, he'll have to pull his men out.'

Portia scowled. 'He can't do that . . . How dare he? I've already lost everything that was in my warehouse. My stock of wine was taken by the looters. All I have left now is this place, and my chest of silver. If I abandon the inn, everything Macro and I have sunk into the business will be gone. I'm not leaving. If those rebels come, I'll be waiting for them.'

Petronella took her hand and gave it a gentle squeeze. 'If the soldiers leave the town, then so must we. There's no point in staying here to die.'

'Pah! I'm an old woman, my girl. Too old to start again. I have put down roots in Londinium and here I'll stay, and if the rebels come for me, well, I'll go down fighting for what is mine, just like my son did.'

Cato was watching her partly in pity, partly in amusement. He could see where his friend had got his stubborn courage from, but laudable though Portia's words were, she had no chance of surviving if she chose to remain and Suetonius and his soldiers pulled out. She had to be made to see reason.

'I'll be honest with you. I doubt there is much chance of holding Londinium, even if the Second Legion were to arrive at this moment. It's a legion in name only these days. Most of the lads in the ranks are still in training before being sent on to reinforce the other legions in Britannia. They lack experience, and who knows how they will perform in their first battle without plenty of veterans to set the example. Then there's the parlous state of the town's defences. The place is wide open. Sure, we could barricade the streets and hold the enemy off for a short time, but if they have the numbers, they will always find a way through or round any makeshift defences we throw up. The only hope is that the rest of the army reaches us before the rebels do. Even then . . .'

'It's as hopeless as that?' Claudia said quietly.

'I think so. The best thing to do is leave. I want you and Lucius out of here.'

'Leave Londinium?'

'Leave Britannia. You should take ship to Gaul while there are still berths to be had. Same goes for you, Petronella, and you, Portia.'

'No!' the old lady responded firmly. 'I'm staying. And if my boy does come back, I'll be here waiting for him.'

Cato sighed. 'Please be reasonable.'

'Damn reason. I'm too old to leave. If this is where it ends for me, then so be it.'

'You don't mean that.'

Portia grasped the handle of the cleaver and wrenched it free. 'Try me.'

Cato raised his hands in mock surrender. 'Enough! I give in. Perhaps we can talk again in the morning.'

'What do you think will be different then?' she challenged him.

'Let's just see,' he temporised, and pushed his empty bowl away. 'Now I need some sleep.'

'I have the room next to Lucius,' said Claudia. 'The bed's comfortable enough for two.'

'You read my mind. But first I have to see my son.'

They rose from the table and bade the others goodnight, then made for the staircase off the passage behind the bar, taking the lamp there to guide their way. Claudia led him to the room where Lucius slept. Quietly opening the door, Cato entered and stood over his son. For a moment, the horrors of the wider world dissolved and his heart filled with tenderness and the deepest love for Lucius. It was hard to resist the urge to stroke his fine hair and hold him close, but it was the middle of the night, in a dark world, and he thought it would be a small mercy to let the boy sleep on. He was curled into a ball on his side and snoring softly, his small hands bunched into fists as he frowned and muttered some defiant nonsense from a dream.

'I see Portia's rubbing off on him,' Cato whispered.

'I think his uncle Macro rubbed off on him long before she did.'

Cato chuckled as he regarded his son fondly for a moment longer before following Claudia to her room. It was no more than ten feet across, and the rafters angled down across it so that he had to crouch slightly as he approached the bed: a simple wooden frame with a feather mattress that felt delightfully soft to his touch. Claudia helped him to strip off his armour, boots and tunic so that he sat on the bed with only his loincloth remaining.

He could feel his groin stirring beneath the thin folds of the cloth. She had set the lamp down on the table beside the bed and now removed her stola, revealing the soft contours of her skin. As she unpinned her hair and let the short tresses fall to her shoulders, Cato reached up and cupped her breast before leaning forward to kiss her nipple softly. She let out a quiet moan of pleasure and stroked his dark curls as he buried his face in her soft flesh.

'I want you,' he said simply.

'You'll be needing to return to your men at first light, I suppose,' she mused both sadly and practically, in the way soldiers' women did.

'Yes. That's why I want you now.' He bent his head to kiss her stomach, and then grazed the fringe of her pubic hair and was rewarded with another soft moan.

'You can have me,' she said, gesturing to the wall that divided them from Lucius. 'But keep the noise down, eh? Let him sleep, poor lamb. He refuses to think Macro is gone.'

Cato paused and looked up. 'I hope he's right.'

'We all do.' Claudia sat down on the bed, then lay back on the covers and beckoned to him. 'Come to me, Cato. I want you inside me . . .'

CHAPTER THIRTEEN

Cato had fallen into a deep, exhausted sleep after he and Claudia had made love. They lay entwined on the covers for a while before she stirred to use the chamber pot in the corner then took a spare cover from a chest in the corner and gently laid it across Cato before slipping in next to him. He turned onto his side, away from her, and she snuggled up to him and kissed him between the shoulder blades before closing her eyes and trying to sleep. Her heart was filled with relief that he had come back to her from the campaign in the mountains. And yet her relief was tempered by the dread of the danger facing not just those in Londinium, but all Romans across the province.

The immediate threat did not come from the enemy, but the bands of looters marauding through the streets. Every so often she heard shouts, screams and the crash of doors being battered in. Mostly from some way off, but sometimes too close for her to be at ease. Twice she rose from the bed and crossed to the shuttered window overlooking the street, slipping the latch and opening the shutters fractionally to peer out. The first time she saw a large group of men, perhaps twenty or so, race around the corner of the junction – dark shapes, like rats. A moment later, a military patrol came running after them, kit jingling as the pounding of their studded boots rattled off the buildings on either side of the street. The second time she was woken by the piercing scream of a woman, but when she looked out over the street again, nothing moved and all was silent.

As the night hours passed, the sounds of violence and robbery became less frequent, and Claudia began to relax, eventually falling asleep with one arm across Cato's side and her hand resting on her lover's chest. In her dreams, her past returned to haunt her: the years she had spent as the emperor's mistress, until Nero's advisers grew wary of her influence over him and contrived to have her sent to exile in Sardinia, where she and Cato had met. She dreamed that she was being hunted through the streets of Londinium by Nero's men. She was running hard, dodging gangs of looters as she glanced back over her shoulder. Her pursuers were in the uniform of the Praetorian Guard and wore determined expressions as they chased after her. Sometimes they appeared to be closing the gap, and she ran faster. Sometimes she tried ducking into a side alley or hiding inside a shop, only for them to spot her again and resume the chase. At length she ran into a blind alley that backed onto a temple and they caught her.

Dragged in chains before Nero, who had somehow materialised in Londinium, along with the imperial palace, she was dumped in front of his dais. He loomed above her on his throne, his heavy cheeks quivering with rage as he raised a pudgy hand. 'I sentenced you to exile for life!' he screamed. 'No man was to touch you again after I had you and discarded you! That was my will. SO WHO IS THIS MAN LYING NEXT TO YOU? I will have him crucified along with you in front of the mob! Crucified!' Claudia threw her hands up and tried to break free of her chains, desperate to save herself and Cato. Then the image of the emperor faded and everything went dark as she awoke in the bed with Cato to discover he was now lying across her arm.

She pulled it free and sat up, breathing hard, still haunted by the shadows of the dream even as it faded. She glanced at Cato's dark form and heard his easy breathing, and was grateful that she hadn't disturbed him, though she longed to tell him about the nightmare and seek his reassurance. In the fetid heat of the summer night, she felt the uncomfortable patina of sweat on her skin. Her heart was beating quickly and she found that she had developed a terrible thirst.

Easing herself out of bed, she crossed to the door and made her way along the small landing to the stairs. There was still some water in the jars drawn from a municipal well three days earlier, when she and Denubius had dared to venture out after the first day of looting. The lamp in the bar was alight, and there was enough light to see her way to the passage that led to the yard. She was about to enter the kitchen when she heard a shouted challenge, cut off almost immediately, and froze.

'Denubius?' she called out softly. She stood still, not breathing, as her ears strained to pick up any further sounds. At last a faint squeal of rusty iron came from outside in the yard, followed by low, urgent voices. Fear clamped her heart. She padded towards the door and could see that it was fractionally open. Peering outside, she made out several dark shapes in the yard and more entering through the open gate.

She pushed the door to and reached for the bolt at the top before easing it across into the sturdy bracket on the frame. As she reached for the bolt halfway down, she heard voices approaching from outside, and an instant later the latch was lifted. She slammed the bolt across and reached down to fasten the lowest one just as a loud thud came and the door lurched. She ran back down the passage, shrieking to raise the alarm.

'Wake up! Wake up! Cato!'

By the time she reached the top of the stairs, Petronella was already standing at the door to her room at the far end of the landing, holding a lamp that betrayed her lack of sleep. She was barefoot but wearing a loose tunic. Portia emerged too, and her eyebrows rose as she saw Claudia's nakedness.

'What's the meaning of this, my girl?'

Claudia ignored her as she rushed back into her own room and gave Cato a violent shake. 'Wake up!'

He woke like any veteran, at once alert, swinging his feet off the bed and standing, ready to act.

'There are men in the yard trying to get in!' Claudia explained as she grabbed her stola from the end of the bed and pulled it over her head.

Cato snatched up his tunic and sword belt and dashed out onto the landing. 'Wake Lucius and tell him to get dressed,' he barked at Portia.

He ran down the stairs towards the sound of the pounding on the door to the yard. From the end of the passage he could see that the bolts were holding for now, and quickly pulled his tunic on and slung his sword belt over his shoulder. Hearing footsteps behind him, he turned to find Petronella at his shoulder.

'Where's Denubius?' she asked.

'I don't know. Last time I saw him he was on watch in the yard. He said he'd come in when things died down.'

'Then he should be inside. He usually sleeps behind the bar, when Portia doesn't want him.'

'He must be inside, the door's bolted.'

'That was me,' said Claudia as she joined them. 'I came down for a drink, heard a noise and looked out and saw the men.'

'How many?' asked Cato.

'Eight, ten. Can't be sure. I think they must have overpowered Denubius.'

'Shit . . .'

The pounding on the door stopped for a beat, then there was a loud splintering crack as someone swung an axe at the timbers.

'We need to reinforce the door.' Cato turned to the bar. 'Claudia, give me a hand with one of the benches. Petronella, get some of those knives and cleavers ready. Looks like we're going to need them.'

By the time he and Claudia had carried the first bench into the passage, the axe had opened a small split in the timbers and they could see its edge as it struck again, sending splinters flying. Cato rammed the bench at an angle so that it reinforced the bolt halfway up.

'We need more.'

They carried more benches through and placed a heavy table on its end to block the passage as one of the timbers in the door shattered and a large, jagged piece of wood burst inwards. Petronella let out a cry as a splinter gashed her brow.

'Another table!' Cato ordered. 'Quickly!'

More axe blows, and then a hand thrust through, grappling with the middle bolt and sliding it free. The men outside battered the door again, and the remaining bolts bulged before the one at the top gave way. A moment later, the bottom bolt went the same way and the ruined door shuddered inwards. It was short work to push the benches aside, and the first man shoved his way past the wreckage and obstacles to gain entrance to the passage.

Claudia and Petronella came up with the second table and Cato helped them to ram it against the one that was already barricading the passage. Fingers appeared around the edge of the first table, and Cato clambered on top of the second, drew his sword and hacked at them, severing a forefinger. There was a howl of agony as the hand was snatched back, and then another hand made a grab for the other side of the table. There wasn't enough room for Cato to effectively swing his sword, and he turned to Petronella. 'Give me a cleaver!'

She handed him a heavy blade with a leather handle and

he sheathed his sword. The new weapon proved its worth in the confined space as he struck two more crippling blows before the attackers drew back. There was a brief, muted exchange, then a handful of men scurried out into the yard, from where the moans and agonised howls of the injured sounded.

'Get back into the main room,' Cato ordered. 'They may try the street entrance. I can hold them here. Go!'

Claudia and Petronella hastened down the corridor as Cato risked a glance over the top of the table. There were two men squeezed into the narrow corridor, and when they saw him, one punched an iron-studded club at his face. Cato ducked, and the tip of the club hit the boards of the ceiling with a loud crack. Grit and dust fell over his head, causing him to blink. A moment later, he heard the men in the yard return, grunting with effort, and a growled command for those watching Cato to move aside. There was a pause before the voice counted to three, and then a jarring crash as the table shuddered under the impact of a makeshift battering ram. Perhaps one of the hitching posts from the yard, Cato guessed, as a second blow struck and he felt the impact through the surface of the table beneath his bare feet.

'There's nothing of value to be had here!' he called out. 'Nothing worth risking your lives over. Begone! Find yourselves some easier prey, you bloody fools!'

'Nothing of value, he says,' a voice responded. 'Hear that, lads?'

There was some harsh laughter.

'It's no secret that the landlady has a small fortune. And if we can't find it, then there's the women to be had, eh? Besides, you've taken off the fingers of some of my lads and there's a score to be settled one way or another. Tell you what, friend. You let us search the place and we'll do you no harm. You and any others here. If we find Portia's strongbox, that'll satisfy us, right, lads?'

His companions grumbled their assent before their leader continued. 'Let us in and hand over the silver and we'll go our separate ways. Can't say fairer than that under the circumstances. What d'you say, friend?'

Cato was not fooled, and could guess at the fate intended for himself, the women and Lucius if he agreed to the man's terms.

'I say that you and those bastards with you had better have made your peace with the gods before choosing to rob the Dog and Deer. This is the last warning I'll give you – "friend". Get out of here while you still can.'

Their response came a heartbeat later as the table shuddered under a fresh attack and one of the trestles broke with a loud crack. Cato could see that it would give way after a few more blows, and he scrambled back and jumped to the floor before running down the corridor to the main room and slamming the door closed behind him.

'They're coming through! Help me here!'

As splintering crashes sounded from beyond the door, the three of them hurriedly braced the interior door with more benches and then a heavy table.

Cato stood back, his expression anxious in the dim glow of the oil lamp hanging from a chain at the end of the bar. The interior door was a less sturdy affair, constructed to give Portia privacy rather than keep raiders out, and would have even less chance of withstanding an assault by the men even now smashing their way past the tables. For the moment they ignored the closed door at the end of the corridor and busied themselves with searching and ransacking the storerooms and kitchen on either side. Cato knew that Portia used one of the smaller rooms as her office, and turned to Petronella.

'Do you know if she keeps her strongbox where she does the accounts?'

'No. She takes it up to her room each night.'

'Damn, they'll not find what they want out there then.' He slapped a hand on the door. 'This won't keep them out for long. We're going to have to retreat and barricade the stairs. Claudia, go and tell Portia. Get her to help you ready some bed frames to block the way.'

She nodded and disappeared up the stairs. Cato glanced at the cleavers and knives laid out on the counter.

'Get those upstairs, Petronella, and help the others.'

She picked up the bundle of makeshift weapons, then hesitated. 'What about you?'

'I'll try and buy us some time.'

'You can't hold them off on your own.'

'I'll try for as long as I can. Then I'll join you upstairs. Don't worry,' he forced a smile, 'I'm not going to throw my life away. Claudia would never forgive me.'

Petronella laughed nervously. 'Not the kind of woman to enrage, then.'

He gave her a gentle shove. 'Go. I'll be fine.'

As the stairs creaked beneath her footsteps, Cato drew his sword again, transferring the cleaver to his left hand. He would have preferred the familiar weight and balance of a legionary dagger, but the heavy blade would do far more damage if he was able to land a firm blow.

'Nothing here!' one of the men called out. 'Just bloody pans and jars.'

'Same here!' another added.

'All right, lads. We'll have to take the rest of the place apart. Kill that bastard who took the fingers off Albacus. You can do what you like with any women you find. But I want the strongbox. Anyone who's thinking of taking it for themselves better think something else. I'll carve the balls off any of you who try it on. Get me?'

There was a pause before the leader cleared his throat. 'Right then, let's get on with it.'

Cato raised his weapons as the latch rattled and a violent kick shook the door. The table held firm as he braced his foot against the edge of it.

'Fuck, he's barricaded this one and all. Pick up that post, lads. We're going to need it again. Same as before. On three . . .'

When the blow came, the door's timbers gave way on the first attempt and crashed against the top of the table. The impact jarred Cato's knee, and he stepped away and made ready to strike as more blows landed, breaking down the door and forcing the benches and table back across the flagstones.

'That's it! We're through. Clear that lot away and let's get it done.'

The post was hauled away and discarded, and the first of the men wrenched the ruined door apart and shoved the table to one side. Cato stepped forward, thrusting his sword towards the man's face, and the point caught him on the chin, opening up his cheek. He jumped back with a pained gasp, and at once was replaced by another man, holding a buckler before him as he brandished a club. By the light of the oil lamp, Cato could see the wary hunch of his shoulders and the watchful gleam in his eyes. He looked like a man who knew how to fight.

Cato stabbed his sword forward, but the strike was easily deflected before his opponent stepped through the opening and shoved the table and benches aside before swinging his club in a vicious arc. Cato dodged round to the front of the counter before he struck again. Once more his foe blocked it and swung the club horizontally, forcing him back. Behind the club-wielding man, one of his companions emerged from the corridor and made towards the far end of the counter to work his way round and take Cato in the flank.

Cato saw that there was no way of holding his position any longer. This time he swung his cleaver at his enemy. The club came up to block the blow and the heavy blade bit deeply into the shaft and drove it down onto the counter before Cato made a hasty cut with his sword and caught the man below the elbow.

The cleaver was solidly embedded, and Cato released his grip, turning and running across the room to the foot of the stairs and up to the floor above. He found Claudia and Petronella heaving a solid bed frame along the narrow landing while Portia held a lamp aloft with one hand and clutched Lucius to her side with the other.

The child lurched from her grip. 'Father!'

Cato caught him in his arms and gave him a quick hug before squatting down so that they were face to face. 'I've missed you, son. But we can't talk now. You need to let Portia take care of you.'

The old woman took a firm grip on the boy's hand while Cato turned his attention to helping the others position the bed frame over the opening above the stairs. The sounds of crashing furniture and crockery came from beneath, then the pounding of feet. The bed frame lurched as the raiders tried to heave it up. Cato leaned his weight on it and called over his shoulder.

'Get some mattresses! Anything heavy we can put on top!'

The pressure from beneath ceased, and he could hear muted exchanges from the inn's main room as the men planned their next step.

He became aware that his son was crying, and softened his voice as he spoke. 'Lucius, be brave and stop your tears.'

'But I'm afraid, Daddy,' the boy quavered.

'Of course you are. But being brave is about doing what we must even if we are afraid. Do you see?' Cato smiled encouragingly, then added as an afterthought, 'Would Uncle Macro have cried?'

Lucius shook his head. Macro was the man he admired most in the world.

'He'd have said brush those tears away and be ready to show the enemy how a Roman soldier fights, wouldn't he?'

'Yes . . .'

'Then do us both proud, son.'

Lucius nodded and cuffed away a tear as Petronella reappeared dragging a mattress. Cato helped her heave it onto the bed frame, and did the same with the clothes chest that Claudia added. Then he stepped back and examined their efforts.

'It should hold them off for a while,' he said, more to encourage the others than out of any conviction. He turned to Portia. 'Your strongbox, is it up here?'

'Yes,' she replied warily. 'So?'

'Where exactly is it? We may need it.'

'It's mine. Belongs to me. No one else.'

He regarded her coolly. 'Listen. It's all we have left to bargain with. Those men downstairs will finish searching the rest of the inn before long, and then they'll force their way up here and kill us all. If we let them take the strongbox and go, there's a chance we may come out of this alive.'

'I'm not giving it up,' Portia replied firmly. 'And certainly not while I have any fight left in me. I'm no coward.'

'Nor am I. And I'll do what I can to keep them at bay. But if it's clear that we can't keep them from gaining this floor, then we have to try something else. In that case, I want the strongbox. What use will your coins do you if we're all dead?'

He was aware of how upsetting his words might be for Lucius, and stepped over to rest his hands on the lad's bony shoulders. 'It's time for you to prove yourself, son. Can you be brave for me?'

'I-I'll try.'

'Good man. Now listen. We're in a desperate situation. We can't leave this place. The windows are too small for us to get out. But you can squeeze through and climb down into the street.'

'I'm not leaving you to die!'

'I'm not asking you to. I need you to be a hero and see that we are saved. Can you do that?'

'How?'

'Once you are in the street, I want you to make your way to the governor's headquarters.'

'The big building at the end of the street?'

'That's it. Go there and find a man called Centurion Tubero. Tell him that you are the son of Prefect Cato and say that I want ten of his men to come back here as soon as possible. Tell him that our lives depend on it. Is that clear, son?'

Lucius nodded, and Cato felt his heart lurch with anxiety at the danger his son would face in carrying out the task.

'Make sure you stay in the shadows along the edge of the street as far as you can. If anyone comes your way, keep still and be quiet until they are gone. If they see you, run as fast as you can. Can you do that?'

'Yes,' Lucius replied with a determined expression.

'Good, then let's get going.' Cato led him into Claudia's room and opened the small square window, a little more than a foot across. 'Climb out and hang on to the sill. Claudia, pass me that blanket.'

When Lucius had done as he was told and his bare feet dangled some six feet above the ground, Cato fed out the woollen material until he was holding the corner. 'Use it to let yourself down, son.'

Lucius grasped the folds tightly and worked his way down, dropping the last two feet and landing in a crouch. He took a last glance up at his father as Cato stuck his head out of the window.

'Go, my boy! As fast as you can.'

The small figure darted along the side of the building and was quickly lost from view. Cato was still, his ears straining for any indication that the boy had been spotted, then ducked back inside.

'Do you really think he can get help in time?' asked Claudia.

'I don't know. All I can hope is that he is safer outside than in here. And if he reaches headquarters, he will be looked after. Tubero is a good man. He'll do right by my son.'

There was a deep, dull thud from the landing, and they rushed from the room just as the chest on top of the mattress lurched as a jarring blow struck the bed frame. Cato realised the men must be using the same post as before, but this time the angle would make it more difficult for them to strike with the same momentum.

'Stand ready, lads, we can hold this ground,' he said instinctively. 'Sorry, ladies . . .'

It amused him to see himself in a desperate last stand with women for comrades. Not an ending he had envisioned for himself in all his years as a soldier. But if it came to it, he would fight and die with them and count it as much of an honourable end as any other.

The men below continued to batter away at the bed frame, and soon there was a splintering noise and a cry of triumph before the assault was renewed. Cato was standing with his sword and one of the cleavers that had been taken upstairs. He was poised to strike when Claudia took a step back and cocked her head to one side. Then she grabbed his arm.

'Listen!'

At first he could not make out what had drawn her attention, but then he heard it: a softer thudding from somewhere behind them. He turned swiftly, and this time he was certain of it.

'Stay here! If they poke their heads or hands up around the mattress, you know what to do.'

Petronella hefted her cleaver in acknowledgement.

Cato padded back along the corridor, checking the first two rooms and finding no sign of danger in either. As he opened the door to the third room, he heard a thud and a crack, and by the glow of a fire outside he saw one of the floorboards burst upwards. Another blow drove up the one beside it, then a hand wrenched at the splintered boards and tore one free, thrusting it to the side of the opening. Cato walked softly across to the far side of the hole in the floor and crouched there, cleaver raised as he balanced his weight on his haunches.

'That's it, boys,' a voice said from the room beneath, one of the cells used during working hours by the prostitutes employed at the inn. 'Get the next one out of the way and we'll go up there and deal with 'em.'

The next floorboard was quickly loosened, and another blow smashed it in two. Hands pulled at the fragments and Cato held his breath as he waited to strike. A moment later, two arms reached up and he saw the top of a man's head as his comrades hoisted him.

'How's it looking?'

The man drew himself up so that his shoulders were clear of the opening. He paused and glanced at the door. 'No one here.'

Cato raised the cleaver, took aim at the centre of the man's head and struck him a savage blow. The heavy blade cracked the skull like an egg and carried on deep into the brain, almost as far as the jaw. The man's arms thrust out, fingers splayed, as he spasmed violently. Bracing a foot on his victim's shoulder, Cato wrenched at the cleaver, tugging it from side to side.

'What the fuck you kicking me for!' a voice called out from below, then, more plaintively, 'Fesculus?'

The cleaver came free and Cato shoved the man's shoulders back through the opening so that the body dropped heavily on those below amid a chorus of angry shouts.

'Fesculus! You clumsy bastard, what— Oh shit. He's fucked . . . Look at his head!'

'I warned you!' Cato called down through the hole. 'Get out of here while you can! I've sent for help. There will be soldiers here soon. If they capture you, I swear I'll make sure every one of you is crucified! You have my word on it. Go while you still can.'

'There ain't nobody coming!' the looters' leader responded. 'No one's got past my lads. You're on your own, and you're going to pay for what you've done to my men. You either throw your blades down to us and give in, or you stay where you are and fry. If you try and escape the blaze, my lads will cut you down. If you give us the old cunt's money, I'll let the women go. Not you, though. Not now you've done for Fesculus.'

Cato glanced up and saw that the glow was brighter than when he had entered the room. Crossing to the window, he looked out over the back of the inn and saw that two of the storerooms in the yard were alight. Flames licked through small gaps in the shingle roofs. By the light of the flames he saw the body of Denubius sprawled on his back by the burning building, a dark patch around his head. Already the flames were spreading towards the rear of the inn.

'What d'you say?' the man below shouted. 'Surrender or burn. What's your choice?'

Cato ignored him and made his way back to the corridor to explain the new danger to the others.

'My inn?' Portia's expression was horrified. 'My beautiful inn!'

'What do we do?' asked Claudia.

'They mean to kill us either way,' said Cato. 'They'll probably take longer over it with you women.'

195

His meaning was clear, and Petronella gave a growl before she replied. 'I'll burn rather than give those bastards the satisfaction of cutting me up.'

'We're not done for yet. There's still time for Lucius to raise the alarm and bring help.'

'Why did they have to set fire to the place?' Portia moaned. 'What good does it do 'em to burn it down and lose any chance of taking my coin? The fools!'

'You can be sure they'll search the ruins once it's over. They'll not want to leave anything behind for Boudica's people to find.' Cato pointed to the room he had come from. 'Petronella, you go in there. There's a hole by the bed. Take a swing at anyone who shows their head.'

She nodded and disappeared through the doorway.

The pounding on the bed frame under the mattress had paused following the killing of one of the looters, but now it resumed with a more urgent rhythm. Cato could hear the wooden boards shattering one by one, and then the mattress sagged as the smashed frame gave way and the fragments were torn away by the looters. A moment later, it gave a lurch and was drawn downwards.

'Ready?' He glanced at Claudia, and she gritted her teeth and nodded. 'Any moment now . . .'

He saw the tremor in her arm and reached across to give her a reassuring squeeze. She glanced at him, and he tried to conceal his concern and the painful guilt gnawing at him for not being able to protect the woman he was devoted to.

She swallowed nervously. 'Is this what you go through before every battle?'

'Battle?' He forced a smile. 'This isn't even a skirmish, my love. Barely more than a brawl. So let's show them what we're made of, eh?'

There was no time to hope that his words had had a reassuring

196

effect as the mattress was ripped away and the faces of the looters were revealed at the foot of the stairs, their features illuminated by one of the inn's lamps.

There was a beat before their leader bellowed, 'What are you waiting for?'

With a roar, the first man pounded up, dagger raised in front of him, the point aimed at Cato's chest. Cato braced himself, sword and cleaver poised to strike, while Claudia crouched at his shoulder, brandishing her knife. He let the looter stab at him, then parried the blow to the side and lashed out at the man's shoulder with the cleaver. It was a hurried attack, and the blade struck only a glancing blow, but the numbing impact was enough to cause the looter to drop his weapon and retreat a couple of steps before one of his comrades thrust him aside and came on. Cato hacked at the head of the second man's club, and the edge of his sword split the wooden shaft down its length and lodged firmly. Both men wrestled with their weapons, wrenching them from side to side in the narrow stairwell. Cato's left hand struck the wall hard and he lost his grip on the cleaver, which tumbled down the stairs.

'Ha!' The looter grinned. 'Now I've got you!'

As he went to tug his club back again, Claudia let out an enraged shriek and stabbed at his arm, over and over, piercing the limb so that droplets of blood spattered the three of them and streaked the walls on either side of the stairs. As the looter released his grip, she thrust herself forward onto the top step and stabbed again, this time at his face, lacerating his cheeks and brow, his howls of pain competing with her animal cry.

Cato caught her arm and drew her back. 'Easy there! Behind me, now!'

He ripped the sword free of the club and brandished the blade at the men below. 'Who's next?'

Their leader shoved one of his men forward. 'You go.' When

the man hesitated, he shoved again. 'An extra share of the loot for you when you cut him down.'

'Sod that! I'm not going up there to face that bastard and his mad bitch. You want the silver so much, you go.'

The leader squared off against his follower, and for an instant Cato thought they might fight each other. But then another man rushed in from the direction of the yard.

'Soldiers!' he shouted. 'Coming down the street!'

Cato saw the anguished expression on the leader's face. 'Right, lads, let's go. Before they trap us in here. Move!'

The looters disappeared and there was the sound of crashing furniture as they blundered through the ransacked inn and fled towards the yard. Cato waited to be certain they had gone before lowering the sword. 'I think we're safe now.'

'Safe?' Portia wailed from the far end of the landing. She was standing by the window overlooking the yard, her thin face lit up by the flare of the flames. 'What about my inn?'

Above the crackle of the fire, Cato heard shouts to the rear and the sound of boots below. He tensed again, and then saw the face of Tubero looking up from the bottom of the stairs.

'Sir, are you all right?'

'We are now.' He grinned. 'So my boy came through for us.'

'Aye. I told him to wait at headquarters and leave this to us. But he wouldn't have it. Here he is.'

Lucius came running up the stairs, and Cato knelt and wrapped an arm around his small body and held him tight.

'I did it, Daddy. Just as you ordered.'

He kissed the top of the boy's head, then held him at arm's length. 'You're a brave one and no mistake. As brave as the best of my soldiers.'

Lucius beamed proudly.

'What's going on?' Petronella demanded as she came out of the room where she had been guarding the hole in the floor. Her

198

eyes widened as she caught sight of the boy. 'You little treasure!' she exclaimed.

From further down the landing, Portia backed away from the window as a billow of smoke curled around her. 'If you've finished with all the congratulations, perhaps we can get your men to put that bloody fire out before the whole place goes up in flames . . .'

CHAPTER FOURTEEN

As dawn broke over Londinium, the acrid smell of burning hung in the air. There were several fires still raging, and columns of smoke plumed into the pale sky, adding to the thin brown haze that hung over the town. Cato had snatched some sleep after he and his men had finally managed to put out the blaze at the inn. However, all the storerooms and their contents had been lost, and their blackened remains surrounded the yard. There was also damage to one end of the inn itself.

The five men Tubero had left behind to guard the Dog and Deer were slumped against the wall inside the gate, asleep. Emerging from within, Cato was tempted to bawl them out, but instead jabbed his toe at the nearest auxiliary to wake him.

'On your feet. You keep watch. If there's any sign of trouble, wake the others.'

The soldier scrambled up and saluted wearily. 'Yes, sir.'

'If you fall asleep again, I'll have you on latrines for the next six months,' Cato warned him, before going over to the trough and leaning down to dip his head in the cold water. It was fortunate that Portia had installed a pipe that fed off one of the streams that ran through Londinium. The water, used for horses and to flush out the inn's toilet and other spoil, had saved most of the building. Cato turned his face from side to side to refresh himself before standing up with a shake of his head. His skin was streaked with grime and his clothes still stank of smoke, and he would have liked nothing better than to spend the morning at one of the bathhouses to cleanse himself and get a massage for his stiff limbs. But there was no time for that. The town had experienced the worst night of lawlessness and chaos since Decianus had lost control of the streets, and Cato would be needed at headquarters.

The thought of that drew him on to a consideration of the wider situation. Anticipation of the arrival of Boudica and her host would only worsen the disorder as looters sought to make off with as much as they could carry before the town fell to the rebels. Clearly it was not safe to let the women and Lucius remain at the inn while he made arrangements to evacuate them. There were still many ships moored in the river. Finding berths should not be difficult, even if he had to pay a premium. As the situation became more desperate, it would be more difficult to escape, and he resolved to speak to one of the ships' captains as soon as possible. First, though, he must report to the governor.

He adjusted his scale armour and sword belt before reaching down for his padded skullcap and helmet.

'When will you be back?'

He turned and saw Claudia emerging from the scorched rear door of the inn, barefoot. Her eyes looked puffy from lack of sleep and she regarded him with an anxious expression. As she approached, she glanced down and grimaced at the patch of dried blood where Denubius had been killed. His body had been scorched by the flames and Cato had ordered his men to take it inside and place it in one of the prostitutes' cubicles. Portia could make arrangements for the burial, if there was time for that.

The old lady was in a poor state. She had watched in horror as the soldiers had fought the blaze, and then slumped down when it was over, shrunken and defeated. The smoke had got to her lungs, causing her to cough and gasp for air, and Petronella had helped her back to her room and sat with her for the rest of the night.

Claudia wrapped her arms around Cato and drew him close as he replied.

'Hard to say. Depends on what plans Suetonius has been making.'

'Plans?'

'Unless the Second Legion arrives very soon, there's little chance of us being able to hold Londinium. In the meantime, he has to keep order here while he decides whether to evacuate. I need to get you and the others out of the town until the rebellion is over.'

She looked up at him, her hazel eyes widening beneath the fringe of dark hair she had dyed to help conceal her identity. 'You're sending us away?'

'I have to, my love. You can't stay here, and it's too dangerous and difficult for you to march with the column if Suetonius abandons Londinium. There will be a battle as soon as he has gathered sufficient forces to face Boudica, and there's no guarantee that our side will win.'

'Where will you send us?'

'If we are defeated, there will be no place safe for Romans anywhere in Britannia. You must go to Gaul until it's over.'

'Gaul?'

'It's not that far. Two days' sail, three at the most. I'll send for you the moment the rebellion has been put down.'

'And if it isn't?'

He lifted her chin tenderly. 'Then I want you to take Lucius and the others back to Italia. There's a small villa outside Pompeii that came with my father-in-law's estate. It's a quiet spot, far enough from the towns and coastal resorts where you might encounter anyone who recognises you from your time at the imperial palace. The rent from the house in Rome and my savings

202

will be sufficient for you to live comfortably. All I ask is that you raise Lucius as if he was your own son, and look after Petronella and Portia.'

'You've thought it all through, it seems,' she said sadly.

'I've tried to.' He smiled affectionately. 'One less thing to worry about while I do my duty.'

'What if I don't want to go to Gaul?'

Cato sighed inwardly. He had anticipated this might be her response. 'I'll go to face the enemy with an easier mind if I know that you and the others are safe. You must do this for me. I have to know that you and Lucius are not in danger, whatever happens.'

'Have you spoken to Petronella or Portia about this?'

'Not yet. I'll do it later.'

'What if they say they won't go?'

'Then I'll tell them it's what Macro would have wanted, for the same reasons I'm giving you. There's even less reason for them to remain here now that he's gone.'

'Do you think there's any chance at all that he's still alive?'

Cato thought a moment. 'I wish he was, with all my heart . . .'

'But?'

'But I cannot see how he can have survived the fall of Camulodunum. He would never have abandoned his post. I fear he can only have met the same fate as the rest of the defenders. He may have bought us a few days. The best way to honour his sacrifice is to use that time wisely and get those he loved to safety.'

'I understand. I'll speak to them while you are gone.'

He kissed her. 'Thank you. Now I must go.'

He put on his skullcap and helmet and fastened the straps before striding towards the auxiliary on watch by the gate. 'Lock it behind me,' he ordered. 'Then make sure you stay awake until I return or you are relieved. Understand?'

'Yes, sir.'

He lifted the bar and eased the gate open, glancing out into the street. All seemed quiet in the cool blue light and shadows of the coming dawn. In normal times there would have been people going to their places of work and traders with their handcarts making their way to the forum to set up their stands. Three mangy-looking dogs were lapping at a pool of blood a few feet from the body of a man lying beside the wall of the inn. His head was a misshapen mass of blood, bones and brain, and Cato realised he must be one of the looters from the previous night, most likely the man he had struck down attempting to climb up through the hole in the upstairs room.

He closed the gate behind him and heard the soft grate of the locking bar being replaced by the auxiliary. Looking from side to side, he made his way the short distance to the crossroads giving out onto the town's main street. He gave the dogs a wide berth, and they paused to watch him warily until he was a safe distance further on before they resumed their gruesome meal.

When he had arrived the day before, the damage to the town had seemed bad enough, but after the night's violence and looting, Londinium looked as if it had been sacked by a rampaging horde of barbarians. There was hardly a house or business where the doors had not been beaten in. He passed several that were burned-out ruins and two more that were still alight. A family and their neighbours were struggling to contain the fire by forming a bucket chain to a nearby well. A sobbing woman and two infants sat opposite the second burning building, a pitiful pile of personal effects beside them.

Cato was tempted to pause and tell those fighting the fires that their efforts were futile. There was little of the buildings that could be saved, and what was left was almost certainly going to be destroyed when the rebels reached Londinium. It would be better for them to salvage what they could and flee. They would realise that soon enough. For now, though, they clung desperately to the life they had built for themselves in the new province, determined to protect it until the last moment. It was irrational, but understandable.

He continued down the street towards the looming mass of the provincial headquarters, passing small clusters of civilians carrying their belongings and leading children and heavily loaded mules towards the western and northern gates of the town. As he reached a minor intersection, he glanced down a narrow street and saw a group of twenty or more burly men making their way from the wharf district, bales of bright material under their arms. They were drinking from small jars, the contents sloshing over their faces as they exchanged cheerful jests. They paused as they caught sight of Cato in his officer's uniform, then, seeing that he was alone, continued on their way.

He increased his pace, hand resting on the pommel of his short sword. A short distance from the headquarters gate, he encountered one of Tubero's patrols. Two of the men were wounded and being carried by their comrades. The optio in charge saluted as his superior approached.

Cato indicated the injured men. 'What's the story, Optio?'

'Run-in with a street gang down on the wharfs in the middle of the night, sir. They had us badly outnumbered, so we retreated into a warehouse and held out there until first light.'

'I see. Get yourself some food and rest once you've taken those lads to the surgeon.'

'Yes, sir.'

Cato strode on. If the patrol's experience was anything to go by, the auxiliaries who had been sent out to restore order had failed in their task. There was no longer any semblance of control over Londinium's streets.

A strong guard, two sections of Suetonius's personal bodyguard, was posted at the gate and parted to let him through. Outside the main building a line of carts was being loaded with official records and the more portable of the other contents. Clerks were being helped by men from the column that had ridden down from Mona, while others prepared the morning meal by campfires lit around the perimeter of the courtyard.

Suetonius was in his office with his tribunes. Cato noted the haggard look on his face and guessed that he had not slept through the night and must be as bone-weary as he himself felt, with the additional burden of many more years of service. The governor frowned as he looked up at him.

'Seems your men were able to do little to keep order.'

'I'm sure they did their best, sir.' Cato hesitated before he continued. 'There are just too few men for the job.'

'Then we'll have to accept that Londinium is a lost cause as far as the rule of law goes. At least until after the rebellion is over.' Suetonius sighed heavily. 'Whether I give up the town to Boudica is the next question. I cannot hope to fight enemies from without as well as within.'

'There's always the rest of the army marching to join us, sir,' Tribune Agricola ventured. 'If we and the Second Legion can hold the headquarters compound until then, the balance may shift in our favour.'

'Centurion Macro and his veterans didn't manage to hold Camulodunum, despite its natural defences,' Suetonius pointed out.

'He had far fewer men, sir. We might not be able to hold the town, but we could make a stand here. Use what time we have to fortify the walls and fetch sufficient supplies of food from the warehouses. Once the Second arrives, we'll have over six thousand men to defend a relatively short perimeter.'

Suetonius ran a hand through his thinning hair and closed his eyes for a moment as he considered the idea. When he opened them again, he looked directly at Cato. 'What is your opinion,

Prefect? You're the only man here with almost as much experience as myself.'

Cato thought carefully. It was possible that the question might be taken at face value, but he sensed that he was being pressed to pick a side, and that meant Suetonius had doubts about the idea of trying to turn the headquarters compound into a fortress strong enough to defy the rebels. Yet there was some merit in the tribune's argument and Cato made a mental note that Agricola might be a young officer with a future, should he choose to dedicate himself to the military rather than the political career path that was open to men of his background.

'I believe we could hold the compound with six thousand men, sir. There are places where the outer ditch has been filled in, but we can dig that out easily enough, and there are plenty of spare arrows, slingshot and javelins in the stores. We've seen how effective they are against the tribesmen in the past. I'm confident we could hold out until the rest of the army reaches Londinium and we can take the fight on more even terms. There are other reasons why it might be wise to hold our ground here, sir.'

Suetonius arched a brow. 'And what might they be?'

'The ranks of the rebels are swelling with every victory they achieve. If we let them walk into Londinium unopposed, they'll have taken the most important Roman settlement in the province. You can imagine the effect that will have on those tribes still wavering over whether or not to throw their lot in with Boudica. But if we can stop her here, even if the rebels destroy the rest of the town, and force her to abandon the attack, the setback might well put off others considering joining her cause. It might also undermine the morale of those who are already fighting under her banner. You know how fickle irregular forces can be, sir.'

'That's true,' Suetonius mused.

'There's one other thing that occurs to me,' Cato continued. 'Go on, Prefect.'

'I wonder how it would look to those back in Rome if we were to give up Londinium without a fight. You know how it is, sir. There are plenty of armchair generals sitting on the cushioned benches of the Senate who will pass judgement on those of us fighting the rebels in the farthest-flung province of the Empire. They won't have any understanding of the conditions we face in this situation, yet they'll bend the ear of the emperor and suggest that we lacked the moral fibre to hold our ground. Careers and reputations are on the line as well as the fate of the province.'

There was an awkward pause as those in the room weighed his words. Cato had chosen to refer to them all rather than just the governor, yet it was clear where the burden of responsibility and blame lay. That was the price of high command.

Suetonius cleared his throat. 'That was a rather fuller and more frank appraisal of the situation than I was looking for, Prefect Cato. Nevertheless, you speak true and I respect that in my subordinates. Very well, we shall prepare our defences here at the headquarters compound while we wait for the Second to reach Londinium. I'll give the orders to begin the work as soon as this morning's briefing is over.'

Cato saw the look of satisfaction that flitted across Agricola's face before the tribune forced himself to hide his pride that his suggestion had been vindicated. Cato himself was rather more sanguine about the outcome. His words might have swayed the governor into taking a path that would get them all killed if the defence of the compound failed. With the information to hand, it seemed like the best choice, but as past experience demonstrated, even the best of plans was at the mercy of the slightest shift in the forces at play.

'There's one other pressing matter,' Suetonius continued. 'We don't have any intelligence on the precise location of the enemy. We don't know how much time we have before they attack.

Frankly, I'm surprised they aren't already here. I need to know how close they are and what their strength is. Prefect Cato, I want you to take your cohort out to the east of the town and scout the approaches. You are to avoid contact with the enemy as far as possible; I cannot afford to lose any more men. So no glory-hunting. You are just to observe them. Is that clear?'

Cato bridled at the implication that he was motivated by glory. He was experienced enough to know that the 'thrusters', as the men referred to such commanding officers, usually paved the road to success with the bodies of those who served under them. Glory was a bauble used by aristocrats to impress their friends and to dangle before the mob. He had long since eschewed the notion and instead dedicated himself to his duty and protecting the backs of his comrades. Perhaps it was because he lacked a family tradition, he mused. He swallowed his irritation and nodded his agreement.

'Very well,' Suetonius went on. 'Have your men ready to march as soon as possible. You are to report back to me once you have sighted the main column of the rebels. Don't tangle with their scouts or vanguard.'

'Yes, sir.'

'Then get going, Prefect.'

Cato found Tubero and the other officers enjoying cups of heated wine around one of the cooking fires. He relayed the governor's orders. As the others headed to their men, shouting commands, he held Tubero back. 'There are still five men posted at the inn. Send one of the headquarters clerks over with orders for them to remain there until further notice.'

'Yes, sir.'

'One other thing. Just a moment.'

He trotted across to the administration building, returning with a wax tablet and stylus, and hurriedly composed a message for Claudia explaining his absence and asking her to try and find a ship's captain willing to take her and the others to Gaul.

He replaced the stylus in its groove and snapped the tablet shut. 'Make sure this is handed to the woman called Claudia at the inn.'

'Yes, sir.'

'And tell her I'm sorry, but I have my orders.'

Tubero lingered a moment, but Cato shook his head. 'There's nothing else to say. See to it.'

'Yes, sir.'

As orders were barked across the courtyard, the men of the Eighth Cohort's mounted contingent set aside their morning meals, doused their fires and prepared their mounts. Cato was glad he'd had the foresight to ensure that his men had been issued with extra rations and feed after reaching Londinium. They would be able to sustain themselves for a further two days in the field. He did not anticipate having to spend any longer than that in tracking down the rebel column. The enemy must surely be within thirty miles of the town by now. No more than two days' march. That should give Suetonius enough time to prepare the compound to withstand a siege when the Second Legion arrived, as they surely must any hour now. Lacking siege weapons or any sophisticated understanding of siegecraft, the rebels were at a distinct disadvantage. Their usual tactic of working themselves up into a fervour and hurling themselves forward in a mad charge would prove futile against a ditch and rampart defended by professional soldiers.

Once the men were mounted, Cato led them through the compound gate and out along the street in the direction of the east gate. The sun had risen and more of the town's inhabitants had dared to venture outside their homes. They regarded the column of horsemen with sullen looks, and one man spat in the path of Cato's horse before brandishing his fist.

'Bastards are abandoning us!'

Tubero made to steer his mount towards the man, but Cato gestured to him to hold his position and ride on. What good would it do to upbraid the fellow or explain their purpose?

Once they had passed through the dilapidated gatehouse that now served as more of a toll gate than any credible defence, Cato increased the pace to a trot, keen to put some distance between himself and the acrid tang of burning overlaying the stench of sewage and other urban odours. The sky was clear and promised a fine day ahead. The sun shone on the vibrant green foliage and golden fields of cereal crops and pastureland. Many of the farms along the road to Camulodunum appeared to have been abandoned, but some people still worked their smallholdings, heedless of the looming danger. For a moment Cato's imagination overlaid the peaceful rural idyll with columns of smoke above the torched villas and farms of Roman settlers, whose bodies lay strewn across the land in the wake of the vengeful rebel horde. Once more he felt a surge of bitter rage directed at Decianus, who had done so much to provoke the crisis. How much blood was on that man's hands? How much more would there be? At some point there must be a reckoning. But what punishment could possibly measure up to the tidal wave of death and destruction that Decianus had unleashed across the province?

Forcing himself to set aside such speculations, he focused his thoughts on the task before him.

'Tubero!'

'Sir?'

'I want the column closed up. And tell the men to have their eyes open and their wits about them. The enemy is at hand.'

CHAPTER FIFTEEN

Cato estimated they had covered fifteen miles by noon and gave the order to halt at one of the inns that lined the road to Camulodunum. The owner had already abandoned the premises but through some quirk of habit had left everything in neat order, as if he had been hoping to return once the rebellion was over and resume business where he had left off. Cheap samianware cups and bowls lined the shelves behind the counter and the tables and benches were neatly aligned inside and underneath the sheltered area facing the road. A stunted grape vine struggled to thrive amid the wooden lattices that provided shade for customers. Six large wine amphorae and stocks of flour, barley, cheese and cured meats were in the pantry. The only sign that the inhabitants had left in a hurry was the empty strongbox in the corner of the pantry where the innkeeper had kept his takings, and the open clothes chest and unmade bed in the two rooms at the rear overlooking the empty stables.

Tearing a shred of meat from a strip of dried beef, Cato emerged from the entrance and spoke quietly to Tubero. 'The place is nicely stocked. Have a section fetch the food out and distribute it to the column. There's wine too. Make sure the optio doesn't let his men get at it. They're not to pocket any personal effects either.'

'Better our lads have them than let the enemy loot the place.'

'Better the enemy drink themselves insensible and fight over the loot than our lads, Centurion. In any case, we need clear heads if we are to locate the rebels and get away without any trouble. If some fool gets drunk and falls from his saddle, we'll leave him where he lies and let him take his chances with Boudica's followers. Make sure everyone understands that. I'll not risk any lives to cover up for the foolishness of an individual.'

'Yes, sir.' Tubero hesitated a moment. 'Strange that we haven't seen any of them yet, I'm thinking.'

'Indeed.' Cato glanced to the east, where the road climbed a low ridge before disappearing. He had expected to come across at least some small bands of marauders in advance of the rebel column, keen to make the most of easy pickings before the horde descended on the farms and villas in their path. He had spotted some distant columns of smoke across the landscape to the east, but nothing close enough to cause concern. 'Where are their scouts?'

Tubero's gaze shifted to the fringes of a forest less than a mile to the north of the road. 'I'd hate to think we were being lured into a trap, sir.'

'So would I.' Cato made a dismissive gesture. 'See to the food, Centurion.'

As Tubero made off, Cato bit into the tough strip of meat and tore off another chunk as he scanned their surroundings. There was no sign of anyone else in the surrounding landscape. Not even in the cluster of native huts beside a small villa to the south of the road. It might be a trap, he conceded. The enemy could be staring back at him from the forest, waiting until the small mounted column had moved on before cutting off their line of retreat. It was time to divide the cohort into squadrons to spread out across the line of march and forestall the risk of ambush. As soon as the men and horses had rested and were ready to remount and continue the advance.

He swallowed the softened meat and tossed the rest of the strip aside. It was too tough to eat and had made his jaw ache. Turning to the inn, he glanced towards the ridge and paused mid stride. Was it his tired imagination, or was there a faint haze smearing the horizon? He shaded his eyes and stared a moment longer before striding back towards his mount.

'First Squadron! On me!'

The men scrambled back into the saddle as the rest of the cohort looked round to see what was happening. As soon as the last of the riders was mounted, Cato waved his arm forward and led the way to the ridge at a steady canter, glancing to left and right, searching for any sign of the enemy. He was wary of what might be beyond the rising ground and made ready to order a swift about-turn and gallop back to their comrades at the inn.

As they reached the crest, the rolling countryside beyond was revealed. It was as if some vast monster was crawling across the landscape with tendrils reaching towards the farmsteads and small settlements it was passing through. A dark mass of humanity, perhaps half a mile across and several miles in length. The dust haze kicked up by the feet, hooves and wheels of the host shrouded the rear of the rebel column and made it difficult to estimate its size. At least fifty thousand of the rebels were visible, Cato guessed, and he felt his stomach clench in despair at the scale of the force bearing down on Londinium. Not all of those he could see were combatants, but even allowing for half or a third of their number, it was clear that the compound could not be held.

'Fuck me . . .' one of the auxiliaries at his side muttered, as they filed off the road and extended either side of Cato. 'Looks like every one of the bastards that lives on the island is out for our blood.'

'We're dead men,' said another.

'Shut your mouths!' Cato snapped. 'Silence in the ranks!'

He turned his attention to the enemy. The head of the column was perhaps five miles away, led by a vanguard of armed men whose weapons and armour glinted in the sunlight. Parties of horsemen were criss-crossing the countryside in front of them, while small bands of men on foot were foraging for food and loot in the homes and settlements abandoned in the path of Boudica's host. Cato could not help a nagging feeling that something was odd about the manner of the rebels' advance. Then it struck him. The horsemen were not riding in the direction of Londinium as he would have expected if they had been scouting any distance ahead of the column. Instead they seemed to be scouring the landscape, as if they were searching for something.

A thrumming of hooves from behind caused him to turn, and he saw Tubero galloping up the slope to join them, reining in abruptly in a puff of dust as he caught sight of the rebels.

'Sweet Jupiter's balls . . .'

'Why are you forward?' Cato demanded.

'There's movement to the north, sir.'

He pointed, and Cato saw that there was another small plume of dust beyond the forest he had scrutinised earlier. For it to have appeared in the time it had taken him to reach the ridge indicated that the second force was moving at a swift pace.

'Looks like cavalry.'

'Then it is a trap, sir. We'd better get out of here.'

'Stay where you are!' Cato glared at him. 'We are not in immediate danger, and I'm damned if I will be rushed into a headlong retreat like some green tribune on his first patrol into enemy territory just because one of his officers loses his head.'

He regretted his outburst immediately. In all the time he had served with Tubero he had never let his composure slip to such a degree. It was exhaustion talking, he realised, but that was no excuse to berate the centurion in such a caustic manner. He took a deep breath and forced himself to continue more calmly.

'Go back to the column, Centurion. Have the men prepared to discard their feed nets if the need arises. We may have a hard ride ahead of us on the return to Londinium.'

They exchanged a salute, and Tubero galloped back down the road, leaving Cato to return to his assessment of the horsemen riding in front of the rebel column, no more than two miles away. Whatever or whoever they were searching for, they were making a determined job of it. Every copse and ditch was being inspected, while screens of riders picked their way through fields of crops, scanning the ground before them.

'Sir!'

One of the auxiliaries thrust his arm out towards a cluster of huts surrounded by a low stockade just under a mile from their position. A figure was standing in the doorway of the hut nearest the ridge, waving his arms as if trying to attract the attention of Cato and his men.

'Looks like someone's left it too late to get away,' a voice muttered. 'Those riders'll be taking his head the moment they reach him.'

Cato saw a group of ten men on ponies trotting towards the farmstead. It was likely to be as the auxiliary had said: the man, and any others hiding in the huts, was as good as dead already, unless he pledged loyalty to the rebellion. Even then Cato doubted he would be spared. This was Catuvellaunian territory, and the rebels of the Iceni and Trinovantes bore a grudge against their old oppressors from the years before the Roman invasion. He pitied anyone still in the farmstead and had no desire to witness their end. He was turning his mount about when one of his men gave an amused snort.

'He's a game one. Look at that!'

Cato glanced over his shoulder and saw that the man had emerged from the hut. A sword glinted as he scurried in the direction of the ridge where the Romans were positioned and ducked into cover behind an empty cattle pen. Then he turned to the auxiliaries on the crest and waved his hand frantically, beckoning to them. Cato could see no sign of any other inhabitants of the farmstead and surmised that the man was alone. Perhaps he was a looter who had taken advantage of the abandoned property and had tarried too long. The rebel horsemen had already reached the stockade and would be sure to find him when they began their search. Even though he had a sword, he would have little chance against them.

He was about to give the order to his men to rejoin the column when some sixth sense stayed his hand. There was something about the man that caused a flicker of hope deep in his heart. Something about his physique and the way he carried himself. A quick glance over the rebel search parties showed that none was making a move towards Cato and his men. They had been spotted, since two of the groups of riders had stopped and were looking in their direction as a messenger raced back in the direction of the main column. To the north, the other enemy formation was still some miles off. There was plenty of time.

Down in the farmstead, the rebels had dismounted and were going from hut to hut, then three of them moved in the direction of the cattle pen. The fugitive risked a quick glance and hurriedly sheathed his sword. An instant later, he bolted towards the stockade. The rebels broke into a run as they chased after him. With admirable strength and agility, their prey heaved himself up over the timbers and began to sprint across the open ground towards the ridge. Behind him, two of the rebels clambered over the stockade and set off in pursuit, while the third man ran back to the huts, waving his arms. A moment later, his comrades were running from the huts and mounting up.

As Cato weighed up the relative distances between the fleeing man, the two pursuers on foot, the eight riders galloping out of the gate of the farmstead and the auxiliaries on the crest of the ridge, it was clear that the fugitive was doomed. He would not cover half the distance before he was ridden down and killed. Even if he could reach the Romans' position, what then? Could Cato allow one of his men to be slowed by the burden of a second rider on his mount?

'Sir?' one of the auxiliaries prompted, gesturing down the slope. 'What are we going to do?'

'Quiet!' Cato replied harshly. He was staring at the figure sprinting towards them, and as the distance closed and he began to make out his features, a cold shiver flowed up his spine and clenched the back of his neck in an icy grip. 'I don't bloody believe it . . . It can't be!'

'Sir?'

And yet in his heart he knew who it was as surely as his mind told him it could not be. Grasping his reins, he urged his horse down the slope. 'Follow me!'

Digging his heels in, he drew his sword and held it out to the side where it would not endanger himself or his mount as he charged towards Macro and his pursuers. He did not look back, but heard the drumming of hooves as the auxiliaries swept downhill behind him. With the incline favouring the men of the Eighth Cohort, they were moving faster than the rebel horsemen, but it was impossible to calculate who would reach their target first.

Macro stumbled, ran on a few steps with his arms swinging frantically as he tried to retain his balance, then tumbled forward into the tussocks that covered the slope, disappearing from view.

Cato felt his heart lurch at the sight, and he roared at his horse in frustration. 'Come on, you brute!'

Rising to his feet, Macro glanced back and ran on, drawing his sword again. A hundred paces behind him, the rebel horsemen began to lower their spear tips as they bunched up, eager to be the one to make the killing thrust. Cato realised in horror that they were going to reach the centurion first. He was close enough to see the anguished expression on his friend's face as he gritted his teeth and put all his strength into running for his life.

The closest of his pursuers hunched forward and drew back his spear arm. At the last moment, Macro hurled himself to the ground and the spear passed over his head. Even as he fell, he hacked at the legs of the pony as it swept by, and with a toss of its maned head the beast staggered to the side and went down, rolling on top of its rider. Macro rose into a crouch and stabbed his assailant in the throat before releasing his grip on the sword. Snatching up the spear that had fallen into the grass, he turned to confront the next two pursuers, the first of whom veered aside. The second was made of sterner stuff and came on, weapon poised to thrust at the centurion. The blade caught Macro in the folds over the left shoulder of his coarse tunic and he spun slightly under the impact. His own spear hit the rider in the midriff, and he was torn from the saddle and crashed to the ground, wrenching the shaft from Macro's grasp.

Cato raced past his friend, his gaze fixed on the rest of the rebel party. They had slowed, having witnessed the fate of their companions. But it was too late to avoid the Roman horsemen. Cato plunged into them, parrying a panicked thrust before the mounts clashed flank to flank and the smaller native pony reeled back under the impact, hooves scrabbling to recover balance. Swivelling in the saddle, he struck out to the other side and landed a blow on a rebel's raised shield, and then he had passed through the group and tugged on the reins to turn his horse back towards the skirmish.

His men had charged home at speed and scattered the rebels, and now an unequal battle was being fought on the slope around Macro, who had recovered his sword and kept the point raised as he crouched and turned amid the flurry of weapons and horseflesh. Despite being outnumbered three to one, the rebels fought on with determination, and when the chance arose, they attempted to close on Macro and strike him down. Cato blocked the first thrust and battered the spear aside with the flat of his sword, then remained in position to cover his friend from further attacks. In short order, the survivors were driven away from the ring of auxiliaries surrounding their commander and the erstwhile fugitive, and they turned and rode off, shouting curses over their shoulders.

Cato watched them for a moment to be certain they had abandoned the fight, then sheathed his sword and swung himself down from the saddle. Macro lowered his blade and straightened up, chest heaving from the exertion of his escape. Sweat gleamed on his brow and a thick growth of stubble fringed his grime-streaked cheeks. For a few heartbeats they regarded each other before Cato could not help an astonished laugh.

'I thought you were dead.' He shook his head in wonder.

'Nearly was . . . Would have been if you hadn't . . . ridden down those bastards. What kept you? I was waving . . . my arms like a fucking . . . windmill to get your attention.'

'How could I be expected to know it was you? I was hardly going to risk my men to rescue some vagrant looter.'

'Sir!' one of the auxiliaries interrupted. 'We're going to have company very soon if we stay here.'

Cato looked down the slope and saw that several parties of rebel horsemen had turned in their direction, the nearest no more than half a mile away. He glanced at Macro and saw a glistening dark patch on his left shoulder. 'You're wounded. Can you handle a mount?'

Macro flexed his arm and grimaced. 'I'll manage.'

Cato rounded on his men. 'Any casualties?'

There was no reply, thankfully, and he pointed to the pony of the man Macro had impaled and unseated. 'Take that one.'

He helped his friend into the saddle, then remounted his own horse and took up the reins. More of the enemy patrols had turned towards them, and a glance was enough for Cato to estimate that at least five hundred riders were now in pursuit of Macro and the squadron of auxiliaries.

'Let's go!'

With Macro riding at his side, left arm hanging limply, Cato led the way up to the crest and down the far side towards the inn. Tubero and his men were already mounted, facing in the direction of Londinium.

'Thank the gods you didn't come for me with just these lads,' said Macro, clearly grateful for the increased security of numbers.

'We didn't come for you at all, brother. We were just sent to report on the position of the enemy.'

'And now you know, so let's get the fuck away from them.'

There was a certain dread in Macro's tone that told of the horror of recent days, and Cato shot him an anxious glance before taking the chance to check on the position of the enemy column beyond the forest. The haze had moved to the west, ahead of the inn. They were either attempting to cut Cato's cohort off, or they had other orders.

Cato led the squadron past the rear of the mounted column and took up position at the head of the cohort, where Tubero joined him, regarding Macro with curiosity.

'Tubero, let me introduce you to Centurion Macro.'

They exchanged a curt nod before Tubero's eyes widened in surprise. '*The* Centurion Macro?'

Macro chuckled. 'Seems I have a certain reputation that precedes me.'

'We thought you were dead. We were certain of it after we heard about Camulodunum,' Cato explained.

Macro's expression became concerned. 'What about Petronella and the others? Are they safe?'

'They reached Londinium safely. We can talk more later. Now we have to move.'

Cato gave the order for his men to cut loose their feed bags and advance at the canter. As the column moved forward down the road, the first of the enemy patrols crested the ridge behind them. They reined in at the sight of the modest Roman force below, and waited for more of their men to arrive before continuing the pursuit. By then the auxiliaries had won nearly two miles' head start. Cato was confident that his men had the better mounts and would manage to remain ahead of the enemy long enough to reach the relative safety of Londinium. Then he snorted with derision at the notion. The town was far from being safe in any sense now that he had seen the size of the host bearing down on it. Even with the Second Legion adding its strength to the soldiers already preparing to defend the compound. Londinium would have to be given up to the rebel host. That meant it would be sacked and razed to the ground, and any inhabitants foolish enough to remain would be massacred.

They kept up a steady pace, increasing it when the enemy drew closer and slowing to a trot when they fell a safe distance behind. After ten miles, late in the afternoon, the rebels gave up the pursuit, and when they were no longer in sight, Cato gave the order for the column to walk their tired mounts. A milestone indicated that they were five miles from Londinium, and he estimated that they would reach the town by sunset.

'We should be safe now,' he announced, and saw Macro's shoulders ease in relief. 'How's the wound?'

The torn material over the centurion's shoulder was drenched with blood, and his features looked pale beneath the grime.

'I'll live,' Macro answered wearily as he peeled back the cloth and saw that it was only a shallow flesh wound. He grinned. 'The gods must smile on me.'

'Smile? Seems to me that you're their darling. How in Hades did you escape from Camulodunum before it fell?'

The grin abruptly gave way to a haunted look. 'I didn't escape.'

As they rode on, Macro related the details to his friend. He spoke of the assault on the colony's defences and the fine manner in which the veterans and the volunteers who had remained to defend their homes had repulsed the early attacks. His account became more halting as he described the final stand amid the building site where a temple to Claudius was under construction.

'I lost the boy, Parvus.' He swallowed as he recalled the inferno that had caused the temple's partly completed roof to collapse on the injured, where Parvus and Cato's dog, Cassius, had been sheltering. 'Poor little sod didn't stand a chance.' He was silent for a moment as he looked down.

'I'm so sorry,' Cato said. 'I know he was like a son to you.'

'Yes . . . he was. I'll have to tell Petronella. She felt the same way.'

'I know.'

'Parvus wasn't the only close one to be lost.' Macro looked up. 'There was Apollonius, too.'

'Apollonius?' Cato was surprised, if only because the Greek spy was singularly adept with weapons and had an unparalleled survival instinct. 'He stayed with you to the end?'

'His end, yes. I tell you, Cato, he was one of the bravest men I've ever met. He died saving me. I did him a great wrong, you know. I always treated him with suspicion and unkindness over the few years we served together. In our last days at Camulodunum, I finally got to know him well enough to call him a friend. I wish that had happened long before.'

'He wasn't an easy man to understand, Macro. Don't blame yourself for that.'

'Maybe, but I grieve for him nonetheless. Him and all the others who fell at the colony.'

Cato felt a shadow come between them as he braced himself to address the unasked question that required an answer before Macro reported to the governor.

'How did you survive, brother?'

Macro glanced at him. 'There have been moments when I wish I hadn't. Any man who comes back from the dead when all his comrades have fallen is bound to be viewed with suspicion. There will always be some who question what I say happened. Even if it happened exactly as I say it did.'

'I will not question it,' Cato replied. 'You know that.'

'I know.'

'So tell me, brother.'

Macro collected his thoughts and told his best friend of the fate of those who had been taken alive when the temple compound at Camulodunum had fallen. He spared no detail of the torture and executions, the duel with Boudica's champion, his escape from the rebel camp and the long hours spent in hiding as the enemy scoured the countryside looking for the Roman prisoner who had been promised to the gods of the Britons in sacrifice. After his stolen horse had stumbled on a rabbit warren and become lame, he had been forced to continue on foot, hiding in daylight hours and proceeding cautiously in the direction of Londinium under cover of darkness. At some point he had become feverish and was forced to hide in a forest close to the abandoned farmstead. On recovery, he had emerged and sought what food he could find, and then slept. He had woken to discover the enemy patrols sweeping the landscape around him, and that was when he had spied the auxiliaries on the ridge and decided to attract their attention.

'By Jupiter, Best and Greatest, you were my last hope. If you and your lads had ridden away, I was determined to turn on the rebels and go down fighting. I wasn't going to be burned as a sacrifice. Not that . . .' he concluded with a shudder.

Cato had listened to the account with a mixture of horror at the trials his friend had endured and also unbridled admiration at his fortitude and good luck. Macro was Fortuna's favourite.

'There's one other thing I have to tell you, brother,' the centurion added in an undertone as he gestured meaningfully at the men riding behind them. 'But only you.'

Cato trotted forward a short distance before he slowed down again, and Macro fell in alongside him a moment later.

'Well?'

Macro moistened his lips as he gathered the will to speak. 'The rebellion, it's my fault that it began.'

Cato looked at him directly. 'Your fault? How is that possible?'

Macro's expression was pained. 'You recall that Decianus was sent to collect the debt owed by the Icenians? And that I was to command his escort?'

'Yes.'

'Decianus went well beyond his orders. When Boudica failed to come up with the coin, he had her taken hostage, along with her daughters. He also confiscated all the portable valuables our men could find in the Icenian capital before marching back to Londinium.'

Cato shook his head. 'The fool. He couldn't have offended the tribe more effectively if that was his aim.'

'That's not the worst of it,' Macro continued. 'One of Decianus's men fell behind the column and I took some lads back to look for him, but he had already been killed. While I was away, Decianus had Boudica flogged, and then let his men rape her daughters in front of her . . .'

Cato clenched his eyes shut for an instant and swore a silent vow to put an end to Decianus, slowly and painfully. No man who had caused so much bloodshed deserved a merciful death. He turned to Macro with a frown.

'How could that be your fault? You were away from the column when it happened, you say?'

'Aye, and when I got back and heard what Decianus had done, I went to his tent intending to throttle the bastard. I wish I had done, instead . . .'

'Instead?' Cato prompted. 'Instead of what?'

Macro looked at him with an anguished expression. 'I helped them to escape, lad. Boudica and her daughters. We know her, you and I. We fought at her side. I count that an honour, as you do. How could I let her be treated like that and dragged to Londinium in chains? Besides, I wanted her to know that Decianus is not Rome. We are better than that. So I cut them free and sent them back to their people. I told Decianus that they must have found a small blade in the cart they were tied to and used that to cut their bonds . . .' He paused. 'Do you understand now?'

Cato saw it all in an instant – Boudica returning to her people with wounds on her back, her daughters distraught from their ordeal. After the indignities imposed on them by Decianus and the governor, this outrage would have been the final act of oppression that tipped the tribe into open rebellion. Decianus could not have acted in a more provocative manner, and maybe that was his true purpose. Cato knew that there were many in Rome who wanted Nero to withdraw the legions from Britannia. What better way to achieve that than cause this terrible rebellion that had already cost the lives of the veterans at Camulodunum and was now about to deliver a similar fate to Londinium? Even if that was so, the plotters had underestimated the true danger of their scheme.

While the responsibility for the abuse of Boudica and her daughters lay at the feet of Decianus alone, Cato saw clearly the source of Macro's torment. If he had not effected the queen's escape, all those at Camulodunum might still be alive. As well as the thousands of legionaries from the Ninth Legion who had been ambushed and annihilated. It was a horrific moral burden for any man to bear. But would he himself have acted any differently had he been in Macro's place? He could not imagine it. Macro's sin, grave though the consequences were, was surely less damning than the atrocity perpetrated by Decianus that was the immediate cause of Macro's action and all the suffering that had flowed from it.

'You couldn't have known what would happen,' he said at length.

'I should have known. There was a risk that the outcome would be as it is. I acted in the moment. It seemed the right thing to do . . . In my place, you would have thought it through, lad. And you know it.'

Cato shook his head. 'Who can say, Macro? I was not there.'

His friend shrugged resignedly, then his brow creased up. 'Something else I discovered. Later, when I was a prisoner of the rebels. Boudica sent for me. The night before the execution of the other prisoners. There was something she needed me to know before I died. A secret that would die with me. She told me that Prasutagus was not the father of Bardea, her elder daughter. I am her real father.'

Cato instinctively reached out his hand and rested it on Macro's unwounded shoulder. 'I was wrong about the gods. I thought they looked out for you. Now I see that you are their plaything to torment again and again in a bid to break you. But you have not broken. You have survived. You have defied their best efforts to crush you and your spirit. That you live is proof of your strength, and that is what Rome needs now, in her darkest hour. Be strong, Macro. Rome needs you. I need you, and Petronella needs you.'

Macro looked at him bleakly, but forced himself to nod. 'Maybe . . .'

'Whatever you may think about the situation, I urge you to keep the part you played in it to yourself. No good will come of saying anything at the moment. Save it for after the rebellion.'

Cato stared down the road in the direction of Londinium. In the late afternoon light he could clearly make out the brown stain in the sky that lingered over the town when there was no breeze. They would surely reach their destination before it was dark. Then there would be something that he and Macro must attend to. A deed that would not change the outcome of the rebellion but would resolve one of its injustices at least.

'Decianus must pay the price for his actions,' he announced.

'Yes. Is he still in Londinium?'

Cato nodded. 'For now. The garrison centurion had him arrested before he could flee to Gaul.'

'Remind me to buy that centurion a drink some day.' Macro smiled thinly.

'Whatever else happens when we return to Londinium, Decianus must pay with his life. This I swear before Jupiter, Best and Greatest. On my life. I will kill him with my own hands,' said Cato.

His friend turned to him, and they exchanged a look of understanding before Macro replied, 'If not you, then me. Either way, the bastard dies.'

CHAPTER SIXTEEN

'Bloody hell, what's happened here?' asked Macro as they entered Londinium's east gate at dusk. He took in the looted buildings, abandoned and stolen possessions scattered in the street and several bodies sprawled amid dry patches of blood. He turned to Cato. 'You've really let the place go since I moved to Camulodunum.'

Cato smiled, gratified that his friend had recovered some of his customary dry humour. 'By the time the rebels arrive, there won't be much left for them to raze to the ground.'

'Has any damage been done to the inn?'

'Some. There was a fire the other night . . . Last night,' Cato corrected himself, shocked at how much had happened in so short a time. 'We put it out before the flames did much damage to the main building, but your mother's taken it hard.'

'Not surprised. She put all her savings into the business. And a good deal of mine too. Now I've lost the farm outside the colony and my home in Camulodunum, and my share of the inn is going to be burned to the ground when the rebels arrive. I've lost everything. Nothing to show for all the years I put into the army.'

'You still have Petronella, and your mother.'

'There's that, I suppose.'

'I have savings in Rome, and property. More than enough to go round,' Cato offered.

Macro nodded. 'Thanks, lad.'

'You'd do the same in my position.'

They made straight for headquarters, where the garrison and the men of Suetonius's mounted column were making preparations to defend the compound, bodies gleaming with sweat as they laboured by the light of torches and braziers set up around the perimeter. All quite pointless now, following the reconnaissance, Cato reflected. He noticed that there was no sign of men from the Second Legion yet and wondered what was delaying them. They should surely have arrived by now.

He dismissed his men and dismounted before turning to Macro.

'The governor will want your report before you can make for the Dog and Deer. I've posted some men there to guard the place, so Petronella and the others are safe for now. If I'm detained here, you'd better let them know that Londinium will have to be abandoned and the best thing is for them to leave Britannia at once. I planned to get them on a ship before I was sent to scout out the rebels. You'll have to do that if I can't get back to the inn.'

'All right, lad. I'll take care of it.'

Cato glanced towards the entrance of the headquarters building and took a breath as he removed his helmet. 'Let's go and break the bad news to Suetonius.'

Cato led the way when they were ushered into the governor's office once Macro's wound had been hurriedly cleaned and dressed. Suetonius was listening to a report from Agricola, and raised his hand to silence the tribune as he looked up.

'Prefect Cato? Back so soon. That can only be bad news.'

'I'm afraid so, sir. The main rebel column is no more than a day's march away. Their cavalry and light troops could reach

230

Londinium by dawn at the latest. I dare say the first of them will arrive in the town during the night.'

'The defences should be completed by first light, sir,' said Agricola. 'We'll be ready for them.'

'No,' Cato cut in. 'We can't remain here, sir. I estimated at least thirty thousand men under arms. There's a separate column working its way round to the North of us. There will be more out foraging, as well as those joining Boudica's host all the time. And I could not make out the end of the column. There could be well over a hundred thousand in all.'

'A hundred thousand?' Suetonius repeated incredulously. 'How can that be possible? There can't be that many in the entire Iceni tribe.'

'It's not just the Iceni, sir,' said Macro, stepping up at Cato's side. 'It's the Trinovantians and many contingents from the other tribes who have grievances against Rome. They're coming from further afield all the time. I've seen them with my own eyes.'

'Who is this vagrant?' Suetonius demanded, then did a double-take before he leaned forward. 'Centurion Macro? How in Hades are you still alive?'

'I was taken prisoner at Camulodunum, sir. Along with a dozen other men. I was the only one who lived to escape. I was saved from the enemy when I encountered Prefect Cato and his men.'

'Really?' Suetonius responded suspiciously. 'I'll have the full story out of you the moment there's time for that. For now, I must know if you can bear out the prefect's estimate of enemy strength.'

'From what I have seen, his report can be counted on, sir.'

'I see.' Suetonius considered what he had been told for a moment. 'If Cato is right, then we're in more danger than I calculated, gentlemen.'

'How many of those are trained warriors, sir?' asked Agricola.

231

'No more than a fraction, I'd wager. The rest are merely levies. Poorly armed and with fragile morale. Hardly a match for the auxiliaries defending the compound, let alone the legionaries marching to swell our ranks.'

Macro gave a dry chuckle. 'Those mere levies, as you put it, made mincemeat of the Ninth Legion. The lads of the Second are almost all fresh recruits. I wouldn't put too much faith in their battle-readiness, Tribune.'

Agricola did not take the rebuke well and tilted his chin haughtily. 'They couldn't perform any worse than the veterans at Camulodunum, I would imagine.'

Macro took a step forward, fists clenched as he growled, 'You dare to question those who fought and died for Rome at the colony?'

'Not all of them, evidently.'

'Say that again outside, you cocky little bastard.'

'Enough!' Suetonius slammed his hand down on the desk and stood, drawing himself up to his full height. 'The arrival of the enemy is imminent. I will not have you squabbling shamefully when every moment counts.'

He glared at the two men in turn, defying them to continue the exchange. Then he took a sharp breath and continued. 'The men of the Second Legion are untried, it is true. The battle for Londinium will be their chance to be blooded. Besides, there are five thousand of them to add to our thousand. The main body of the army is no more than seven days away. When the two forces are joined, we'll be a match for the enemy. We need to hold our nerve and stand firm. I know how tired you all are, but we cannot afford division in our ranks. Every one of us must stick to the purpose. We will meet the enemy here.' He jabbed his finger towards the floor. 'And defeat them.'

There was a sharp rap on the door, and it swung open as a clerk stepped into the room.

'What is it now?' Suetonius said harshly.

'Messenger from the acting commander of the Second, sir.'

'At last.' Some of the tension drained from the governor's expression. 'Send him in.'

The clerk stood aside and beckoned. A nervous-looking tribune, not yet twenty by Cato's reckoning, entered and saluted the governor. He looked to have ridden hard and was spattered with mud, his brown hair matted with perspiration. He took out a sealed leather tube and set it down on the table. It was a reticent gesture, and Cato guessed that the tribune was the bearer of bad news.

The governor hesitated before he picked up the tube, broke the seal and extracted the scroll inside. The others in the room watched in silence as he scanned the lines of the message, his lips pressed together in fury. Then he paused a moment before reading the message aloud.

'"To Suetonius Paulinus, governor of Britannia, I send greetings. In accordance with instructions issued to me, I ordered the Second Legion to march on Londinium with all due dispatch. At some distance from the town, my scouts reported that there were columns of smoke rising from the area, and on further reconnaissance it was apparent that sections of Londinium were on fire. I halted the legion and conferred with my officers, and the consensus was that the rebels had arrived before us and were sacking the town. Therefore I decided that the prudent course of action was not to risk the legion in a futile attempt to drive the enemy out. Mindful of the dire threat posed to the province by Boudica and her host and the consequent need to concentrate our forces against the rebels, I therefore ordered the Second Legion to retreat and await further orders from you."'

Some of the officers stirred uneasily, and Suetonius raised a hand to silence them as he continued.

'The best is yet to come, gentlemen. Our worthy Postumus goes on, "Some three days after reversing our direction, the column was overtaken by a scout sent from Londinium to report on our progress. It was from him that I learned the town was still in Roman hands and the fires were the result of civil disturbance and not enemy action. After conferring with my officers once more, I determined that it was likely to be too late to march back to Londinium in time to play any useful part in its defence. Moreover, the legion had almost exhausted its marching rations and I resolved to retreat to our base and await further orders from you.

"'I have sent three copies of this message. The bearers were instructed to head north to the army at Mona, and to the fortress at Deva, while the last was to return to Londinium in the unlikely event that the town is still in our possession and that you or the procurator are present. I await your orders, sir.

"'Your obedient servant, Poenius Postumus, Camp Prefect, Second Legion, at Deva.'"

Suetonius lowered the scroll and let it drop on the desk as if it was some soiled object of disgust. Cato regarded the other faces in the room and saw the contempt and anger in their expressions over the shameful actions of the camp prefect. A man who had attained that rank must be one of the most experienced men in the army, having worked his way up the seniority ladder of the centurionate. How could it be that Postumus had been so indecisive and exposed himself to the inevitable accusations of cowardice? The contents of the scroll had damned his reputation for ever. When Nero heard about it, the very best he could expect was public disgrace and banishment. More likely he would be paid a visit by the Praetorian Guard and required to fall on his sword. Despite everything, Cato felt a moment's sympathy for a man who had clearly been promoted beyond his ability.

'The fate of Londinium is sealed, gentlemen,' Suetonius announced. 'We must abandon the town before it becomes our grave. Tribune Agricola?'

'Sir?'

'Order the men to stop work on the defences. They are to gather their kit and prepare to leave. We'll fall back on Verulamium. Let's hope we get away before the second rebel column identified by Prefect Cato envelops the town, otherwise we'll have to fight our way clear.'

'What about the civilians, sir?' Agricola asked.

'They'll have to look out for themselves.'

'They won't stand a chance. We should let them know, sir.'

'I can't do anything to help them, Tribune. What do you think will happen if we warn them we're pulling out? They will come out in the streets to beg us to stay, and how will we get clear of the town then? And if they try to come with us, they will only hamper our progress. They're on their own from now on. Understand?'

Agricola nodded.

'Good. Let's get moving, gentlemen.'

As the officers stirred, the tribune sent by Postumus cleared his throat. 'Do you wish me to carry a reply back to Deva, sir?'

'Reply?' Suetonius's lips curled. 'What reply could ever measure up to such calumny? Let Postumus stew in silence. He and his men are too far away to make any difference now. As for you, young man, I need every sword that can be raised against Boudica. You will serve with me until the rebellion is over. It's death or honour for you now. Count yourself fortunate in that. Either way you are spared the shame of Postumus.'

As the officers filed out of the headquarters, Cato took Macro to one side and spoke urgently to him. 'Get back to the others at the inn as fast as you can. Then take them down to the wharf and get them aboard a ship to Gaul. There'll be no time for discussion.

One way or another they leave tonight. It might be best for you to be on the ship with them.'

'What? And miss all the fun? I've got my own reasons for wanting to stay and fight. I have to set things straight, given my part in this.'

'All right. I understand. Get them on the ship and be back here as soon as you can. You don't want to be in Londinium when Boudica and her people turn up.'

'Believe me, I know.'

'The men from the cohort at the inn, take them with you when you make for the wharf. Whatever Suetonius may think, word will get out that the army is leaving. Once that's common knowledge, things will get bad very quickly.'

'I'll manage. Trust me, lad.'

'With my life, and those of my son and Claudia.'

Macro punched him lightly on the chest. 'They'll be safe. You have my word.'

'That's all I needed to know. I'll wait for you here as long as I can.'

Macro nodded and trotted off across the courtyard. Cato watched him go before making for the horse lines of his cohort as the interior of the compound echoed with shouted orders. Then he stopped dead and turned to look back at the building, recalling the pact he and Macro had agreed earlier as he mouthed the name. 'Decianus . . .'

Macro was grateful for the darkness as he hurried along the street, keeping his distance from the gangs of men abroad. Many of them were drunk and some were fighting. There were women too, keen to share the wine that had been looted from inns and warehouses. He regarded them with pity. They were as good as dead if they caroused in this fashion rather than escape from the trap that the rebels were setting for them. If the treatment of the prisoners taken at Camulodunum was anything to go by, there would be a bloodbath in Londinium as appalling as any scene from a sacked town that he had ever witnessed.

When he reached the inn, he could see from its silhouette how much damage the fire had done. The Dog and Deer's destruction would be completed when the town was consumed by a sea of flames after the rebels had finished slaughtering its inhabitants and looting its buildings, just as they had razed Camulodunum. All that would remain was another vast sprawl of blackened ruins and the stench of burned bodies.

The windows and doors fronting the streets on either angle of the crossroads were closed, and when he tried the main entrance he found it securely barred, so he made his way to the side street where the yard lay. He rapped on the gate and a voice called back.

'Who's there?'

'Centurion Macro. Let me in.'

'Don't know any Centurion Macro. Piss off.'

'Listen, friend. My mother owns this place. Portia's her name. If you don't let me in and she finds out, she'll have your balls for breakfast. Now open that gate while you still can, eh?'

The bar rattled and the gate swung in enough to admit Macro, then was quickly closed behind him and secured again. He found himself facing the dark shapes of four men with drawn swords. Another came up to them with a raised oil lamp to inspect their visitor.

'Easy there, lads. I'm telling the truth.'

'From the state of you, I'd say you were a beggar. Centurion? We'll see about that. Tifernus, fetch one of the women to see if his story holds up.'

Macro sighed and folded his arms while the man entered the inn. There was a brief delay before the door crashed open and Petronella came running across the yard. She barged her way through the soldiers and locked him in a tight embrace.

'I knew you were still alive!' she sobbed. 'I never stopped believing it! Oh, my love . . .'

Macro held her tightly, kissing the top of her head as he muttered affectionate blandishments. 'You think I'd ever leave you alone, eh? Come on, my sweet . . . There, stop those tears now.' He looked towards the inn. 'Where's my mum?'

'Inside.'

'Does she know I'm here?'

'She heard the soldier say so.'

'Then what's keeping the old girl? I'm already braced for her tongue-lashing.'

Petronella pushed herself away and held him at arm's length. 'She's in bed, Macro. The strain of last night and the damage done to the inn have hit her hard.'

'She's as tough as old boots. If anything dared to hit her hard, it would be flat on its back in short order.'

His wife smiled sadly. 'Once maybe. The years have been kind to her, Macro, but not any longer. She said there was a pain in her heart this morning. It got worse as the day went on and now she's struggling for breath.'

'Take me to her.'

They entered the inn and climbed the stairs to the room that had best survived the fire damage. Portia was in the bed, propped up by a pair of bolsters. Claudia was sitting on a stool to the side, dabbing the old lady's lined forehead with a damp rag. A pair of oil lamps hanging from a stand lit the room. Both women looked up as Macro and Petronella entered.

Claudia smiled warmly. 'I'm so glad to see you, Macro. We thought you were . . .' She caught herself and continued. 'Cato was right, you are the darling of the gods.'

'My boy . . .' Portia reached out a frail arm.

Macro knelt down next to her and took her hand, shocked at

how clammy it was. Even though it was only a few months since he had last seen her, she seemed to have aged years. Her eyes and cheeks appeared sunken and there was a waxy sheen to her skin. The hard-nut demeanour he had always known seemed to have faded, and she actually smiled at him and reached her hand up to stroke his cheek.

'Just when I was on the point of accepting you had gone, here you are, turning up once again like the proverbial bad *as* coin . . . Thank the gods.'

'Did you really think I wouldn't come back to Londinium and make sure you were looking after my investment?' Macro smiled. 'I was right to be worried, judging from the state of it.'

His attempt at gentle humour fell flat as a pained look crossed her face. 'I put the last years of my life into the Dog and Deer. I wanted to leave you something valuable after all the trouble I caused you when you were a kid.'

'Shh. That was long ago, Mum. You've nothing to prove to me.'

'I was not a good mother . . .'

'And I wasn't a particularly good kid, was I? Always getting into trouble and making you angry. No wonder you buggered off with that marine when you had the chance.' He squeezed her hand. 'I wouldn't have got very far in the army if I hadn't inherited your strength and toughness. I didn't get that from my father.'

She looked saddened. 'He was a good man. Too kind-hearted and an easy touch for those with a sob story. I was never going to change him and he was never going to give me the kind of excitement I wanted. He deserved a better wife than me.' She broke into a coughing fit and clasped her hands to her mouth as her thin frame shook. When it subsided, she slumped back and asked for a drink.

'Here.' Claudia picked up a cup of watered wine and guided it to her lips. Portia took two swallows and sighed gratefully.

'Much as I'm enjoying the catch-up,' Macro said, 'we need to get moving. Cato's told me to get you all onto a ship heading for Gaul. We can't delay. The rebels will be here at first light, if not before. Once they appear there's going to be panic. We can't afford to get caught up in that.'

'What about the soldiers?' asked Petronella. 'Surely they'll protect us?'

Macro shook his head. 'The governor's abandoning Londinium in the next few hours.'

'He's leaving us?' Claudia looked up in anguish. 'What about Cato? Where is he?'

'He's with his men. He can't be spared at the moment. I'll find him once you're all safe. Suetonius needs every man when the time comes to confront the enemy.'

Petronella glared at him. 'What? But I've only just discovered you are alive and safe.'

'Alive, yes. But none of us are safe while we sit here gabbling like bloody geese. Get what valuables you can carry. Where's Lucius?'

'Asleep in the next room.'

'Wake him up. Tell him he's going on an adventure. I'll have to carry my mother.'

Petronella nodded and left the room. Macro felt a tug on the folds of his tunic and looked down at Portia.

'Son, I'm not going . . .'

'Of course you are. I'll get you to the ship, and once you're in Gaul, you can find somewhere to rest and recover.'

'I won't live that long. It's pointless. Let me die here, in my own home.'

Macro felt his throat tighten and he shook his head. 'No chance.'

'It's my decision,' she said sharply. 'I'll not be a burden to you and the others while you try to get them out of Londinium.'

'You won't be a burden,' he protested. 'Don't talk this way.'

'Be quiet, boy. My mind is made up. There's one thing you can do for me, though.' She indicated the space under the bed. 'My strongbox. Take it. The others will need coin to pay their way in Gaul. I've no use for it now.'

Macro bent and dragged the chest out. It was a foot and a half in length, oak reinforced with iron bands and a sturdy lock. Portia strained to lift her head and handed him the key hanging from a cord around her neck. Unlocking the box, he lifted the lid and saw a small fortune in silver within.

'I was going to give that to you anyway. Your share of the profits in the Dog and Deer and my other businesses here. If there's any left, you and Petronella can use it to make a new start, somewhere far away from Britannia.'

'I-I don't know what to say . . .'

'That's a first.' She gave a dry laugh and coughed again.

Petronella returned, leading Lucius by the hand. The boy was yawning, still half asleep. As soon as he saw Macro, though, his eyes widened and he smiled with delight as he rushed across and was swept up in the centurion's arms.

'How's my lad?'

His expression became serious for a moment. 'They said you weren't ever coming back.'

'I'm pleased to report they were mistaken.' Macro chuckled and set the boy down, regarding him formally as he tugged his tunic into better shape. 'I know there's much to be said, but we have no time at the moment. You need to be ready to march. Can you do that for me?'

Lucius nodded.

'Good man. Now get some clothes sorted for the journey, and any valuables. I'll meet you all downstairs.'

Once the others had left Macro alone with his mother, he

locked the strongbox. 'Please change your mind. You can come with us.'

'No.'

He hesitated. 'What happens if you're still alive when the rebels arrive?'

'I'll be ready for them.' Portia folded back the blanket covering her and revealed the gleam of a cleaver. 'I'll bury that in the head of the first one through the door. Or I can use it on my own wrists if it comes to that.'

Macro winced and was about to protest when she raised a hand to silence him. 'I've had a good life. Only a few regrets, and you were never one of them, despite the way I've treated you in the past. I've made my peace with life, son. I get to die where I want and when I want. How many of us can say that?'

He felt his throat ache as it tightened. He leaned down and kissed her on the forehead.

'I'll look out for you when it's my turn to cross into the shades, Mother,' he said softly.

Portia closed her eyes and turned her face to the wall, breathing with difficulty. Macro left her that way and closed the door gently behind him. He paused to cuff away the tears that had pricked out of his eyes in the last moments he had been with his mother. Then he took a deep breath and descended the stairs to join the others in the room below.

CHAPTER SEVENTEEN

As Macro's party approached the river, he could see the dark mass of the warehouses that lined the wharf. There were gaps where buildings had been burned down that reminded him of the teeth of some wizened dotard. He led the way, with the two women and Lucius behind him and the soldiers from Cato's cohort on either side. He had given the order to draw their swords to deter the gangs of drunken looters that ranged freely through the town. There were many people trying to escape, making for the gates or the remaining ships before it was too late, and they too kept in groups to protect themselves. The air was filled with the sounds of drunken revelry – singing, shouting, laughing and the pitiful screams of women and children suffering abuse at the hands of their tormentors. Abandoned and broken furniture and household goods littered the narrow streets, forming obstacles that slowed the progress of the party.

At one point, as they approached a crossroads, they saw that the way had been blocked by two carts with a small gap between them, and several burly men were stopping and searching those who wanted to get through to the wharf, stripping them of their valuables. Macro's group backtracked to work their way round to the street that ran behind the warehouses. Beyond, the masts of a handful of ships rose against a clear night sky where stars shone cold and bright, heedless of the chaos and desperation that reigned in Londinium. Locating one of the narrow alleys that ran down to the wharf, he led them towards the far end and then ordered another halt. From the darkness of the alley they could see the crowd that thronged the riverside, pressing forward to try and get aboard the last vessels to quit the doomed town.

'I'll go ahead and find a skipper and try to cut a deal,' Macro announced as he handed the strongbox to Petronella. 'Guard that well. Stay here and keep out of sight.'

Petronella grabbed his arm and gave him a quick kiss. 'Be careful.'

'Aren't I always?'

He stepped out and moved towards the mob trying to board the nearest ship. The crew had heaved it away from the wharf, and a slender plank extended across the dark waters of the river, leading to the deck. It was guarded by four men with staves while the captain negotiated with those ashore for places on the vessel. Working his way along the wharf, Macro came across the same scene at every ship he passed. Some were already so dangerously overloaded that he discounted them at once and continued his search with a growing sense of concern. If such craft were to venture out onto the open sea, there was a clear danger that they would founder and their crew and passengers would drown. There was less of a crush towards the far end of the wharf, and he pushed his way through the throng and cupped a hand to his mouth as he called across to the crew of a sturdy-looking cargo vessel.

'I need berths for two women and a boy!'

It took a few more shouts before he attracted the attention of the captain, who called back, 'We still have a few berths, if you can pay for them!'

'How much?'

'Two hundred sestertii.'

That was nearly the annual pay of a legionary, Macro fumed. However, he was mindful of the need to complete his task as soon as possible if he and the auxiliaries were to get back to headquarters in time to join the rest of the soldiers leaving the town. 'All right. Two hundred.'

'Each!' the captain shouted back.

Macro's first instinct was to charge across the gangplank, pin the captain against the mast and negotiate a fair price at the point of a sword. But he would be overpowered by the other members of the crew before he had taken two paces. He suppressed his anger.

'All right! Two hundred each, you bastard.'

The other man gave a cynical smile. 'There's a surcharge for insulting me and my crew. We're just honest men offering a service.'

Macro stabbed a finger at him. 'Be ready for us when I get back!'

'Be quick then. We'll be casting off soon.'

He left the crowded wharf and hurried back along the edge of the warehouses, where there was more space. When he reached the alley where the others were waiting, he retrieved the strongbox. 'I've found a ship, though it's going to cost us dear. Bloody profiteers . . . Let's go.'

In the same formation as earlier, they moved along the wharf. The angry and desperate people crowded in the restricted space were shouting at the ships' crews and each other as they jostled dangerously close to the water's edge. Halfway along, Macro's party had to pause as there was a sudden surge towards a vessel that had drifted too close to the wharf. Scores of people were leaping across the narrowing gap. One old man mistimed his jump, or was nudged in the back, and fell into the river with a sharp cry. He didn't resurface. Some of the crew thrust at the wharf with their sweep oars to fend the ship away, while others brandished staves at those still tempted to try and make the leap. As the gap increased, the gangway fell into the water with a loud splash, prompting an agonised groan from the crowd as they realised there was no chance of boarding now.

Fifty or sixty people must have joined those already aboard, and the dangerously overloaded vessel began to rock from side to side. The captain shouted an order to the men with staves, who turned towards those who had jumped the gap. With the herd instinct of the desperate, the fugitives crowded together on the far side of the ship, and as the crew closed in on them, the deck began to cant over and the gleaming hull rolled out of the water. There was a cry of alarm, but it was already too late, and the vessel continued to roll onto its side, pitching those on deck into the dark river. The mast snapped with a loud crack and together with the rigging it crashed down amid the people thrashing about in the water. There were piteous cries and splashes as some attempted to swim back to the wharf, while others clung to the upturned hull and tried to clamber up to relative safety. Those on the wharf looked on in horror.

'Keep moving,' Macro urged, and the small group edged past the stricken crowd before it turned to find the next available ship that might offer some hope of escape.

Even with a bright full moon illuminating the scene, Macro struggled to pick out the mast of the vessel they were making for, but he knew they were drawing close to the stretch of wharf where it had been moored. Then a gap opened up in the crowd, and he saw a ship moving out into the current, propelled by its sweeps. It took him a moment to realise it was the same one whose captain he had bargained with. He rushed to the edge of the wharf.

'Hey! Where the fuck d'you think you're going? Get back here.'

The captain must have recognised his voice, as he came to the side and called back, 'Sorry, friend. We sold the last places to someone else while we were waiting. Good luck.'

'Good luck?' Macro repeated softly, before his temper exploded. 'We made a fucking deal! Get your arse back here right now! If you don't, I'll remember you, and the next time we meet I'll tear your balls off and sell them back to you for two hundred sestertii! Each!'

The captain gave a final wave before he turned his back and ordered his crew to row the boat out into the middle of the Tamesis.

Petronella came over and took Macro's arm gently. 'It's too late. They're gone. They won't come back. We'll have to try another ship.'

Macro gestured along the wharf, where the dense mass of people were crying out in panic. 'What other ship? There's only two left now and we'll never get through that mob.'

Petronella looked about, and then pointed to the dark bulk of another ship visible a short distance from the bank. 'What about that one?'

Macro squinted and made out the lines of a warship. One of the smaller class, a liburnian perhaps.

'It's worth a go. I might have some authority there.' He gestured to the others to follow him as he hurried towards the end of the wharf, where a brazier burned, illuminating a squad of marines guarding steps leading down to a skiff tied to one of the posts rising from the riverbed. There were only a handful of civilians at this end of the river, and the marines levelled their spears at any that ventured too near and told them to back off.

Macro raised a hand as he approached. 'Lower those weapons! I'm a legionary centurion.'

'Advance then!' the optio in command of the party replied.

As Macro emerged into the loom of the brazier, the optio

247

scrutinised his bedraggled appearance and gripped the handle of his sword but did not draw it. 'Centurion, eh? Look more like some vagrant. Who are those with you?'

'These men are auxiliaries of the Eighth Cohort, serving under Suetonius. The civilians are the dependents of senior officers.'

The optio seemed to relax his guard as he saw the kit and uniforms of soldiers. He looked at Macro again. 'Assuming you are who you say you are, sir, what do you want here?'

'Berths for the two women and the boy. I'll be joining the lads when we return to headquarters.'

'Nothing doing. We're under orders not to let civilians on the ship.'

'Why are you still here?'

'Waiting for the carts carrying the records from headquarters, sir. Soon as they're loaded and the civilian officials are on board, we're weighing anchor and sailing for Gaul.'

'Gaul? That's good. That's where these three are headed. Just get them on your boat there and row them out to the ship.' Macro made a move towards the stairs, but the optio stepped into his path and shook his head.

'Like I said. We have orders.'

'Listen, if you don't do as I say, it's the governor you'll be answering to, in person. If he hears that you've refused to give these civilians a place on that warship, you'll be demoted to the most junior rowing position on a galley, on a bench above the bilge. If you don't want to make the decision, I suggest you ask your captain to come ashore and deal with it.'

The optio considered the threat before turning towards the Liburnian and calling out, 'Navarch Pallinus! Sir!'

'What is it, Optio?' a voice responded tersely. 'Is it the party from headquarters?'

'No, sir. Some soldiers and a centurion. Says there's two

women and a boy needing to be on the ship. Dependents of senior officers.'

'Really? Dammit . . . Send the boat over for me.'

Shortly afterwards, the captain climbed the steps. He was a slender man in his mid thirties with a bald pate, and he regarded Macro and the others suspiciously. 'Is this a joke? You're a centurion?'

'Lucius Cornelius Macro, centurion – retired – and senior magistrate of the veterans' colony at Camulodunum. Or was, until the rebels burned the place to the ground. Petronella is my wife. The other woman is the wife of Prefect Cato, commander of one of the governor's auxiliary cohorts. The boy is his son.'

Macro sensed the reluctance of the naval officer to help them and decided to try a different tack to win the man round. 'A quiet word with you.'

The two stepped out of earshot and Macro tapped the strongbox. 'If it helps sweeten the request, there's five hundred sestertii for your trouble. Three passengers are not going to be any extra burden to your ship, Pallinus. Besides, if you take them, you'll have my gratitude and that of Prefect Cato. If you don't, and anything happens to them as a result, I wouldn't want to be in your boots.'

'Are you threatening me?'

'No, friend. Just making the situation as clear to you as I can. Some coin and our gratitude, or no money and our enmity. Which is it to be?'

It was the silver that swung it, Macro guessed, as he saw the navarch's gaze shift to the strongbox. He gave it a gentle shake so that the other man could hear the coins shifting inside.

'Well, I suppose three more won't make any appreciable difference. Five hundred then,' Pallinus said quietly. 'Just between you and me.'

'Done,' Macro responded before he could have a change of heart. 'Let's get them and this box on board straight away. Then my wife will sort out the payment.'

They turned back to the others and Macro smiled. 'The navarch says he'll take you.'

Pallinus indicated the skiff. 'Down there, if you please.'

Petronella hugged Macro and they exchanged a desperate kiss before he forced himself to draw away from her. There was a good chance they might never see each other again, but that was too painful to dwell on. For a moment he was tempted to leave the province with her, but then his resolve to avenge the comrades who had fallen at Camulodunum steadied his sense of purpose.

'No time for long goodbyes, my love. You have to go, and the lads and I are needed at headquarters.' He patted Lucius on the head. 'Your father and I will see you again as soon as the trouble here is over. I need you to look after Petronella and Claudia meanwhile. Can you do that for me and your dad?'

Lucius drew himself up and saluted. 'Yes, Uncle Macro. You can rely on me.'

'Of course I can. Now get yourself into that boat. You too, Claudia.'

She touched his hand. 'I'll look after him.'

As the pair descended the steps, Macro handed the strongbox to Petronella along with the key. 'Here, look after that. You'll have to pay five hundred sestertii for the fare. Just make sure you don't blow the rest on shoes while you're in Gaul.'

'I might at that.'

They exchanged a sad smile, and then she kissed him again and whispered in his ear, 'You are the love of my life. Don't die on me again, you hear?'

'I'm like a cat,' he replied. 'Nine lives and that.'

'You used those up long ago, you old fool.'

'Old?' Macro affected umbrage. 'Better get going before I take that personally.'

Petronella turned and went down the steps to join the others, clutching the strongbox tightly. A moment later, the two crewmen cast off and rowed the boat out into the river towards the warship. Macro watched them until he could no longer make out any details, then sighed heavily and looked at the auxiliaries. 'We're done here. Back to headquarters.'

They were about to march off when he heard the trundle of cart wheels approaching. Two vehicles, drawn by mules, emerged from an alley. A handful of men paced alongside the carts and made for the waiting marines.

'Give us a hand unloading, sir,' said the optio. 'One favour deserves another, eh? Won't take long. Sooner it's done, the sooner those civvies get to quit Londinium.'

'All right,' Macro conceded. 'I'll have the auxiliary lads do it.'

Mindful of his shoulder wound, he stood aside as the carts drew up close to the edge of the wharf and the men who had accompanied them threw back the covers to reveal boxes filled with scrolls and waxed slates, and locked chests. The auxiliaries and marines helped the clerks to unload them while the warship's crew rowed a cable ashore and hauled the stern into the wharf before mooring the vessel in readiness for the official cargo. Once the carts were empty, the mules were led into the yard of the nearest warehouse and abandoned. Macro turned to the auxiliaries.

'Time to get back to the cohort. Off you go. I'll be along in a moment.'

They needed no encouragement and trotted off up the street in the direction of the headquarters compound. Macro stepped close enough to the stern of the warship to make out the navarch and called out to him, 'Make sure you treat the passengers well and see that no one tries to rob them.'

'We have a deal, Centurion Macro. I'll honour my side of it. I give you my word.'

'That'll have to do.'

He turned away and was passing by the headquarters clerks when something struck him as out of place. One of their number, the only one with the hood of his cloak drawn up over his head, had backed out of his way more than was necessary. Macro stopped and addressed the dark figure. 'Do I know you?'

The other man waved a hand dismissively and replied in an undertone, 'Never seen you before.'

Despite the attempt to disguise his voice, there was no hiding the cultured accent of a patrician, and Macro felt his guts churn at the recognition that flowed through him like a sickness. He took four quick strides towards the man and reached out to fling back the hood. Decianus recoiled, his face a mask of fear and cunning in the moonlight.

'Optio! Get this man off me!'

The marine hesitated.

Macro already had his hands clenched in the folds of the procurator's cloak and hauled him closer so that they were face to face. 'You weaselly little bastard,' he snarled. 'Trying to escape from all the shit you've rained down on us, eh?'

'I'm the imperial procurator!' Decianus cried out towards the marines. 'The emperor's man. Anyone who touches me commits treason! Arrest this thug.'

'You're a corrupt coward whose time has come.' Macro swung Decianus around and thrust him onto the ground. As the procurator scrambled backwards like a crab, the centurion drew his sword and paced towards him.

'What's the meaning of this?' Pallinus demanded as he climbed onto the ship's stern rail and hopped ashore. 'Answer me, Centurion!'

Macro drew up and jabbed his sword towards Decianus. 'This miserable piece of slime is the cause of all this mayhem. He needs to pay the price for what he's done.'

Pallinus looked down at the cowering procurator. 'Decianus Catus? Yes, I recognise him. I don't know what you think he's done, but he's right about being the emperor's man. You harm him and Nero won't take it kindly.'

'I'll worry about that later.' Macro made to take another step and the navarch caught him by the arm and held it tightly.

'It might not just be your life on the line if anything happens to him. Besides, I have orders from the procurator not to leave Londinium until he's aboard.'

'His orders are worthless. He's been placed under arrest.'

Pallinus shrugged. 'I don't know anything about that.'

Macro was seething with rage and only managed to contain his temper with great effort. He forced himself to take a calming breath. 'I need a moment alone with the procurator to settle a few differences. This man is responsible for countless deaths, and there will be more. Look, I know you're reluctant to take my word for it, but this is not the time and place for lengthy explanations. If you can't sail without him aboard, you have my word that I'll hand him back to you once we've had our little chat. On my honour.'

'All right, but be quick.'

'What?' Decianus looked up at the navarch. 'You can't be serious?'

Macro grabbed him by the collar of his tunic and dragged him to his feet, then propelled him across the wharf to the entrance of the yard where the mules and carts had been taken. Pallinus turned away and ordered his men and the clerks to board the warship and make ready to cast off.

The stars and moon cast a steely hue over the yard as the two men entered, and the mules stirred as if sensing the tension between them. With a powerful thrust, Macro sent the procurator crashing against the side of the warehouse.

'You'll pay for that,' Decianus gasped as he fought for breath. 'You may beat me up now . . . but I'll have you hunted down and held accountable for assaulting an imperial servant . . . if it's the last thing I do.'

'No you won't,' Macro replied coldly. 'This is where it ends, Decianus. This is where you make amends for all the carnage you have wrought. This is where Boudica and her daughters are avenged for what you ordered your men to do to them.'

'This is about that haggard bitch and her whelps?' Decianus laughed. 'She's an enemy of Rome, you fool. You avenge her, you betray your people.'

'One of the girls was my daughter,' Macro replied.

'What nonsense . . .'

'Like I said to the navarch, there's no time for explanations. This isn't a court, Decianus. There are no bent lawyers to defend you. There's only justice, and justice demands that you die. Now. Much as I want to kill you myself, I'd rather see you end your own life, and watch you squirm while you build up the guts to do it.'

He drew the dagger from the sheath on his belt and tossed it to the ground at the procurator's feet. 'Pick it up.'

'Are you mad? I'll do no such thing.'

'Pick it up!' Macro repeated. 'Pick it up before I use it on you myself.' He took a step forward.

Decianus stooped and snatched up the blade and pointed it at Macro.

'That's more like it. Now use the bloody thing on yourself.'

'No. I won't. And you can't hurt me. You gave your word to the navarch. In front of his men.'

'Yes, I did.' Macro smiled thinly. 'And I'm a man of my word. I could make it easy for you and advise you to open your wrists, but we haven't got time for that. So best to strike up under the ribs into the heart, and give it a good twist just to be sure. It'll be nice and quick.'

'I can't do that,' Decianus quavered. 'I can't.'

'Oh, you're pretty good at dishing out harm to others, aren't you? But not when it comes to yourself. You coward. Turn the blade on yourself and do it.'

'I can't! I can't.' Decianus shook his head. 'I won't.'

'Then you leave me no choice.' Macro took another step and reached for the procurator's wrist, but Decianus slashed out with the dagger and gashed the centurion's forearm.

'Treacherous to the last,' Macro observed. He threw a punch with his other hand, catching Decianus on the jaw so that his head jerked back and struck the wall of the warehouse. The dagger began to slip from his fingers, and Macro clenched his hand around the procurator's and turned the blade towards the latter's chest. As the point came up against Decianus's tunic and began to press home, the procurator looked down, eyes widening in panic as he tried to fight back and force the blade away. Macro leaned into him and used his superior strength to keep the blade moving. The tip tore through the cloth and began to penetrate Decianus's flesh under his sternum.

'Nooo!' he wailed as he clawed at Macro's fist with his spare hand.

'Yes,' Macro replied. 'And never has a piece of shit like you deserved death more.'

He felt a warm gush of blood over his fist as Decianus let out a horrified gasp. But still the procurator struggled, and Macro had to use his last reserves of strength to drive the blade up at an angle. Decianus writhed, his face screwed up with pain and the effort of fighting for his life, even though he was already doomed. Gradually, though, his movements weakened, and Macro felt his grip on the dagger handle loosening. Prising

255

the procurator's fingers away, he grasped the weapon and pressed it home.

Decianus let out a thin cry, and his eyes opened wide, staring at Macro as if in surprise that this was how his life should end. Then he slumped back against the wall and slipped down into a squat, his lips moving feebly and blood trickling from his mouth, black in the moonlight.

Macro watched him bleed out, then drew his sword.

Shortly afterwards, Pallinus saw a figure emerge from the yard. As it drew closer, he recognised Macro.

'Where's the procurator?'

There was no reply, and the navarch cleared his throat. 'You gave your word that you'd bring him back alive.'

'I gave my word that I'd bring him back, and as I told him, I am a man of my word.'

'Then bring him here. Right now. We have to get well downriver before the rebels arrive. I can't leave without the Procurator.'

Macro stopped a couple of paces away and swung his arm. Decianus's head landed on the deck beside the navarch with a wet thud.

'There,' he said. 'The procurator's on board. Now you can go.'

Pallinus was motionless for a moment, and then swore softly. 'You fool . . .'

'What's done is done.' Macro shrugged. 'Better get under way.'

He turned and paced to the shadow of the warehouse, watching as the crew slipped the stern rope and used an oar to heave the liburnian away from the wharf. The black mass of the vessel eased out into the Tamesis and the current began to take it downriver. Macro looked on, grateful that Petronella and the others were safe. When he could no longer make out the warship, he strode up the street towards headquarters.

With Londinium lost, and along with it his mother and the businesses she had built up for them both, he had nothing left in the world besides Petronella and the sword at his side. He smiled grimly to himself. As the old saying went, a man who has nothing to lose is the most dangerous enemy of all. He resolved to make certain that the rebels learned the truth of it.

CHAPTER EIGHTEEN

Macro had barely covered half the distance to headquarters when he became aware of a series of panicked cries coming from his right, in the direction of the town's east gate. They might have been part of the ongoing chaos, but he was mindful that some of the more ambitious of the rebel war bands might attempt to enter Londinium that night. The sounds increased and seemed to come from more directions, along with the faint clash of weapons, and he quickened his pace.

As he reached a junction a hundred paces away from head-quarters, he was forced to stop by a large group of civilians rushing by, heading away from the din. He collared a young man and pinned him against the door frame of a looted blacksmith's.

'What's going on?'

'Let me go!'

'I will do once you tell me.'

The youth nodded in the direction of the east gate. 'They're here!'

'The rebels?'

'They're killing people! Let me go.'

Macro released him, and the youth sprinted off to rejoin the stream of fleeing people. The centurion followed them, heading in the direction of the headquarters.

There was a dull red loom above the compound from the

flames of the torches and fires within that was enough to guide those in the street. By the time Macro approached the gatehouse, a crowd had gathered outside and a cordon of auxiliaries were battering people away with their shields. He forced his way through the seething bodies, his ears ringing with their cries of terror and angry demands to be allowed to take shelter within the walls.

The optio in command of the party defending the gate was from Cato's cohort and recognised Macro by the light of the torches burning in the brackets either side of the archway.

'You'd better get inside quickly, sir. Not sure how much longer we can hold on here.'

'It's not the civilians you need to be worried about. The first of the rebels are here.'

'Already? Hope the governor knows what he's doing.'

'We'll find out soon enough.'

As the auxiliaries parted to let Macro past, there were enraged cries of protest that only died down after he disappeared through the single gate that was still open. On the far side, a squadron of Cato's cavalry stood by their horses ready to deal with any trouble. Centurion Tubero was with them.

'Where's the prefect?' Macro asked.

Tubero pointed to a group of officers on the far side of the compound. Striding across the courtyard, Macro saw that the rest of the mounted contingent the governor had brought with him from Mona was ready to ride. A small body of men on foot that comprised what was left of the garrison stood close to several light carts, along with the clerks, servants and slaves who had served at headquarters. It was clear that the column was about to march, although Macro wondered if the governor had left it too late.

Cato saw his friend approaching and greeted him with a relieved expression.

'I heard that you got the women and Lucius away.'

'Not all of them.' Macro explained his mother's decision.

'I'm sorry.'

'We can grieve later,' he said gruffly.

'Thank the gods the other three are safe at least.'

'Assuming the rebels haven't blockaded the Tamesis and they reach Gaul safely.'

'Thanks for the encouraging words, brother,' Cato smiled.

'Pleased to see you again, Centurion,' said Suetonius as he spotted Macro. 'Good timing. We're about to leave.'

'Not so sure about the timing, sir. The enemy are in the town.'

'By the gods . . . Surely not?'

Macro jerked a thumb back towards the gatehouse. 'That's what the noise is about. And unless you recall the section outside, they'll be torn apart by the mob before too long.'

The governor sent one of his tribunes to give the order, then turned to Agricola. 'Get the vanguard going. I want us out of here at once. We have to put as much distance between us and Londinium as possible before first light.'

'Yes, sir.' Agricola saluted and ran across to the mounted unit assigned to lead the column.

A clerk came running from the entrance of headquarters and drew up in front of the governor. 'No sign of the procurator anywhere, sir.'

'That's too bad. I would love to have seen the bastard had up on capital charges. If he hadn't lost his head, we wouldn't be in this mess.'

Macro shrugged. 'It's because of this mess that he deserved to lose his head, sir.'

Suetonius frowned at the gnomic remark before he dismissed the matter. 'Can't worry about Decianus now. He'll have to look out for himself, as ever.'

He turned to address the gathered officers.

'Gentlemen, there'll be no stopping once we set off. If a horse goes lame, we leave it behind. Same goes for stragglers, and any of the carts that gets damaged. If we run into the enemy, we cut through them and leave our wounded. Those are my orders. That goes for you especially, Prefect Cato, as your men will be serving as the rearguard. If any of you get separated, make for Verulamium.' He paused to look at their sombre expressions, illuminated by a brazier on the steps close by. 'I don't like running out on Londinium and its people any more than you do, but there's nothing we can do to save them. Remember this moment. Remember the shame you are feeling now when we eventually turn and fight and repay those rebel bastards in full. Everyone clear?'

His officers nodded and muttered their assent.

'Then get to your positions, and may the gods spare us.'

The group dispersed, and Macro went with Cato to join the men of the Eighth Cohort, who mounted at their prefect's order. As the auxiliaries settled in their saddles, there was a shout of alarm from the main gatehouse. The optio and his men had fallen back and were locked in a struggle to get the gates closed as the desperate crowd outside surged forward. Cato jerked on his reins and, followed by Macro, crossed the compound towards Tubero and his squadron. It was already clear that the fight for the gates was lost as the auxiliaries scrabbled for footing and braced themselves against the timbers edging inwards.

'Take ten of your men and reinforce the gate,' Cato ordered Tubero before he formed the rest of the men up across the courtyard facing the gate.

The extra men managed to hold the gate and ease it back. Cato looked over his shoulder and saw that the rest of the column was moving off round the mass of the headquarters building towards the compound's northern gate, which gave out onto the open ground beyond the town. A Celtic war horn started braying to the east, and then two more joined in from different locations. There was a fresh outburst of cries from outside, followed by screams. At once the gate began to surge back, and the auxiliaries were unable to withstand the pressure.

'Leave it!' Cato called out to them. 'Get to your horses, boys!'

Tubero and his men turned and ran. An instant later, the gate's iron hinges rumbled as the heavy timbers swung in and crashed against the side of the gatehouse. The first of the civilians, mostly men, surged through, and drew up at the sight of the line of cavalry facing them.

'Lower spears!' Cato ordered, and the deadly points dropped and aimed at the mob, causing the leading rank to retreat as those behind who had not yet seen the horsemen pressed forward. As Cato had hoped, it bought Tubero and his men enough time to mount and form up to the rear.

'Centurion! Fall back on the column!'

As Tubero's men wheeled away, Cato tugged at his reins and was about to ride off when he felt a hand grab his ankle. He looked down as a sturdy man with leather bracers reached up towards the hilt of his sword. He tried to kick himself free, but his assailant now grabbed at his leg with both hands.

'Don't think you're going to rat out on us!' the man snarled.

More figures ran into the courtyard, several making towards Cato and Macro. The centurion, sword in hand, was feinting to right and left to scare away those around him. He saw his friend's plight and urged his mount forward, scattering the men in between and slamming the beast's flank into the back of the man attempting to unseat Cato. The man released his grip and was knocked to the ground, where he curled up, trying to avoid the horse's hooves. The two riders galloped free of the mob and charged across the courtyard to rejoin the rearguard trotting around the headquarters block and out of sight.

When they were a safe distance away, Cato looked back to see a dark mass of figures flooding through the gatehouse and running for their lives. A fresh blast of the enemy's horns sounded closer to, and the first of the rebel horsemen appeared, garishly lit by the torches outside. His sword blade glinted red before the weapon slashed down and cut into one of the fleeing civilians. He was followed into the courtyard by more of his companions, amid the torrent of panicking civilians.

Macro reined in, sword arm bunched up, and for an instant Cato feared that his friend would turn and charge back to engage the rebels.

'Macro! On me!'

The centurion glanced at him and then back towards the developing chaos around the gate. A brazier had been overturned and sparks burst into the air, and a woman started screaming as her cloak caught fire.

'Macro! There's nothing we can do for them. Come on!' Cato grabbed at his reins and led his friend's horse a short distance until the scene was hidden by the corner of the headquarters building. Macro pulled his reins back and grasped them tightly. 'Let's go.'

They caught up with the cohort as Tubero was leading the men through the north gate.

Immediately ahead of them were the men on foot, trotting to keep up with the carts urged on by the frightened mule drivers as they kept pace with the mounted men of the governor's column. Even though it was a bright moonlit night, there were shadows across the landscape that made it impossible to detect movement more than a few hundred paces away, and it was easy to imagine bands of rebels closing in from all sides, intent on wiping out the governor and his exhausted column.

Around Cato and Macro the auxiliaries rode in silence, glancing warily from side to side. Behind them they could hear the faint screams and cries of the civilians trapped in the town, and above them the frequent blaring of war horns, whose notes now had an unmistakably exultant tone. Cato's heart was heavy and his tiredness made the weight of the scale vest on his shoulders feel unbearable. It was demoralising enough to be forced to retreat, but to have abandoned the remaining inhabitants of Londinium to be slaughtered by the rebels tarred every man in the column with a sickening sense of shame that would be impossible to forget, or forgive, despite the circumstances.

Riding at his side, Macro's thoughts were more troubled and more personal. Despite being relieved to have got Petronella and the others away from Londinium, he was haunted by his mother's fate. For all he knew, she might already have died, given her failing condition when he last saw her. But she might still be alive. In which case, he hoped she had the sense to kill herself before the rebels found her. Knowing her as he did, he feared she might wait until they came for her and try to exact some revenge for destroying the life she had built for herself in the town. If that was how it ended, he hoped death came quickly. But he would never know, and that doubt would be with him always.

The track from the north gate of the compound angled to the west and joined the main road on the crest of a ridge overlooking the town and river. From there the road led north in the direction of Verulamium. There were already people fleeing along the route, their carts piled high with belongings and, no doubt, items looted since the collapse of law and order some days earlier. Others carried what pitiful few possessions could be fitted into bags or hung from yokes. There would be many more trying to escape now that the rebels were entering the town. Suetonius had ordered the column to march beside the refugees until the way ahead was sufficiently clear to return to the road.

As Cato's cohort reached the junction, a tribune on horseback approached him.

'Governor's compliments, sir. Suetonius wants the Eighth Cohort to hold the junction open to allow as many of the civilians as possible to escape.'

'How long for?'

'Until dawn, sir.'

Cato exchanged a look with Macro. There were barely two hundred men left in the cohort, all of them on their last legs, even if their mounts had been rested. They would be good for one more charge or skirmish, two at the most, before they were spent.

'Very well,' he replied. 'Tell the governor we'll see him at Verulamium.'

They exchanged a salute before the tribune wheeled his horse and cantered off along the edge of the road.

'Doesn't ask for much, your general, does he?' Macro sighed. 'What does he expect us to achieve?'

'The usual – our duty.' Cato forced a smile. 'Be honest, you've missed this sort of thing since you retired from the army.'

'Frankly, if the last few months are the best that retirement has to offer, I'd be safer back in uniform and serving under the eagles again.'

'Well, I'm glad to have you back at my side.'

Cato called for Tubero and relayed the governor's order. 'The cohort will deploy on either side of the road, in line. We'll hold our ground until first light. Hopefully all those civilians who have got out of the town will have passed through by then.'

'What if the rebels come after them?'

'Like I said, we hold our position. Chances are we'll be facing small bands of scouts who'll be after easy pickings in the town or amongst those they've chased down. They won't want to tangle with formed-up cavalry.'

'And if they do?'

265

'Then we go in hard enough to discourage any further attempt.'

Tubero edged closer and lowered his voice. 'The boys have barely had any rest since we reached Londinium, sir. And before that they were at full stretch all the way from Mona.'

'I know what the men have endured, Centurion. And I know their quality. They're good men and they'll do what they are told to do. I'm counting on you to set them an example. Understand?'

'Yes, sir.'

'Good, then take the first three squadrons and form up on the left of the road. Centurion Macro and I will take the others to the right. Keep an ear open for my orders. There might be a lot of noise if the rebels pursue the civilians as far as the ridge.'

'Yes, sir.'

They exchanged salutes and Tubero rode off to position his men. Macro regarded him for a moment before he commented, 'That one seems a little jumpy to me.'

'He's turned out to be a decent officer. The Mona campaign was a big test for the cohort. They did well. It's just that once the island was taken, the army was looking forward to returning to Deva to enjoy the spoils, collect their awards, get drunk and toast the fallen. Boudica caught us all on the hop.'

'It's never over . . .' Macro began.

'Until it's over?' Cato responded.

'And not even then,' Macro chuckled. 'All right, let's see what your men are made of when the other side turn up.'

It was over an hour, by Cato's estimate, before the last of the civilians approached the ridge. Half a mile behind them came groups of horsemen and more on foot spilling out of the town and moving around its perimeter from the east. There were new fires burning in parts of Londinium, lurid glows against the shades of grey in the moonlight. The final cluster of civilians fleeing the enemy were making the best speed they could up the slope when a party of over a hundred rebel horsemen suddenly lurched into a canter and made for them.

'They're not going to reach us in time,' Macro observed.

Cato craned his neck to take in the wider scene before he reached a decision. 'Time to intervene.'

He called out along the line of the cohort. 'The Eighth will advance! Forward at the walk!'

The line of mounted auxiliaries edged forward, moving down from the ridge. Ahead of them the enemy were bunching up as they rushed to catch up with the last of the civilians.

'At the trot!'

The line became more uneven as the pace increased. Cato was relieved to note that the auxiliaries would pass the civilians before the rebels fell on them.

'At the canter!'

This was as fast as he dared in darkness, even though the slope was even and the grass short thanks to recent grazing. The riders passed either side of the civilians and then closed up as they neared the enemy. The latter reacted too slowly to the oncoming danger and turned in confusion in a bid to escape the Roman cavalry bearing down on them. Before they could complete the manoeuvre or build up any speed, the auxiliaries were upon them, thrusting their spears into their opponents and battering them with their shields. Cato and Macro remained side by side as they plunged amid the fighting horsemen. Even though it was night, it was easy to pick out the enemy. The darkness filled with the clash of blades and thuds of blows, along with the war cries of both sides, the gasps of injured men and the high-pitched whinnying of injured and frightened horses.

Cato picked out a rebel ahead of him and steered his horse to the side to enable him to swing his sword. His opponent saw the attack coming and was able to block the blow before making a quick thrust at Cato's face. He lurched backward in the saddle as the dull gleam of the man's blade shot past his nose, barely inches away. Releasing the reins, he grasped the wrist of the man's sword hand and hacked at his arm. There was not much room for a powerful blow, and his blade failed to cut through the thick folds of the rebel's cloak, but the impact was numbing enough to make him release his grip, and his weapon dropped to the ground. Surging in between the two, Macro thrust his sword into the rebel's stomach, twisted the blade and pulled it free before the press of battle forced the wounded man aside and one of the auxiliaries loomed up in his place, spear raised to strike.

'Easy there!' Macro shouted. 'I'm on your side!'

The auxiliary turned away to look for another target. But the skirmish was already over. The surviving rebels were dashing off in the direction of the town, pursued by scores of Cato's men. He swore at their impetuosity and called out to the cohort's cornice.

'Sound the recall!'

A moment later, a short sequence of notes sounded, and was repeated after a beat until the riders returned to form up on the standard. Cato waited until all appeared to have answered the call. They would only discover their losses when there was time to halt on the road to Verulamium.

'The Eighth will fall back to the ridge and form line!'

The auxiliaries picked their way clear of the bodies and weapons and trotted back up the slope. By the time Cato reached the crest, he could detect the first gleam of dawn away to the east. The stars gradually faded until only the moon was visible, ghostly white against the thin light of the coming day. Glancing behind his men, he saw that the last of the civilians were over a mile away, and soon they were lost from sight as the road passed through a forest.

'Almost time to go,' he commented.

'Not a moment too soon,' Macro responded, raising his arm to point down the slope towards Londinium.

At first Cato thought he was looking at the broad loop of the Tamesis stretching across the landscape. Then he realised it was Boudica's host: a vast, unruly column extending away to the east. Ahead of it, large bands of men, hundreds at a time, were marching towards Londinium, while others circled round to surround the town, trapping those still within. A few parties of horsemen, a mile or so off, kept watch on the line of Roman cavalry on the ridge but made no effort to engage them. After a while, they turned to join their comrades looting the town.

Columns of smoke rose in the still dawn air, and Cato and Macro could see that there were no masts left alongside the wharf and the last of the ships was already several miles downriver. A sudden billow of smoke rose from the headquarters compound, and soon the structure was a mass of brilliant flames that raged so loudly the crack and roar could be heard from the ridge. The local seat of government of the hated Roman Empire was an obvious target for the vengeful wrath of Boudica and her rebels.

Macro's attention was fixed on the area of the town where the Dog and Deer was situated, where another fire was burning, though it was impossible to fix its location precisely. A funeral pyre for his mother? he wondered. There would be other fires soon as the rebels finished looting a neighbourhood and put it to the torch. Eventually the capital of the province would be a sea of flame, burning for days before Londinium was razed to the ground and left as a blackened monument to the folly of Decianus and those he had answered to back in Rome.

The destruction of the provincial capital would be a signal to those tribes still nursing grievances against Rome that the Empire was not the all-powerful edifice that crushed all who stood before it. The iron men of the legions could be defeated. The outposts of empire and the towns they imposed on the landscape of

Britannia could be destroyed, and if the tribes of the island could join together in common cause, then every last trace of the invaders could be wiped out and hurled back across the sea to Gaul in abject humiliation. Such a reverse would reach the ears of every person across the Empire and beyond, and all those who dreamed of throwing off the Roman yoke would draw fresh inspiration from the example of Boudica and her rebels.

Standing between the present and that future were the weary, massively outnumbered soldiers of Governor Suetonius.

'I've seen enough,' said Cato. 'Let's be off.'

He gave the order, and the cohort turned away from the sacking of Londinium. The riders formed a column along the road, and once all was ready, they began their retreat, while the smoke rose behind them and the streets of Londinium filled with the screams of those being hunted down and butchered by the rebels.

CHAPTER NINETEEN

Ordinarily, the journey from Londinium to Verulamium could be completed within a day in good conditions. Despite the clear sky and the warm, dry weather, however, progress along the road that morning was slow and chaotic. Many of those who had fled from Londinium over the previous days had carried too much away with them, and there were carts with broken axles and wheels scattered along the road. Most had been abandoned, but some people stayed with them, unwilling to part from the contents while making attempts at repair. Others had been partially dismantled for firewood.

Most people had little idea where to head for and were driven only by determination to escape the wrath of the rebels. They had little thought of where to go beyond Verulamium and trudged along resignedly, occasionally looking back apprehensively for any sign of pursuers. Those who were weary or infirm rested a short distance from each side of the road, huddled around campfires as they recovered their strength to continue their flight. Many were hungry and begged for food from others or from the column of soldiers picking their way through the slow-moving refugees.

'I've never seen the like before,' Macro commented. 'It's pitiful, and shameful that it should come to this.'

'A dark day for Rome indeed,' Cato agreed as he twitched his

271

reins to steer his horse around a wagon left at an angle across the road. He paused to call back to Tubero, 'Have some men get that off the road!'

By noon, Cato estimated that they had covered barely a third of the distance to Verulamium. The only comfort to be had was that the column was retreating towards the army marching south from Deva: the Twentieth and Fourteenth legions, together with several auxiliary units, under the command of Legate Calpurnius. Despite the men lost during the recent campaign to take Mona, the governor would be able to field at least fifteen thousand soldiers when he made his stand against Boudica and her army. The five thousand men of the Second Legion and those of the Ninth slaughtered in the ambush would be sorely missed, however, and the fate of the province rested on a knife edge.

As they rode on, it was impossible not to notice the hostile glances and curses directed at them from many of the civilians.

'Seems like we've lost a few friends here,' said Macro.

'Are you surprised? We're supposed to defend them. Instead, they've lost everything they had in Londinium and they're now terrified of what will happen if the rebels catch up with them, or worse still, defeat Suetonius.'

'There's nothing we could have done to save Londinium.'

Cato caught the edge to his friend's words and correctly interpreted them, as only the closest of friends could. 'You did what you could to save her, Macro.'

'I shouldn't have listened to her. I should have taken her to the ship. At least she would have stood a chance of surviving.'

'She was weak and ill and she knew her time had come. That's what she told you. You're not to blame for any of this. That's on Decianus. Or it was.' Cato looked at his friend meaningfully.

Macro gave a grim smile.

'I thought so . . . I hope his death wasn't quick or clean,' Cato said quietly.

'Quicker than I'd have liked. But time was pressing. Other-wise . . .' Macro left the possible morbid scenarios unspoken. 'All that matters is that he got what was coming to him.'

'As long as there are no consequences for you. I doubt there will be. Decianus had become an embarrassment to those who sent him here to stir up trouble. They'll be content to have him disappear and won't be asking any questions about how that happened.'

'Let's hope. I'm not going into hiding for the rest of my life. If they put my name to his death, I'll be ready and waiting for whoever they send after me. And they'll get the same treatment as that snake did.'

'I'm sure of it.' Cato nodded. 'But we've got more immediate problems. If we get through this, I'll cover your back, brother.'

Macro was quiet for a beat before he spoke. 'That's good to know.'

As dusk fell, the column halted at Sulloniacis, a settlement just large enough to deserve a place name. A small inn stood beside the road and close by was a modest villa. The rest of the inhabitants lived in traditional clusters of round huts amid animal pens and grain pits. Sulloniacis was on a gently sloping hill overlooked by a signal station that was halfway between Londinium and Verulamium. Already thousands of civilians had chosen to stop there for the night, and many had lit cooking fires. The local people, rightly fearing that their livestock might be purloined by the hungry masses, had driven their animals into the pens and stood guard over them.

Suetonius had taken over the villa to serve as the quarters for himself and his staff for the night. The rest of the column and the small baggage train made camp around it. No orders were given to construct a marching fort in the face of the enemy, as the term had it, since there were too few men to excavate a ditch and rampart large enough to contain the auxiliaries and their horses. Besides, they were too tired, and most slumped to the ground and slept where they lay as soon as they had removed their saddles and seen to the needs of their mounts.

Having set the watch and agreed the password for the cohort with Tubero, Cato and Macro made their way to the villa just after sunset. They took a circuitous route, stopping at the signal tower to climb up the internal ladder to the platform, where a sentry was scrutinising the landscape to the south. Around them flickered the fires of those who had fled from Londinium. No more than three miles away, a belt of campfires gave away the position of the rebels cautiously pursuing them. In the distance, a rosy hue marked the town that was still being sacked by Boudica's followers.

'Ain't difficult to see what happens next,' said Macro. 'Those that can't keep up are going to be overtaken by the enemy. The road between Verulamium and Londinium is going to be one long slaughterhouse.'

'I fear so. And when the main body of rebels swings north after they've finished with Londinium, Suetonius is going to lose Verulamium as well. The three biggest settlements in the province will have gone up in smoke. It's not hard to imagine how that will play out in Rome amongst those who want to abandon Britannia. Even if the rebellion is put down.'

Macro gave a wry smile. 'If? Whatever happened to "when"?'

Satisfied that the enemy were settling down for the night, they descended from the signal tower and headed for the villa. Cato's body felt heavy with exhaustion, and he craved the prospect of a long sleep in a comfortable bed after a decent meal. Thought of food made him aware of how little he had eaten over the previous two days, and a gnawing hunger caused his stomach to growl in protest.

Macro's stomach seemed to answer in sympathy, and both men laughed spontaneously, grateful for the distraction.

'Damn, but I hope the owner of the villa has some decent food available,' said Macro. 'If it hasn't already been scoffed by the governor and his staff.'

Cato indicated one of the pens they were passing on the way to the villa. The grunts of pigs sounded from within and a tall tribesman with a boar spear stood guard, watching them warily as they passed by. 'We might have to liberate one of those later. I fancy a bit of crackling.'

'Don't talk about it,' Macro protested. 'Try thinking about something else before you set my appetite off as well.'

The villa followed the usual pattern, with a small gatehouse set into a wall that enclosed the main house, and stables and storerooms around the edges of the compound. Two of the governor's bodyguards were on duty and saluted the officers, waving them through after a curious passing scrutiny of Macro, who had still not had the chance to clean off the filth accrued during his escape, nor trim the beard that had sprouted on his cheeks and jaw.

'We really must get you some replacement kit,' Cato observed. 'Before someone mistakes you for one of those hairy-arsed barbarians you go on about and sticks a sword in you.'

'Anyone who tries that, barbarian or Roman alike, is going to get the same sword shoved up them where the sun don't shine.'

The villa was owned by a retired centurion from the Ninth Legion, Caius Hitetius, a slim veteran with sparse white hair and dark brown eyes. He had opened his house to the governor and his staff and made available the contents of his wine cellar and pantry. He greeted the new arrivals warmly, but frowned disapprovingly at Macro's appearance.

'I have a small bathhouse at the rear of the villa. Leave those rags outside and I'll have one of my slaves bring fresh clothes for you while you bathe and have a shave. When you feel human

275

again, come join the others in the triclinium for something to eat and drink. The cook's heating up mulsum, and that'll set your world to rights.'

Macro thanked him and followed one of the house slaves in the direction of the bathhouse. Once he had gone, Hitetius turned to Cato.

'You look exhausted, young man.'

Cato could not help smiling. Even though he still had a youthful appearance, he was in his mid thirties. He nodded. 'We're all very tired. When this is over, I swear I'll sleep for a month.'

Hitetius patted him on the shoulder. 'I'm sure. In the meantime, you must be hungry. Come.'

He led Cato through to the small walled garden at the rear of the villa, where Suetonius and his officers were seated around a long trestle table quietly consuming the food and wine that had been laid out for them. Cato noted the carefully kept flower beds and neatly trimmed bushes, and the birdbath at the far end, all dimly lit by the braziers burning in each corner. A place of tranquillity that seemed out of step with the world being torn apart beyond the walls of the villa.

'You keep a nice garden.'

'It was my late wife's pride and joy.' Hitetius smiled fondly. 'She died three years ago. I've kept it as she left it. Sit down.'

Cato found a place on one of the benches close to the governor and nodded a greeting to the other senior officers around him.

'How are your men?' asked Suetonius. 'I heard there was a bit of a skirmish before you pulled back from the ridge.'

'Hardly a skirmish, sir. We chased off some of the rebels who were after the last of the civilians. The enemy bolted when we set on them.'

'Any casualties?'

'Two dead, four slightly wounded.'

276

'That's two men we can ill afford to lose, Cato. Right now, soldiers' lives are far more valuable than those of civilians.'

'Yes, sir.'

They exchanged a look as the governor made sure his subordinate understood and accepted the priority. Then Suetonius took a sip of wine from a silver goblet and continued wearily.

'I've had word from the main column. They are still fifty miles north of Verulamium. They are strung out and will need at least another day before the stragglers catch up. So we're not likely to be in any shape to fight until four days from now.'

Cato grasped the point at once. There was no question of making a stand at Verulamium. A third key settlement of the province was to share the same fate as Camulodunum and Londinium. As many as ten thousand more civilians would be forced to flee, or perish if they failed to leave in time. And the pyre of another Roman settlement would be a beacon for yet more tribespeople to swell the ranks of Boudica's followers. By the same token, Roman morale would slump even lower as a result of this latest disaster.

He sighed heavily. 'Every step we retreat might appear to be one step closer to defeat, sir.'

'I know that, dammit,' Suetonius responded sharply. 'I don't need it pointed out to me.'

'I said that's how it *might* appear, sir.'

'I'm pretty certain that's how it looks to everyone partaking in this tragedy, Prefect.'

Cato's mind was dulled by exhaustion, and it took him a moment to marshal his thoughts before he could explain himself clearly. 'Sir, it's not the first time that a string of victories has drawn an army into a false sense of invincibility. So far the rebels have achieved only one notable success – the ambush of the Ninth Legion. At Camulodunum they faced a small force of veterans behind makeshift defences. Even fewer men were available at Londinium, which would have been impossible to defend with or without the Second Legion. Verulamium will fall for the same reason. The Fates have conspired to gift easy victories to the enemy. I've served in Britannia long enough to see how these people inflate even the smallest victory into a great triumph.'

'They may yet get their great triumph.'

'That's possible. But I think that having things their own way will go to their heads and make them rash. They have an appetite for victory now and they will all want to be in at the kill when we turn and face them in battle. That they will outnumber us at least five to one will only feed their arrogance.'

'Yes, imagine that,' Suetonius responded drily. 'They'll walk straight into the trap we have been baiting for them all along.'

Cato bit back his frustration. The governor was too tired to accept the argument he was trying to make. But he must not give in to his superior's despondency. He continued. 'Such odds are not going to be much use to the enemy unless the rebels can bring them to bear on open ground.' He leaned forward. 'On the march down from Mona, we passed a position that suits our needs precisely. It was a day's ride north of Verulamium, as I recall. A place where the road comes out of a forest and gives out onto a sloping vale with the treeline stretching out on either side for nearly half a mile before a large expanse of pastureland. Do you recall it, sir?'

Suetonius rubbed his brow and nodded. 'Yes . . . Yes, I remember it now.'

'If we were to draw up our forces across the vale, our flanks would be protected by the forest on either side. We'd have the advantage of the higher ground and the rebels would only be able to fight us on the same frontage. Their greater numbers would not be so much use to them in such a battle. And when the battle lines meet, our better training and discipline will prove its worth.

If we hold firm, as I believe we can, the rebels will not be able to overwhelm us.'

Suetonius considered the prospect for a moment. 'I can see the sense of what you say, Cato, but it's one thing to hold our ground and quite another to turn that into a victory. We need to beat the enemy decisively if we are to break this rebellion. Not being defeated is not the same thing as being victorious in this case. How do you propose we turn your plan into the outcome we need?'

'I'm not yet sure, sir. I need to think about it. All I know is that we have to inflict some kind of reverse on them as soon as possible if we are to shore up Roman morale and put an end to their string of successes. If we can inflict heavy enough losses, it will weaken their resolve and we may see many of them desert Boudica's army. They'll already have acquired their loot and slaked their desire for revenge and may not have an appetite for another hard-fought battle. They're not professional soldiers. They lack our discipline.'

'That's all very well, and I don't disagree with you, Prefect Cato, but fine words are no substitute for concrete tactics. I'll give consideration to your suggestion once I've had the chance to sleep on it. But for now, let's enjoy this fine spread that Hitetius has provided for us before we rest.' Suetonius raised his goblet to their host. 'Our thanks.'

'It's a pleasure to be amongst brothers in arms again,' Hitetius replied graciously. 'Besides, I'd sooner we finish off my wine and the best my larder has to offer than leave it for the enemy.' He looked round the garden sadly. 'All of this, the fruits of my service in the legions, will be gone by this time tomorrow, so let's make the most of it.' He poured himself a goblet and downed it in one, then rapped his cup on the table with a contented smile. 'I have a favour I would ask of you, sir, in return for my hospitality.'

'Oh?'

'My wife is gone and I have no family. Soon I will have nothing, except the weapons and kit from my army days. I've kept them in good order from force of habit. I'd be honoured if I might march and fight with the legions one last time before I hang up my sword for good.'

Suetonius looked the veteran up and down. 'How old are you, Centurion Hitetius?'

'Sixty-five, sir.' He lifted his chin defiantly. 'I still have plenty of fight left in me, and I can keep up with the column and show some of the young shavers a thing or two.'

Suetonius smiled admiringly. 'Brave words, comrade. Do you have a horse?'

'Yes, sir. I have four in my stables.'

'I'll be taking three of those for remounts. The last you can keep. You may ride with Prefect Cato's cohort. You can replace one of the men he lost today.'

Cato had the good sense not to respond to the jibe. 'I can always use a good man, sir.'

'Then it's settled.'

As the governor spoke, Macro entered the room, clean-shaven, with a rosy hue to his skin where he had scrubbed the grime away. He was wearing a fresh army tunic and boots. He nodded a greeting to the gathered officers and saluted Suetonius before the latter indicated the space by Cato.

'Centurion Macro, I hardly recognised you. You look Roman again.'

Hitetius regarded him. 'My old tunic's a good fit. I dare say some of my armour would serve equally well, if you have any use for it.'

Macro grinned. 'Just the man I needed!'

As Macro adjusted the final strap of the scale armour and shifted it into a more comfortable position, Hitetius nodded with approval.

'It'll do nicely,' said Cato from the corner of the room, where he was leaning against the wall with his arms crossed. 'Although it's perhaps a touch tight around the middle.'

Macro slapped his belly. 'That would be all the fine food and wine you plied us with, Hitetius. I dare say I'll have plenty of opportunity to work it off over the coming days.'

They were standing in the older centurion's study, off the garden. The latter was still and silent now that Suetonius and his officers had retired for the night.

'We all will,' said Cato, before his attention turned to Hitetius. 'Are you certain you want to join the cohort? You could take your horse and whatever valuables you can carry, and ride north to find shelter at Deva until the rebellion is over.'

'I could, but I won't. I've lived a long life. A good life. But since Albia died, I feel as if I'm counting off the days until we are reunited in the shades.' Hitetius crossed to the chest where his army kit was stored, took out his sword and drew it from its sheath. 'I've had this for fifteen years now. Picked it up at an auction of kit belonging to the officers of a unit that was decimated in the early days of the conquest of Britannia. It's a fine weapon, well balanced and with a keen edge. It seems a shame to let it gather dust here when it could be put to good use.' He sheathed the blade and set it down on a small table, then took out some more items from the chest: breast- and backplate, medal harness, helmet, greaves and bracers.

'Sure you can cope with all of that?' asked Macro as he ran his eyes over the other man's skinny frame.

Hitetius glanced up. 'I'll manage just fine, fuck you very much.'

Cato's gaze had been fixed on the sword during their exchange, and now he pointed to the weapon. 'Mind if I have a look?'

'Help yourself.'

He drew the weapon and held it up to the lamp hanging from

a wall bracket. The handle was bound in leather and the hilt and pommel were decorated with familiar designs. But it was the blade that drew his closest attention, and sure enough, the etched phrase he was looking for was still clearly visible on the gleaming surface. He smiled and gave the sword a few swings to test its weight and balance, finding it to be as good as Hitetius had said, and as good as he recalled from many years earlier. He slid it back into its sheath and set it down on the table.

'I know this sword.'

Hitetius looked round with a surprised expression. 'Really?'

'It used to belong to a centurion of the Second Legion by the name of Bestia. You remember him, Macro?'

'He's a hard man to forget. Tough as old boots and trained his men well. Did a good job on you, given that you weren't the most promising of recruits on the face of it. He died of wounds he received in battle shortly after the legion landed in Britannia, as I recall.'

'That's right.' Cato nodded.

'Not what I was told about the sword's provenance, then,' said Hitetius.

'No, that detail is correct,' Cato replied. 'Bestia handed the sword to another man in his will. A legionary at the time. He was promoted to the centurionate later in the campaign, before his unit was dishonoured and sentenced to decimation.'

Macro gave a low whistle. 'That's the sword he gave you, ain't it?'

Cato nodded.

'Bloody hell, small world.'

'It's your sword?' Hitetius picked the weapon up and eyed it fondly.

'Once, but not for a long time.'

'Then you should have it back.' He made to offer it to Cato, but the latter held up his hand.

'No. You've worn it at your side far longer than I ever did. Keep it, and do honour to its former owner.'

'Thank you, I will. Both of them.'

Suddenly Cato could not help throwing his head back in a wide yawn that made his jaw crack. He smiled in apology. 'I have to get some sleep.'

'Go. I will see you at first light when I join the cohort. I need to spend some time saying goodbye to my home. And I'll need to hide my wife's grave. I wouldn't want the enemy to desecrate it.'

'Want me to help with that?' Macro offered.

'No. Thanks, but no. It might be the last chance I have to be close to her in this life. Besides, you look like you need rest too. Go, I'll be fine.'

Leaving Hitetius alone in the study, Cato and Macro left the villa and returned to the lines of the Eighth Cohort. Overhead, the moon gleamed down on the dark landscape, while stars pricked the night sky. Thousands of people, clustered in groups, were sleeping or resting in the open, and there was some muted conversation, punctuated by the occasional wail of an infant or the sobbing of some inconsolable soul grieving over what had been lost or the grim prospects for the future. Many had not eaten for a day at least, and Cato felt a twinge of guilt over the generous feast he and the other officers had consumed earlier.

Macro was troubled by no such concerns. He was feeling rejuvenated by the bath, shave and fresh wardrobe and the kit that Hitetius had kindly provided. The serenity of the night only added to his good mood, until he recalled his mother. But there was nothing he could do about that, aside from silently swear an oath that she would be avenged.

After ensuring that Tubero had an adequate number of men assigned to the first watch of the night, the two officers settled down beside their saddles, pulled cloaks over their bodies and tried to sleep. Macro, as usual, managed the veteran's trick of falling asleep swiftly and settled into a rhythmic snore. Cato took a little longer, his thoughts focusing on Lucius and Claudia and the fervent hope that they would reach Gaul safely. Whether he ever saw them again would in all likelihood be decided within the next five or six days. The old soldier's adage of 'death or victory' had never been more apposite.

CHAPTER TWENTY

The column reached Verulamium the following evening, having managed to shepherd most of the civilians along with them. Those who could not keep up were placed onto carts, even if that meant emptying them of the possessions of the cart's owners, much to their outrage. When there was no more space on the carts, Cato had to harden his heart to those stragglers who couldn't be helped. They were left behind, and their forlorn cries echoed in the ears of the soldiers long after they had faded in the distance. No one doubted the fate that awaited them when the rebels caught up with them.

To the hunger of previous days was added the torment of thirst. The sun beat down from a cloudless sky and the clinging, choking dust stirred up along the road caught in the throat and eyes. There were no rivers and only a few streams along the route, and the water quickly became almost undrinkable as the muddy beds were stirred up. There was no time to venture further in search of food and drink as the enemy was never more than a mile behind the column. Close enough that those at the rear could see the distant figures of civilians being ridden down and butchered as they were overtaken. Twice Centurion Tubero asked for permission to send a squadron back down the road to drive the rebels off and give the stragglers a chance to catch up. Cato denied him curtly. Suetonius's stricture on putting the lives of his soldiers above those of civilians gave him no choice in the matter. Cold reason justified the governor's caution. The disparity in the size of the opposing armies placed a premium on the life of every man under his command.

As Suetonius led the column through the gates of Verulamium, he was met by a deputation from the town's senate. Unlike the colony at Camulodunum, there were few retired soldiers amongst the settlement's administrators. Most owned businesses in the town or were merchants who plied their trade between Verulamium and the rest of the province. Word that Londinium had been abandoned to the rebels had reached them the previous day, and they were anxious to confront the governor.

Suetonius was tired and anxious and was in no mood to heed the demands of the local worthies to turn and engage Boudica's army at Verulamium. The defences of the town, like those that had already fallen, had been neglected for many years, and buildings had spilled out across the outer ditch, making it easy for an enemy to infiltrate the settlement. The dismay and anger of the officials quickly gave way to the desire for self-preservation, and by the time the Eighth Cohort arrived, the streets were filling with those forced to flee their homes as well as the refugees from Londinium.

One of the junior tribunes was waiting for Cato and directed the cohort to the town's amphitheatre, which had been allocated to them for the night. It proved a good choice, as it was on the edge of the town and there was plenty of grazing for the horses in the open ground outside, while the raked seating provided modest comfort for the men to bed down on. Cato found a feed merchant who had packed his family onto a wagon and was on the verge of fleeing. He willingly threw open the warehouse where his grain and straw were stored before driving the wagon off. The horses were groomed, watered and fed before the men took care of their own needs, and as darkness fell, Cato gave the order for the beasts to be brought into the arena for the night and tethered around its perimeter.

Observing the crowded interior, Centurion Tubero scratched his head. 'Are you sure this is necessary, sir? We can post pickets far enough out to give ample warning if the enemy approach the town during the night.'

'We'll do that anyway. In the absence of a marching camp, the amphitheatre gives us something of a rampart and stockade at least.' He indicated the wooden perimeter hoardings rising above the top row of timber benches.

'As you wish, sir.'

As Tubero walked away, Macro addressed his friend quietly. 'Playing safe, then?'

'With the enemy following us so closely, that's the only way to play it. You know how it goes. I'd sooner have defences and not need them than need them and not have them.'

They found Hitetius making himself at home in the box reserved for dignitaries. It had a hide cover for a canopy so that its occupants would not get wet when it rained and would be shaded on hot days, while the other spectators shivered or sweated accordingly. The veteran was propped up on a couch, arms folded behind his head. The remains of the cold meat and bread he had brought from his villa lay in a small wicker basket.

'Not missing the comforts of home, then,' Macro observed.

'Not as comfortable as my bed, but better than sleeping on the ground, or on one of those benches out there. All the same, it's good to be back with the army. I always feel that is where a soldier's true home is.'

'Easy to say with a billet like this. Give it a few days of sleeping in the open, with a bit of rain thrown in, and you'll be cursing your fortune like a ranker.'

'Maybe, but I'll take each day on its own terms. Given that we might be dead ten days from now, that seems to be the sensible thing to do.'

'I've got plans for the future, so I won't be signing up to your philosophy, brother,' said Cato.

Hitetius gave him a thoughtful look before he continued. 'You're still young enough to feel that way. You might be a little more understanding when you reach my age. The imminence of death tends to make plans futile at the same time as it confers a nice rosy glow on the passing moment.'

Macro chuckled. 'Seems like you've found yourself a poet for a companion, Cato my lad. I hope you two won't spend the night swapping aphorisms while I'm trying to sleep.'

'I doubt that would stop you dropping off,' Cato replied, then noticed that Macro had already taken the only other couch in the box. All that remained were a couple of chairs and the floorboards. He chose a chair and placed it beside one of the posts holding up the canopy to give himself something to prop his back against. Then he looked round at the men patrolling the hoardings before leaning back, stretching out his legs and closing his eyes. Despite his concerns about the great peril facing the province and the fate of his son and lover, he was so exhausted that a heavy veil seemed to close over him in an instant. His chin slumped onto his breast and he began to snore lightly.

Macro glanced over with a surprised expression. 'He beat me to it. Never thought I'd live to see the day.'

The blare of a war horn woke all three men instantly. Macro was the first on his feet and went to the rail overlooking the arena. Already the officers of the cohort were rising and bellowing orders for the men to stand to. A moment later, Cato and then Hitetius joined him, as the horn sounded again, some distance away on the far side of the town.

288

'Tubero!' Cato called out across the turmoil within the amphitheatre. 'Centurion Tubero!'

'Sir!' A moonlit figure on the far side of the area waved.

'Have the First Squadron stand by their horses and get the rest of the men up on the rampart!'

'Yes, sir!'

Snatching up his armour, helmet and sword belt, Cato hurried to the rear of the box and climbed the steps between the tiered benches. Macro and Hitetius followed with their own kit. A second horn, closer to, answered the first, and he made his way round the highest level of the spectator seating, shoving past men hurrying to their positions.

'Make way there!' he called out harshly to warn them of his presence in the gloom.

He stopped as he came to the gatehouse over the main entrance, the highest point of the amphitheatre, looking back towards the settlement a short distance off. Though more horns were blowing now, there was no sign of movement, and he could still make out the figures of the mounted Roman pickets a few hundred paces south of the town. Macro and Hitetius caught up with him, the latter gasping for breath. Macro glanced around at the surrounding landscape.

'I can't see anything. Not yet. But they're out there.'

Now they could hear the faint shouts of alarm coming from within the town, and figures appeared along the wall. The last man of the cohort was in place and an anxious quiet settled over the amphitheatre as the auxiliaries stared into the night, looking for any sign of the enemy. Tubero climbed the short flight of steps to the top of the gatehouse and saluted.

'Cohort is ready, sir.'

'Good.' Cato nodded without taking his gaze from the shadowy landscape. He turned to the centurion. 'Which watch is this?'

'Last one before dawn, sir. About halfway through when the horns started sounding.'

More than an hour before first light then, he mused. At least the men would have had a decent rest and be better prepared for any trouble.

The horns fell silent, one by one, and peace seemed to return to the night. An owl hooted in a nearby field.

'What are they waiting for?' asked Macro as he finished tying the chin straps of the helmet he had been given.

They waited a moment longer before Cato shook his head. 'Nothing. Perhaps they're trying to rattle our cage. Keep us on edge before they put in a real attack.'

'Certainly has me on edge,' said Hitetius. 'I'm looking forward to making those bastards pay for driving me out of my villa.'

Cato turned and gave him a wry smile. 'I dare say the rebels share the sentiment, given how much we have helped ourselves to their lands since we invaded.'

Macro, standing at Cato's shoulder, met the veteran's gaze. Hitetius puffed his cheeks before he responded. 'That's a point of view, I suppose. Not a particularly popular one amongst Roman settlers in Britannia at the moment.'

'I dare say, but when the rebellion is over, assuming we are victorious, we're going to have to find a way of living alongside the locals if the bloodshed is to end.'

'Is your friend always like this?' Hitetius asked Macro.

'You can't imagine . . .'

They were interrupted by more unseen enemy horns, closer now. Cato saw the pickets falling back, running for the town gate and the amphitheatre. He could pick out movement – dark masses emerging from the shadowy landscape as they closed on Verulamium. He could hear the distant chant of war cries, and then something else: the thrumming of hooves and the rumbling of wheels. The sound was unmistakable. He turned quickly to Tubero.

'Take the mounted squadron out to cover our pickets while they fall back. That's chariots we can hear. Go!'

Straining his eyes, he was certain he could see several chariots racing ahead of the rebel infantry closing on the town. Below, he heard the groan of the hinges as the gates were opened, and Tubero's order to advance, then the squadron cantered out in columns of two and steered towards the chariots. In between were the dark shapes of the pickets fleeing for their lives.

'Why in Hades didn't they spot the enemy sooner?' Macro demanded. 'Damn sloppy work. Fucking five-day soldiers.'

'The rebels must have crept forward using the darkness. You have to admire their discipline in keeping such large numbers quiet for long enough to get so close. Something I hadn't counted on.' Cato clicked his tongue. 'Fair play to them.'

They watched as the squadron cantered past the pickets and engaged in a loose skirmish with the charioteers – a confused jumble of dark shapes, strident shouts of warning and cries of triumph as blows were landed. Meanwhile, the pickets had reached the safety of the amphitheatre. Shortly afterwards, Tubero and his squadron broke off the skirmish and followed them. The chariots pursued them briefly, then slowed to a halt before turning away to rejoin the rest of the force closing in on the town's southern flank.

'What now?' asked Hitetius. 'Is this a diversion of some kind, as you suggest, or an attack?'

Cato did not answer as he continued to strain his eyes to discern what has happening in the darkness and understand the enemy's intentions. Given how slowly they had moved on Londinium after sacking Macro's colony, it seemed hard to believe that they were about to strike the third town with their full strength so swiftly. Perhaps Boudica and her advisers had realised that their best chance of success in freeing the island of Roman rule was to wreak as much destruction as they could. That might persuade Nero that Britannia was too difficult and costly to sustain as a province. At the same time, they would surely be aware that Suetonius and his column were located here, providing an opportunity to kill the governor and overwhelm his force before it could reunite with the main column marching from Deva. It would make sense to defeat the Romans in detail rather than wait to let them gather in one place and risk all on the outcome of a single battle. Besides, taking the head of an imperial governor and commander of four legions would shatter Roman morale as much as it would feed that of the rebels.

As Cato considered the situation, it became clear that more and more of the enemy were emerging from the darkness and spreading out to envelop Verulamium and cut off the amphitheatre. He sensed the impatience of those waiting on him and came to a decision.

'This is no feint. It looks as if the rebel army is upon us.' He gazed to the east in vain for some sign of the dawn whose coming would make Boudica's intentions clear.

'There's a column heading our way.' Macro broke into his thoughts, pointing out a mass separating from the dark wave rolling towards the town.

It was too late to mount the men and ride out from the amphitheatre, Cato realised. They would have to stay and defend the place until dawn revealed the full situation. He called down to Tubero. 'Get some benches to bolster the gates! And anything heavy you can lay your hands on.'

'Yes, sir.'

Cupping his hands to his mouth, he called out to the rest of his men positioned around the ellipse of the amphitheatre. 'Prepare to receive an attack! Hold firm, lads!'

'Short and to the point,' said Hitetius. 'Just how I like my swords.'

Macro slapped him lightly on the shoulder. 'I think you're going to fit in here nicely.'

While Tubero and his men went to work tearing up the benches and jamming them against the insides of the gates, the rebels, by the thousand, came on at a fast pace. They halted a hundred or so paces away and began to stretch out along the flanks around the outside of the amphitheatre. There was no longer a need for silence, and they jeered at the defenders and broke into chants as they pumped their weapons up and down and worked themselves into a battle frenzy. Those inside the amphitheatre had witnessed the spectacle many times before and had long since ceased being intimidated by such displays.

Macro crossed to the nearest stretch of the hoardings that ran around the amphitheatre and wrenched it to test its strength. The planks were cheap and thin, a makeshift material put in place until such time as the town could afford a permanent masonry structure. He shook his head. 'It might look like a stockade, but it'll be easy enough to pull apart or pierce with a good weapon.'

'It's all we have,' Cato replied.

There was a roar from the direction of the town as the rebels swept towards its defences, accompanied by another outburst from their war horns. The din was taken up by those surrounding the amphitheatre, and at once they surged forward, the fastest amongst them opening up their formation as they raced ahead of the others, keen to have the honour of being the first to land a blow on their enemy. Around the arena, the auxiliaries readied their spears and adjusted their grip to stab down at their opponents.

The dark wave rushed towards them, and then the foremost rebels were scrambling up the steep turf slope, grasping at tufts of grass to help them gain purchase as they clambered towards the waiting auxiliaries. Cato saw the first of the enemy, a lithe man with a long-handled axe, reach the base of the hoarding and strike at the wooden surface, splintering the planks. He managed two blows before he was pierced through the shoulder by a spear thrust. He stumbled back, fell and rolled down the slope, dislodging two of his companions before disappearing into the mob beneath.

As he watched from the gatehouse, Cato was reminded of an ants' nest he had seen as a child; a mound covered with agitated black shapes. The angle of the slope was difficult to negotiate, particularly for those rebels armed with shields and armour, and the auxiliaries made the most of the advantage of height as they stabbed their spears down at the enemy climbing towards them. The air was fraught with the war cries of the rebels and the thud of weapons striking shields and the surface of the hoarding.

Some of the rebels were armed with bows, but the press of bodies and the darkness made it almost impossible for them to shoot with any accuracy. The shafts of arrows, invisible in the night, splintered the hoarding, struck fellow rebels in the back or passed over the Romans to fall amongst the horses in the arena or clatter against the benches on the far side. Only a few shots struck the defenders, one smashing into the jaw of a man on the gatehouse beside Cato. He stumbled back, dropping his shield and spear as he reached for the wound. As he went down on his knees, Cato leaned over him, squinting in the moonlight as he made out the shaft buried in the shattered bone and teeth. Taking hold of it in both hands, he broke it six inches from the wound as the man let out a gurgling howl of agony.

'Get him down into the arena,' Cato ordered the nearest of his men before warily returning to his station above the gates, trying not to imagine an enemy archer taking aim at him. He picked up the wounded auxiliary's shield to protect himself and looked round at the fighting raging along the ellipse. So far his men were easily holding their own and had kept the attackers at bay. Rebel bodies littered the bottom of the slope, and the wounded were limping through the lines of their comrades pressing forward to take their place.

'Look there!' Macro called out, pointing towards the rebels massing before the gate, the leading rank hammering at the sturdy timbers that had been reinforced by Tubero and his men. Thirty paces out, men were clearing a path for two groups of their comrades carrying some lengthy burden. Cato feared they might have rams, but as they drew close, he saw that they were ladders.

'Stand ready, boys,' he called out to the others on the gatehouse. 'Here they come!'

Those at the gate fell back, and the ladders were angled up so that they slapped down against the hoarding of the gatehouse. At once the first men were clambering up the rungs, before those above had a chance to thrust the risers away from the structure. Hitetius lunged for the first ladder and tried to tip it to the side, but the weight of the two rebels climbing towards him was too much, and he dropped back in disgust at himself, instead drawing his sword and aiming the point between the risers. A hand appeared, and then a face, eyes widening in shock before the point of the veteran's blade plunged through the left socket and into the brain. He tore the blade back and the rebel dropped out of sight.

'Ha!' Hitetius snarled. 'One for my home!'

Cato and Macro stood ready at the other ladder as a second enemy appeared, more wary than his comrade, holding a buckler above his head as he drew a short sword and feinted at the defenders. Cato hacked at the buckler as Macro grabbed the riser and, with a supreme effort, dragged it along the edge of the gatehouse until it overbalanced and toppled aside, carrying the men on it to the ground. Cato turned to see Hitetius cheering them on just as another rebel came up the remaining ladder and kicked a leg over the hoarding.

'Look out!'

The warning came too late. The rebel swung his axe at the veteran, catching him high on his left arm, below the shoulder. The blow was powerful, the edge of the weapon keen, and it cut through the muscle and shattered the bone, driving the veteran stumbling to his side. The rebel landed, feet braced and twirling his axe in an arc to keep the auxiliaries back. Raising his shield, Cato waited until the axe head had sailed past him, then charged home, battering the man against the hoarding and stabbing his sword into his thigh and groin. Macro came at him from the other side, twisting the axe from his grip and hurling it amongst the rebels at the bottom of the remaining ladder. Then he thrust the man against the hoarding and pushed him back.

'You've outstayed your welcome. Over you go!'

The rebel plummeted down the ladder, knocking off another who was halfway up and depositing both in a heap at the base. Macro seized his chance to thrust the ladder aside so it fell away on top of the enemy.

Turning to Hitetius, Cato saw that the veteran's wound was bleeding badly, the arm hanging from the shredded flesh and splintered bone below his shoulder. Hitetius was staring at the mangled limb with a surprised expression, but did not cry out as he stumbled to the rear of the gatehouse, sheathing his sword with his good hand. There was only a moment to detail one of the auxiliaries to get him to a cohort medic before Cato returned to his position.

To the east, he could see the first faint smudge of daylight lining the horizon and already he could make out more details of their surroundings. The auxiliaries were holding the line and had inflicted scores of casualties on the enemy in exchange for a handful of their own. A body lay still on the rampart on the opposite side of the arena, and several men were with the medics at the makeshift dressing station halfway up the raked seating.

'They're falling back,' Macro called out, and Cato saw the rebels edging away from the amphitheatre, those at the top of the turf slope skittering down and rejoining the ranks slinking off. The walking wounded limped away, while those who were more seriously stricken were carried to safety by their comrades. The dead and mortally injured were left where they had fallen, their bodies ringing the amphitheatre.

Cato looked beyond the rebel mass towards the town and saw that the fighting there was continuing in earnest. For the moment, the remainder of Suetonius's flying column and the town's small company of militia held the wall. It was a valiant effort, but as the light strengthened, he could see thousands more of the enemy debouching from a nearby forest, and many more approaching along the road from Londinium. The defenders were almost certain to be overwhelmed before the sun rose. Already the first civilians had forced the northern gate and were fleeing down the road. If the town fell, those Romans in the amphitheatre would be certain to be annihilated if they remained where they were.

'We have to get out of here,' he decided. 'Now.'

He hurried to the rear of the gatehouse and called across the arena, 'To horse!'

At once his men abandoned their positions along the rampart and hurried down to their mounts. Several of the beasts had been wounded by arrows and were rearing and snorting in torment. Cato ordered Tubero to clear the gate, then took one last look towards the enemy who had assaulted the amphitheatre and saw that they had turned away and were heading towards the town. He beckoned to Macro, and they made their way down into the arena.

Those mounts that were too badly injured to ride were led to a rail on the far side of the arena and leashed there. The wounded auxiliaries and Hitetius, whose injury had been hurriedly dressed and the limb strapped to his side, were helped into their saddles and assigned a man each to protect them. Four men stood ready at the gates to open them on Cato's order.

Once he was mounted, he called for silence to make sure all could hear his orders clearly. 'When we leave the amphitheatre, we make for a meeting point on the road ten miles north of Verulamium. If you get separated, make for the meeting point on your own. No man is to stop for any reason. May Fortuna be merciful, and may Jupiter, Best and Greatest, protect us from the enemy! Open the gate!'

There was a groan from the hinges as the heavy timbers were drawn inwards, and Tubero led the First Squadron out, followed by Cato with the standard and bucina close by and Macro behind him leading Hitetius's horse by the reins. The veteran's initial shock had faded, and now he was in agony as the horse jolted his arm at every step. The rest of the cohort followed, with the men who had opened the gates joining the rear.

They emerged at a trot, turning west to skirt round the town before making for the north road. The enemy saw their intention at once, and hundreds of them began to peel off from the main force in a bid to cut off their escape. They already had a half-mile head start on the Eighth Cohort, and Cato felt his guts clench with anxiety as he saw enemy infantry forming a crude line ahead of them, stretching to a cluster of huts on the verge of a small wood. He wondered about turning south and working their way round the far side of the trees before getting back onto the road further north. That would mean heading directly into the path of the rebels marching up from Londinium, however, and if they failed to clear the wood before the mass of the rebels reached it, they would be trapped and cut to pieces. No, the best hope of escape lay in breaking through the line ahead of them.

He called ahead to Tubero, 'Form a wedge!'

The centurion acknowledged the order, and the men following him fanned out on either flank in echelon.

Cato had the order passed down the squadrons, and the formations closed rapidly on the waiting infantry, who were already several ranks deep. As he readied his shield and prepared to draw his sword, he calculated the progressive increase in pace before unleashing the charge, then glanced back to ensure that Macro and Hitetius were close behind him, where he could best protect them when they tore into the enemy. The light was now strong enough for him to pick out details in the rebels' line and see the mix of weapons and armour they carried, much of it looted from the dead of the Ninth Legion and the veterans who had fallen at Camulodunum. There were also many of the kite shields and Gallic helmets that the tribal warriors had hidden away rather than surrender them to Roman officials as they had been ordered by a previous governor.

'At the canter!' he called, and Tubero increased the pace of the squadron, followed by each unit in turn. When there was scarcely two hundred paces between the centurion and the enemy, Cato gave the order for the gallop, and as the gap closed, he roared, 'Charge!'

Tubero drew his sword and waved it in a wild circle over his head as his men lowered their spear tips and hunched forward to brace themselves for the imminent impact with the enemy. Cato drew his own weapon, but held it raised and slightly out to the side as he grasped the reins and shield grip in his left hand and felt the reassuring pressure of the saddle horns holding him firmly in place. The ground rumbled with the pounding of hooves, and he could hear the bellowing snort of his horse's breath as the strands of its mane tossed in the air flowing past. His heartbeat quickened, and despite his tiredness, the ache in his muscles disappeared and he was filled with exhilaration.

It was no easy thing to stand before an oncoming cavalry charge, and Cato saw a handful of the enemy scurry out of the path of the oncoming auxiliaries. He guessed that many of those forming the line had never faced mounted men before and would be equally fearful.

Then the passage of time, which seemed to have slowed moments before, suddenly came on in a rush as the leading squadron ploughed in amongst the rebels with a thud of horseflesh on shields, flesh on flesh and the clatter of weapons and the sharp whinnying cries of horses as they knocked men down and took flesh wounds from those with the presence of mind to strike back at the horses and the men riding them. Tubero and his squadron plunged deep into the mass of rebels and drove their horses on, scattering the enemy with spear thrusts and battering others with their shields. Before the momentum died, Cato and the second column charged into the gap carved by the centurion and his men. There was still a scattering of rebels on their feet, and most tried to avoid the riders of the second wedge, but a few, more courageous than their comrades, fought back. Cato steered for a man wielding a long-handled axe and ran him down before he could strike. His horse stumbled as it trampled the rebel's body but managed to remain on its feet as it plunged on.

The first two squadrons merged into one disordered mass as they drove forward, cutting their way through the line. To his right he saw a sturdy rebel warrior with a boar spear firmly planted under his foot impale an auxiliary in the stomach, ripping the man from his saddle. His body slammed against the cross-piece behind the point of the weapon and his limbs flailed briefly before the warrior tipped him aside and onto the ground, where he wrenched the bloodied spear free. The riderless horse galloped on, weaving through the fighting until it burst into the open and tore off across the open ground.

Cato hacked to one side, twisted in his saddle and hacked to the other, working his horse left and right as he cleared a path for Macro and Hitetius. He burst through a cluster of lightly armed rebels, who hurled themselves aside, and then he was in the open beyond the line, along with several men of the First Squadron, who were about to turn to continue the fight.

'NO!' he bellowed at them. 'Keep going!'

They kept their mounts moving at speed, away from the battle and racing towards the road that led from the town's northern gate. There amongst the fleeing civilians were more mounted men, riding in groups, and Cato could easily pick out the crested helmets and scarlet cloaks of Suetonius, his staff officers and bodyguards as they made their escape. The governor must have realised that any attempt to fight off the attack was hopeless, and that flight was preferable to heroic destruction, which would have presented Boudica with one more prestigious and grisly trophy to brandish before her followers. Close behind them came the first of the rebels, who had chased them through the streets, slaughtering the easy prey of the civilians as well as falling upon any of the stragglers from Suetonius's small force.

The rest of the Eighth Cohort had broken through the enemy line, though at some cost, and now closed up with their comrades as they made for the road. Cato urged his mount alongside Tubero and the survivors of the First Squadron and took charge of the direction they were headed. The chaos and carnage on the road persuaded him to lead the cohort a short distance to the side, where they would not become entangled.

As they rode on, terrified screams from close by filled their ears. Cato saw three rebels hacking a family to death with their long swords. The father thrust himself in front of his young daughter and was felled by a blow to his neck that almost severed his head. Having killed the others, the rebels pinned the girl to the ground as the first of them planted his sword in the ground and lowered his breeches. Further on, a group of rebels were looting a cart around which lay the bloodied bodies of its owners. Nearby, two unmounted auxiliaries stood back to back, engaged by at least ten of the enemy. As the first was speared in his right side the rebels swarmed over his companion in a frenzy of blows from their swords and axes. The orgy of violence had a vengeful lust that Cato had not witnessed before, and he tore his gaze away and urged his mount on.

The first rays of the rising sun stretched over the horizon, casting long shadows in the lurid rosy glow that only added to the horror of what was happening. Two miles further along the road, Cato saw that they had outrun all but a handful of mounted civilians, and the enemy had given up the pursuit as they exulted in their latest bloody triumph. He halted the cohort once they had rejoined the road on high ground, and turned back to see that the first fires were already blazing in the fallen town. Beyond Verulamium, he could see the vast, unruly column of Boudica's followers crawling northwards across the gently rolling landscape.

Tubero shook his head. 'How can we ever hope to defeat that? We wouldn't stand a chance even if we had twice the number of soldiers in Britannia. We're fucked. Completely fucked.'

'Shut your mouth,' Cato snapped, then lowered his voice as he continued in a fierce tone. 'Don't you dare spew that kind of defeatist shit in front of the men. Pull yourself together, Centurion.'

Tubero took a calming breath and nodded.

'That's better. Now get the men formed up and ready to march.'

The centurion wheeled his mount and trotted back down the column to cajole the tired men into re-forming their squadrons.

'He's losing his grip, that one,' Macro commented as he steadied Hitetius in his saddle. The veteran was grasping one of the saddle horns tightly with his right hand as his left lay limply on his thigh.

'Tubero's a decent enough officer. He's just close to the limit of his endurance, like the rest of us.'

'If you're going to be a centurion, you set your limit beyond what the rest of the men can endure.'

'Fair point,' Cato conceded. 'How's the old boy doing?'

Hitetius looked up with a frown. 'The old boy is still capable of speaking for himself. I'm not some witless geriatric. I've still got one decent arm left and I'll knock you out of that saddle if you treat me like one.'

Cato raised a hand to pacify the veteran as he smiled wearily. 'Apologies, Centurion. We'll get that wound seen to the moment we rejoin the rest of the column.'

Hitetius nodded, then grimaced before he mastered the pain and clenched his jaw.

They waited while the stragglers from the other cohorts caught up with them, then Cato gave the order to advance. As they marched north towards the appointed meeting place, the clear sky behind them was stained by the coiled pillars of smoke rising from Verulamium.

CHAPTER TWENTY-ONE

It was an hour or so past noon when they caught up with Suetonius and most of the survivors of the other units in the column. They had overtaken the stragglers, some on foot leading lame or wounded horses and others who had lost their mounts, and these continued to drift in over the following hours. The governor and his staff were seated at tables outside an abandoned inn. Tribune Agricola's arm was in a bloodstained sling, and some of the others had dressings. A medic was attending to a gash in the governor's arm and was busy putting in the last suture as Cato dismounted and made his report.

'The Eighth lost thirty-four men, sir. Though there might still be a few who got away by a different route and may turn up later.'

'Thirty-four? You got off lightly compared to the rest of us. I doubt if half the column has survived.'

Cato glanced round at the men and horses surrounding the inn. Many had been wounded, and some were still being treated by the medics. The rest looked bone tired, and there was a despondent quietness about them that defeated troops often had. The officers surrounding the governor shared the same demeanour, and he could not help wondering how men in such a condition could hope to prevail against a much larger army, regardless of the disparity in training and discipline that advantaged the Romans.

'Any response from Legate Calpurnius, sir?'

Suetonius nodded, then made a face as the medic tied off the last suture and dabbed the blood away. 'He's sent word that his scouts have found the position you mentioned and reported that it might suit our purpose. He aims to reach that point tomorrow night. I've told him to halt there and rest his troops and let the stragglers and baggage catch up with him, particularly the artillery train. We will join the main column there sometime tomorrow afternoon if we march hard.' Suetonius glanced up at the sky. 'We've got several more hours of daylight to put some distance between us and the enemy before we camp for the night.'

'Begging your pardon, sir, I'm not sure it's wise to stop tonight. We'd be better off marching through the night so we reach Calpurnius in the morning. You saw how quickly the rebels moved up from Londinium to take us by surprise. Why wouldn't they do the same again? In their place, that's what I'd attempt.'

'Oh, would you?' Suetonius mused in a tone that suggested such a move would be bad manners.

Cato ignored the response as he continued. 'They know how few men are with you, sir. They'll be likely to send a large enough force of cavalry, and maybe some chariots, to catch up with us and make sure they take you, dead or alive, this time. We can't allow that to happen.'

'I appreciate your concern for my personal safety, but I need to think for a moment.' Suetonius dismissed the medic and flexed his arm.

Cato waited. He was not so much concerned about the personal safety of the governor as what that safety represented for Roman interests.

'You may rest assured that I won't let those barbarian scum take me alive,' said Suetonius. 'Whatever happens. As for your suggestion, it would be prudent to ensure that we keep ahead of

305

our pursuers until we reach the main column. Very well, we will march through the night. That will not make me a popular man, Prefect.'

'Goes with the rank, sir.'

'Yes, it does. I'll give the order to move once your men have had the chance to rest their horses.'

'Yes, sir.'

Cato made his way back to the column and gave the order to fall out and water the horses at a stream a short distance from the inn. The cohort's surgeon, Phrygenus, a wiry easterner, had removed Hitetius's dressing and was examining the wound as Cato approached. Macro was standing to one side, looking on with a concerned expression. Although there was no more bleeding, the flesh was puckered in purple hues, and it was clear that the veteran's arm would be useless for the rest of his life.

Cato was on the verge of speaking to the surgeon when he caught himself and addressed Hitetius instead. 'How are you doing?'

'It's bloody painful. Next dumb question?' The veteran ground his teeth before continuing. 'Your man here says I'll have to lose the arm. Can't fix it and there's a risk of it going bad and killing me. So off it comes.'

'When can you do it?' Cato asked the surgeon.

'Now would be best, sir.'

'We can't do that. The column is about to get back on the move and we'll be marching through the night. You'll have to get a fresh dressing on it quickly.'

The surgeon shook his head. 'Sir, we're lucky that the ride so far didn't open an artery. If a shard of bone shifts, it could cause heavy bleeding. He'd be dead in moments. His best chance is to have the limb removed and then cauterised.'

Hitetius, the surgeon and Macro all looked at Cato, waiting for his response. He balanced the risks. If Hitetius rode on, there

306

was a good chance he'd die. If he was left behind, the rebels would kill him if the wound didn't.

'How quickly could you perform the amputation?'

'I have the instruments. I'll need a fire to heat the artery clamps and the pitch. Say an hour or so.'

'An hour might be too long,' Cato replied. 'The rebels could be here before then.'

'Or they might not,' said Macro. He hesitated a moment as he considered the situation. If there was a chance to save Hitetius, that would go some small way to alleviating the guilt that burdened him. 'Look, I'll stay with the pair of them and get them away when it's done. If the enemy come close, we'll have to dress the wound and take a risk with the ride.'

There was a shout from behind, and Cato turned to see the prefect of the leading cohort, the Tenth Gallic, giving the order for his men to mount up.

'Very well. I'll leave you some men for an escort.' He paused and faced the surgeon. 'I'll not order you to stay and do this, Phrygenus. Are you willing to?'

'I'd rather not, but it's the best chance the centurion has of making it, sir.'

'I'll take that as a yes. Get it done then, as quick as you can, and catch up with the cohort.'

'Yes, sir.' The surgeon hurried over to his kit box to select his tools.

The First Squadron of the Tenth was already setting off, and Suetonius and his officers were making their way to their horse line.

'I'll see you on the road, or in camp tomorrow,' said Cato, as he clasped forearms with Macro, and then, more carefully, with Hitetius's uninjured limb. 'Good luck.'

He strode away to find Tubero and give the orders for ten men to remain behind and the rest to resume the march. Once he was back in the saddle, he let his column file by before giving a final wave to Macro and then cantering to take up his position at the head of the cohort.

Macro watched for a moment before he turned to the surgeon, who had cleared one of the inn's outside tables and set up his instruments on another, a gleaming assortment of fine blades and saws.

'What do you need us to do?'

'I'll need a fire going and a pan to heat this.' Phrygenus handed him a jar, and Macro removed the top and smelled the acrid contents.

'It has to be as hot as possible when I apply it,' the surgeon explained.

In the kitchen at the back of the inn, a bed of warm ashes lay below the iron griddle. Kindling and wood were stacked neatly at the side, together with a tinder box. Macro got a fire lit and put one of the heavy iron pots on it, then poured in the pitch and ordered one of the auxiliaries to keep an eye on it. Two more men were sent to the top of a nearby hill to keep watch along the road. Hitetius was sitting on a bench staring into the distance, and Macro crossed to him.

'Are you ready for this?'

'Would it make any difference if I wasn't?' The veteran smiled bleakly. 'It's a shame. When this is all over and I go back to what's left of my home, the gardening is going to take twice as long.'

'So take up another hobby. That's what I did when I took my discharge and lived in Camulodunum. Only need one hand to drink.'

'I could use a drink now.'

'There's some wine inside. I'll get it for you.'

'No. Better not be drunk when I get back in the saddle after Phrygenus has done his work.'

The auxiliary left in charge of heating the pitch appeared at the doorway to the inn and announced that it was ready.

'It's time,' said Macro.

The two men went to the tables the surgeon had prepared.

'If you'd lie here, sir.' Phrygenus gestured.

Hitetius eased himself up and lay flat. Phrygenus handed him a thick length of wood covered in leather. 'Bite down on that when the moment comes. Better than severing your tongue.' He looked at Macro. 'You'll have to hold his shoulders down. Another man for each leg and one for his good arm.'

When everyone was in place and Macro had pinned the veteran's shoulders against the tabletop, Phrygenus spoke gently. 'Best to turn your head away and close your eyes.'

'Fuck that.' Hitetius stared straight up at the sky as he clamped his teeth on the bit.

Phrygenus adjusted the centurion's arm so that it extended at a right angle to his body, then reached for a scalpel from the other table and bent over the wound.

He worked quickly, and the keen edge of the scalpel made short work of the torn flesh, exposing the bone, streaked with blood. Hitetius's face creased in agony and he made a low keening sound deep in his throat as he submitted to the process. Putting the scalpel to one side, Phrygenus picked up a rag to clean his hands before he reached for a delicate-looking saw. He turned to the auxiliary from the kitchen. 'Have the pitch ready the moment I call for it.'

Hitetius's jaw strained and the muscles of his neck stood out like thick cords of rope as the surgeon lowered the saw blade to the bone. A soft grating noise accompanied his actions, and Macro, despite long years of familiarity with wounds, felt his stomach lurch.

The bone parted with a crunch, and Phrygenus called for the pitch. The auxiliary came out with the pan, a thick piece of cloth wrapped around the handle, and set it down where the surgeon indicated.

A drumming of hooves caused Macro to look up, and he saw one of the lookouts galloping down the hill towards them. A moment later, he slewed to a halt a short distance from the table where Hitetius was stretched out.

'Sir, we've sighted the enemy! Fifty of them, led by three chariots, coming up the road.'

Macro nodded to the surgeon. 'Get it done. Quick.'

Phrygenus used a small scoop to apply the simmering pitch to the exposed bone and withered blood vessels. Hitetius's jaw sagged and the bit dropped to the table as he passed out and went limp. The surgeon added more pitch to cauterise the flesh until he was satisfied that he had done what was necessary.

Macro turned to the lookout. 'How far off are they?'

'Less than two miles, sir.'

'Shit.' He looked at Phrygenus. 'What's left to do?'

'We have to wait until the pitch dries and hardens enough for me to close the wound by stitching those folds of skin together.'

'How long?'

The surgeon shrugged. 'Not long.'

Macro hissed at the unhelpful response and switched his attention to the lookout. 'Get back onto the hill. When they're within a mile, come back here. Both of you.'

The auxiliary wheeled his mount and galloped back to the man still watching from the hill.

As they waited for the pitch to turn dull and harden, Phrygenus hurriedly wiped down the instruments he had used and packed everything back into the chest, save for the suture needle and thread. Hitetius stirred and opened his eyes, then his head lolled to the side and he lost consciousness again.

'Will he be able to ride in time?' asked Macro.

'Not by himself. Best to have him strapped to the saddle with a man on either side.'

'That's going to slow us down.'

As Macro glanced back to the hilltop the two lookouts started down the slope.

'Phrygenus, I don't care what you think about the pitch. Finish it off now.'

The medic made no protest. He picked up the needle in one hand and overlapped the folds of skin with the other and began to stitch them together over the ugly dark mass of the pitch. Hitetius grimaced and muttered something unintelligible as Phrygenus put the sutures in place.

The lookouts drew up and Macro glanced down the road. He could see the dust stirred up by the approaching enemy. 'Where are our friends?'

'Less than a mile away, and they've increased the pace, sir.' The auxiliary took in the severed arm and the smears of blood on the table, and glanced at his companion before he ventured a further remark. 'We should get moving, sir.'

'I'll give the fucking orders!' Macro glared at him and bunched his fists. The other man looked away, shamefaced. 'And you two get to ride either side of Hitetius.'

Phrygenus tied off the last suture. 'You can get him onto his horse now.'

Macro and the others who had been holding the veteran down lifted his body into the saddle and strapped him in place.

'They're coming!' one of the lookouts cried.

Macro saw the leading chariot trundle around the corner of a copse no more than half a mile away. The warrior on the bed of the chariot turned to call to his followers, and the other chariots and mounted men cantered into view, increasing their pace as they caught sight of the small group of Romans outside the inn.

311

Their war cries and the rumble of wheels and hooves carried across the open ground.

As soon as Hitetius was secure, Macro ordered his two escorts to get moving, then ran to his own mount. Phrygenus had closed his wooden chest and was struggling with the straps as the centurion passed him.

'Leave it, you bloody fool! It'll only weigh you down!'

The surgeon hesitated, then shoved the chest aside and rushed to his horse. The auxiliaries galloped off, followed by the two men either side of Hitetius, with Macro and Phrygenus at the rear. Looking over his shoulder, Macro saw that the enemy were scarcely three hundred paces behind. The mounted men drew steadily ahead of the chariots, light and nimble though the latter were, their riders leaning forward as they urged their horses on.

As the chase continued along the road, the gap between the Romans and their pursuers closed at points, only to open up again. Having been rested while Phrygenus had carried out the amputation, the Roman horses were a little fresher and managed to stay ahead. But it was becoming clear that the rebels were steadily closing and would soon overtake Macro and his party.

The way ahead climbed and then dipped into a vale where a wide river flowed languidly between beds of reeds. The road ran across a narrow stone bridge, wide enough to take a wagon, before climbing the far slope and passing into a forest. As the first of the auxiliaries reached the bridge, Macro called out to them. 'Stop there! Halt, damn you!'

As the leading men reined in, dust swirling around them, Macro drew a breath and gave his orders. 'You three men, stay here with me. The rest keep going until you catch up with the cohort. Phrygenus, you're in command. Make sure you get the centurion to safety. Go!'

As the riders galloped away up the slope, Macro assigned one man to hold the horses on the far side of the river and ordered the other two to join him on the bridge. He took the spear and shield of the horse holder and led the trio to the narrowest point between the low stone walls on either side.

'Shields up and spears advanced,' he instructed them as the first of the rebel horsemen approached, slowing down at the sight of the three men blocking his way.

'What the fuck are we doing here?' the man to Macro's left hissed.

'Our duty, lad. It's what you get paid for.'

'Then they aren't paying me enough.'

'I ain't disputing that,' Macro chuckled as he braced his boots and lowered his body to absorb the impact of any charge the enemy attempted. 'We'll take the pay issue up with the prefect when we see him next, eh?'

The rebel drew his sword and urged his mount onto the bridge at a canter. The points of three spears feinted towards the horse and it drew up and reared. The rebel gritted his teeth, turned the animal to the side and swung his sword at Macro, who took the blow on his shield as he lunged his spear at the rider's midriff, driving the point into his ribs. Withdrawing it, he dropped back a step into alignment with the two auxiliaries as the rebel turned his horse away, blood running down his side and soaking through his tunic.

As soon as the first man was off the bridge, two more riders came forward and tried in vain to get close enough to use their weapons. The large oval auxiliary shields blocked any blows and the Romans' spear thrusts wounded both the horses and another of the men before they withdrew to rejoin their comrades. From the crest of the bridge, Macro witnessed a heated exchange between a pigtailed warrior on the nearest of the three chariots, clearly their leader, and another man on horseback. With a snort of derision, the chariot-borne warrior gave an instruction to his driver, who steered the two yoked ponies towards the bridge at speed.

'They're going to try and run us down,' said Macro. 'Down on one knee and brace your spears!'

The three men knelt behind their shields, spear butts braced against the heels of their boots and points angled at the chariot. Macro could see the warrior gripping the rail with one hand as he raised a javelin and hurled it at the Romans. The shaft was deflected to the side and splashed into the fast-flowing river under the bridge. He could make out the fierce expression on the man's face and realised that there was no chance of the chariot stopping or drawing up before it reached them. Even if the ponies baulked at the spear points, they were trapped in their harnesses and bound to the yoke and would be driven onto the three men defending the bridge by the momentum of the vehicle behind. The warrior clearly placed little value on the lives of his animals.

'Oh shit . . .'

That was all there was time to utter before the right-hand pony impaled itself on the spear of the man next to Macro. The spear shattered and the auxiliary was knocked onto his back. The other pony managed to veer into the parapet before being drawn up by his stricken companion. The charioteer released his grip on the traces and sprang up onto the shaft, running forward and hurling himself at Macro. He was stabbed in the side by the other auxiliary and fell across the collapsed pony. The warrior who had been riding the chariot drew a long sword and plucked up a shield from the bed of the vehicle before jumping down between the dying pony and the one caught against the parapet. Macro rose to his feet and presented his shield, holding his spear in an underhand grip, arm muscles bunched as he readied himself to strike.

The warrior wore a mail vest under his cloak and a thick gold torc around his broad neck. He took a step towards Macro and thrust his shield out to test his opponent's reactions. Macro flinched, and the warrior sneered before suddenly rushing in, sword swinging, to force the centurion to block the blow. Too late Macro realised the man's intention as the warrior slipped his shield inside the shaft of the spear and with a mighty wrench flipped the Roman shield aside and thrust his sword at Macro's throat. There was no time for Macro to react, and in a moment of clarity, he felt sure that he was about to die. Then the shield of the auxiliary to his left blurred across his face and took the blow with a sharp thud.

Macro stepped back a pace to give himself space to wield his spear. The warrior had also stepped back, and snarled in frustration as he swung his sword in a display of dexterity, as if to challenge the Roman to come forward against him.

'Happy to oblige,' Macro growled as he resumed his balanced poise and feinted with the spear. He tried a short series of thrusts, but the warrior deflected each one with ease.

The centurion drew back and risked a glance over his shoulder. The rest of his party had ridden out of the vale and had a good head start on their pursuers. He looked back at the carnage on the bridge: the dying pony and mortally injured charioteer, the tangle of traces and the chariot jammed across the narrow space between the parapets. To one side, several rebels had walked their horses down to the reeds and were picking their way towards the open water. He had to put an end to the delaying action before it became a trap instead.

'All right, boys, fall back and get mounted. Have my horse ready for me when I come.'

The auxiliaries retreated a few paces and turned to trot back across the bridge to their comrade holding the reins of the four horses.

'Just you and me now.' Macro grinned at the warrior as he inscribed small circles with the tip of his spear. He took a half-step forward, then feinted again, and an instant later hurled his shield at the rebel. The latter was caught by surprise and

315

instinctively recoiled, giving Macro the briefest opportunity to strike. He lunged and thrust the spear, and it struck the warrior's right shoulder, penetrating to the bone. The rebel's sword dropped and he backed towards the chariot, raising his shield. Macro was tempted to finish the job, but several of the warrior's followers were already running onto the bridge.

'Your lucky day, sunshine.' He rose and hurled the spear over the warrior towards his men, then sprinted back towards the waiting horses.

Climbing into the saddle, he took the reins and turned away from the bridge, the auxiliaries urging their mounts into a gallop alongside him. They pounded up the gentle incline to the top of the vale before Macro looked back. The horsemen who had tried their luck in the river were being swept downstream as they did their best to get their mounts to make the crossing. On the bridge, the warrior was clutching a hand to his wounded shoulder as his men began to clear away the wreckage and bodies so they could continue the pursuit.

Macro felt a moment's satisfaction at winning enough time for Hitetius and the others to get clear of their pursuers. They were a couple of miles ahead of the centurion and his three companions, and a few miles ahead again he could make out the dust haze of Suetonius's column. Far enough away to frustrate any attempt by the rebels on the bridge to run their prey down once they were over the river.

CHAPTER TWENTY-TWO

The main column of Suetonius's army had only reached the meeting point an hour or so before the governor and the survivors of his flying column arrived. The legionaries were toiling away with their picks to prepare a ditch and rampart to surround the army's marching camp. Further out, auxiliary infantry screened the approaches to the camp and watched for sign of the enemy. Pegs marked the lines where the soldiers would erect their tents once the defences were complete. The command tents were already pitched, occupying a large area in the heart of the camp.

The riders coming from the south approached at a steady walking pace, the horses and men weary after their march through the night. Many of the riders were drooping in their saddles and had to be nudged awake by their comrades to keep from falling to the ground. It had proved a wise expedient to push the men on and not risk being overtaken by the rebels. The governor had halted the column at dusk and ordered scores of fires to be lit in the hope of fooling the enemy into thinking they were making camp for the night and luring them into delaying while they prepared another surprise attack. In the meantime, the column had won a few miles' head start before the ruse was discovered.

Hitetius had been in a poor state throughout the night, haunted by bad dreams in between episodes of wakeful agony. But as the sun had risen, his mind had cleared and he regarded the stump where his left arm had been with morbid interest. He wore only his tunic and boots. His sword belt hung from his saddle, while his armour had been carried by a packhorse of the Eighth Cohort.

'Your fighting days are over for good this time, I'm afraid,' said Cato when he had fallen in alongside Macro's group to see how the veteran was faring.

Hitetius raised his right hand. 'I'm still capable of using this.'

'That's not going to be much use to you in the line with other infantry, and you won't be able to ride and fight with the cavalry.'

'I'll find a place for myself when the time comes.'

'If you have fully recovered your strength, then maybe.'

Macro was surveying the camp site. 'That's not two full legions over there. Where are the rest of them?'

'Aside from the campaign losses, there'll be plenty still on the road from Deva,' said Cato. 'The stragglers should catch up within the next day or so.'

'They'd better. At the rate the rebels are advancing, they'll be on us soon.' Macro yawned and rubbed his eyes. 'Another thing. We'll need a rest before we're battle-ready. Our lot and the lads from the main column both.'

'Let's hope Boudica is kind enough to grant us that,' said Hitetius.

'Oh, I think she might.' Cato could not help a yawn of his own. 'After all, she's been pushing her army to keep on our tail ever since we quit Londinium. They're going to be as tired as we are. Maybe more so, since the vast majority are on foot. And there's the usual circus as they work themselves up into a battle fever.' He paused to force his weary mind to estimate the period of grace that Suetonius and his army might have before battle was joined. 'I'd give it at least two days. Maybe more if she waits for the baggage and camp followers to catch up.'

'Why would she do that?'

'She'll want her people to witness the spectacle of Suetonius and his army being wiped out. A story they will pass down the generations to set an example for those who may one day have to face the legions again. She knows this might be the hour of her greatness and that of the Iceni tribe who led the way. She has personal reasons too. She wants the largest audience possible to witness the punishment of those who flogged her and raped her daughters.'

'Sounds like you know the woman well enough.'

Cato and Macro exchanged a look. 'We do. She is brave and intelligent and was a loyal ally of Rome until some men of influence abused that relationship and made her into our enemy. When this is over, whichever way it goes, I hope those men will be held responsible and will pay the price for the bloodshed they have unleashed.'

'One of them already has,' said Macro. 'Good riddance to the bastard.'

'The procurator was merely the agent of those who sent him to stir up trouble. It goes close to the top of the political establishment. Some of them are probably members of Nero's inner circle of advisers.'

Hitetius shook his head. 'You can't be serious. Why would anyone be mad enough to provoke a rebellion?'

'For a number of reasons. There are some who believe that Britannia will never generate enough wealth to justify the cost of occupation. Others oppose the Senate faction that Suetonius belongs to. If he is defeated, his supporters' reputation is tarnished, and there will be an opportunity for any would-be general to take command of whatever punitive expedition is sent to Britannia. Whatever the motive, I dare say those behind it never dreamed the situation would become so dangerous. They underestimated the hatred towards Rome that many tribes felt.

And they underestimated Boudica. I hope that Suetonius has learned how dangerous that can be.'

'Are you certain he will turn and fight?' asked Macro. 'You've served with him in the field long enough to know his quality.'

Cato considered the question thoughtfully before he replied. 'Yes, I believe so. He doesn't have a choice. The big question is *where* he chooses to fight, and whether the rebels will accept battle on ground of our choice.'

'That's two questions,' Macro commented.

'Cut me some slack,' Cato grumbled. 'I'm shattered, Macro. Can barely string a coherent sentence together as it is.'

'We'll get some shut-eye tonight, safe and sound inside the camp. Jupiter's balls, I can hardly wait to get my head down.'

Up ahead, Cato saw Suetonius leading his staff through the half-constructed gatehouse and on towards the command tents. As each unit of the column reached the camp, one of Calpurnius's tribunes assigned them tent lines. Cato smiled wryly. They had no tents with them, having left them with the rest of the kit that had been abandoned when they set out from Mona. They would have to sleep in the open once again, until the baggage train arrived with their equipment.

'Has the rest of the Eighth Cohort arrived yet?' he asked the tribune. 'I'm their commanding officer.'

'Yes, sir. Prefect Cato. I recognise you. The infantry contingent of the Eighth are escorting the artillery train at the rear of the column. It'll take them a day or two to catch up.'

'I see. Send word to me the moment they arrive.'

'Yes, sir.'

They exchanged a salute, and Cato led his weary men through the gatehouse.

The site of the marching camp was well chosen. There was good grazing for the horses on the land between the fort and a meandering river where they could be watered. The auxiliaries

320

dismounted and led their horses to the lines, where they removed their saddles and saddle cloths before brushing the sweat from their hides. While Macro organised a shelter to provide some shade for Hitetius, Cato made his way across the camp to headquarters to find the supply officer. There were few rations to be had for the men or their horses until the baggage train arrived, he was told. Forage parties had been sent to scour the surrounding area and he was assured that the Eighth would be accorded their share of whatever was brought back to camp.

As he was leaving the supply officer's tent, he encountered Tribune Agricola. The young man was still covered with grime from the previous two days, and where it had soiled his face, it made him appear several years older. His eyes were red-rimmed with tiredness and he responded sluggishly to Cato's muted greeting.

'The governor's holding a meeting of all senior officers at dusk. He's resting until then,' he explained. 'Those of us who rode with him would be well advised to do the same. I will, the moment I can get hold of a sleeping mat.'

'Good luck with that.' Cato smiled. 'I'll see you at dusk then.'

When he returned to the Eighth's lines, the men had finished attending to their mounts and were dozing or sleeping on the bare ground while the duty squadron led strings of horses down to the river to drink and graze. Macro and Hitetius were already asleep under a goatskin awning with spears serving as tent poles. Leaving orders with the decurion on duty that they were to be woken an hour before dusk, Cato rolled up his cloak to act as a bolster and lay down, closing his eyes with relief. He was aware of the sounds of the camp for a moment before sleep closed over him like a warm, soothing fog.

When Tubero shook him gently, Cato was fully awake in an instant from force of habit. He sat up and looked around. The

321

marching camp was largely complete. A packed-earth rampart surrounded the neat rows of tents that had been erected as he slept, and the final stretches of the palisade were being driven into the ground. Closer to, the men of the Eighth Cohort were stretched out in the downtrodden grass. Hitetius and Macro were still asleep. The latter's mouth sagged open and a faint rattle sounded from the back of his throat before he took a snorting double breath and turned onto his side.

'An hour or so before dusk, near as I make it, sir,' said Tubero. 'Thank you.'

As the centurion walked off to continue his rounds of the men on duty, Cato stretched his arms, wincing. Almost every joint and muscle in his body seemed to ache, and he walked stiffly as he made his way out of the camp and down towards the river. Horses grazed on the lush grass in the late-afternoon sun as butterflies flickered amongst them. There were a number of soldiers bathing in the river, some splashing about in the shallows while others sat immersed up to their shoulders enjoying the cold flow of the water.

On the far bank, some seventy paces away, several enemy scouts were keeping watch on the Roman camp. Two men remained with the horses while their comrades sat on the riverbank, sunning themselves. Every so often, one would cup his hands to shout something insulting to the Roman bathers. A reply would be shouted back, and sometimes both groups of men would laugh if the gist was clear and amusing enough. Watching them for a moment, Cato found it strange how men dedicated to each other's extermination often sought out some sign of kindred spirit in such moments. Perhaps it was the serenity of the setting, and the joy that men found in bathing in a river.

After the tension of recent days, Cato needed a moment alone. He found himself a small gap between clumps of reeds, opposite a small shrub-covered island in the middle of the river. Stripping off, he entered the chilly water, grimacing as it closed round his groin. He rose on his toes and braced himself, then threw himself forward and swam a few brisk strokes to get used to the temperature before striking out towards the island, angling upstream to make sure he didn't get carried past the open stretch of pebbles he was aiming for. The current became stronger the further out from the bank he swam, and by the time he emerged onto the island, his heart was beating fast. He felt refreshed and clean and decided to rest there briefly before swimming back.

Closing his eyes, he enjoyed the remaining warmth of the sun sinking towards the west. He tried to clear his mind to enjoy this brief escape from his cares and responsibilities, but found his thoughts shifting to Lucius and Claudia, wondering whether they had yet reached safety. It must be the same for Macro with regard to Petronella, and selfishly he longed for the time when neither of them had had any dependents to burden them with worries about their well-being. It was no wonder the army had long since forbidden soldiers from being married. Not that it made much difference, since men formed long-standing relationships, had children and made wills that were as binding as any relating to a civilian marriage.

A flurry of splashing nearby caused his eyes to snap open, and when he sat up, he saw a swimmer in difficulties a short distance upriver. He dived back into the water, heading to intercept the man. As he drew close, the swimmer started to go under, his gleaming dark hair plastered to his scalp and his arms flailing in his struggle to keep afloat. Reaching him, Cato placed his hand under the man's chin and turned on his back as he struck out for the island. The man resisted weakly before allowing himself to be towed to safety. As soon as his feet could get a good purchase on the riverbed, Cato pulled the swimmer out of the water and onto the pebbles. It was then that he saw the swirling tattoos on the man's chest and the plait on the back of his head.

The tribesman was as naked as Cato, and since he was exhausted and spluttering for breath, he constituted no immediate danger. Even though he was the enemy and it would have been easy to crush his head with a rock or drag him back into the river to drown him, Cato had no wish to harm him. It would be a cowardly and unworthy act. Instead he squatted down a short distance away and waited for the rebel to recover enough to prop himself on an elbow. He nodded his thanks, and his eyes narrowed suspiciously as he realised his rescuer was a Roman.

'How are you doing?' Cato asked in the Iceni dialect he had learned during the time he had spent with the tribe.

The man looked surprised before he coughed and replied, 'Been better.' He tapped his chest. 'Tongdubnus. Iceni.'

'I thought so.' Cato indicated the horse-head designs amid the tattoos on the rebel's chest. 'My name is Cato. I'm from . . .' He gestured pointlessly in the direction of the fort, as if the Icenian had any doubts about his identity.

'You speak our tongue well. Not many Romans I have met ever tried to.'

'I learned from my Iceni friends . . . At least, they were my friends before the rebellion.'

'Those days are gone. Perhaps you Romans should not have treated your friends so badly.' The warrior eased himself up into a sitting position and regarded Cato warily.

'Not all Romans are the same,' Cato protested. 'I would have done all I could to save that friendship. But . . . Politics. You understand?'

'Your politics, Roman . . . Cato. Not ours. How could we remain friends when you outraged our queen and dishonoured our tribe?'

'I know. I cannot tell you how much I regret that. The man responsible is dead. To that extent Boudica has been avenged. Some justice has been done.'

'It's too late for that.'

Cato looked at him directly and nodded. 'True.'

'Rome forced us to rise up. We endured being robbed of our lands and property for long enough before our queen was humiliated. Now we will hunt you down and kill you all and Britannia will be free again.' Tongdubnus spoke with passion, then regarded Cato anxiously, fearing that he had overstepped the mark.

'There's no need for killing here and now. Not between us. Not after I saved your life. There's been enough bloodshed already, and there will be more. But for now, let us have this moment of peace. Agreed?' Cato reached out his hand. The rebel hesitated, then grasped it firmly as he nodded.

They lay in the glow of the late-afternoon sun, talking about the people and places both men were familiar with and listening to the jovial exchanges being shouted across the river further upstream. At length Cato knew he must return to the Roman-held bank of the river.

'I have to go now.' He stood up.

Tongdubnus rose too, and nodded. 'I thank you for saving my life. You know my people well enough to understand what that means. I am in your debt. But I will not be able to repay you. In a few days our armies will meet in battle and the Romans will be defeated. You will all die. I will be sad, knowing that you are amongst the dead.'

'Maybe my side will win.'

'No. That is not possible. Our gods have foretold our victory. We have nothing to fear when we go into battle.'

'Even the gods make mistakes.'

They clasped hands one last time, then Cato waded out into the river. He looked back at the rebel. 'May your gods protect you, Tongdubnus, and see that you return safely to your home and hearth.'

'And you also, Cato. Wherever your home is, as long as it is not in Britannia. Perhaps one day I may meet you as a guest in our land, rather than an invader.'

Cato struck out across the current, swimming hard towards the gap in the reeds where he had left his clothes. When he reached the bank and emerged from the water, he looked back across the glittering eddies, but Tongdubnus had gone. As he dressed and did up his boots, he reflected on the encounter and wondered if either of them would survive the coming battle. He set off for the headquarters tent with a sense of regret at the failure of governance the rebellion represented.

Even though the sweltering heat of the day had passed, the side flaps of the headquarters tents were rolled up for the comfort of the governor and his staff. Cato was the last to arrive, water dripping from his matted hair as he found a space at the end of one of the benches. Suetonius was quietly conferring with Legate Calpurnius, but when he saw the late arrival, he turned to the assembled officers.

'Now that we're all here . . . The most recent reports from the tail of Calpurnius's column indicate that the rest of our forces will reach us by the end of tomorrow. By then we shall be able to field eight thousand legionaries and as many auxiliary troops, together with forty serviceable bolt-throwers in the artillery train. We have limited supplies of caltrops but no means of casting any more. Our men are in good condition and will be battle-ready once they have rested. Our scouts have been keeping watch on the enemy vanguard. They are a day's march away, with the bulk of their forces and baggage a day behind the leading elements. That gives us two days' grace. Barely sufficient if they choose to attack at once. But I suspect they will also need to rest and gather their strength for the battle. It's likely, therefore, that the issue may be decided three days from now.'

He paused to let his officers digest the prospect, then continued, 'I have discussed with Legate Calpurnius the possibility of attacking the enemy before they have a chance to gather their full strength, but the scouts report that even their vanguard outnumbers us two to one. Therefore it is my decision that we must fight a defensive battle on ground that advantages us. Prefect Cato has identified a potential site a few miles north of the marching camp. Legate Calpurnius passed through yesterday and he confirms that it may be suitable and offer us a number of advantages. I will inspect the site for myself tomorrow morning before I make a decision. Assuming it is satisfactory, we will move the army there the day after tomorrow and draw up our battle lines and prepare the ground.'

'Excuse me, sir,' Tribune Agricola responded. 'But what if the enemy decides not to fight us on our ground? They're familiar enough with our ways to refuse to take the bait. What if they use their numbers to manoeuvre round us and turn the position into a trap?'

'It's a fair question. But I've been considering the speed with which they pursued us from Londinium compared to the time they took marching there from Camulodunum. It's my conviction that Boudica wants to win her victory as soon as possible. She might need to. The tribes of Britannia, as we know, have rarely made good bedfellows. The people of this island are a fractious lot. Traditionally more divides them than unites them. She has finally provided them a common purpose through their shared hatred of Rome. Some will have satisfied that hatred through the destruction of three of our largest settlements and the booty they have claimed in the process. They will be looking for a reason to slip away. Then there will be those amongst her advisers who have different views on how the rebellion should play out. Some will no doubt be harbouring ambitions to replace her as leader. Time is therefore against Boudica and she may need a decisive result while she has the authority and the numbers to achieve it. I believe she will fight us wherever we choose to let her find us.'

'I suppose so, sir,' Agricola commented. 'I hope so, at any rate.'

'I think there's good reason to believe that,' Cato commented. Suetonius and the other officers looked in his direction, and he continued, 'I had a conversation with one of their warriors while I was swimming in the river earlier.'

Suetonius looked at him curiously. 'You had a conversation with one of the rebels?'

'I speak some Iceni, sir. The man came from Boudica's tribe. I saved him from drowning and we got talking.'

'Prefect Cato . . . I swear that as long as I live, I shall not meet an officer more likely to surprise me at almost every turn with some new ability or scheme. Go on. What did your new-found acquaintance have to say?'

'He said that the rebels have been told that their gods have promised a great victory. If that's the case, she won't be likely to try and outmanoeuvre us if the battleground is not entirely to her liking. If any of us were in her position, we'd think twice about it, but for Boudica tactical issues are only part of what is driving her. She has the numbers, the blessings of her gods and the desire to crush us as swiftly as possible before the eyes of her people. I believe she will attack us wherever we offer battle.'

Suetonius considered his words. 'I hope you are right about all of that, Prefect. Everything is riding on the decisions I make now.'

'There is something else we need to consider, sir,' Cato continued. 'The fate of the civilians outside the camp. We need to make arrangements for their safety before the battle takes place. We can't just leave them while we move the army into position. They're bound to try and follow us. The last thing we need is to be encumbered by them and their baggage.'

'What do you suggest?'

'We have to get them out of the way. Sufficiently far that they won't get in the way of our preparations for the battle. At the moment, they are tired, but more importantly, they're hungry. Most of them left Londinium several days ago. They'll have exhausted what food they might have brought with them. So let's offer to feed them from our supplies. At an appointed place as far north of the battlefield as we can get them to in the time available. There's plenty to go round in the baggage train Legate Calpurnius brought with him from Deva.'

'It's true that we have enough to feed the army for five more days,' said Calpurnius. 'But if we hand over most of that to the civilians, what are the soldiers going to eat two days from now?'

'If we are victorious, we'll find far more to eat than we'll ever need amongst the rebels' baggage train,' Cato pointed out. 'And if we are defeated, it won't be a problem that concerns us, since we'll all be dead.'

Suetonius could not help a smile. 'When you put it like that . . . Very well. Calpurnius, have an announcement made throughout the civilian encampment that the army will be providing them with food twenty miles further up the road. First thing in the morning. That should get them on the move and out of our way in plenty of time.'

'Yes, sir. Should I say anything about your decision to give battle? It might be good for their morale.'

Suetonius considered the suggestion briefly, then shook his head. 'I think not. They have enough worries already. It would be kindest to say nothing. The more astute amongst them will know what the position is in any case but will be keeping it to themselves. Just tell them about the food.'

'Yes, sir.'

Suetonius was quiet for a moment. 'I think that's all there is to say tonight, gentlemen. Make sure your men and horses are rested. Get as much sleep as you can. Tomorrow we'll inspect the site that Prefect Cato has chosen for us, whether it's the place where we win a victory as famous as any in the long history of Rome, or the place that will become the graveyard of the Roman army in Britannia. Dismissed.'

CHAPTER TWENTY-THREE

As the last of the civilians trudged out of sight along the road cutting through the forest, Suetonius's senior officers surveyed the landscape from the top of the gentle slope, while the governor himself walked off a short distance to consider his plans. To the right and left of the road, the treeline angled away downhill to a broad expanse of low-lying grassland, where a stream flowed from left to right. The road cut directly across this and ran south over gently undulating countryside interspersed with copses and small woods. There were several farms, some of which had not yet been abandoned. The fine weather continued, with blue sky broken up by the fluffy shapes of brilliant white clouds drifting serenely. There was the lightest of breezes to provide some relief from the oppressive heat of the noon sun.

'So this is the place you recommended we should make our stand,' Tribune Agricola commented to Cato as he rested his hands on his hips and looked over the main features of the landscape. 'It's true that it gives us the advantage of the high ground, but that slope is gentle enough that it won't tire the enemy when they start up it. And the flanks are covered by the woods. The trees and the undergrowth look dense enough to hinder an attack, but that cuts both ways. If we have to beat a quick retreat, those trees will pose quite an obstacle to our men. The only other route would be along the road, and that would be congested in short order.'

'There's truth in what you say,' Cato replied. 'However, I'm not sure Suetonius envisages any kind of retreat once battle is joined. That would be almost as bad as a defeat, given the strategic situation. It would be delaying the final destruction of what remains of the army. No, I think he means for us to leave this battlefield as victors, or die here. If I was in his place, I'd feel the same way.'

Agricola shook his head. 'That's madness. To bet everything on one throw of the dice and have no contingency plan – what kind of general would do that?'

'Do you think Suetonius is unaware of the potential dangers of this site in the event we are defeated? Our men will know the score the moment they see this position. They will understand that there is little chance of escape if the battle goes against us. That will certainly harden their resolve when the fighting starts.'

Agricola looked at him closely. 'That's what you had in mind when you told him about this place.'

'Certainly,' Cato admitted. 'We're vastly outnumbered, and the fate of the province hangs by a thread. In such a predicament, it's vital that the men know there is no escape. They must conquer or die. It's a simple incentive to motivate them to fight to the best of their ability, and beyond.'

'May the gods preserve us from the reasoning of professional soldiers . . . There has to be a better place to make our stand than this.'

Cato gestured to the surrounding landscape. 'Be my guest. If you can find a superior position in the time it takes for the enemy to arrive, you're a better soldier than me.'

The challenge went unanswered by the young aristocrat, so Cato continued patiently explaining in a manner suggestive of a teacher trying not to display irritation towards a student who had read but one book on a particular topic and assumed the hubris to behave as if they were the greatest living expert on such matters.

'The overriding factor in determining where we should draw up our battle line is the huge disparity in numbers. Therefore, we need somewhere we can force the enemy to fight us on a narrow front.' He examined the ground and pointed to a milestone on the road halfway down the slope. 'There. If our army is drawn up across the slope from that point, our flanks will reach the trees and be protected by them, and we will have sufficient depth to withstand a series of charges. Each of those charges will be compressed between the woods on either side as the enemy closes on our narrow front. So it doesn't much matter how many more men they have, as only a limited number will be in contact with our line at any moment. Man for man, our soldiers are better trained and equipped than the rebels. The first time they charge us, they will be in for a rude shock.'

He indicated the sprawling landscape in front of the position. 'That's where they will mass before they charge. They will know their numbers and see how few we are in comparison. That will embolden them, and when they rush in, they will be pressed together. Easy targets for our bolt-throwers and then our javelins before their charge hits our line and the close-quarter fighting begins. They will be shaken by their losses and their charge will be robbed of some of its impetus.'

'You make it sound as if we have the battle in the bag.'

'Not quite, Tribune. The danger to our side will come if the enemy manage to whittle our numbers down to the point where we cannot maintain a long enough line. Then we'll have to fall back to a narrower point between the trees, or thin out our ranks and take the risk that the rebels may break through. If that happens and they get enough men into the gap, then it's as good as over for us. They'll roll up our line, trap us against the forest and then cut us to pieces.'

333

Cato reflected briefly. 'What it comes down to is a simple calculation: will they be able to absorb sufficient casualties to wear us down to breaking point? This won't be a battle where a smart manoeuvre wins the day. It's going to be a long, hard fight with victory for whichever side has the stomach to outlast the other. Even if we win the battle, it may come at such a cost that we still can't put down the rebellion. Both sides will be fighting to completely destroy the other. The problem for us is that we have to kill four or five of them for each man we lose. It's possible. History has handed down enough examples where the smaller army triumphs over the larger.'

Agricola looked down the slope, as if trying to visualise what was to come. 'If any of that was supposed to offer a crumb of comfort, you've failed.'

'We're soldiers. We deal with realities. We leave the honey-coating of harsh truths to politicians and lawyers.'

'You are a little ray of sunshine, aren't you?'

'You sought out my views and I'm telling you what I think based on my experience. I've been at this game for nearly eighteen years now. You were probably still sucking at your mother's tit when I joined the Second Legion. It was quite a different unit at the time. One of the best. It pains me to think of the shame they have earned recently. I've seen enough to know how the battle will be fought. You'd do well to listen to those with experience if you want to rise to senior command. I can already see that you have the makings of a decent officer. In a way, you're fortunate. Most tribunes come and go, serving out their two years' enlistment without doing anything more useful than drawing up watch rotas. Few get to take part in a battle. You will learn a lot about yourself and the men around you in the next few days. If you survive, the experience will be useful to you later on. Make sure you stand your ground and let the men see you are unshakeable, even if your every instinct tells you to run . . . Anyway, here comes Suetonius.'

They turned to the governor as he strode towards his officers, drawing up a short distance away to address them. 'This place suits our needs well, just as Prefect Cato said it might.' He nodded his gratitude. 'We'll be able to make the enemy conform to the length of our battle line. The Fourteenth and Twentieth legions will occupy the centre, here.' He stabbed a finger towards the ground. 'The auxiliaries will form up on the flanks. Tenth Gallic and Eighth Illyrian on the right, the Second and Fifth Macedonian on the left, with the remaining cohorts in reserve, along with what's left of our mounted contingents. The artillery will be divided into three batteries behind the centre and each of the wings. I want most of our baggage train left on the other side of the forest. We'll have some wagons brought forward to where the road enters the trees, to create a redoubt where the army's surgeons and medics can treat the injured.'

He hesitated, and Cato guessed what was in his thoughts. If the battle went against them, the redoubt would be where the remnants of his army would gather to make their final stand. There was no need to elaborate. The experienced officers got the point without needing to be told. If they had to resort to using the redoubt, it would be a matter of taking as many rebels with them as possible, and ensuring that the wounded were not taken alive for the enemy to torture and mutilate.

Facing back down the slope, Suetonius continued, 'I expect the rebels to occupy that slight rise in the ground a mile or so off. When they begin their attacks, they'll go full pelt downhill, and hopefully the steeper slope on our side will wind them a bit before they make contact. The bolt-throwers will open up the moment the enemy come within range. Since we occupy the high ground, our shots will travel further. When they get closer to, the front ranks of the infantry will throw javelins and be fed more from weapons from the rear ranks. They can replenish stocks between charges.

'Between the distance the rebels have to cover, the slope and the missiles raining down on them, they won't be able to hit us with much impetus. And then it's down to our men to keep their shields up and stick it to the enemy with their swords. We will be able to throw back the first charge well enough, and the second, and those that follow. However, they will have fresh men to push forward each time. We won't. There will be casualties on our side and our strength will be steadily sapped as the battle goes on. It's going to be about endurance and courage. Whoever possesses most of those qualities will win the day. I believe that will be us,' he added firmly. 'We have the best men and the best training, and besides,' he gave a wry smile, 'we have nowhere we can run to for help or shelter. It's on us, and only us, to win this battle. May the gods save the emperor, and Rome!'

Even though the officers echoed his cheer, Cato was alert to the anxious expressions and half-hearted gusto of some and the grim resignation of others. It was clear that every one of them understood the high stakes Suetonius was playing for. When the battle began, all of them would have to fight as never before. Every ounce of their courage, strength and skill at arms would be tested to the utmost. Anything short of that risked certain defeat and death.

Suetonius waited for the clamour to die down before he spoke again. 'Our scouts report that the main body of the enemy will be in striking distance of our camp by the end of tomorrow. If we remain there too long, we may be surrounded and besieged. Therefore we will abandon the camp and move the army here. That has the additional benefit of cutting the distance for the last elements of the main column to join us. You will receive your orders after we return to the camp. Prefect Cato . . .'

Cato sighed inwardly. Here it comes, he thought, another stint at the thankless and exhausting job of handling the rearguard. 'Sir?'

The tone of his voice caused Suetonius to smile. 'I think the Eighth Cohort has performed admirably as the rearguard of the mounted column . . . However, you and your mounted contingent will be the first unit to leave the camp tomorrow. You are to proceed north until you link up with the rest of your men and the artillery train. We must have the bolt-thrower batteries prepared by the end of the day. Understand?'

'Yes, sir.'

'You'll need to have your men ready to march before dawn to ensure they reach the artillery train in good time.'

'They'll be ready, sir.'

'I don't doubt it. If the last few months have proved anything, it's that your lads are the finest auxiliary unit in Britannia. I dare say they'll be adding a fresh decoration to their standard before long.'

'Thank you, sir.' Cato acknowledged the praise self-consciously, aware of the admiration on the faces of most of the other officers. 'May I pass your words on to the men?'

'By all means. Anything that inspires them to fight their hardest.'

It was hard to tell from the remark whether the governor was earnest about his words of praise a moment earlier, or whether it was a ploy to wring out every last ounce of effort from the men under his command.

'They will, sir. They always have.'

The first glow of dawn was seeping over the eastern horizon as the Eighth Cohort left the marching camp. The legionaries of the Twentieth were already at work taking down the palisade stakes and breaking up the ramparts to refill the ditch. Within a matter of hours, the only trace of the camp would be the heaps of loose soil that marked its boundary. There would be nothing left that the enemy could occupy and use for defensive purposes of their own. That the legions could construct and dismantle marching camps so efficiently was one more tribute to the finely tuned war machine that Rome had created, and Cato looked on with a feeling of pride as the legionaries went about their task.

Beyond the Roman camp, on the far side of the river and covering a vast expanse of the landscape to the south, glittered the fires and embers of the rebel horde. The woodsmoke created a veil that obscured the lowest-hanging stars. By the light of the nearest fires still being fed, Cato could pick out the figures of those sleeping around them or stirring to scrutinise the movements in the Roman camp. He wondered if Tongdubnus was amongst those looking in his direction. Was the Iceni warrior still as certain of victory, or was he harbouring misgivings now that battle was imminent?

Thanks to his years of service across the Empire, Cato was aware of the mixed feelings that soldiers experienced before battle. There was always excitement at the prospect of contributing some small part to a page of history about to be written. There was the nervous cheerfulness of the inexperienced and the stolid reflectiveness of veterans. Some men were boastful about their intended exploits. Sometimes to try and conceal their fears. Sometimes because they truly relished the thrill and danger of combat and liked to imagine themselves saving the life of their general and being handsomely rewarded for the deed. There were others who convinced themselves that they were fated to die, or suffer a cruelly disabling wound that would reduce them to the humiliation of begging for a living. For them there was often the additional shaming prospect that they might try to turn and run when the battle began. The army had long since found a way to deal with such men: any attempt to flee would be met by a blow from the weighted staffs carried by the optios as they patrolled the rear rank of their units. In most cases, the presence of other men on either side, behind and before, was enough to stiffen resolve. The army was a brotherhood that fostered the deepest of bonds in order to make the prospect of letting down your comrades almost unthinkable.

It would be somewhat different in the enemy camp, where the tribal warriors still clung to the ideal of the individual heroic warrior striving to outdo the exploits of his peers. It was not their way to consider themselves part of a formation. That drive to win personal acclaim was what made the Celts formidable opponents in single combat, but almost unmanageable in battle.

'Quite a sight, isn't it?' said Macro as he drew alongside Cato and rested his hands on one of his saddle horns. 'I have never seen anything like it in all my days serving with the eagles.'

'Numbers aren't everything.'

'True.' He nodded. 'But sometimes they are. I hope this isn't one of those times.'

They walked their horses on in silence for a moment before Cato spoke again. 'This isn't like you, Macro. The odds have never daunted you in the past.'

'I don't think the odds have ever been so stacked against us, brother. Besides, men are born with only a certain amount of luck. Some have very little and don't last long. I've been blessed. Truly I have. I might have been killed on many occasions, but I survived. However, these last few months I feel that I've used up whatever luck remained to me. The gods eventually get bored of their playthings. I fear I may have outlived my entertainment value to the fuckers.'

Cato was used to his friend's rough piety when it came to the gods, the Fates, the Furies and, once in a while, the Muses. He tolerated it, as friends did, to a point.

'Macro, has it occurred to you that your survival owes as much to your toughness and ability as it does to luck and the whim of the gods?'

'Hmm. Fair point . . . In any case, if they ever choose to give

339

up on me, then fuck 'em. I'll manage on my own.'

Cato looked at him askance, and Macro was only able to keep a straight face for a few beats before he roared with laughter. 'Ha! Got you. I'll be fine. Just as soon as I've made an offering to Fortuna before the battle to keep her happy. I'll put in a word for you too. As always.'

Cato shook his head. 'You're bloody hopeless . . .'

They met the main baggage column, along with the artillery train, some eight miles north of the position Suetonius had chosen to face the enemy. Cato's servant, Trebonius, and Centurion Galerius, who had been left in command of the Eighth Illyrian Cohort's infantry, gave broad smiles as they greeted their prefect.

'Good to see you again, sir!' said Galerius.

'I trust you haven't let the cohort go to rack and ruin in my absence?'

'Not a bit of it. We picked up the stragglers from the mounted column along the road, so we should have all the available men ready for action.'

Cato introduced Macro and Hitetius, before Galerius's smile faded as he looked at the denuded ranks of the cavalry contingent marching up behind. 'The rest of the men . . . Lost?'

Cato nodded.

'We heard the news about Londinium and Verulamium from the civilians we passed yesterday.'

'Without the rest of the army, there was no chance of saving either town. Now that you've finally turned up, the governor's going to make a stand a short distance down the road. He sent me to hurry the artillery train along.'

Galerius nodded. 'Good. Let's see how brave those rebel bastards are when they go up against three legions and the auxiliary cohorts.'

'There'll only be two legions. The Fourteenth and the Twentieth.'

'What's happened to the Second, sir?'

Macro snorted with contempt. 'What indeed? Their acting commander got cold feet and is holed up in the fortress down at Isca Dumnoniorum. You'd think one of the other officers would shame him into growing a spine, or take the initiative and relieve him of his command and get their lads moving. Pah! To think that the Second, of all legions, should have sunk so low.'

'I take it you served with them?'

'For most of my career,' Macro replied. 'Bloody fine legion. Once.'

'Crying shame,' Hitetius added with feeling. 'It's going to be a long time before their reputation recovers.'

Cato interjected. 'Much as I'd like to spend time reminiscing about the glory days of our old unit and bemoaning its present condition, we need to get the artillery train moving.'

'Easier said than done, sir.' Galerius indicated the long line of wagons and carts stretching out ahead of those being escorted by the infantry of the Eighth Cohort. 'That lot have been holding us up most of the way from Deva.'

'Not any more they won't.' Cato turned in his saddle. 'Tubero! Take your men forward. You are to clear the baggage train off the road while the artillery moves on. Tell any supply officer who gives you trouble that the order comes from Suetonius himself. If there are any complaints, they can take them up with the governor after the battle.'

'Yes, sir!' Tubero chuckled and turned the men about to follow him back down the road, repeating Cato's orders to the drovers and wagon masters he met along the way. Where there were protests, a handful of auxiliaries were left to make sure the vehicles moved aside. The reluctance to obey was understandable, Cato reflected. The ground on either side, while generally even

341

and dry, sometimes gave way to softer surfaces or dips, and there was a risk of the heavier wagons getting stuck, or worse, rolling over. But that could not be helped. The bolt-throwers were the priority, and they had to be reassembled and in position as swiftly as possible. Cato turned to Trebonius.

'If any choice items of food or wine happen to fall off the back of any of those wagons, that would be appreciated.'

His servant grinned. 'Be a sin to waste good food and drink, sir. I'll see to it.'

The nearest vehicles began to pull off the road, to the accompaniment of the shouts of the drovers as they whacked their canes against the rears of their harnessed oxen and mules.

'Let's go,' Cato barked, and the order was repeated down the line, the mules of the artillery train straining against their harnesses to get the carts moving. As they passed the men of the baggage train, Cato ignored their surly looks and muttered resentment. Soon they would have more important matters to occupy their thoughts.

It was late afternoon before the artillery wagons, accompanied by the Eighth Cohort, emerged from the forest road and looked down the slope at the site Suetonius had chosen for the army. Most of the units had already arrived and been assigned their positions. The legionaries of the Fourteenth had been posted to the left of the road, and the Twentieth were to the right. Sounds of sawing and chopping came from the trees either side, and Cato saw men carrying roughly hewn stakes down the slope to be deposited in piles close to where Suetonius had indicated the Roman battle line would make its stand. The combined mounted strength of the auxiliary contingents came to little more than eight hundred riders, and most of the mounts were being watered at the stream running by the bottom of the slope. In the distance, the two infantry cohorts of the rearguard were approaching along the road with small groups of rebel cavalry hanging on their flanks, just beyond javelin range.

The positions chosen for the artillery batteries had been marked out by stakes with red strips of cloth tied to the top. Fifty paces behind the battle line, the artillery crews would have a clear view of the enemy as they approached. The rebels would come within range of the bolt-throwers once they had crossed the stream, Cato calculated. Suetonius had assigned twenty of the weapons to each flank battery and forty to the centre.

Once the carts had been handed over to the artillery crews of the legions, Cato led his men to their position on the extreme right of the line. As they passed the Tenth Gallic, he raised his hand in greeting to its commander, Prefect Thrasyllus. His auxiliaries were cutting away the turf and soil in front of their position to create a ledge, some three feet above the ground in front of them, from which to fight the enemy. Some of the men were driving stakes into the earth at the foot of the ledge, angled towards the enemy, before they were sharpened with adzes.

'Hot work, Cato!' Thrasyllus called.

'So I see.'

'Suetonius wants the field works completed by nightfall. You'd better get your lads to it straight away.'

'We'll manage.'

Thrasyllus squinted towards the sun, calculating the hours of daylight left, and shook his head. 'I doubt it.'

The ground marked out for the Eighth Illyrian extended across a front of a hundred paces from the treeline to the flank of Thrasyllus's cohort. The Eighth was one of the larger, combined cavalry and infantry cohorts, with over nine hundred men on its roll when they had begun the campaign to take Mona. Combat losses, injuries and sickness had reduced that to less than half its original strength. With the mounted contingent being withdrawn to the reserve with the rest of the cavalry, Cato would be left with three hundred men to hold his section of the battle line. Three ranks deep then, he thought. Hardly enough to stand their ground against a determined charge. He could only hope that the governor's plan to break up the charges with missiles and field defences succeeded.

Once the men had downed their marching yokes and taken out their picks, their centurions set them to work preparing the fighting ledge to be occupied by the Eighth. It was clear that the auxiliaries were dog tired after the long day's march, but there was no time to let them rest. Cato decided he needed to set an example to show them how vital it was that the army was prepared for battle as swiftly as possible. Removing his helmet, he took up two of the spare tools from a cart and handed one to Macro. 'Let's show them how it's done.'

They took their place where the ledge constructed by the neighbouring cohort ended and began to swing the picks, breaking up the earth into clumps of rooted grass and loose soil. The men looked on with surprised and amused expressions to see their commanding officer laying into the earth. After the first few swings, Cato paused and stood up to address them.

'What? You think your prefect is too high and mighty for such work? Let me tell you, long before I was a prefect, I was a ranker in the legions. Now, if you gentlemen have finished gawking, you'd better get stuck in before Centurion Macro and I finish the job for you!'

The comment was greeted with laughter, and the men fell into line and set to, and soon the ledge began to take shape. The work was accompanied by the usual banter, and the centurions had no need to use their canes to urge the men on. Dusk was settling over the landscape when the task neared completion, and Cato lowered his pick and mopped the sweat from his face with the back of his forearm. He examined their efforts with satisfaction before sending Galerius and his century to fetch some stakes to complete the cohort's field defences.

Reaching for his canteen, he took a generous swig before turning his attention to the spectacle developing to the south. The rearguard had reached the modest ford that crossed the stream and were tramping up the slope to join the rest of the army. The groups of rebel horsemen that had been shadowing them drew up a few hundred paces further back to regard their enemy's preparations. Beyond them, some miles to the south, the last rays of the setting sun cast a red hue across the dry countryside and the vast dark mass of Boudica's army and its camp followers. Above them hung a rosy veil of dust, and there was an endless ripple of glints as the sun caught the weapons and armour of the rebel warriors.

The other men of the cohort, and those all along the slope, paused to regard the vast column inching its way closer like some titanic swarm of insects. A peculiar silence fell over them as they looked on in awe. Only a few had seen the full scale of the enemy host as it approached Londinium. Now Suetonius and every man in his army could see the peril for themselves and understand the magnitude of the struggle that faced them.

'It's like . . . it's like a great flood,' one of the auxiliaries near Cato commented artlessly. 'Come to sweep us away.'

Macro had untied his neckcloth and was mopping his face. 'Ain't nobody going to sweep us anywhere, boys. The Roman army is the rock on which enemy armies break.'

'And sometimes they don't . . .' Cato said softly to himself.

He drew a breath and shouted an order across the slope. 'Back to work! I want the stakes positioned and sharpened while there's still light! Get moving!'

CHAPTER TWENTY-FOUR

Through the night, more and more campfires were lit in a broad arc around the Roman position, the nearest on the slight rise in the ground a mile beyond the stream. From there, thousands of red glints stretched away until they appeared to meet the cool white glitter of the stars. The faint hubbub of voices and whinnies reminded Cato of the sounds that came from the Circus Maximus in Rome before the races began. He knew that the tens of thousands of people gathered around the fires shared the desire to destroy every Roman settlement and kill every Roman soldier, civilian and collaborator in Britannia. And yet he could not help finding the spectacle quite eerie and, in its way, beautiful.

Around him, the preparation of the Roman fieldworks continued in the darkness as the engineers oversaw the construction of the batteries' defences and the siting of an assembly of bolt-throwers. Further back, a line of wagons had been formed across the narrowest point between the trees either side of the road to act as the final redoubt. By the light of braziers, men were fixing logs across the wheels to deny access under the vehicles. Others were building up the sides of the wagons facing the slope and constructing a gatehouse over the road.

Elsewhere, the units that had completed their field defences were resting in position. There were no tents, as Suetonius did not want the army to be encumbered by them if the enemy attempted a surprise night attack. So the men lay on the ground, trying to sleep, or sat up and stared at the enemy camp, mesmerised by its scale. Conversation was muted, and a sole effort to raise spirits with a marching song was abandoned after the first two verses.

After walking the line of his pickets, two hundred paces down the slope, making sure they were alert and that they knew the correct challenge and reply, Cato continued to the fire lit for the officers of the Eighth Cohort. Behind them, planted firmly in the ground, was the cohort's standard. The gold crown that had been awarded to the Eighth in Mona was attached to the staff just below the plaque with the cohort's name and number. Above that was the silver likeness of the emperor, clearly cast by an artisan who had never seen Nero in the flesh. Most of the centurions and optios were with their men, but Galerius and Tubero were sharing a couple of flasks of wine with Macro and Hitetius as Trebonius prepared some stew in an iron pot resting on an iron griddle positioned over a campfire.

'Mind if I have some?' asked Cato as he sat down.

'Of course, sir. My pleasure,' Galerius replied, holding out his flask. Cato took a sniff, made an impressed face and took a swig.

'Good stuff.'

'The old boy got it for us.' Galerius indicated Hitetius.

'There's an inn on the other side of the forest. The owner's a former optio of mine,' the veteran explained. 'He managed to keep back some of his best stock when the army marched past. You know how it is with the legionaries. They'll help themselves to everything and never pay if they can get away with it. I had to give him a very good price for as much as I could carry. I went back for it while you and your lads were busy.' He tapped the large purse on his belt. 'Not much point in hanging on to my silver if there's a chance I won't live to spend it, eh?'

347

'You'll still be around,' Cato said, though the veteran's defeatist comment had soured his enjoyment of the wine. 'Once we've beaten the rebels, you're going to need every sestertius you have to rebuild your life.'

'Fat chance of that,' Hitetius replied, waving the leather cup that covered his stump. 'What good is a one-armed man to anyone?'

'One arm or two isn't going to make much difference to keeping a woman happy,' Galerius leered, his voice betraying the quantity of wine he had already consumed.

Hitetius's expression became sad. 'There'll never be another woman. Not after Albia.'

'Never say never, especially with regards to women!' Galerius reached for the flask, but Cato held on to it and shook his head.

'You've had enough, Centurion. I suggest you go and see to your men. Tell them to get their heads down, and you do the same. I want every man of the cohort rested and fresh for battle tomorrow.'

'Yes, sir,' Galerius responded in a surly tone before rising unsteadily to his feet, saluting, and striding off into the darkness.

'Bit harsh,' Macro commented.

'He's a good officer, and I want to keep him that way. He may get promoted to command a cohort of his own one day. He needs to know when he's drunk enough and stop there.'

Cato turned to Hitetius. 'I apologise for what he said a moment ago.'

The veteran waved his hand dismissively. 'He didn't mean any harm. He never knew Albia. If he had, he would understand why I am no longer interested in other women.' There was silence before he spoke again. 'How about you, Prefect? You have a wife?'

'I had a wife once. A woman I loved and thought I could trust. Turns out I was mistaken. She's dead now and I've moved on.

348

We had a son. Lucius. He's a good boy. Wants to be a soldier when he grows up, although I think that's because he's become too used to having the likes of me and Macro around.'

'It doesn't sound like you're keen on the idea.'

'It'll be his choice when the time comes. As long as it makes him happy, that's all that matters to me.'

'Fair enough. Where is he now?'

'Not here. Safe, I hope. I sent him away from Britannia when the rebels came for Londinium. Him, and Claudia, who I hope to make my second wife one day.' Cato smiled fondly. 'I think she's the one. Like your Albia. I can see myself growing old with her at my side.'

'Then you have something to live for, my friend. Be thankful for that. How about you, Macro?'

'I have Petronella,' Macro grinned. 'The best woman in the Empire. Brave as a lion, tough as a first spear centurion, and she throws a right hook that would knock a professional boxer on his arse. She can hold her drink and she's a wildcat in the sack . . . By the gods, I miss her. She's with Cato's boy and Claudia, making sure they're both safe.'

'Sounds like a keeper,' Hitetius said wryly. 'From your description of her, the prefect must either be feeling fortunate that she's looking out for his loved ones, or terrified of what might become of them under her influence.'

Macro scowled. 'She's a good woman. Won't have a bad word said about her. If you want to keep that head on your shoulders, I'd be careful what you say.'

'I've no wish to lose another piece of my body,' Hitetius chuckled, and handed Macro a fresh flask of wine. 'Have one on me, for your Petronella.'

Macro raised the flask. 'For Petronella, Claudia and the memory of your Albia. Bless 'em all.' He took a swig and passed the flask round as the toast was echoed by the others, then looked

349

wistfully across to the enemy camp in the distance.

Cato knew that his friend was thinking about Boudica, and the daughter whose existence he had only recently been made aware of. There was a time, long before she became Queen of the Iceni, when she might have been more than a passing flame to Macro, but for an arranged marriage to Prasutagus, a warrior hero of their tribe. It was possible, thought Cato, that had she chosen differently back then, the bloodshed of the last few months might have been avoided. History was a fickle bitch, he concluded, smiling inwardly. It was the kind of abbreviated aphorism Macro might have come up with.

'Whatever happens tomorrow, and whatever has happened in recent days, she is a fine woman too, Macro. And a mother who would fight to the last to protect her children.'

Macro looked at him guiltily before he nodded. 'I know. I just wish . . .' He shook his head and took another swig. 'That's the way things go. The fucking Fates will play their bloody games with common soldiers and queens alike.'

'That's what I thought you'd say,' Cato chuckled. 'Let me have that flask before you finish it all.'

They continued drinking until half the small supply of wine remained, and Cato told Tubero to take the rest to share with the men, rather than let himself or Macro risk becoming drunk at such a critical time.

'I'll keep one back for myself,' said Hitetius, putting the flask quickly into his sidebag before Cato could volunteer it for common consumption. 'For medicinal purposes tomorrow, if needed.'

'You won't be doing any fighting,' said Cato. 'I want you to the rear, helping out with the cohort's medical orderlies.'

'What good would I be with one arm?' Hitetius countered angrily. 'I could hardly tie dressings, thread a needle or suchlike. I've still got my sword arm, and that's all I need to fight.'

'And how will you carry a shield?' asked Macro. 'You'll need one of those if you're to avoid being skewered by the first rebel with a spear who comes at you. Besides, we can't afford any gaps in the shield wall.'

The veteran was about to protest again when Cato cut in firmly. 'I've made my decision, Centurion Hitetius. I am the prefect of the Eighth. You asked to join the cohort and that means you obey my orders. If that's not acceptable to you, you have no place here. You'll be treated as a civilian and removed from the battlefield. Is that clear?'

The veteran struggled to his feet and offered an exaggerated salute before he strode off into the darkness.

Trebonius approached with the first two mess tins of stew and arched an eyebrow. 'Just the two of you eating, sir?'

Cato nodded as he took the stew and carefully tested it. 'Good. Very good. Have some yourself.'

'Yes, sir. Thank you.' Trebonius touched his brow in salute and returned to his fire. The two officers ate in silence before Macro cleared his throat.

'Was that necessary? What you said to Hitetius.'

'Yes.'

'He's a proud man. You know how it is with some old soldiers, they never really get over having to retire. The army is their life. That's all the old codger has now that his wife has gone and his home has most likely been ransacked and torched.'

'I can't help that. I'm commanding a cohort, not a social club for veterans. Besides, I'm too tired to get into an argument over it. I've made my decision. He has his orders and he'll damn well obey them. If you want to make anything more of it, the medics can always use an extra pair of hands.'

Macro raised both hands. 'You make Hitetius's argument for him . . . He's not much use to the wounded with only one of these.'

'Oh, shut up, Macro. I'm going to get some sleep. You'd be wise to do the same.'

Cato eased himself onto his side, back to the fire, raising his arm to act as a headrest. He closed his eyes and tried to clear his head. The preparations for the battle had been completed. Tubero would handle the changing of the sentries, and if there was an attack, the alarm would be raised across the army's position and every man would be on his feet and in formation in an instant. His last waking thought was about his treatment of Hitetius. Perhaps he could have handled it more sensitively. But that made no difference to Macro's point about the veteran being a liability to a battle line. In any case, if things went against Rome, Hitetius would have his way after all.

A foggy weariness closed over his mind, and within seconds he was asleep.

Macro woke him at first light, and Cato stirred and groaned as the stiffness in his limbs and back made itself felt. He momentarily regretted the work he had done alongside the men the previous evening.

'Upsy-daisy!' Macro said cheerfully as he hauled him to his feet.

Around them, the rest of the cohort was stirring with weary mutterings. Some of the men had already started cooking fires to prepare a substantial enough meal to see them through whatever the day brought. A fine mist hung over the slope, and the shapes of the men were vague and spectral, while the sounds coming from the other units of the army were muffled.

'Anything to report?' Cato asked.

'I spoke with Galerius when I went for a piss a moment ago. He was just coming off watch. Not a peep from the enemy. I imagine they want to be rested for what's coming today as well.' Macro looked to the west as the first rays of the sun stretched out feebly, struggling to pierce the mist. 'That is the last sunrise many men are going to see . . .'

'Yes,' Cato answered flatly, then glanced round. 'Where's Hitetius?'

'No idea. He didn't come back to the fire last night. He might have joined the medics in the redoubt. That or he's buggered off to join the civilians heading north, given the way you spoke to him.'

The critical edge to Macro's words was hard to miss, but Cato had said his piece and made his decision and saw no reason to go back on it.

As the sun rose, the mist steadily thinned and seemed to recede down the slope, where it stopped over the stream and continued to hang there. On the rising ground beyond, the rebels were already on the move. Large bands of men on foot marched out of the enemy camp and took up their positions in an arc facing the Roman army. They strode forward confidently before they were halted and marshalled into position by their chieftains, gradually forming a line at least three times as long as that of the Romans, with a depth that extended up the slope almost as far as the ridge. The rebel cavalry moved to the flanks, several thousand of them, and then sent their mounts to the rear as they closed up on their comrades on foot and waited for the battle to begin.

Behind them, the first wagons and carts appeared and formed up along the crest of the far slope. There they were unharnessed and pushed together to form a solid-looking barricade that gradually lengthened beyond the flanks of the army and curved round some distance beyond. Cato could just make out many thousands of figures climbing onto the vehicles, women, children and old men, packed in tightly.

'What's going on there?' asked Macro as he squinted towards the barricade. 'Looks like they're preparing their own fieldworks. Surely they can't be thinking we'd be mad enough to attack them?'

'It's not for that purpose,' said Cato. 'Looks to me like Boudica wants to give as many of her people as possible a grand view of proceedings. Like an audience at the theatre, except that admission is free and the bloodshed is real.'

Once the first enemy bands were in position, the warriors sat down while they waited for more formations to arrive. The mist over the stream faded as the sun climbed above the horizon. There was a noticeable dullness to it, and a haze obscured the sky so that it appeared tawny rather than the clear azure of previous days. A bank of dark clouds lingered to the north, and the air was still and felt close and uncomfortable.

The enemy line was at least four hundred yards back from the stream, and small groups of warriors came down the slope to fill waterskins to take back to their comrades. Despite the haze, it was going to be a hot day, Cato realised, and he gave orders for each of the centuries in his cohort to send a section down to the water, carrying the canteens of the rest of the men. He watched curiously as some of the auxiliaries and their opposite numbers exchanged comments, and even traded rations and small items whose details he could not make out.

'It's a strange business,' he commented to Macro. 'Those men down there appear to be getting on well enough. In a few hours' time, they'll be trying to gut each other with their swords. I'm not sure I should be indulging them.'

'Leave 'em be. What harm can it do?'

'I suppose.'

As the early-morning hours passed and there was no sign that an attack was imminent, the mounted men of both sides took their horses to the stream to drink, and there was further trading of banter and trinkets. Three hours or so after sunrise, however, Suetonius sent tribunes down to order the troops back to their lines. The rebels strung out on the far side of the stream looked on in disgust and loudly booed the young Roman officers.

354

Once all the men were back in position, the governor made his way along the Roman line from left to right, stopping at each cohort to address the men and offer them encouragement and promises of the loot to be had once the rebels were defeated. The fact that most of the loot in the enemy's hands had formerly been the property of Romans and their tribal allies was neither here nor there. Each time, he was cheered loudly by the men, and jeered from the far slope.

Once he had spoken to the Tenth Gallic, he rode to where Cato and Macro were standing near the standard and called out, 'How are your heroes of the Eighth Illyrian Cohort this fine morning, Prefect Cato?'

'Well rested and keen to get stuck in, sir!'

Suetonius walked his horse along the line of men standing at ease and then turned back towards Cato.

'A hard-looking bunch of soldiers you have here.'

'Yes, sir,' Cato called back, playing along. 'Hard as they come.'

'I hope they fight hard too. Every one of them looks like the meanest scoundrel from the criminal gangs of the Subura!'

The governor reined in halfway down the line and called out again. 'Are you men ready to teach those hairy-arsed barbarians a lesson?'

The soldiers were grinning as they responded in a loud chorus, 'Yes!'

'Are you going to make Rome proud?'

'Yes!'

'Do you love your emperor?'

'Yes!'

'Will you show the rest of the army how its best men fight?'

'Yes!'

'And do you love your general?'

'Nooooo!'

The men roared with laughter as their commander affected a disgusted expression and urged his horse back towards Cato.

'Like I said, bloody scoundrels! Every damn one of them! I don't know about the enemy, but they put the shits up me!'

The men laughed again, and Suetonius bit his fist and shook it at them as he rode off back towards his command position.

'That was nicely done,' Macro commented. 'I dare say every second unit was treated to the same performance.'

'Of course, but it has paid off. The men are in a better mood than they were.'

A distant outburst of cheers caused them to look towards the massed ranks of the enemy. The sound swelled into a continuous roar as a single chariot rounded the end of the rebel line and began to proceed along its front at a slow pace. Even at that distance, it was easy to make out the red hair of the woman standing on the chariot bed brandishing a spear.

There was a watchful stillness across the Roman army as they witnessed Boudica's parade before the multitude of her followers. The cheers would have drowned out even those of the wildly exuberant crowd at the Circus Maximus as a chariot race reached its climax. They reached a new crescendo as one of the enemy horns sounded, and others joined in until they provided a continuous blaring note to accompany the cries of the rebels. As fists punched the air and swords, spears, axes and helmets were brandished, the horde seemed to seethe like the surface of a boiling cauldron, and the air reverberated with the din.

As Boudica reached the end of the line, then turned her chariot and travelled back towards the centre, a column of people, roped together, were dragged through her warriors and led out in front of the army, where they were forced to kneel. Cato saw that their hands were tied behind their backs. As Boudica's chariot approached, two men thrust the first of the prisoners onto the ground, on his face. The horses trampled the prone figure

356

before the chariot wheels crushed his skull and spine, and the rebels let out a fresh clamour of lustful exultation. One by one the prisoners went under the wheels. Somehow a handful survived the first encounter with the chariot, and writhed in agony on the ground until it came back to finish the job and grind them into the earth.

Macro, his expression furious, strode out in front of the Eighth Cohort, who had been watching in silence. 'Never forget what you saw just then! Never! That is what they intend for any of us they take alive. And our civilians! Our families! Our children! Keep that thought in your mind when the battle begins. Make those animals pay dearly for outrages they have committed against our people.'

He glared at the auxiliaries, defying them to harbour any shred of mercy for the enemy, before marching back towards the standard, his lips pressed together in a tight line. As Cato glanced at him, he realised that the horrors his friend had endured during his captivity ran deeper than Macro had let on.

The centre of the enemy line parted to let Boudica's chariot pass through to take up position on a small knoll overlooking the rebel army. The cheering continued, but now took on a rhythmic quality, rising and falling as individual warriors rushed out and brandished their weapons at their enemy, bellowing insults and challenges.

'They're working themselves up for the first charge,' said Cato. He turned to Galerius. 'Form the men up!'

As the centurions and optios echoed the order, the auxiliaries took their place in the line, shields grounded at their sides. The men at the front had javelins to hand, while those behind were ready to pass theirs forward when the time came to unleash the opening volleys. All along the Roman line, the men of the auxiliary and legionary cohorts made ready, while the crews of the bolt-throwers fitted the sturdy cords to the ends of the torsion arms and wound them back to ease out the slack, ready to load the first bolts.

The heaviness of the air seemed to have intensified, and looking to the north-west, Cato could see that the dark band of clouds had drawn closer. Distant thunder rumbled like a menacing omen.

More and more of the enemy warriors came forward to issue their challenges, and the front line of the massed rebels appeared to undulate as their wild cheering reached a new pitch of excitement. It took a moment before Cato realised that the horns had been silent for a while. Then there was a sudden blast from several of them at once: three notes, the last of which occasioned a final endless roar as the first wave of enemy warriors surged forward over the open ground, racing to have the honour of striking the first blow of the battle.

Cato cupped his hands to his mouth and shouted out, 'Here they come! Eighth Cohort will stand to and prepare to receive the charge!'

CHAPTER TWENTY-FIVE

As soon as the order was given, the front rank of the cohort took up their shields and readied their grip on their javelins. Along the Roman line, the other infantry cohorts followed suit as their officers bellowed orders and encouragement to their men. The sharp metallic clank of the ratchets sounded from the artillery batteries as the crews hurriedly worked the small windlasses to draw the torsion arms back to the furthest notch for maximum range. Once ready, they placed the short, heavy projectiles into the waiting grooves and signalled to their officers that their weapons were ready to shoot. All eyes fixed on the enemy swarming towards the stream and splashing through it in sheets of liquid silver droplets before they reached the far side and rushed towards the bottom of the slope leading up to the Roman position.

Cato heard the order from the commander of the battery a short distance behind his cohort.

'Release!'

There was a rapid chorus of sharp cracks, and a veil of dark streaks whirred over the heads of the auxiliaries and seemed to converge as they drew towards the mass of rebels rushing forward. The missiles disappeared amongst the enemy, though their impact could be easily discerned as they knocked men off their feet. Some created a furrow as they tore into three or four of the rebels in turn. The first gaps opened in the leading wave as men moved round the dead and dying. The other batteries joined in, and scores more were cut down. The battery nearest to Cato reloaded with a clatter of ratchets, and another volley arced towards the onrushing enemy, yet the rebels' battle cries only grew more frenzied as they continued to close the distance.

'Shoot at will!'

The clank of the ratchets, the crack of the torsion arms and the whirr of the flighted bolts merged into one deafening cacophony as the deadly weapons devastated the leading ranks of the charging rebels. As they closed on the post that marked a hundred paces' distance from the front line, Cato shouted the order. 'Ready javelins!'

The men of the second rank stepped back two paces as those at the front braced their boots and drew back their arms, angling the iron heads of the javelins high to achieve the best range. Cato watched the distance to the leading rebels and waited until the nearest of them was in range.

'Release!'

Just as the shafts from the bolt-throwers had given the impression of being part of a veil, so did the javelins, a hundred of them rising towards the hazy sky before their trajectories flattened and they plunged amid the horde charging towards the Roman line. The deadly points impaled their victims, or punched through shields, or missed completely to bury their tips into the ground while the shafts quivered momentarily. Twice more, fresh javelins were passed forward and hurled, and Cato noted with professional satisfaction how the leading wave had been thinned out so that the rebels would reach his men in a piecemeal manner without inflicting the usual crushing impact of a Celtic charge.

'Shields front! Swords out!'

The large oval shields swung round as the men braced

themselves and drew their swords. They rested the flat of the blades against the trim of the shields so the points projected like steel teeth ready to tear into their prey. Individual rebel warriors, the fleetest of foot who had survived the volleys of missiles, charged up to the Roman line heedless of their lack of support and were forced to slow down to thread their way past the stakes before they struck home at the shield wall with their weapons. With the slight but significant advantage of height, the auxiliaries were able to keep their shields low to protect their feet and shins as they thrust with their swords. Immediately in front of Cato, a warrior slashed his sword through the shield trim of his chosen target. The blade lodged in the splintered wood, and before he could wrench it free, the auxiliary to the right stabbed him in the side, while the man to his left thrust a sword into his chest. The rebel staggered away before collapsing to his knees between the stakes and clutching his hand to his profusely bleeding chest wound.

More rebels arrived singly or in small groups, and soon the entire front line of the cohort was engaged. The air filled with the clatter and clash of weapons, the thud of blows landing on shields, and the continued war cries of the enemy, as well as the more distant cheers of encouragement from the host of spectators and the warriors being held back for renewed charges or to reinforce breakthroughs. The Roman soldiers fought largely in silence as they maintained their shield wall and struck at any enemy who attempted to clamber onto the ledge or came within stabbing distance of their short swords.

There were casualties amongst the defenders. Men who were wounded through gaps between the auxiliaries' shields or hit by undamaged javelins that had been recovered as the rebels swept forward. Some attempted to make their way to the dressing stations at the rear, while others, more seriously hurt, were aided by the walking wounded. The dead and mortally injured were hauled to the rear and left on the ground, where they would not impede their comrades. The gaps left by the casualties were filled by the men in the second line without hesitation, Cato noted with pride.

Behind the cohort, the battery had ceased shooting as the last of the rebels from the first charge were now obstructed by the defenders.

Macro was looking along the rest of the line, where the battle was raging as more and more of the rebels pressed against those who had reached the enemy first. Their keenness to get to grips with the Romans was the undoing of their comrades directly engaged, as they had no room to avoid the points of the short swords flickering in and out from between the auxiliaries' shields.

'They'll not keep this up for long. They're losing too many men.'

Cato nodded, without looking round, and then pointed to a sudden swirl of motion to the right of the centre of the cohort. A huge warrior had vaulted onto the ledge and thrust aside the auxiliaries as he wielded a large axe.

'Galerius! Cut that fellow down!'

The centurion snatched up a javelin and surged forward, shield raised, flanked by two men from the rear rank. He slammed into the warrior, knocking him off the ledge to tumble onto his comrades, taking several down with him, then hurled the javelin into the huge man's chest. There was an audible groan from those around the impaled warrior as one of the rebels pulled the javelin out and four more carried him back through the press of bodies. Cato realised that he must be a renowned hero and his wounding had caused those around him to lose their resolve. As if a cold wind had blown through the hearts of the rebels, they flinched away from their enemy and began to move back, through the stakes, still facing the Romans. Macro seized the chance to break their spirit further.

'Javelins!' he bellowed. 'Hit 'em with the javelins!'

It took a few beats for the men in the front line to recover their wits enough to obey the order. There was no attempt to use volleys as the missiles arced over the growing gap between the two sides. The compact ranks of the rebels meant it was almost impossible to miss, and their retreat became more hurried, those at the rear turning away to trot back down towards the stream. More and more broke away as those closest to the Romans suffered ever more casualties from the weapons tearing into them. As the first wave in front of the Eighth Cohort steadily disintegrated and streamed back down the slope, past the dead and injured, Cato ordered his men to cease throwing. There was a pause as they caught their breath, and then a ragged cheer spread along the line as they saw their enemies in full flight.

As soon as the rebels fell back far enough to be under the sights of the bolt-throwers, the throwing arms leaped forward once again, hurling their deadly bolts and skewering several more before they crossed the stream and fled out of range.

Looking to his left, Cato saw that most of the enemy had fallen back right along the line, and the fighting continued in only a few places before even the most ardent rebels broke contact and withdrew. The officers indulged the excited cheers of the Roman soldiers for a moment longer before ordering them to be quiet.

Cato singled out the senior centurion in the front rank of his cohort. 'Flaccus! Take fifty men forward to recover any usable javelins and ballista bolts.'

'Yes, sir!'

The centurion hopped down off the ledge and picked his way through the bodies of the rebels as his men followed suit, pausing to finish off any of the enemy that were still alive with sword thrusts to the throat or heart. A glance to the rear of the cohort revealed fourteen Roman casualties. Three were dead. Cato did a quick inspection of the injured and had the three most seriously hurt carried up the slope to the redoubt, while the others had their wounds dressed and fell in at the rear of the line.

He joined Macro on the left flank of the cohort and they surveyed the corpses littering the slope.

'How many do you make it?' asked the centurion. 'Four hundred?'

'Nearer five, I'd say. And there'll be many more who were wounded and won't be playing any further part in the battle.'

'What about our lads?'

'If the casualties of the Eighth Cohort are anything to go by . . .' Cato reckoned up the strengths of the two legions and six cohorts that formed the Roman battle line. 'I'd say we have suffered no more than a fifth of the losses the enemy has taken.'

'That's a good start, then.'

Cato gestured to the massed ranks of the rebels as the horns began to bray again and another wave of warriors began to issue a challenge to the Romans. 'Boudica can afford to lose five of her men to every one of ours and still have plenty to spare.'

'It ain't just a question of maths, Cato. We've repulsed the first attack with ease. That will have put a dent in their morale. We'll do the same to the second charge, when it comes. And the third. Each time, they'll find it a little harder to find the courage to go forward.'

'You may be right, but the other side of the coin is that our lads will be whittled down each time, and their morale will take a hit as well. It'll be interesting to see whose spirit gives way first.'

Macro looked at him. 'Interesting?'

They were interrupted by the shrill notes of the bucinas at Suetonius's command post sounding the recall. The men sent forward to recover undamaged missiles hurriedly climbed the slope back to the Roman lines. Cato gave the order for the first rank of his cohort to move to the rear, and the files opened to allow them to withdraw. A second order had the formation take

364

two paces forward to form a battle line along the ledge once again. There were gaps in the new front line where men had stepped up during the fighting to replace casualties, and these were now filled by men from the new follow-up line, whose gaps in turn were filled by those who had been pulled back to the rear of the cohort. This meant that fresh men would face the next charge and the enemy would be presented with a shield wall that was no different in length to the first.

Besides managing the weariness of the men, the manoeuvre had the additional advantage of making it seem to the enemy that the Romans had beaten them off with negligible losses. Of course, the longer the fight went on, the fewer men there would be in the third line of the cohort, until there came a point when there would only be enough to fill two lines on the same frontage. Later still, there would be barely enough for one rank. If it came to that, Cato hoped Suetonius would have the sense to pull the men back up the slope to present a narrower front and allow the line to increase in depth once again. It was that or risk it being too thin to withstand an enemy breakthrough.

'Here they come again,' said Macro as the rebels surged towards the stream once more. Their charge was uneven, as the fastest and the most fearless raced ahead of their comrades. Cato noticed that they struggled to get across the stream, churning up mud on either side, and this caused them to bunch up before they reached the bottom of the slope. The artillery was presented with a perfect target, and most of the heavy shafts hit two or three men each time. As the charge climbed the slope, hundreds more bodies were visible littering the stream and the banks on either side. Once the artillery ceased shooting, the enemy came within range of javelins and were subjected to an even more devastating, albeit short-lived, barrage.

This time there was less cheering by the rebels as they charged home. Nor was this such a wild, thoughtless attack. While the fighting raged across the front of the Roman line, small groups of warriors were busy tearing up the pointed stakes and carrying them off to the bottom of the slope. Cato was watching the performance of his men closely and saw that they were holding their ground even as the enemy pressed them for longer this time, causing more casualties and thinning out his reserves. A glance to the left revealed that Thrasyllus's cohort was equally affected.

'The other side are making hot work of this,' Macro observed.

Cato nodded, then glanced up at the sky. Even though it must be close to midday, there was less light than before. The haze had thickened and the dark clouds were drawing closer to the battlefield and he could hear the low rumble of thunder above the din of the men locked into their deadly struggle. There was only the lightest of breezes, and he felt sweat breaking out across his body. His men's heavy clothing, armour and equipment would be more burdensome than the lighter garb of the rebels under any circumstances, but in this heat it would exhaust the Romans more rapidly. It was something he had not considered earlier when calculating the effects of a prolonged battle.

This time the attack broke down in the centre as the rebels recoiled from the steadfast legionaries of the Twentieth. They withdrew much more quickly this time, Cato noticed, in order to escape the worst effects of the javelins and the artillery batteries. Even so, the intensity and duration of the second attack had been greater, and as the rebels regained the far bank of the stream, it was clear that it had cost them thousands more of their men, particularly at the feet of the Roman soldiers, where the bodies were piled deep enough to reach the lip of the ledge in many places.

Cato ordered men forward once more to retrieve undamaged javelins and ballista bolts, and to clear the bodies away from the fighting ledge and dump them ten feet down the slope, where they would serve to break the impetus of the next charge in the absence of the sharpened stakes that had been carried off. The cohort had suffered fourteen dead, including two of his centurions, Annius and the recently promoted Lenticulus. Cato knew that many of those who would have to take the brunt of the third charge had already been engaged, and that his reserve rank would be reduced to little more than two sections of his men.

Worse news followed, as Galerius's party returned from sweeping the slope for reusable javelins. They had recovered only a handful, which they added to the dwindling stock at the rear of the cohort.

'The rebels must have collected them as they withdrew, sir.'

'They learn fast,' said Macro. 'I dare say we're going to be on the receiving end of those when they return for the next round.'

'Very well.' Cato addressed Galerius. 'Get back to your position and make sure the men take a good swig from their canteens. I don't want anyone passing out in this heat.'

'Yes, sir.' The centurion mopped his brow and turned to march away.

Once he had reordered his lines, Cato sent a runner to Suetonius's field quarters to notify them of his casualties and the certainty that the Eighth would be reduced to two ranks after the next attack. It was possible that the message would be taken as being defeatist, but he hoped it might at least prompt the governor to be ready to shift the line back to defend a narrower front. Meanwhile, Cato would have to make some contingency arrangements of his own.

'Macro, I'm going to pull the men out of the third line and create two flying squads. You take Annius's men on the left and I'll take the rest of Lenticulus's lads to the right. If the enemy

367

threaten to break our line or push us back, don't wait for orders. Plug the gap and force them out.'

'I'll manage.'

Cato smiled. 'I have no doubt.'

There was a delay before Boudica and her commanders sent in their third attack. Cato could see their wounded being laid out in the grass in front of the long line of carts and wagons packed with spectators. Parties were sent to the stream to fill up waterskins, and groups of riders led their horses down to drink at the extremity of the battlefield, where they would be out of range of the bolt-throwers. Taking advantage of the lull, some of the Roman commanders sent their own watering parties down: men laden with canteens, with an escort bearing shields. As soon as the enemy spotted them descending the slope, a line of slingers trotted forward and unleashed their missiles, striking down several of Suetonius's soldiers and causing him to signal a hurried recall. His men would have to put up with the sweltering heat, and those who had already emptied their canteens would have to endure their thirst until the battle was over.

The dark clouds were now above the left flank of the Roman army, and there was a tension in the breathless atmosphere smothering both armies. The arrival of the storm felt imminent. The third wave of Boudica's warriors moved forward with much less cheering and brandishing of weapons. As they massed out of range of the bolt-throwers, large numbers of cavalry gathered on the flanks, while fifty chariots rumbled into position behind each cavalry force.

'Looks like they're going for broke this time,' said Macro as he observed the enemy's preparations. 'It's going to be tough sending that lot back down the hill.'

'Time to get in position,' said Cato. He picked up his shield and reached out his arm to Macro. His friend looked at him curiously as they grasped forearms.

'A formal farewell?'

Cato smiled self-consciously. 'Let's hope not. I'm just grateful you're here when my men and I need you most.'

'Look here, Cato. I can't be expected to win this battle single-handed,' Macro joked. 'You and your lads will need to do your bit too, you know.'

'We'll try our best. I'll see you later.'

'Later then. You can count on it.'

They parted and gathered their small parties of reserve troops, and took up their positions behind the cohort while the rest of the men readied themselves in the two remaining lines. There were enough javelins left for two volleys. After that, the rebels would only be exposed to the bolt-throwers, as long as their ammunition endured. Cato felt a growing disquiet that the balance of the battle was shifting in the enemy's favour.

A blast of horns announced the opening of the attack. There seemed to be no rush to get to grips with the Romans as Boudica's infantry walked down to the stream, squelching through the mud to the far side. The batteries did not shoot until the enemy were well within range, and Cato took that as a sign that they were having to conserve ammunition. The rebels were a hundred paces beyond the stream when the familiar crack of throwing arms being released came from behind him. As soon as they saw the dark shafts rising into the sky, they let out a roar and burst into a dead run up the slope, their ranks opening to minimise casualties.

'Steady, boys!' Cato called to his men. 'Ready javelins!'

The auxiliaries in the front rank hefted their weapons and held them back, ready to hurl. Cato waited until the leading rebels were no more than thirty paces away. Then he saw the first shafts arcing towards his men from the enemy ranks and cried out quickly, 'Release!'

The javelins crossed paths in the air and men on both sides were struck down. One of the enemy's weapons came over the line close by, forcing an optio amongst Cato's reserves to leap aside to avoid it. As he resumed his position, a number of his comrades blew loud raspberries to mock his reaction.

'That's enough!' Cato snapped. 'Silence!'

The auxiliaries' second volley was launched just in time for the men to draw their short swords and engage the rebels clambering over the line of bodies and charging the defenders on the fighting ledge. The rolling thud of blows landing on their shields spread along the line and merged with the clatter and clash of blades into one deafening sound. It drowned out the rumble of thunder and the rustle of leaves in the nearby trees as a sudden breeze heralded the coming of the rain.

Cato drew his own sword. Turning to the standard bearer, he instructed him to keep the standard high, where it would be clearly visible above the confusion of the battle for the men to rally to if necessary. Then he fixed his attention on the fighting along the line of the Eighth Cohort. His men were bracing their legs and leaning into their shields to counter the shoving from the other side, and taking advantage of any exposed enemy limbs to hack at them or thrust their swords into the bodies and faces of the rebels. To his right, he saw the second line forced back a step as their comrades in front gave ground. Then one of them was hauled from the ledge and out of sight. Before the gap could be closed, three of the enemy had climbed up and thrown themselves on the auxiliaries, creating space for more of the rebels to get onto the ledge. The auxiliaries tried to push them back, cutting down two warriors who had recklessly sacrificed themselves to open the way for those behind. There were now eight rebels on the ledge and more climbing up behind them, and Cato decided it was time to intervene before the situation got any worse.

He trotted towards the danger point and forced himself

between two of his men in the rear line as he shouted, 'Come on, boys! Push those bastards back!'

His reserve party charged in bodily, carrying Cato and the men of the second line with them as they closed up on the knot of enemy warriors desperately trying to enlarge the foothold they had gained within the Roman position. Directly in front of Cato was a square-shouldered man of his own height wearing a legionary helmet and cuirass over his black and green striped tunic. Braided hair hung down from beneath the cheek guards either side of a thick red beard and moustache. His lips were parted in a snarl as he lifted his oval shield with a white horse's head on it and raised his long sword to strike at the Roman prefect's neck.

Cato surged forward, lifting his own shield to block the blow before it could gain any momentum, and the warrior's forearm slammed down on the surface, the pommel of his sword crashing on the bulge of the handguard, making a deafening ringing sound that numbed Cato's left ear. Boots braced in the soil to give him a solid grip, he thrust once more. The warrior's rear foot came off the edge of the ledge, and he gave a cry of alarm as he lost his balance and fell backwards onto the men packed below. Cato spared him no more attention and immediately turned to push against the man to his left as the rest of his party pressed forward, using their superior numbers to drive headlong into the rebels. One after the other, the enemy warriors toppled back from the ledge and the gap was plugged.

'Close up!' Cato shouted, and the auxiliaries in the front line shuffled towards him until he was able to step back and withdraw his squad a few paces behind the rear line. Breathing hard, they stood ready to respond to any further trouble. He glanced towards Macro's squad and saw his friend tap the point of his sword against the brim of his helmet in a salute. The Eighth were still holding on.

371

Beyond Macro, Cato saw men from Thrasyllus's cohort running to the rear and towards the left flank of the Eighth. Behind them, he realised with horror, enemy chariots had broken through the gap between the Tenth Gallic and the next unit in the line, the First Cohort of the Twentieth Legion.

A cold surge of fear coursed through his veins as he grasped the peril now facing the Roman army. If the chariots widened the breach sufficiently, the infantry following them would pour through and roll up the line. Disaster threatened, and Cato's men, clinging on to their own position, had no chance of intervening.

CHAPTER TWENTY-SIX

'Fall back to the battery!' Cato ordered his reserve squad. 'Wait for me there. If any of those chariots come your way, protect the bolt-throwers. Go!'

As the men turned to trot up the slope, he ordered the standard bearer to follow him and ran to Galerius, pulling him out of the second line. 'You're in command here. The standard bearer stays with you. Hold the line. If the rebels break through, fall back to the battery. But buy me as much time as you can.'

'Where—' Galerius began.

'Later.' Cato slapped him on the back to urge him into line and ran across the rear to Macro, where he paused, breathing hard. 'I need you . . . to hold the left flank. Don't let those chariots get in amongst us.'

'What about the rest of the line? They're going to need support.'

Cato conceded the point. 'Detach ten men under an optio. The rest hold the flank with you.'

'What are you up to?'

'There's no time to explain. Just do as I ask.'

'All right. But it better be good.'

Cato looked along the line. Thrasyllus's left was giving ground as the charioteers drove their horses into the Roman ranks, sacrificing them to break up the line. Turning away, he ran up the slope to the battery overlooking the Eighth Cohort and found its commander, a young legionary centurion, no more than thirty, watching the Tenth being forced back.

'Turn your weapons on those chariots!' Cato ordered him.

'We're down to the last few bolts, sir. I've got strict orders to save them for the next attack.'

'There won't be another attack if we don't fucking stop this one,' Cato snapped. He thrust his arm towards the chariots. 'Shoot them down! That's an order.'

'I answer to Legate Calpurnius.'

'Well, he isn't here and I am your superior. Obey my order.'

The centurion hesitated, and Cato raised his sword. 'Do it, or I'll kill you where you stand right now!'

The young officer took one more look at the crazed expression on the prefect's face, then cupped his hands to his mouth and called out to his crews, 'New target! Enemy chariots to the left! Shoot at will!'

Cato remained long enough to see the bolt-throwers traverse towards the chariots shattering the Tenth Cohort's flank and begin to shoot across the Roman rear. The third shot plucked a charioteer from his yoke and hurled him back into the warrior on the chariot bed. The sudden pressure on the reins caused the ponies to swerve to the side, overturning the vehicle.

'Good shot!' he said to the centurion. 'Keep it up, down to the last bolt if necessary.'

'Yes, sir. But you'll answer to the legate when this is over.'

'I'm sure I will.'

Cato ran through the line of carts and near-empty ammunition baskets and continued up the slope to where the cavalry reserve was waiting, the men already mounted. Tubero was there with what remained of the Eighth's mounted contingent, along with no more than four hundred other men drawn from the auxiliary cohorts under the command of Prefect Quadrillus, a veteran in his mid fifties, commander of the Fifth Hispanic mounted cohort, one of the units that had suffered heavy losses in the Mona campaign. As Cato approached the formation, Quadrillus leaned forward in his saddle and trotted his horse along the front of the cavalry reserve.

'What are you doing up here, Prefect Cato?'

'We have to break up the chariot charge. Before the enemy infantry follow through. I need a horse.'

'I have none to spare.'

Cato pointed to one of Quadrillus's men. 'You, hand your mount over.'

As the man swung his leg over the saddle, Quadrillus shouted, 'Stay in your saddle, damn you!'

The auxiliary froze, looking from one superior officer to the other. Cato grabbed his arm and pulled him down so that he was forced to dismount or fall to the ground. A moment later, he was in the saddle and had taken up the reins. He urged the horse forward and stared anxiously towards the developing breach. The battery was doing a fine job of cutting down the chariots, and the wrecked vehicles, wounded horses and crews were piling up amid the disrupted ranks of the Tenth. Closer to, Macro and his men had formed a short line to protect the left flank of the Eighth, and the artillery crews had won a brief reprieve for Cato's men. Beyond the chariots, he could see a dense body of enemy infantry pushing through the gap between the Twentieth Legion and the Tenth Cohort.

'We have to charge. At once. Give the order!'

Quadrillus's mouth opened to protest, then he looked past Cato at the grave situation developing and grasped the need for swift action. He called the order – 'Cavalry reserve will advance at the trot! On me!' – then urged his horse down the slope, angling to the left of the artillery battery as the centurion there hurriedly called on his men to cease shooting.

The mounted reserve rode on towards the remaining chariots

and the infantry spilling through the gap. Cato fell in alongside Tubero as the formation pounded across the downtrodden grass towards the rebels. The left flank of the Tenth had been torn to pieces, and he caught a glimpse of Thrasyllus desperately rallying a group of his men to form a flank guard at right angles to what was left of his main line, still battling the enemy along the ledge. A small group of chariots, ten or so, had broken away from the rest and were running down the auxiliaries who had fled the initial charge. Cato raised his sword and led his men to take the enemy in the flank.

The chariots were so intent on their prey that they only became aware of the cavalry bearing down on them when it was too late. Cato plunged through the gap between the two nearest chariots before wheeling to his right. Leaning from his saddle, he hacked at the charioteer and caught him on the side of the skull, cutting deep into his cheek and severing the top of his ear. The man instinctively jerked away and pulled on the traces to swerve the chariot clear of his attacker. The warrior in the rear of the vehicle shouted angrily as Cato moved out of range of his spear.

Cato steered his mount away and towards the rear of another chariot in the middle of the small group. Tubero and the rest of his men had charged in amongst the enemy, spearing horses and those on the chariots alike. There was a panicked cry as one of the auxiliaries collided with a pair of ponies; before he could recover, the charioteer had run along the yoke and swung an axe into his neck. The auxiliary instantly folded over his saddle horns, his shield and spear dropping from his nerveless fingers as his mount swung away and galloped off. The charioteer had little more than a heartbeat to celebrate his victory before he was run through from the other side and collapsed across the rump of one of his ponies, before sliding off and falling under the chariot with a cry of anguish that died in his throat as the wheel crushed his chest.

All but three of the chariots had come to grief now, and the survivors turned and careered down the slope, attempting to flee along the side of the infantry pouring through the widening breach. Quadrillus had increased the pace as his cavalry approached diagonally, and now, with fifty paces to go, he gave the order to charge. The auxiliaries lowered their spears and bent forward, locking their thighs against the flanks of their horses as they galloped straight at the mass of enemy warriors. There was no time for the rebels to react before the cavalry charge crashed into them. The momentum flattened some of them, hurled others aside and crushed the rest back into the tightly pressed column trying to force its way through the Roman line. The lethal points of the auxiliaries' spears stabbed out, and when the shafts broke or the weapons were torn from their grip, the riders snatched out their long swords and laid about them at the tightly packed ranks of the rebels, who were forced back before them.

Cato rallied his men to the cohort's standard and led them past the bodies of their comrades who had been cut down by the chariots only moments before. Quadrillus and the rest of the cavalry reserve had carved their way deep into the enemy ranks, and the rebels were recoiling under the impact, with some already fleeing back down the slope. Cato steered his men to the right to clear the enemy from the flank of Thrasyllus's men, who were already pushing forward now that the crisis had passed. The failure of the breakthrough was swiftly turning into a collapse all along the front as the rebels wavered.

Seeing his chance, Cato wheeled his party into the flank of the warriors still fighting the Tenth Cohort. He could see the terror in their faces as they backed away from the auxiliaries and turned to face the new threat. He knew that there were too few of his men to roll up the enemy flank, but maybe there were enough to break the rebels' spirit. He shouted wildly as they slashed and stabbed to right and left and their horses snorted and swerved, knocking men back and rearing as they were injured in turn. Then, with a roar, the auxiliaries of the Tenth jumped from their ledge and charged over the bodies below into the disordered enemy ranks. They slammed their shields into the rebels, and hacked and stabbed with their swords, blood spraying through the air and spattering shields, armour and exposed flesh.

Attacked on two sides, the rebels' resolve crumbled, and hundreds of them peeled away and ran back down the slope. As they fled, so too did their comrades facing the hard-pressed Eighth Cohort, quickly pursued by Cato's men, as Macro bellowed the order to charge.

Overhead, the dark clouds covered most of the battlefield and the first drops of rain began to fall, while the breeze tossed the branches of the trees at the edge of the forest. As the enemy ran pell-mell, the mounted auxiliaries gave vent to their excitement and chased down the nearest rebels, stabbing them in the back or delivering deadly overhead blows that split skulls and shattered shoulders and spines. A hundred paces down the slope, Cato reined in and called on his men to halt. Some, lost in their battle rage, took a moment to respond. When they had formed up around him and the standard, he looked about, but there was no sign of Tubero. Or over a third of the mounted contingent. The same was true of the rest of the cavalry reserve as Quadrillus recalled his men. They were a spent force. Some of the wounded were still in their saddles. Many others lay amongst the rebel bodies that carpeted the slope to the Roman front and were heaped around the point where they had almost achieved their breakthrough.

Thrasyllus and Macro were also bellowing at their men to cease the pursuit, and they drew up wearily, gasping for breath. The rebels ran on long enough to open a safe gap between the two sides before slowing down and retreating across the stream to rejoin the rest of the horde waiting in sombre silence. One of the auxiliaries raised his sword and cheered wildly, but his call was unanswered and he quickly fell silent. Every man knew how close they had come to defeat, and that if the enemy attacked again, they might easily overwhelm the denuded and exhausted Roman army.

The auxiliaries and legionaries who had pursued the enemy a short distance were rounded up by their officers and turned back up the slope to their original positions. There were almost no serviceable javelins to be retrieved, and as the artillery batteries had exhausted their ammunition, it was clear that the next time the rebels came forward, there would be no way of breaking the impetus of their charge. No missiles, no stakes and now no effective cavalry reserve to counter a breakthrough on the right of the Roman line.

Handing his horse to one of the mounted contingent, Cato made for the Eighth Cohort and found Macro having his thigh dressed by one of the medics.

'How serious?' he asked.

'Flesh wound. One of their lot was playing dead when I was about to step over him. He didn't have to play it once I'd finished with him.'

They exchanged an edgy smile, elated that they had both survived and at the same time shocked at how close they had come to defeat.

'That was quick thinking,' said Macro as he nodded up the slope to the men of the cavalry reserve walking their horses past the battery. 'Good work.'

Cato reflected briefly. It was almost as if he had not thought it through at all. He had acted on instinct and it could easily have gone the other way. Looking past Macro, he saw that his men had suffered more losses in the last attack than in the first two combined. There were barely a hundred and fifty still standing.

Not enough to form two ranks. They would offer little more than a skirmish line when the rebels attacked again. The same was true of Thrasyllus's cohort, and further along, only the legionaries appeared to have suffered less proportionately. Which was as well, he thought, as only the iron men of the legions could achieve victory now that the batteries, the auxiliary cohort and one of the cavalry reserves were spent forces.

The rain was falling steadily, pinging off men's helmets and dripping off their armour as they trudged back into position while the wounded were carried away. Before them lay the carnage of the first three attacks. Well over ten thousand of Boudica's followers must have fallen, and the cries and moans of the wounded carried through the hiss of the rain. Beyond the stream, the rebel army was re-forming its shattered formations. The war horns sounded once again, but there was no cheering now, and Cato sensed a reluctance to renew the fight. And yet . . . and yet their leaders and their Druids had stepped out in front of the line to cajole and urge them on to make one final, decisive effort. They knew they must conquer this day, before their followers sank into a despondency that would jeopardise the struggle against the invader. They still had a chance, and their leaders knew it, Cato mused. It all depended on whether they could get their side forward in sufficient numbers to decide the issue.

'By the gods, they're going to try again,' said Macro, peering down the slope with his hand to the brim of his helmet to keep the rain out of his eyes. He surveyed the enemy line edging forward as their leaders rounded up every man who could still fight, while their families looked on in silence from the wagons and the higher ground curving around the battlefield. He moved closer to Cato as he muttered, 'I'm not sure we can survive another attack.'

'You may be right. I'd hoped we might have shaken them enough after the failure of the last attempt. Shit . . . You can't help but admire their courage. If only we'd had the good sense to treat them as allies instead of grinding them under our heel. Imagine what could be achieved with ten trained cohorts of such men.'

'They still might achieve something notable even without that training, the way things are going. However, whether we win or lose, there'll be fools back in Rome who will never accept that those barbarians could match us man for man.'

A tribune came trotting up from the direction of the field headquarters. He reined in and saluted Cato.

'Governor's compliments, sir. He says to congratulate you on your swift action to close the breach. He also asks that your men hold their position one last time.'

'Last time?' Macro said caustically. 'Not sure if we should be encouraged by that.'

The tribune looked affronted. 'That's not what the governor meant, sir.'

Macro looked at Cato and rolled his eyes before he replied. 'Glad to hear it. Now run along, young man. Before I say something I regret.'

The tribune turned and galloped off as Macro shook his head sadly. 'Where on earth do they find such material? I leave the army for a few months and it goes to the dogs.'

'You haven't left it, though,' Cato pointed out. 'It's true what they say. You can take the man out of the army, but you can't take the army out of the man. I almost think someone had you in mind when they came up with that aphorism.'

'They?'

'Don't get me started.' He turned his gaze towards the enemy. The dark clouds had blotted out the sky and the rain was falling so hard the rebels were only visible as a grey mass in the mid distance. A moment later, he could see that they were advancing for the fourth time, and he felt his heart sink at the prospect. He instinctively knew that this would be the last attack of the day. It was do or die for both armies.

He called to his men to make ready, and the auxiliaries wearily returned to the ledge. There was no longer any changing of the ranks. The surviving officers put the least tired and those who were not yet wounded at the front, while the rest formed two parties under Cato and Macro, ready to reprise their role as stopgap reserves. Behind the Eighth Cohort's position, the legionary artillery crews filed out of the battery and returned to the ranks of the Twentieth. Quadrillus and his small body of cavalry stood by, ready for a final charge if they were called upon. Cato had little doubt that they would be before the battle was over.

The rebels crossed the stream, slowed down by the thick band of churned mud, and advanced in one vast mass, more than forty thousand strong. They were silent and did not try to rush the Roman line as before. They had no need to fear the bolt-throwers, nor were there any javelins remaining. They themselves had expended their small force of chariots, and the slope was too muddy for their cavalry, so every man was obliged to fight on foot. The final round was going to be a brutal struggle to the death over the body-strewn slope, made slippery by blood and rain.

It seemed to take an age for the horde to make their way up to the waiting Romans. As they came on, sheets of dazzling lightning burst amid the clouds, momentarily illuminating the two armies in a pearly white gleam, as if they were ghosts, before the gloom instantly closed in once more.

'We're dead men,' said one of the auxiliaries in Cato's party.

The prefect turned instantly. 'Who said that?'

The man next to the culprit could not help glancing at his comrade, and Cato strode up to the auxiliary and glared at him.

'No one, and I mean no one, gets to die unless I order it. Understand?'

The man raised his eyebrows in surprise but nodded all the same. 'Yes, sir.'

'That's better. Now there'll be no more of that nonsense. Pull yourself together and do your duty.'

'Yes, sir.'

Cato returned to his position. He might not have cured the man's fear, but he had done enough to preoccupy him. His comrades grinned and shook their heads before their attention was drawn back to the approaching enemy.

The rebels were no more than a hundred paces away, but it was impossible to discern their features through the rain. Cato tightened his grip on his shield handle and saw that Macro was inscribing small circles with the tip of his sword as he waited for battle. The enemy was moving more slowly now, and when they were fifty paces away, they shuffled to a halt. Their chieftains and warrior champions stepped forward and yelled their challenges, then waved their men forward. None moved. Their leaders shouted at them, alternating between appeals to their courage, threats, insults and pleading. To no avail. But neither did they back away.

'What are you waiting for?' an auxiliary cried out. 'Come and get it, you fucking barbarians!'

'Silence!' Galerius shouted, his voice straining. 'Silence in the ranks!'

The rain fell with a soft roar, interspersed with lightning and thunder as the storm passed overhead. Both armies seemed frozen. Then a solitary figure burst out from between the Tenth Cohort and the legionaries of the Twentieth and ran until he was halfway between the two sides. Turning to face the Roman line, he brandished his sword in the air.

'Hitetius,' Cato muttered. 'What are you doing?'

'Why are you standing there?' the veteran screamed in rage. 'They burned your towns, slaughtered Roman citizens and destroyed your comrades of the Ninth . . . What are you waiting for? Kill them! Kill them all!' He spun round and charged down the slope towards the waiting rebels. 'For Albia! For Rome!'

He slammed into the shield of one of the warriors. Immediately, another cut at his wrist, disarming him. Then hands grabbed him and hoisted him into the air, and he was passed along the front line, being stabbed as he went. Even as he was wounded again and again, he continued to shout his war cry.

A groan rose from many of the Romans, and then Macro's voice could be heard, clear and commanding.

'You heard him! Kill them! Kill 'em all!'

He surged forward, his party following as he burst through the front rank, and then, as if possessed by one will, the Eighth went with him.

'No . . .' Cato murmured in despair, but he found himself running with his men. The Tenth followed their example, and then the legionaries of the Twentieth trotted forward with a great roar, still in formation.

Leaping over the gleaming bodies of the dead and dying, the auxiliaries slammed into the enemy line, the impetus of the charge thrusting the front rank back on their comrades. To his left, Cato saw the heavy infantry of the legions cutting their way into the centre of the enemy line, driving it down the slope so that a broad wedge was developing as the outnumbered Romans pressed forward. The surprise of the charge and the frenzied hacking and thrusting of the Roman swords caused the enemy to recoil onto themselves, their ranks so tightly compacted that they could not wield their weapons easily.

Cato fought as his men did, without reason, without thought, stabbing and stabbing at the bodies trapped in front of him. Scores of the rebels were being cut down by his men as they fought like

Furies, punching with their shields and striking out with their swords, killing and moving on over the dead and dying as they forced their way down the slope, pace by pace. A great cry of despair rose from the enemy mass, drowning out the rallying cries shouted by the few chieftains and warriors that had survived the Roman onslaught. The lightning caught and froze vivid tableaus of snarling and terrified features, sprays of blood, and the tangle of weapons wielded above the two sides like a field of silver thorns.

A gap opened up ahead of Cato, and he saw that the enemy were breaking and running for their lives, slithering and stumbling down the slick muddy slope. Some abandoned their shields and weapons in terror as they strove to escape the vengeful wrath of the Romans sweeping all before them. A rush of movement to his right caught his attention, and he saw the dark shapes of Quadrillus and his men racing into what was becoming more of a massacre than a battle. The cavalry broke up the enemy flank and set about those that attempted to run from them.

As Cato drew close to the stream, he felt his boots sink into the mud. Filthy water, streaked with blood, sprayed as the men of both sides waded through the glutinous quagmire. Many of those that fell caused others to tumble on top of them, and they flailed desperately until they drowned or were stabbed by blades plunged through the surface. The Romans forced their way across, the water now running with blood, raindrops exploding off the disturbed current. Cato's lungs were burning with the effort of wielding his sword and shield as he struggled through the expanse of mud on the far side of the stream. He could hear the terrified cries of the enemy camp followers as the first of the fugitives reached the dense line of wagons and carts and revealed the scale of the unfolding disaster.

Some of the enemy found the courage to turn and fight. Small clusters of warriors and larger warbands grimly held their ground as their leaders urged them to sell their lives dearly. Their efforts proved futile as the Romans steadily surrounded and crushed them before moving on over their bodies to find fresh prey.

Cato's limbs felt increasingly heavy and sluggish as he killed and moved on to kill again. He was conscious that the pace of the Roman advance was flagging and that the enemy retreat was slowing. As a new gap opened between himself and the rebels, he paused, chest heaving, and looked up to see a terrible spectacle. Many of the rebel camp followers had been sitting or standing in front of the wagons and carts, and now they were crushed against them as the warriors were pushed back until they were too tightly packed to move, let alone fight. The air filled with shrieks and wailing as the legionaries and auxiliaries hacked at their helpless opponents, then climbed onto their bodies to kill those behind without mercy. All cohesion amongst the cohorts had crumbled away, and each man indulged himself in the exhausting slaughter of the enemy warriors and their women and children. There were those who begged for mercy, but their pleas were ignored by men who had heard the reports and rumours of the atrocities inflicted by Boudica's followers.

Stepping back from the slaughter, Cato looked round to take stock and see what had happened to his cohort. But it was impossible to distinguish his men from those of Thrasyllus amid the mud- and blood-streaked figures wearily continuing the massacre. He picked out the crested helmet that Macro had been given by Hitetius and stumbled toward his friend across the heaped bodies of the rebels.

Macro had grounded his shield and was bent over it as he struggled for breath. He looked up at Cato as if he could not remember his face. Then he blinked and wiped the gore from his sword before sheathing it. Swallowing and clearing his parched throat, he attempted to acknowledge his friend.

'I'm fucked . . . Completely fucked.'

386

They stood side by side, breathing hard as the rain continued to fall. The storm was moving on. The lightning was some miles away, and the thunder that had crashed overhead with the sound of tortured metal was now the rumble of a titan disturbed in his sleep. Around them, the men of Suetonius's army were spent, too tired to continue the slaughter. Thousands of the enemy, including some of the women and children, were climbing over the bodies heaped against the wagons and carts and making their escape. There was no attempt to pursue them. It was pointless. The enemy had been crushed, defeated to an extent that Cato could never have imagined. Tens of thousands of corpses lay spread across a huge expanse of ground either side of the stream, and the mud made it impossible to distinguish rebel from Roman. Somewhere out there lay Hitetius, Tubero and many others Cato had come to know.

'It's over,' Macro said flatly. 'Over.'

'Yes.'

'I hope she got away . . . Boudica.'

Cato nodded. For all that had happened in the last month or so, he could not bring himself to wish her dead. If she was out there, amongst the corpses, he hoped she would not be found. She deserved better than for her head to be brought to Suetonius as a trophy.

As he looked out over the battlefield and the carnage that had been unleashed in front of the wagons, he felt more appalled than he had ever done before. No other battle he had fought had been like this. Not in scale, desperation or cost in lives. He resolved that as long as he lived, he never wanted to see its like again.

CHAPTER TWENTY-SEVEN

Londinium, five days later

They could smell the town some time before it came within view. An acrid stench of charred wood, roast meat and decaying flesh borne on the summer breeze. There were still a handful of fires burning, and a few hundred rebel stragglers were searching the ruins and abandoned buildings for what loot remained. They were chased off by Roman patrols or killed on the spot if they were captured.

The streets were filled with blackened rubble, broken furniture and crockery that had been cast aside. And bodies. Hundreds of them. Some were burned, or partly burned. Others showed signs of torture as well as the wounds that had killed them. The rebels had spared no one. Men, women, children, the old, the infirm, Roman and Briton alike had been slain without mercy. A desolate quiet hung over the town, aside from the odd shout and the barking of dogs as they fought over scraps of meat and human flesh. They made off at the approach of the soldiers, padding into the alleys and disappearing around piles of debris.

Cato and Macro, together with the remaining fifty men of the mounted contingent of the cohort, were making their way along a street parallel to the main thoroughfare, looking for signs of survivors. So far they had encountered none. The only people they had seen had been five drunken rebels in the yard of what had been a wine merchant's business. They had been killed before they were even aware that the men coming towards them were Romans.

Some distance behind the advance parties scouring the ruins of the town marched the main column. The thinned-out ranks of the auxiliary and legionary cohorts included many men who bore the bloodied dressings of the wounds they had received in the fight. Behind them in the baggage train came wagon after wagon carrying the seriously injured, groaning and crying out with pain at every jolt of the clumsy vehicles. Over a hundred men had died en route, and the remains of their funeral pyres marked the places where the army had made camp each night. As for the Roman dead on the battlefield itself, their bodies had been stacked onto the abandoned enemy wagons and cremated the day after the battle.

After the slaughter was over, the men of the army had slowly made their way back to the Roman lines to sleep for the night. Most had been so exhausted that they had lain down their shields and weapons and slept in the open, heedless of the rain that continued for another hour after night had fallen. Cato was haunted by the vision that had been revealed the next morning, when the sun rose into a clear sky. The slope below was covered with bodies, singly and in tangled heaps. Some still twitched or moved feebly until they were dispatched by parties of soldiers looking for their comrades. He had found the body of Hitetius amid the corpses of the enemy and had given orders for the veteran to be given the honour of a personal burial. His sword, that had once belonged to Cato, was lying beneath him and Cato was sad to retrieve it after so many years under such circumstances.

Other men were out searching for booty, bending over the corpses to take torcs, rings, brooches and other valuables from the dead. Crows had descended on the carrion to feast and pluck at the torn flesh, and flapped into the air with raucous cries whenever they were disturbed by looters.

The slaughter had been so great that only a handful of prisoners had been taken, and these were sent out with the search parties to find the bodies of Boudica, her daughters and the ringleaders of the rebellion. There were many of the latter, tribal chiefs and the warrior leaders of warbands, but no sign of the queen, or at least none that the prisoners were willing to identify. Cato and Macro found it hard to believe that she would have abandoned her people and fled. That was not like her, from their experience. And then, at noon, a mortally wounded woman was found, half buried by bodies in front of the wagons. She claimed to have seen the queen carried away by her royal bodyguards as the army were routed before the Roman charge. She might have been lying to preserve the notion that the rebellion lived on as long as Boudica was alive. She died with a fanatical gleam in her eyes shortly after giving her account of the last moments of the battle.

After the funeral rites had been observed for the Roman dead, the enemy corpses were left where they had fallen. Some would be retrieved by those who had escaped before the end of the battle. The rest would have to be dealt with later, as they could not be left there to rot. As the army marched away from the scene, not a man looked back on the haunting spectacle.

Cato reined in as they reached a junction of two of Londinium's streets. He looked to his left before he spoke to Macro. 'I think this is where the inn is.'

His friend took a moment to get his bearings, then nodded. 'It is. Up that way.'

They turned in the direction Macro indicated, although little remained of the once familiar surroundings. He felt his throat constrict as they approached what was left of the Dog and Deer – a pile of rubble, timbers and roof tiles, all blackened by flames.

One gable still stood, stained with soot, and a short stretch of the upper storey where the bedrooms had been, but there was no sign of any beds or bodies.

Macro dismounted, wincing as he clasped his hand to his bandaged leg. He bent to retrieve the scorched sign that had hung outside the entrance before tenderly touching the painted figures of a small black dog prancing around the legs of an aloof-looking deer. He stared at it a moment before leaning it up against a charred length of the door frame, and then climbed back into the saddle. He trotted a short distance ahead of Cato and the other men so that they would not see the tears brimming in his eyes.

Picking their way along the main street that ran through Londinium, they made for the headquarters complex and the compound surrounding it that had served as the seat of provincial government. The huge building that had dominated the compound was no more. Only a blackened skeletal tracery remained within the outer walls. A squad of the governor's Praetorians stood guard at the gatehouse, and they exchanged a salute with Macro and Cato as they led the riders within.

There was one last horror to witness, and Cato felt his guts twist as his eyes swept over the posts that had been set up around the interior of the compound. Each one carried the impaled remains of victims of the rebels. Men and women, their skin blotchy and dark after several days' exposure to the sun and the onset of corruption. Two squadrons of cavalry auxiliaries were already taking down the posts and removing the bodies.

Tribune Agricola approached Cato as soon as he saw the riders enter the courtyard.

'Governor's compliments, sir. He asked for you and Centurion Macro to join him as soon as you reached headquarters.'

'Headquarters?' Macro sniffed. 'What headquarters?'

Cato looked round but could not see Suetonius or his small retinue. 'Where is he?'

'Round the back, sir. There's a few rooms of the old slave quarters still standing. He's using those for the moment, until the reconstruction gets under way. If you'd follow me . . .'

Agricola led them between the rows of posts with their grisly remains, and around the ruins of the main building to the large courtyard at the rear in front of the gatehouse that Suetonius and his mounted column had passed through when they had abandoned Londinium to the rebels. Some clerks and staff officers had set up makeshift tables and benches outside the drab slave accommodation blocks. It seemed hard to accept that the business of running the province could be resumed so soon after the traumatic events of recent months. And yet Cato knew that was how Rome endured. No catastrophe was final. Even in the darkest days of the wars against Hannibal and the appalling defeats he had inflicted on the Republic, the people and soldiers of Rome had turned themselves to fashioning their recovery and ultimate victory.

Agricola waved them through a doorway into the largest of the slave blocks. It was a long, narrow building with slits for windows high up in the walls. The coarse sleeping mats had been rolled up and piled at the far end. In front of them, Suetonius was sitting on a fire-damaged chest as he dictated orders to a pair of clerks sitting on the floor, who were taking down his words on their wax tablets. He paused as he saw Cato and Macro, and beckoned to them.

'Find any survivors?'

'None, sir.'

'Not surprised, given the display in the main courtyard. It seems they spared nobody.'

Cato gave a sombre nod.

'Too bad. I had hoped some would have been able to hide themselves away and bear witness to what happened here.'

'I don't think they would have been able to tell us anything we couldn't have worked out for ourselves, sir.'

'No . . . I suppose not.' Suetonius collected his thoughts for a moment before he continued. 'There's still no confirmation about Boudica. We know that thousands of her followers escaped the destruction of her army. They will have gone east, towards Iceni territory. If she's still alive, that's where she will be.'

'I imagine so, sir.'

'You and Centurion Macro know her well, I understand. You also know something of the terrain. Is that right?'

'Some of the settlements and tracks, sir. Not as well as most of the merchants and veterans at Camulodunum did.'

'Well, they're all dead now. That leaves you two as the best informed of my men with regard to Boudica, her people and their lands. We may have defeated her army, and destroyed most of it, along with the camp followers, but Rome will not accept that the rebellion is over until we produce Boudica and the surviving ringleaders, and those men still under arms who serve her. I want them all. Dead or alive. I don't care which, as long as I have heads to send to the emperor. I'll give you the pick of the army to get the job done. And a squadron of warships once the fleet returns from Mona. You can make a start on choosing your men the moment the main column reaches Londinium. There won't be much time to rest them before you begin the campaign. When you do, I want you to bring fire and the sword to the Iceni tribe. They must never again be able to rise up against us. Their fate must act as a stark warning to every tribe in Britannia of what happens when you defy Rome.'

He gave Cato and Macro a long, steady stare before he concluded. 'Are you both clear about what I am asking of you?'

'Yes, sir,' they replied.

'Good.' Suetonius clasped his hands together. 'Boudica. Dead or alive.'

393

AUTHOR'S NOTE

Boudica's rebellion could not have come at a worse time for the Roman invaders of Britannia. Envisaging a swift conquest of the island and the establishment of a new province for the Empire, they had been frustrated by the Celtic tribes who had chosen to resist. The struggle had been going on for over seventeen years when the uprising occurred. A bad harvest, the unanswered grievances of the Iceni and Trinovante tribes and the outrages perpetrated against Queen Boudica and her daughters provoked the downtrodden to rise up and take advantage of the dispersed Roman forces in Britannia.

The governor, together with the bulk of the legionary and auxiliary forces, was on the far-flung island of Mona (Anglesey), mopping up the remnants of the Druids and their followers. The Ninth Legion at Lindum (Lincoln) had given up four of their ten cohorts to bolster the ranks of Suetonius's army. In the West Country, the Second Legion was based at Isca Dumnoniorum (Exeter). It is reasonable to suppose that they had been ordered to give up their best troops to serve in the Mona campaign. It is also likely that some of the senior officers of both legions had joined the governor to gain experience and share the glory. This was particularly unfortunate in the case of the Second Legion, who, in the absence of their legate, were under the command of an apparently irresolute camp prefect. When he was called upon to act, he failed disastrously, and answered for his sins grievously at a later date.

There has been some interesting speculation about the failure of the Second Legion to intervene during the rebellion. Some have argued that the legion might have been a training formation, given that it was situated close to the southern coast, where it could have operated as a receiving centre for recruits. These would have been given initial training before being sent as replacements to the other legions in Britannia. If so, the raw quality of such men might well have caused the hapless camp prefect to waver. Whatever the truth of it, the fact remains that the Second Legion failed to respond to orders and sat out the rebellion behind the walls of their fortress. By contrast, the Ninth displayed no such caution when they marched out of Lindum to go to the aid of the veterans of the military colony at Camulodunum (Colchester). Somehow they allowed themselves to be caught in an ambush, and only the legate and his mounted escort managed to extricate themselves. They then fled to a fort on the road to Lindum and played no further part in proceedings. One can imagine the frustration, despair and anger of the governor on having to confront the rebel horde without these two legions joining forces with the main army rushing back from Mona.

The only other soldiers available to Suetonius were the remnants of the Londinium garrison and small detachments of auxiliary troops scattered across the province. Morale, badly shaken by the failures of the two legions mentioned above, was dealt a series of hammer blows with the destruction of Camulodunum, Londinium and Verulamium (St Albans) in succession. Given such setbacks, it is a measure of the resilience of the governor and his army that they were still able to confront and comprehensively defeat the rebels a short distance north of Verulamium.

As for the rebels, the string of victories emboldened them and rallied recruits to swell their numbers. We cannot be certain of the size of the horde that Boudica led, nor whether she was accepted as their commander. Given the fractious nature of Celtic tribes, it is likely that there was some dissent amongst the leadership about how to direct their forces against the Romans. This might go some way towards explaining the long delay between sacking Camulodunum and advancing on Londinium. It seems extraordinary that Suetonius and his mounted column managed to march over 270 miles to reach the town days before the rebels covered the 60 miles from Camulodunum. Perhaps the rebels had surprised themselves with the easy victories over the veterans of Camulodunum and the Ninth Legion and had no clear plan what to do next. Perhaps there were heated debates over what course of action to follow. We shall never know.

Looking back, it's clear to see that any hope of success depended upon the swift destruction of Roman forces in detail accompanied by the demolition of infrastructure on a far wider scale. The devastation of Roman assets and military units would have gone a long way towards persuading Rome to give up the troublesome province. As it was, the rebels' lacklustre advance gave Suetonius the opportunity to concentrate his forces. Rather than pursuing the proven success of guerrilla tactics eventually deployed by Caratacus, the rebels opted for a set-piece battle, despite previous demonstrations of the superiority of Roman discipline and training in such situations. They vastly outnumbered the army facing them, and that may have caused them to ignore past experience and thus commit themselves to battle.

The precise location of the battlefield is unknown, although the 'destruction horizon' (the dark band in the layers of remains that marks the immolation caused by Boudica's rebels) uncovered by archaeologists indicates that the rebels did not get much further than Verulamium, and so I have set the scene to coincide with the archaeological evidence rather than going with the various topographical claims that have been made for likely locations. It is a shame that the sparse descriptions of the rebellion provided by Roman historians tend to observe more fidelity to genre than to facts. Tacitus gives us invented speeches made by the leaders of both sides, while Cassius Dio cites the number of combatants as 10,000 Romans and 230,000 rebels. He later states that the Romans lost some 400 men as against the enemy's 80,000. Most modern historians don't give much credence to such claims. I have tried to provide a more balanced description of how the battle might have occurred, albeit within the realm of historical fiction. I imagine it would have been hard fought, given what was at stake for both sides, and casualties would have been high before the rebel army broke and was defeated.

Neither Roman historian can provide a definitive account of Boudica's fate. If she died in the battle, her body was not identified. If it had been, we can be sure that the historians would have mentioned it. She may have been wounded and died elsewhere. She might have taken poison rather than face capture. We simply don't know. Equally possible is that she and some of her followers escaped and were determined to continue the struggle for as long as possible. That is for Macro and Cato to discover in the next novel . . .

Discover more enthralling
Eagles of the Empire novels:

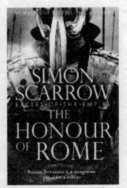

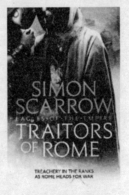

Available now from

HEADLINE

Don't miss the epic story of Caratacus: a barbarian king who led the tribes of Britannia against mighty Rome . . .

AD 18, BRITANNIA.

The Roman Empire rules much of the known world. Beyond the northern frontier lies Britannia, where ceaseless feuding amongst the Celts leaves the island vulnerable to Rome's ambitions.

Caratacus, son of a powerful king, has no premonition of destiny when he is dispatched to train with the Druids. A brutal regime transforms the young prince into a warrior with unparalleled military skills – and the strategic cunning essential to outwit a stronger enemy.

Nothing can prepare a man for the vicious reality of war. When Caratacus's father takes a stand against aggressive neighbouring tribes, the combat exercises are over; this is a fight to the death. Only the most ruthless of tactics offer any hope of victory. But Caratacus, and the loyal comrades willing to ride with him into hostile terrain, are ready to do whatever it takes – and endure any hardship – to defeat those set on destroying their kingdom . . .

As mayhem and carnage spread across the land, everywhere can be felt the malign influence of Rome. Even if the battle is won, conflict with the Empire lies ahead.

Originally published in 5 ebook novellas

Available now

HEADLINE

Discover Simon Scarrow's first thrilling
CI Schenke novel

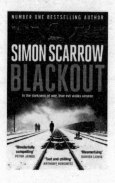

BERLIN, DECEMBER 1939.

As Germany goes to war, the Nazis tighten their terrifying grip. Paranoia in the capital is intensified by a rigidly enforced blackout that plunges the city into oppressive darkness every night, as the bleak winter sun sets.

When a young woman is murdered, Criminal Inspector Horst Schenke is under pressure to solve the case, swiftly. Distrusted by his superiors for his failure to join the Nazi Party, Schenke walks a perilous line – for disloyalty is a death sentence.

The discovery of a second victim confirms Schenke's worst fears. He must uncover the truth before evil strikes again.

As the investigation takes him closer to the sinister heart of the regime, Schenke realises there is danger everywhere – and the warring factions of the Reich can be as deadly as a killer stalking the streets . . .

Available now

HEADLINE

Join CI Schenke in another exhilarating read from Simon Scarrow . . .

BERLIN. JANUARY 1940.

After Germany's invasion of Poland, the world is holding its breath and hoping for peace. At home, the Nazi Party's hold on power is absolute.

One freezing night, an SS doctor and his wife return from an evening mingling with their fellow Nazis at the concert hall. By the time the sun rises, the doctor will be lying lifeless in a pool of blood.

Was it murder or suicide? Criminal Inspector Horst Schenke is told that under no circumstances should he investigate. The doctor's widow, however, is convinced her husband was the target of a hit. But why would anyone murder an apparently obscure doctor? Compelled to dig deeper, Schenke learns of the mysterious death of a child. The cases seem unconnected, but soon chilling links begin to emerge that point to a terrifying secret.

Even in times of war, under a ruthless regime, there are places no man should ever enter. And Schenke fears he may not return alive . . .

Available now

HEADLINE